D

Planting one foot on the creature's body to hold its writhing mass in place, Optimus Prime yanked out the energy spear. It left his opponent's flesh with a dripping *slorp* and a crackle as it chewed through even more bone and plating. The creature writhed and howled in agony as Prime lifted the spear once more—

And waited.

"Why do you hesitate?" the Judge demanded. *"The victory is yours. Make the kill."*

"I will not," Prime said confidently. To kill in wartime was one thing, to take life when it was the only way to stop an enemy—*that* he could accept. "Find your amusement elsewhere."

"As you wish."

Suddenly, one of the human spectators cried out in alarm as invisible pincers yanked her high into the air, holding her tight by her midsection.

"Wait!" she screamed. "No, I have a family, don't—"

The pincers snapped shut with a sharp hiss, spewing gore and a rain of blood over the heads of the crowd. The two halves of the still twitching corpse tumbled to the ground and terrified people darted like animals to avoid them.

"All of them next," the Judge said wistfully. *"Your choice."*

SCIENCE FICTION UNIVERSES
published by ibooks, inc.:

TERMINATOR 2:
THE NEW JOHN CONNOR CHRONICLES
by Russell Blackford
Book 1: *Dark Futures* • Book 2: *An Evil Hour*
Book 3: *Times of Trouble*
[coming September 2003]

BATTLESTAR GALACTICA
Battlestar Galactica Classic
Battlestar Galactica Classic: The Tombs of Kobol
by Glen A. Larson and Robert Thurston

Battlestar Galactica: Resurrection
by Richard Hatch and Stan Timmons
Battlestar Galactica: Rebellion
by Richard Hatch and Alan Rodgers

THE MICRONAUTS
by Steve Lyons
The Time Traveler Trilogy, Book 1

THE TWILIGHT ZONE
Book 1: Shades of Night, Falling
by John J. Miller

HARDWIRED

SCOTT CIENCIN

ibooks

new york
www.ibooks.net

DISTRIBUTED BY SIMON & SCHUSTER, INC.

To Denise

Special thanks to Marc Cerasini and Loren Coleman

An Original Publication of ibooks, inc.

Copyright © 2003 Hasbro
ALL RIGHTS RESERVED.

TRANSFORMERS®, all associated logos, characters, and their respective likenesses are trademarks of Hasbro, under license from Takara Co., Ltd., and used with Hasbro's permission.

All rights reserved, including the right to reproduce this book or portions thereof in any form whatsoever.
Distributed by Simon & Schuster, Inc.
1230 Avenue of the Americas, New York, NY 10020

ibooks, inc.
24 West 25th Street
New York, NY 10010

The ibooks, inc. World Wide Web Site Address is:
http://www.ibooks.net

The Hasbro World Wide Web Site Address is:
http://www.hasbro.com

ISBN 0-7434-5898-2
First ibooks, inc. printing July 2003
10 9 8 7 6 5 4 3 2 1

**Special thanks to Joshua Izzo,
for going above and beyond the call of duty.**

Cover art of Optimus Prime by Dreamwave Productions
Copyright © 2003 Hasbro

Cover design by j. vita

Printed in the U.S.A.

CHAPTER ONE

Their war had raged for four million years.

Staring into the cold, soulless eyes of his mortal enemy as they battled yet again, this time against a backdrop of chill night and hammering rain, in a sparkling city filled with terrified, innocent humans, Optimus Prime truly believed their conflict might go on for four million more... *unless* he and his fellow Transformers found a way to end it, once and for all, this very night.

Optimus Prime and Megatron, two metallic goliaths, each several stories tall, tore into each other without mercy. Steel fists the size of automobiles smashed against faceplates of ancient—and alien—manufacture. Buildings burned and people within them shrieked in sheer agony, the victims of Megatron's arm-mounted fusion cannon. Death and destruction surrounded Prime, holding him in an inescapable iron grip far stronger than anything ever created on their homeworld of Cybertron.

The once-teaming streets of the Ginza district of Tokyo were, under more normal circumstances, a blinding electric sea of flashing lights and neon. For over a century this vibrant area was the center of Japanese sophistication and consumerism. The first place in the nation to wholeheartedly embrace the influences of the West, Ginza was a glittering showcase for cutting-edge trends, modern architecture, and contemporary affluence. Elegant shops, restaurants, bars and boutiques lined the teaming streets, each with brilliant banks of neon, or state-of-the-art digital displays arcing or flashing across their ultra-modern façade.

Citizens of Tokyo have long remarked that there is so much light in Ginza that daytime never ends there. But tonight, as two menacing giants were locked in mortal combat in the middle of its battered streets, those same lights blinked and wavered—and then went dark. Power grids, smashed by flying chunks of steel, brick, and mortar, exploded and burned. Banks of neon burst in a shower of sparks as the pummeling rain clashed with naked electricity. With a deafening crash, a multi-storied glass façade shattered. A million shards of razor-sharp glass plunged earthward, mingling with the sheets of rain. Down on the broken streets, there was a sharp explosion. A hundred sirens wailed.

The titans grappled, knocking one another off balance. They plummeted toward the street below. Prime heard screams, but could see nothing beyond the malevolently smoldering crimson eyes and the obscenely pure ivory of Megatron's hated sphinx-like face.

For Prime, time seemed to slow, almost to stop. He and Megatron plunged into a stage that had been erected on the roped-off street the night before. His cybernetic brain, its functions bolstered by the power of the Matrix long ago been embedded in his chest, isolated the panicked voices rising from the stage, allowing him to identify the humans who were about to join the ranks of collateral damage in this war that was not of Earth's making. The clearest voice belonged to Isolde Holden, a television reporter who had been broadcasting live when the battle began.

Isolde had been one of the few humans on the planet who had remained a staunch supporter of Prime and his fellow Autobots—even when public sentiment had swung dangerously far from their favor after their surprising resurrection and public resurgence.

All the Transformers were thought to have been destroyed in the *Ark II* tragedy. That ship had been created to ferry the Transformers and a handful of humans to the Transformers homeworld, and it had been built after the nations of Earth joined together and sided with the Autobots in a final and successful attack on the Decepticons. The *Ark II* blew up in the sky, and mechanical negligence was initially blamed, though many suspected sabotage.

Later, remains of the Transformers began to turn up. Megatron was found by a known terrorist, the Decepticon's power restored so that he, and other Transformers, could be used as ultimate weapons sold to the highest bidder. Meanwhile, the United States government—with help from Spike Witwicky and a remnant of the Matrix—found and restored Optimus Prime, who sought out other Autobots.

Megatron slipped his chains quickly, and another full on conflict erupted between the Autobots and Decepticons, one that ended with a nuclear weapon exploding off the coast of Los Angeles. Through it all, Isolde had championed Prime and his warriors.

Now, her voice alone was calm and strong, though her crushing death was only an instant away. "I do not blame the Autobots," she said.

Prime braced himself, knowing all too well there was nothing he could do. They were falling toward her, and Megatron's weight would crush her instantly. Yet inwardly, he chanted, *I cannot let this happen. I cannot. I will NOT—*

Isolde shrieked—but more from surprise than terror, or so it seemed to Prime as he and Megatron slammed to the ground. Prime's audio sensors were overwhelmed by the deafening, concussive blast of their impact as Megatron's back hit the street, Prime's weight added to him. The concrete tore itself apart, crackling in welcome. Yet the splintering of the wooden stage, the sickening sound of human flesh and bone being flattened into pulp... *those* sounds never arrived.

Prime rolled off the momentarily stunned Megatron, careful to avoid any humans who had not yet fled the area or, failing that, taken cover. Wreckage from a half-dozen buildings, and the burning hulks of a hundred cars, littered the streets. Smoke, pelted by rain, hung low over the choking streets. In the distance, more sirens shrieked as fire engines raced to the scene—more innocent lives soon to be snuffed out, unless Prime could end this confrontation now.

Prime quickly scanned the area. A thousand audio buffers filtered out all but the sounds the Autobot needed to anticipate his adversary's next move. Vision sensors shifted from normal spectrum to infrared, as Prime's cybernetic brain gauged the destruction all around him. He saw that a hundred fires burned, and for every blaze smothered by pelting rain, a dozen others intensified, fed by broken gas mains, broken walls, and shattered debris.

Shifting his sensors to ultra-high frequency microwave radar mode, Prime instantly sensed the presence of other Autobots. Instantly data filled one corner of his faceplate—more information than any mere biological brain could hope to comprehend in a lifetime. After the nanosecond it took for Prime to collect, sift, and absorb the data, the Autobot automatically switched to long-distance vision mode. He now used his full-spectrum vision to pierce the rain and darkness. Filtering out any biological signs—including the hundreds of humans still trapped in the shattered rubble—the Autobot scanned only for signs of his team.

Telescopic sights focused on the stage over a block away, and on the long skidmarks leading all the way back to the fallen warriors. Above and to one side of the quaking humans stood Bluestreak, another Autobot. His narrow vision slits were focused on Prime. His barrel-like chest was thrust outward, his armored car doors spread wide. Fresh scorch marks stained his shimmering silver and black armor. In his powerful grip he clutched his mammoth blaster at the ready, prepared to direct a rain of destruction on the enemy.

But Prime himself stood in the line of fire.

Then, with a great whirr of tires, a sports car dislodged itself from the base of the stage, drove a hundred yards from it, and spun on the rain-slicked pavement. There was more than meets the eye about this vehicle. In seconds, the car *unfolded*, piece by piece, transforming into Jazz, the third and final Autobot on the scene. His peaked head rose over the enormous chest plate. Inside the armor of the enormous Autobot, servomotors purred and pneumatic gears locked into place as Jazz rose to upright position, to tower over the humans around him.

Jazz had saved Isolde and the others!

"Maybe we can help," Bluestreak said. The Autobot nodded in the direction of the fallen Megatron. "Heads up, Prime. This isn't over."

Whirling on his enemy, Prime saw Megatron slowly raise his arm and take aim with his fusion cannon. The weapon was angled in the direction of Prime's *head*, and if Prime moved out of the line of fire, either Bluestreak would be hit, or, more likely, an office building behind him would take the brunt of the blast. Once again, Prime's visual and heat scans had registered hundreds of innocent people in that building.

Advancing with surprising speed, Prime raised his right hand and sent a highly distinct signal from his cybertronic brain that rocketed through his entire system. Energon stores were rerouted and his hand folded up into his wrist, a purely mechanical act, and a surge of blazing fire erupted, a glowing Energon Axe of pure blinding light taking shape where his hand had been.

Megatron brought himself up to settle on one knee and was about to fire when the sweeping arc of Prime's blade swung in close and severed Megatron's arm with surgical precision. The twitching hand, the jerking forearm, and the now useless weapon attached to it fell away, while blue-white sparks hissed against driving sheets of rain. The Decepticon howled in rage as the dead limb, sliced cleanly off just above the elbow, dropped to the ground, punching into the roof of a bus with a thunderclap of its own. Both sides of the thankfully abandoned bus ballooned out as the bus's metal frame screamed and its glass windows exploded, sending a shower of glass at a handful of people still on the street. Out of the corner of his eye, Prime saw two fall: a man and a child. Then the weapon detached from the arm, rolled from the ruined bus, and clattered on the ground—before smashing a third person up against a wall. A teenage girl this time. Prime heard Jazz race toward her, then stop. She'd been crushed instantly. He was simply too late.

For every action Prime was forced to make in this conflict, there was more than an equal and opposite reaction...there was slaughter of the innocents.

This is all there is, Prime thought. *One battle after another. The endless war. I'm a prisoner to this life... and Megatron holds the key to my freedom. If he dies, the war will end. The Decepticons are nothing without his leadership.*

If he dies...

I can live.

Prime swung his axe at Megatron's head, but his enemy's remaining arm changed suddenly, his left hand folding in on itself, retreating into his wrist, an Energon Morning Star firing outward in place of his hand. Megatron brought the weapon across in time to block Prime's arm.

Megatron jammed the still sparking stump of his arm at Prime's face, forcing the warrior to withdraw long enough for Megatron to stand on both powerful legs and gain his center of gravity.

He's insane, Prime thought. The notion really shouldn't have come as a complete surprise, yet it was jarring nonetheless. Megatron had always been ambitious, power-mad even, but he had always acted logically, methodically. And unlike so many of their previous encounters, this assault had come without warning, without provocation, and seemingly without purpose—except to strike out, alone, at those he hated.

The evening had started uneventfully. As part of a good will effort arranged by the U.N. to help stem the tide of protest and the public backlash against the

Transformers ever since the Los Angeles incident, Prime, Jazz, and Bluestreak had been flown to Tokyo to engender some positive public relations for their cause. Officials knew that nothing could ever wipe out the memories of the horrible last battle between Megatron's legions and the followers of Optimus Prime, but every effort had to be made to restore some luster to the tarnished steel of the Autobots' reputation as defenders of the innocent. The Decepticons, scattered though they appeared to be, were still out there, and the public's cooperation was necessary if they were all to be found and brought to justice for their many crimes by the special task force headed by the Autobots.

Prime certainly didn't blame the people of the world for turning on them. A nuclear weapon detonated off the coast of southern California during that battle. The bomb had been sent by a lunatic military commander named Hallo *without* the authorization of the President. Further, the blast had cost the life of Prime's trusted friend and fellow Autobot warrior Superion, a giant among giants, an invaluable resource on so many fronts, whom Prime had sent to his death so that the bomb would not strike Los Angeles.

Yet there had been no way to evacuate all of Los Angeles when the attack came. Collateral damage had been wracked up, innocent lives lost both in the battle and in the ensuing tidal wave that struck the city in the nuke's wake. Fearing black clouds of radioactive fall-out, a huge percentage of the populace had left L.A. behind. For months now, the news reports coming out of L.A. had been filled with stories of the search for survivors in the rubble, and of the looting and riots resulting from lack of law enforcement and the overall terror everyone felt over what had happened... and could happen *again*.

The entire entertainment industry had abandoned the West Coast. Hollywood was now a ghost town. The work of those producers, actors, musicians, and so on, had barely skipped a beat—New York, Florida, North Carolina had all benefited. Production in Australia and New Zealand had skyrocketed. So many in other fields had lost their jobs, their homes, and had been forced to start over. Insurance covered nothing. Government relief funding had been a joke.

Yes, there was a great and understandable bitterness directed toward the Transformers, and Prime felt the weight of it fully. The positive work the Transformers had been doing since the L.A. incident hardly seemed to balance the scales. There were people who had helped the task force, but there were also countless false leads on the whereabouts of the Decepticons, several fostered by humans who simply *liked* seeing the Autobots race around for no reason, who desperately wanted some power over these living machines which seemed to have ultimate power over them.

Thus Prime, Jazz and Bluestreak had come to put on a simple dog and pony show. A "Q and A" with the press, a few meet and greets with some Asian officials and celebrities, and what promised to be a *lot* of standing around looking like damn fools at the center of a fire works display later on in the evening at a near-by theme park. Hardly the stuff of heroes.

The only Autobot who seemed to be enjoying himself during the trip had been Jazz because he got to meet his idol, Jackie Chan, at one of the meet and greets.

Prime had not been looking for or expecting a fight as he stood gleaming uncomfortably in the spotlight of fame, notoriety, a living metallic symbol of a nation—and a world's—attempt at reinvesting the public's confidence in beings once thought of as the greatest peacekeepers and deterrents against worldwide terrorism and other manifestations of human evil that had ever walked the planet. The role of hero and protector was never one he had ever asked for, but Prime understood the value in playing this part in his adopted world. Earth was peopled by many noble, brave, and valiant souls. There were countless innocents and flesh-and-blood heroes who deserved every measure of protection from Megatron and other dangers that only a being such as he might provide.

Then, in a blink, it was over. Prime's fragile moment of peace, his instant of hope that the negativity directed at the Transformers might indeed be turned around, had all melted away. The ground shook, a building exploded, and Megatron launched himself out of the smoking ruin, blinding streams of energy firing from his fusion cannon, as the surviving members of the crowd fled in a mad panic. Jazz and Bluestreak did their best to protect the people, even taking blasts from Megatron to save human lives. Then it fell to Prime to keep the leader of the Decepticons busy while his fellow Autobots saved as many people as they could, even when it meant saving them from themselves. Despite the Autobots' efforts, humans trampled and crushed one another as they tried to escape.

As he grappled with Megatron, Prime had tried, and failed, to make sense of his enemy's sudden appearance. Along with the efforts from the private sector, every global security agency in the world had been searching for clues to the whereabouts of Megatron and his fellow Decepticons. There had been countless false leads: some accounts had the Decepticons hiding in the arctic, or amidst mountainous terrain, or even beneath the sea. Anywhere that might be hidden from satellite imaging technology. Many believed the evil Transformers were hiding in plain sight: A truck here, a jet there—anything seemed possible.

Only a month ago, one of the greatest naval military commanders of the past decade had sworn that he had seen lights and shapes in the depths that might have been a Decepticon city or fortress. Prime himself had been to the spot that Hugo Fortuna, the naval commander, had sworn that he had seen strange lattices of blue and crimson light, strange hulking metallic shapes moving behind them.

He had found nothing.

The mystery remained. Megatron had been here, somehow smuggled into the city, but by who? For what purpose?

If Prime took the Decepticon's life, he might never know the answers to those questions...and lack of intelligence of that sort could mean the difference between life or death for millions on this planet, perhaps even for the world itself.

His great and powerful hands were once again bound. He had to capture and interrogate Megatron, not kill him.

Prime smiled inwardly as Megatron launched yet another attack. *Doesn't mean he has to stay in one piece.*

With savage speed, Prime raised his axe and brought it slashing across Megatron's chest. Sparks hissed and ripped into the sky, the closest Prime would see to fireworks this night. Megatron howled in fury and brought his morning star to bear. Prime easily evaded his opponent's clumsy blow, and swung his axe at Megatron's forearm. The Decepticon went off-balance, unintentionally saving himself from the crackling sweep of Prime's axe. Only grazing his enemy's arm instead of taking it off completely, Prime reached for Megatron's throat. He would hold the Decepticon still while he relieved him of his weapon.

The Decepticon darted forward before Prime's hand could reach his neck. In the time it took Prime to realize Megatron's lumbering blows had been feints, his enemy brought the morning star, which sported long, sharp *spikes,* and buried it in the side of Prime's neck.

Pain unlike any that Optimus Prime had ever experienced tore through his living metal frame. A soul grinding agony nearly made him forget that he, too, was armed, but when he tried to bring his axe around, he was stopped by Megatron yanking the spiked morning star back and forth in his neck, severing more and more connections, tearing his screaming steel skin apart. Prime's cybernetic brain swam in the pain, and all he could do was jerk about like a helpless puppet as Megatron tortured him.

Prime had heard the distant rumbles of Jazz and Bluestreak speeding away only moments ago. Unable to get around the two behemoths so that they could grab Megatron from behind, they had transformed into vehicles and drove away, seeking side-streets and parallel roads they could use to box their way around, motor up behind the Decepticon, and transform again, only now in position to truly help Prime stop Megatron.

There would be no help from either of them. Not in time. Megatron had played the madman, luring

Optimus into reckless and overconfident behavior, and the plan had worked perfectly.

"Die, you sanctimonious heap of scrap metal," Megatron said with a sharp metallic hiss as he dragged the morning star out of Prime's neck, then struck at his skull with it, partially dislodging the Autobot's faceplate with an echoing clang that rose above the steady drizzle of the storm, that drowned out a thunderclap from the heavens.

The present shorted out as a hailstorm of ancient memories became Optimus's world.

Optimus, once known as Optronix, or Orion to his friends, had never wanted to be Prime. He had been a simple archivist, safe and secure in his structured, regimented, boring existence. Then he had received word from the Council of Ancients that *he*—of all Transformers—had been chosen by the very Matrix itself to become the next Prime, the greatest champion and defender of their world.

Wracked with doubt and misgivings, he had journeyed to the sprawling Chamber of the Ancients and tried to explain why it made no sense for him to assume this mantle. He was not a warrior, he told them. He had no training, no experience. They were in the middle of a civil war and they wanted a glorified *librarian* to lead them? It was madness! Thus he urged the Ancients to abandon tradition and choose a different Prime.

He also felt strongly that the civil war led by Megatron's factions served no purpose. If Megatron wanted their world, then why not leave Cybertron behind and let him have it? Those who did not wish to accept Megatron's rule could easily build a new home elsewhere.

What he didn't understand was that for Megatron, the fight wasn't about property, not directly. It was about subjugating the rights of individuals, transforming them into property, making them little more than slaves who would bow to Megatron's will.

Bowing to the will of the council, yet inwardly certain that he would not survive the initiation ceremony, Optronix accepted The Matrix into himself and became Optimus Prime... just in time to deal with the Decepticon's first attempt to assassinate him.

His first official act as the new Prime was to order the evacuation of Cybertron. He would not have any more Autobots lose their lives in this civil war. But he didn't understand the depths of Megatron's hatred of the Autobots. Megatron not only wanted Cybertron for his Decepticons, he also wanted the Autobots wiped out of existence. Optimus's order to evacuate Cybertron only made the conflict worse.

It was not an auspicious beginning for a new Prime.

Optimus later learned that Megatron's real plan was to turn Cybertron into a moving War World, a weapon that could strike at any planet in the universe until every living thing was under Megatron's thumb? Optimus was sickened with himself when the truth became clear. A Prime who had been truly worthy would have seen that Megatron had just been trying to create distractions for his larger plan and would have been able to defeat him without any further loss of life.

On and on it had gone, one decision after another that filled him with regret, that made him wonder, deep down, if his initial instinct had been right, if he never should have been Prime at all.

Now, falling to his knees before Megatron, his mind

racing, his memories blurring together then fading as control over his body was lost to him, all he could think about was his failure. How he would die a failure.

This was the great destiny the Matrix had seen for him, he realized bitterly. This was the role he had been destined to play.

It was how he had been programmed.

How he was hardwired.

"It's not your fault," a strong, deep voice said.

With the last of his strength, Optimus Prime turned his head to one side, and looked up at the shadowy figure who stood where Megatron had been only a moment earlier.

No, Optimus thought. *This is impossible.*

An Autobot stood in the rain-drenched street, a sudden flash of lighting revealing his proud, regal bearing and features. The blue, gold, and silver plates and ribbing were much like his own, and his face, like that of Optimus, was expressionless, guarded by a serrated plate that covered the planes below his blue-white eyes, across to his cheek guards, and down to his chin. His blue hands were balled into shimmering fists.

He was a giant.

A legend.

And he had been *dead* for a *very* long time.

"Sentinel Prime," Optimus choked. He was looking up into the face of his predecessor, and he could only imagine the Autobot's shame and disgust.

"I'm not a ghost," Sentinel Prime said. "I'm as real as anything else in your mind, and to your senses. The Matrix within you chose this form to communicate with you."

Optimus almost laughed. This wasn't happening. It couldn't be happening. "Not the best time…"

"You were right to think that an error was made. It never should have been you, Optimus. You should have been free to choose the life you would lead. This burden of leadership had been meant for another. It is only after many years of detailed self-diagnostic routines that the flaw has become apparent."

"No…"

"You need to hear this, Optimus," Sentinel Prime said calmly. "You were chosen to fail. Chosen by Megatron himself."

"That can't be," Optimus whispered, his body shaking like a frightened child even though Optimus himself knew no fear. A sense of calm had descended on him. He was dying. Perhaps even dead for all intents and purposes, except for a few flickering impulses of energy racing about in his brain, trying to make sense of what was happening, trying to absolve him of the guilt he felt at allowing Megatron to defeat him.

"Not to absolve you," Sentinel Prime said, clearly aware of Optimus's thoughts. "To free you. Just because Megatron chose you to fail doesn't mean you should let him kill you here and like this. Fight the battle he never believed you could win. You've done it before. Do it now…and you can be free. Leadership of the Autobots can be given to another. You've served well. Now save yourself…carve out a future beyond that which was destined for you. It is the reward you have earned. *Now claim it!*"

A sudden surge of energy exploded within Prime's damaged body as power was routed from one subsystem to another, and his faltering lifesigns dramatically peaked. Lightning flashed again, and this time he saw Megatron standing over him, morning star raised high, a final blow that would surely shatter his skull to pieces about to descend.

No—it was descending. Time was elongating once again to his enhanced senses. A trick, of course, a simple illusion stemming from how quickly Optimus Prime was actually moving. The speed and the strength to do what was necessary was within him. All he needed now was the will.

Behind Megatron, Optimus saw the towering figures of Jazz and Bluestreak. They were close to Megatron, but not close enough to stop him with their bare hands. And any other choice, any use of weapons, would have meant risking even more innocent human lives. Optimus Prime could reach out with ease now and detect the number of human heartbeats within a five-block radius: It was two hundred and twelve.

So it would remain.

With a triumphant shout, Optimus Prime raised his right arm and brought his energy axe across the legs of his hated enemy—chopping them off at midthigh.

"Wah—what..." Megatron said, his upper body falling backward, into the hands of Jazz and Bluestreak, while the Decepticon's energy spitting legs quivered then fell, one at a time, to either side of the street.

Optimus Prime rose, the final reserves of energy that had flooded into his system now, at the last, already beginning to fail.

He had no idea if the vision he had seen of Sentinel Prime was anything more than a product of his fevered, guilt-ridden mind. At this moment, it hardly mattered. The burden of leadership would indeed be taken from him by the darkness he felt clawing at the outer reaches of his mind, fighting to take him down to oblivion one final time.

"I must name my successor," Optimus Prime told his startled companions, who had secured the shocked, speechless form of Megatron on the slick street.

Before he could say another word, a brilliant blue and crimson lattice of spiraling energy burst in the storming night sky. At first, Optimus thought this might be another illusion of his fevered and dying mind. Then he studied the expressions of his companions, who were equally perplexed and disturbed, and knew he wasn't the only one witnessing the light show.

Is it the fireworks at last? Optimus wondered, his limbs threatening to give out under him once more.

But the whiplike energies did not quickly dissipate. Nor did they remain stationary. Instead, the huge net expanded and descended, dropping rapidly as humans screamed and Autobots readied weapons that they could never fire in time—and would not help even if they could.

The energies struck quickly, silently, slicing through Optimus and the others, bringing a cold, stinging, curtain of darkness upon them. The huge blue and crimson net covered five city blocks, passing harmlessly through buildings and vehicles, sparkling just a little brighter only when it touched organic or metallic matter.

Then, as quickly as it came, it was gone...

And so was *everyone* it had touched.

CHAPTER TWO

Cleveland, Ohio

Spike was sitting on his favorite stool in his favorite diner, an out of the way dive called the BuzzKill, downing his morning coffee, when the stranger approached and the trouble began. Though the diner was a riot of clashing post-modern styles—silver aluminum siding on the exterior, exposed duct-work along the high ceiling, white tile on the floors and walls, and a long counter of marble lined with high, scarlet-upholstered stools—the dominate theme at BuzzKill's was retro-1980s.

The staff was decked out in a variety of 1980s attire, everything from executive suits and power ties to full punk regalia. One waiter, an African-American with slick hair and chiseled features, wore a leather bandleader jacket, tight black pants, white socks and dancing shoes—and a single, white-spangled glove. A waitress hustled by carrying a tray on one shoulder. She sported black leather pants and a bustier, and her head was shaved except for a spiked plume of platinum blond projecting from the center of her scalp. With eyes surrounded by dark makeup, and ebony lipstick plastered on her lips, she was the embodiment of mid-1980s Goth. A second waitress sported a cuddly, Jennifer Beals look, with leg warmers, jogging pants, and a sweatshirt with the neck cut out, revealing one slim and toned shoulder.

BuzzKills was pretty lively for a brilliant, but still too-cold February morning. Most of the booths were full, and even the counter was busy. The Ohio sunlight poured in through the tall windows, illuminating the already bright interior with a rosy gold glow.

Spike was twenty-two, with dirty brown hair, an innocent, youthful, heart-shaped face, and ice-blue eyes. He wore jeans and a sweatshirt, his factory wear sitting neatly folded in the back seat of his car. He preferred to change in a deserted woods near the plant so that when he arrived, he would always look sharp, not a wrinkle in his outfit. Prime had taught him to think and act like a soldier all too well, even though, technically speaking, he had never served any branch of the government in an official capacity. It had always been covert ops. And, from the look of things, he was being aimed, like a precision weapon, in that direction once again.

The difference was that unlike a weapon with no mind or soul of its own, Spike could more than make up his own mind about things. In this situation, he already had. He flagged down the woman behind the counter, but she pretended not to notice him. Clearly, the man beside him, or an associate, had already bought her off, or threatened her into submission. The conversation with the man beside him would be private.

"You really have to go out of your way to find a place like this," the stranger said. He was a strong-looking guy with sculpted features, icy soft blue eyes, and a well-toned physique hidden under a beige ribbed sweater. Spike had been able to tell instantly, from the man's bearing, the square set of his shoulders, the way he stared at a person without blinking—that he was, or had been, military.

"Twenty minutes out of my way to work, every morning," Spike said as he took a final sip of his coffee and hauled out his wallet to take care of his tab. He wouldn't be returning here—not for a very long time. He hated when he got made like this.

Halfway off the stool, Spike felt the man's vice-like grip clamp onto his forearm, his companion's reflexes were nearly as blinding as that of an Autobot. The grip relaxed instantly, and the forced, friendly smile the stranger wore now broadened.

"What's your hurry?" the man asked.

"Late for work," Spike said.

"No you're not. You called in sick." The man took out a slim line micro cassette player, wound it back to its zero mark, and played back a call between someone who sounded *exactly* like Spike and his supervisor at the plant.

Sure enough, "Spike Witwicky" had indeed called in complaining of the severe flu that had been going around. The only problem was, he hadn't *sounded* sick, and when his hard-ass boss called him on it, "Spike" had cursed him a blue-streak...and lost himself one of the few jobs that had been available to him after his long absence during the California disaster and its terrible aftermath.

"Voice simulator?" Spike asked, settling back down on his stool. He wasn't defeated, not by a longshot, but he knew from experience that he would have to hear this guy out eventually: his type never quit until the desired audience sat still and listened to the pitch. Spike was nothing if not a practical guy.

And sitting here for a while gave him a chance to size up what kind of threat he was truly facing—and to come up with a plan for burning the bastards who'd sent his companion. Spike had a young son at home, who he was raising with his wife Carly. And there were the massive gambling debts his brother, Buster, had wracked up in the months following the news that his dad had died in the *Ark II* tragedy. He *needed* the meager income he'd been earning at the plastics manufacturing plant just to put food on the table and to keep very bad men from doing very bad things to his brother, who was now trying to clean up his life and face his demons, though he could not do it alone. So this whole thing had really pissed him off... not that he was going to give the stranger the satisfaction of knowing that. Not right away.

Not until he had a plan for dealing with the creep.

"Voice sim?" the stranger asked. "I guess we could have done it that way. But why go all high-tech when the old-fashioned way still works?" With that, the stranger raised his deep, throaty growl of a voice up an octave, smoothed out his diction, and repeated a phrase from the recording in a startlingly accurate impersonation of Spike.

A vein began to throb in Spike's temple and his face and neck flushed. Still, he remained perfectly still. "I don't suppose we could just go to the part where you tell me who you're working for and what you want?"

The stranger shrugged. "No problem. Franklin Townsend, officially N.S.A., but currently reassigned to a special U.N. taskforce to investigate the disappearance of the two hundred and twelve people in Tokyo last night. Here to recruit you to the dark side, natch."

Spike narrowed his gaze and twitched a little, despite himself. His memories of General Hallo's traitorous acts were still fresh enough for him to flinch at the idea of anyone making a joke out of what had happened. Hallo had, without authorization from the President, launched the nuclear weapon that had cost Superion's life, and all but transformed the southwest coast of the United States into a ghostly shell of what it had been, a frightening new frontier that the authorities were still arguing over. Was martial law necessary? Should those who were foolish enough to remain be forced to sign "hold harmless" agreements with the government for any potential health hazards they might encounter due to the occasional charcoal clouds and black rain that struck the city...sign or risk the loss of citizenship?

It was a nightmare out there. And last night, for more than two hundred families, a new nightmare had unfolded.

"Not interested," Spike said firmly.

"But you're intrigued."

"I feel terrible for the families of the people who were taken. But I don't see what I can—"

"Taken," Franklin said. "Interesting choice of words. So you fall in with the rest of us who believe those people are still alive somewhere, that they weren't just blown away somehow by a weapon that only kills people."

"You mean humans."

"Pardon?"

"Prime, Megatron, Bluestreak, and Jazz... they're missing, too. And disappeared is the phrase you used, so it sounds like you've made up your mind, too."

Franklin laughed. "From your response, it seems that *you* would classify Prime and the others as 'persons.' Not just machines."

"They're living machines. I thought you did your homework. Get on AOL and run a search for it, if you need the info. There's a ton of websites about them. Just leave me alone."

"There are very few hard and fast facts about these things," Franklin said. "All we have to go on is what they tell us."

Spike shook his head and was about to rise once more when Franklin added, "It's not like anyone of *us* ever walked a mile in one of *their* shoes."

That stopped Spike. Did Franklin know what had happened to him all those years ago? Or was he just guessing?

"Let's just say I have reason to believe you possess unique insights into the Transformers. As a result, I believe you can help us infiltrate the Followers."

Spike winced. Even the mention of that group grated on his nerves.

He had been approached directly by the Followers a good half-dozen times, and when it had become clear he would not join their ranks simply by dint of invitation, other means had been employed. Candayce Simmons, a beautiful young woman he thought loved him, had turned out to be a covert member of the Followers. Her task had been to entice him subtly into becoming a part of their movement... and, in the process, to gain whatever information he had about the Transformers. In the afterglow of making love she would ask what it felt like to *ride* on the back of a Transformer, to be taken into the air and feel the strumming of their pulsating machinery beneath you...

It became a game with her, a sexual fantasy she finally admitted to, a little dirty talk here and there in a restaurant while her fingers did the walking and his did the same. A topic raised as he took her on a rooftop at night overlooking the city, or in an elevator, dangerous places, one kink added atop another so that he would not question her minute, probing inquiries into the exact mechanics of the great living machines and *precisely* what they might transform into. And Spike had fallen for it, even hinting once that a car in which they fulfilled their mutual needs was more than meets the eye.

Then there were the people who tried to get to him through his son and his brother... the whole deal sickened him.

"You think they're involved in what happened last night?" Spike asked, interested despite himself. The urge for payback against the Followers was strong inside him.

"Among the missing, there are at least *two* known members of the Followers," Franklin said. "I could write that off to coincidence, except that they were both Americans, they both left their jobs with no notice the moment the press deal was set up in Tokyo, and the credit cards used to pay for their flights, hotel rooms, and expenses, all trace back to the organization."

"Huh," Spike said, taking a sip of his now ice-cold coffee.

"The Followers have never done anything actionable," Franklin went on. "No overt criminal activities. They're just obsessed with all things related to the Transformers. Some of them seem to worship the Autobots as gods, most of them just appear to be curious. Every person recruited by the organization has had his or her life impacted, in one way or another, by the presence of these alien, living machines on Earth."

"And no one knows who's paying for what they do."

"No one."

Spike thought about it. "You think they might have found a way to teleport the Transformers from Tokyo to some private spot for study."

"Ignoring the fact that no known science on Earth allows for that kind of matter transfer… who knows? We live in a world where alien robots tear up the planet on a semi-regular basis. That in itself kind of expands the realm of what's possible and what isn't, don't you think?"

"I suppose," Spike said, remembering the days when he ran with the Transformers…and the brief time, when he had been dying, and had, himself, become *something more*.

Franklin looked around the diner and grinned. "I can understand why you choose to hang out in a place like this. Lots of good memories, right? Back when things were black and white, good versus evil, you were just a kid and your father was going to live forever. Back before you knew any better."

"Don't mention my father," Spike said, his voice cold and practically robotic. *"Nothing* gives you that right."

Franklin sighed and got off the stool. "You know what my offer is. You know what the stakes are. I'll be outside for the next hour. If you want to pursue this, that's how long I'll be waiting."

"Uh-huh."

Spike watched the man leave. His waitress came over, unwilling to meet his gaze, and refilled his coffee.

He watched the clock carefully as he made his decision.

At exactly one hour and five minutes, he went outside. As he suspected, Franklin was *still* waiting.

"My terms," Spike said. "My way."

"Of course," Franklin acquiesced.

Spike, of course, didn't believe him for a second.

Tokyo, Japan

Reporter Chris Killah, formerly of *The Times*, hurried through the streets of the cordoned off zone in which four Transformers and over two hundred people disappeared the night before. He was not alone. The sandy-haired, green-eyed reporter, recently promoted to on-air reporter for Music News Television, a cable network that was another holding of the Times megaconglomerate parent company, raced ahead with his bulky, red-haired cameraman Joe Chuckry and his sound engineer, the salt-and-pepper haired wiry Tom Hyroon. Killah's signature black leather duster grazed bits of rubble and his ribbed dark gray sweater and blue jeans absorbed the golden light from above as surely as his Neo-influenced Raybans.

Because they were all looking up—and not paying attention to the ground—each nearly tripped over scattered debris a dozen times before they caught up with their quarry: A pair of Autobots searching the scene of the disappearance: Prowl and Bumblebee, in the metallic "flesh."

The one called Bumblebee scanned the scene impassively. His canary-yellow armor gleamed in the morning sun. Standing tall on his column-like legs, Bumblebee resembled a Viking with a horned helmet. The mechanical smile on his faceplate lent this Autobot an air of perpetual cheerfulness, even in such a grim, post-apocalyptic setting.

Prowl, on the other hand, projected an almost demonic air, no doubt because of his impassive gray face, and the long scarlet sensor arrays that projected from his robotic forehead like devil horns. He used his sensors to scan the combat zone for any clue to the alien energy that washed over the Ginza district just a few hours ago.

Seemingly oblivious to the presence of these mechanical titans, a host of rescue workers dug through the ruins. Some waded through knee-deep drifts of broken glass and shattered masonry in an effort to find those still trapped beneath the wreckage. A huge, bowl-shaped blast area several blocks long and five blocks wide marked the boundaries of last night's combat. Inside the battle zone the streets were all but impassable—not even heavy equipment could be brought in to clear the thoroughfares. Nearer to the scorched edges of that ruined zone, the streets were mostly clear. There, several dozen ambulances waited, motors idling and emergency lights flashing, to rush survivors to nearby trauma centers. In numerous areas, firefighters still poured water on scattered fires that smoldered beneath the ruins, sending up thick black smoke that hovered over the rest of Tokyo.

"Okay, okay," Chris said, desperately trying to wrangle in his excitement as he addressed his crew. "We've talked about this. No matter what happens, *keep shooting*. Got it?"

Both crewmembers nodded. A hot link would broadcast their footage to Rhona Jay, their producer, who was back in the van. She was making sure it was bounced to their live satellite feed from the dish atop the vehicle.

"Everyone scared out of their minds?" Chris asked.

Joe and Tom nodded like eager puppies.

"Good," Killah said. "Best way to be. If this plays out, I'll be on the cover of *Newsweek* and the two of you will be looking at bonuses big enough to buy your dream houses, or whatever it is you geeks are into."

"Keep it frosty, gentlemen. We're going in."

It took nearly ten minutes for the reporter to get the Transformers' attention, deliver his pitch, and secure their agreement to the interview. Chris came across as passionate and concerned, much like his totally manufactured on-air persona. He explained that the U.S. administration, along with the U.N., were concerned about the impact this current situation would have on younger viewers, many of whom worshipped the Transformers as great heroes and had been highly disturbed by reports of the previous night's events. Just *seeing* a couple of Autobots, alive and well, would go a long way toward settling the fears of today's youth.

It was crap, of course. Their boss, media mogul Iolus Monk, had paid off the right people in the right places to land them an exclusive. But the pitch sounded good, and these strong, but simple creatures, *always* responded to nobility and all that garbage.

These two proved to be no exception. Soon, Killah had them posed before a ruined office building that he was certain they weren't even aware was in the shot. A little added "show don't tell" to stir things up, scare the public even more, and drive the ratings through the roof.

The effervescent Bumblebee elected to speak first,

as Prowl, the always-logical warrior, looked out impassively beside him.

As he spoke, he was all business. The drill here was simple: Soften them up, then go in for the kill.

"This is Chris Killah reporting live from the site of last night's mysterious event in Toyko. Joining me now are the Autobots Bumblebee and Prowl. Bumblebee, would you tell us in your opinion what happened here last night?"

The nervous Autobot pointed at the camera. "Um... I... Gee, is that thing on? Really?"

"Really," Chris confirmed.

Bumblebee's glowing eyes seemed to widen. Or perhaps it was a trick of the light. Bumblebee certainly wasn't ignorant of Earth culture in any way, shape or form. He had been with Spike all the time, after all. So it wasn't as if he didn't know what a camera was, or wasn't aware of the media...he simply wasn't used to being the center of media attention.

The reporter had seen this kind of thing all the time. He'd interviewed a brilliant scientist last week and the man had turned into a nervous, bashful kid the moment a camera was pointed at him. Media attention was flattering and disarming and could put anyone who wasn't used to being interviewed off their game, making them stutter, leaving the most articulate at a loss for words. That meant the advantage went to the reporter.

"Gee, uh... I don't know what happened. That's what we're here to find out." The sleek angular planes of Bumblebee's yellow horned metallic face turned slightly... amber. It was as if he were blushing. Another trick of the light, more likely than not. "Hopefully, I mean. Hopefully we'll find out. We want out friends back."

The reporter nodded thoughtfully. "Every one of us in the media is very well aware of the good the Transformers have done for this planet. This must be a very trying time for all of you?"

Bumblebee nodded.

"Did you know that Isolde Holden is among the missing? We've lost one of our own, and Isolde has been a champion during even your darkest days."

"I heard about that," Bumblebee said. "Bummer, isn't it?"

Chris had to keep himself from inwardly shrieking with delight. He knew damn well that Bumblebee had no intention of sounding callous, but that phrase, on its own, would be plastered over headlines throughout the world, and the haters, always the most vocal and powerful minority, would seize on it and keep it alive for *years*.

"We're all greatly concerned," Prowl said, butting in.

The reporter ignored him. Bumblebee was the innocent and vulnerable one here. He was the target.

"Are you aware of the rumors?" Killah asked. "And the avenues of speculation that the leading analysts have thus far suggested?"

Bumblebee shook his head and shifted his weight uncomfortably from one massive foot to the other. "No, uh, not really..." He cleared his throat, a strange mechanical sound clearly patterned after human emotional responses. "No."

"Theories fall into two distinct categories," the reporter said. "In the first, Prime, Megatron, Bluestreak, and Jazz were taken—along with several hundred innocent humans—from this very spot to parts unknown. By who? Or what? There are quite a few theories on that as well. The second category suggests the Autobots, the Decepticon and all of these people are dead, that they were reduced or *transformed* to nothingness. So let's start with that. Alive or dead, Bumblebee? What's your feeling?"

Bumblebee drew back, flustered. "Well, um... I'm not sure—"

Suddenly, Prowl stomped in front of his companion, causing the camera crew to leap back and nearly lose their balance from the thumping vibrations of his feet, each of which were the size of busses.

"The buildings are still standing," Prowl said calmly, pragmatically. "We know of no force that could target both organic and technological life forms, destroy them and the inorganic matter they were wearing or carrying, and leave everything else standing. No, if they had been destroyed, this place would be a smoking pit."

Killah was unconvinced. "But some force *did* target only the Transformers and the humans in this area. The question is whether it destroyed them or took them somewhere."

"Suggestions have been made that the Transformers themselves caused this to happen."

"Ridiculous," Prowl said calmly.

"What about Megatron?" the reporter continued, battering his giant subject with the force of his disturbing questions. "He was here. Alone. Up to *something*. Authorities are baffled as to how he got into the country and his reasons for doing so. Aren't you at least mildly curious? Is it beyond all reason, in your experience, to consider that Megatron may have lured the others into some kind of trap?"

"Enough," Prowl said matter-of-factly. "You must see, logically, that this is pointless. We don't have any answers—we've come here looking for them just like everyone else. We pray that everyone is safe. For right now, until we learn more, that is all we can do."

"Hey, wait," Bumblebee said. "I caught something on the news on the way over here. There was some guy, a navy dude, commanding a submarine or something. He said that a couple of months ago, he was out there in the Pacific, somewhere deep, and he saw lights just like the ones that came up just before everybody blinked out."

Killah switched tactics, obviously intrigued. "So you are suggesting there is yet *another* alien race to be factored into this equation?"

"This has become sensationalistic," Prowl said. The Autobot reached down at the cameraman and casually sent a highly targeted, low energy pulse directly at their equipment. Their signal was blocked out, their transmission ended.

"Hey, what'd you do that for?" asked the cameraman, not lowering his camera.

Prowl bent low, his faceplate becoming the world for the camera crew and the reporter. "People will say whatever they want to say because of their fears or because they think they can elevate themselves into the public eye by attacking us. Fine. We accepted that a long time ago. The bottom line is that none of us has enough hard data to draw any reasonable conclusions. We need to work together to find the truth—or get the slag out of each other's way."

"So you want to control or suppress the people's right to know?" Killah asked.

Prowl shook his head sadly. Even though they were no longer broadcasting, his camera was still working...and everything the Autobot said and did was being taped.

"No comment." Prowl said with a sigh. Then he

rose, grabbed Bumblebee's arm, and led his fellow Autobot away.

"Nice meeting you!" Bumblebee called over his shoulder.

You say that now, Killah thought. *Just wait until this footage hits the air...*

Prowl appeared disquieted to Bumblebee.

"Something bothering you?" Bumblebee asked.

"I believe that reporter was attempting to manipulate both of us and that his concern over how children were going to handle this situation was a smokescreen. He was looking for sound bites and we gave him everything he needed."

Bumblebee just looked at him blankly.

Prowl sighed and turned away. He had an idea of how much worse public sentiment was about to get for them, but there wasn't much he could do about it now. "There's nothing here for us. We've scanned the area for leftover ambient energies a dozen times now, looked for any kind of tech that might have been used in the abduction, the kind that human senses and equipment wouldn't pick up, and we're still at square one."

"So what do you think happened?" Bumblebee asked quietly.

The Autobots looked to the sky. Prowl said, "I'd like to think they're in a better place. But somehow, considering the trouble that always follows us around, I tend to doubt it."

CHAPTER
THREE

"So, Prime," Jazz muttered, "think they're ever going to turn on the lights in this place?"

Optimus Prime sat totally still in the darkness. No, it was *more* than darkness. He was in a void, an area that defied all of his senses and eluded every scan. Darkness was never a problem for those of his manufacture: Unlike humans, whose ocular capacities were severely limited, Prime could read every possible spectrum band. Plus, he could reach out with sonar, examine heat patterns, and employ many other "enhanced senses" to know the exact strengths and weaknesses of any battlefield at any given time.

None of those abilities were doing him the slightest bit of good. All he could feel was that he was alive, intact, miraculously restored, and sitting upon some flat surface, a bench or shelf of some kind. The sudden intrusion of Jazz's voice had startled him because it meant that at least some of his senses were operating at capacity... while others were *not*.

Or were being blocked.

He could hear Jazz, and from the sound of his friend's voice, pinpoint the Autobot's location. Prime now knew that Jazz sat fifteen meters away, at an 80 degree bearing... but that was *all* his senses would tell him. He still could not "see" or otherwise get a sense of the place in which they were being held. Nor could he tell if they were alone.

"Bluestreak?" he asked, surprised again to be able to hear the sound of his own voice. Then, hesitantly, "Megatron?"

There was no reply.

"I think we're alone," Jazz said, breaking the silence.

"What happened? Was it the Decepticons?"

"If it was, Megatron didn't know a thing about it. I was looking right at him when the lightshow hit. He was as surprised as the rest of us." Jazz sighed. "As far as how long we've been here... No idea. My time sense is all messed up. I feel like it could have been a few minutes ago when we were all in Tokyo, or maybe it was a few million years back."

Optimus had also been robbed of any sense of the passage of time, however, his internal diagnostics revealed complete repairs to all his damaged sectors. He revealed as much to his friend.

"Well, that's good," Jazz said. "I really wasn't ready to deal with you naming your successor."

Optimus thought back to the last battle and wondered if perhaps he *should* abdicate responsibility.

No, not until we know what's going on, not until we get out of... wherever "here" is.

"How long do you think this is going to go on?" Jazz asked. "I hate that I can't move."

"Anyone who's ever seen you dance already knows you can't move, Jazz," Optimus said.

"Oh, right. Kick an Autobot when he can't kick back."

Optimus hadn't realized it at first, but he was testing his friend. *Was* Jazz up to the role of commander if anything happened to Optimus? He had to know.

"You've got that mouth of yours," Optimus said. "You usually don't have any trouble using *it* as a weapon."

A surprisingly soft and smooth voice intruded. *"Yes. Test your boundaries. Attempt to discern if you have any strengths that are not measured by the physical. This is an excellent beginning."*

Optimus and Jazz sat waiting for a stretch that felt like a very long time to them, hoping that the voice would say more.

It did not.

"Who are you?" Optimus Prime demanded. "Where have you taken us?"

The voice remained silent. Though there was no physical change in the atmosphere surrounding the Autobot, Prime had a strange sense that a shift had occurred, that whoever—or whatever—was monitoring them had suddenly become bored, or disappointed by these questions.

The voice had seemed far more interested and entertained when it appeared that Prime and Jazz might fight, even if it was only a mild bout of verbal sparring.

"Only those with something to hide refuse to show their faces," Optimus Prime said, switching tactics as he endeavored to elicit some response from the observer. "Or those who are afraid."

Nothing.

"Bored now," Jazz said in a lilting voice, quoting from one of those TV programs he enjoyed so much. Prime understood immediately that Jazz was far from bored, he was pretending so that he could get a rise out of their captors—and it worked like a charm.

"You're bored?" the voice inquired. *"Your fate is uncertain. The matter of your immediate continued existence is up for debate. You are little more than a few impulses of energy racing about a cybernetic brain, all else is uncertain, a mystery. Yet you are bored."*

"There's nothing to see," Jazz went on, continuing to playact that he was disinterested when the truth was just the opposite. "Nothing to do."

"You see no value in pondering your current state?"

"Nope. It's dull," Jazz said, driving the final nail into the coffin of their captor's patience and tolerance.

The voice hesitated. *"Then behold!"*

The darkness about them lifted.

No...

It simply changed. The infinite void surrounding Optimus Prime and Jazz melted away and was replaced with the deep black abyss of space. Stars flickered and came into focus—and Prime saw that they were in some type of sphere revealed only by intermittent flashes of blue and crimson lightening.

Prime was well pleased. Jazz had cleverly manipulated the entity who had been speaking to them into revealing this incredible vista.

At least, Prime *thought* it had been part of a clever ploy.

Or maybe Jazz had just been bored.

Able to move slightly, Prime looked to either side and saw that their sphere was not the only one in this deep and, at a glance, unfamiliar area of space. More than a hundred such translucent balls of energy stretched outward in either direction, only a dozen yards separating one from the next. Optimus saw Bluestreak and Megatron—who had also been restored—in one off to their immediate left. The rest were filled with human beings.

Prime tried to get a fix on the constellations, but they matched no starscape in his database. Ahead was a swirling mass that Prime had first thought was a spiral galaxy. It was not. He was looking at a world, one unlike any he had previously envisioned. Lattices of blue and crimson energy like that which captured the Transformers on Earth bound an insane collection of asteroid fragments and wrecked generation ships, each the size of a small continent on Earth. Larger objects had also been pulled into the mad menagerie. Prime saw moons yanked out of their orbits and carcasses of beings that were altogether impossible. The latter were the size of worlds. Some were vaguely humanoid, others formed bizarre geometric shapes. Still others were impossible collections of bones, limbs, muscular structures, organisms that, in life, seemed to have followed no rhyme or reason, almost a conglomeration of billions of individuals fused together for some unfathomable purpose.

What was this place? Why had they been brought here?

"How does a place like this exist?" Jazz asked.

Prime was certain that his comrade did not expect an answer, however...

"It exists because we will it to be so. It serves a function... as will all of you."

"Look upon me and despair, for I am *vast*," Jazz whispered. Prime recognized the words from some book written on Earth.

"We're moving. We must be," Optimus said. "I can't feel it. My sensors are deadened. But—"

"Our perspective keeps changing," Jazz finished. "Either that thing is moving toward us, or we're headed for it."

In the blink of an eye, the vision before them faded and the void was restored.

"It hasn't been that long," Optimus said.

"What are you talking about?" Jazz asked.

"All those people are still alive. Maybe they could have been frozen somehow, like we were millions of years ago, but my instinct tells me that's just not the case."

"Yeah, that and Mister Creepy-Voice," Jazz said. "Someone does this much talking, it's because he wants an audience *now*. So how did we get somewhere so far from Earth?"

"Wormhole travel is the only possibility I can come up with," Optimus admitted. He refrained from adding that wormholes were usually two-way streets.

"You have seen your final destination," the voice rang out. *"There is no way out of the Labyrinth. And where you have been taken, there is no hope of rescue."*

Jazz hrmmphed. "I think he's insecure about it. They're not showing us the exact way in because then we'd know the way out."

"Not at all," the voice chimed in. *"We have learned from past experiences that your minds simply could not contain all you would experience should we allowed you visual and sensory stimulus. And, damaged to such a degree, you would hold no value for us."*

"Who are you?" Prime demanded.

"We are the Keepers."

"Wow, that's really specific," Jazz mused.

Optimus could not help but recall his time before he became Prime, when he confessed his lack of faith in the cause for which he would soon be made to fight.

"We know of your homeworld. We know more about it than any of you. We know when it was built. We know why. And we know by whom."

"Don't listen," Optimus said.

Jazz laughed hollowly. "I'd like to... but he just won't shut up."

"We know what's inside you. Each of you. You can aspire all you want to be something more or something

different, but your evolution stopped a long time ago. The experiment that produced you ran its course to disappointing effect and was then... neglected."

"They're lying to us," Optimus said quickly. "They'll say anything to confuse us, to try and control us."

The disappointed tone returned to the voice from the darkness. *"Controlling you is a simple matter. You are immobile right now because that is what we wish. You see and hear only what we allow. We want you to understand your options. We want you to revel in your own power as you never have before."*

"Then set us *free*," Prime raged.

"That you must do for yourself. We can only attempt to guide you. Surely you have had other... mentors... in your lives."

There was one that immediately came to Optimus's mind, but it was a figure he desperately did not want to think about. In fact, he would do practically anything to keep from thinking about his vision during the battle. A malfunction, certainly, a result of the punishment he had sustained from Megatron.

Yet the words of Sentinel Prime haunted him, causing him pain and doubt, even now.

He had led his fellows and the innocent humans to this fate. It was all on his shoulders, and he had to fight to keep the burden from becoming crippling.

"Why did you take the people?" Prime asked. "What are you planning to do with them?"

"Free yourself of concern. They're safe... for now. They will remain unharmed so long as you comply with our commands."

"They're hostages?" Jazz spat with contempt. "Why not just reprogram us? Make us do what you want? You're forcing us, anyway."

"No, we're not. You have always possessed free will,

whether you realized that or not. Your physical strength is not the only measure of your power, and that is something you must learn."

"Go to hell," Optimus Prime muttered.

"From your limited perspective, it may soon seem as if we had come to that mythical place. You have arrived. Now look upon this..."

The void's walls faded and suddenly Prime and Jazz were on their feet standing above a great arena. Simple physics did not seem to apply in this place. They stood upon nothing yet they did not fall. They were surrounded by luminous, blue-gray arching walls and a concave ceiling that felt disquietingly familiar. Optimus felt as if he were in the belly of some beast, but what surrounded him was not organic. His scans revealed traces of something that had been techno-organic.

This arena had been placed within the remains of beings.

Below, two aliens grappled as large, monolith slabs, or panels, slid out from under them and slammed toward them in an ever-moving shuffle. Beneath the panels lay a fiery abyss.

At first, Optimus Prime thought he was staring out at two wild beasts locked in a primal struggle for survival. If his sensors were to be believed, each was as tall as a Transformer. One was vaguely bird-like, with a sharp, pale, curved beak, a blood red skull, and a frill with dark spikes reaching out behind its head. Dark wings spread behind the creature, flapping occasionally, but not lifting it into the air. A long neck with serrated plates led down to a deep blue egg-shaped torso, and raking talons spread out from the hands and feet of its long, thin, yet very powerful arms. It moved with grace, agility, and speed, darting back and biting or tearing at the heavier body of its foe. The other alien had a face that looked as if it might be more at home on that of a panda back on Earth, only one that had been put through a funhouse mirror and stretched to an obscene length, turning it into more of a coyote-shaped, a furry white-and-black death's head. The body was powerful and not unlike that of a marsupial... except for the great, curled claws at the end of its club-like hands and feet.

But they were not animals. They wore jewelry and armor, and the scabbards of now discarded edged weapons were belted around their waists. On the ever-shifting panels beneath them lay an ion sword and two cutlasses crackling with blue and crimson energies.

Both combatants were bloodied. The devil bird's tactic had been one of wearing down his larger and meatier opponent with an endless supply of thin, deep cuts and ragged wounds threatening to spill intestines or to expose ivory bone. The death's head creature circled like a wrestler, watching and waiting patiently for his opponent to miss leaping upon a panel, lose his balance, or get distracted in any way so that he might seize on the opening and crush the winged fighter. From the odd angle at which one of the devil bird's wings was set, certainly not natural, and a dent that must have signaled internal injuries in the plating over the bird's ribs, it was clear the death's head alien had landed at least two solid and punishing blows.

A crowd rose into view on either side of the combatants. It was comprised of two sets of aliens corresponding to the fighters, one group of winged "devil beasts," another of the thicker-set "death's head marsupials." Each set was kept a fair distance from the other, yet each was stationed close enough to have a "ringside" view of the fighting and to have their mad cheers and bloodthirsty urgings heard by each of their "champions"...if that was the right word for the two monstrous beings fighting to the death. Perhaps the warriors were lawbreakers and this was their punishment. Prime had no way to know. He had tried to speak several times since this tableau was revealed, to ask the "Keeper" why this was happening, to issue some protest at very least, but that simple act, like forward motion, had proved impossible.

The shifting tiles upon which the fighters danced merely to stay in place stopped moving suddenly—surprising not the winged beast, but instead the death's head fighter. The devil bird darted in swiftly, risking its own long neck, to strike at the throat of his opponent. A torrent of blood splashed across the tiles, a thick, ugly red rain, and the tide turned. The tiles beneath the winged beast slid and blurred with savage frenzy, while those under his enemy remained still. Despite the increased difficulty in reaching his prey, the devil bird alien struck a dozen more times, until the death's head beast collapsed, no longer able to raise a single blocking arm in his own defense.

From that moment on, there was no longer a contest. It was simple slaughter.

"Turn away now, if you will," the unseen Keeper instructed.

Optimus realized that control of his body had been returned to him—within limits. He could do exactly what the Keeper suggested, but nothing more. Instead, he remained stock still, while Jazz shuddered and looked away. Then, shamed, Prime's fellow Autobot fixed his gaze firmly on the horror below.

The Keepers would *not* dictate their actions. The Autobots had free will. If the only way of proving that and defying their captors was to watch this atrocity, then that was what they would do.

"Now think long and hard of your future... and your purpose."

Optimus Prime and Jazz felt the Keeper depart. There was no specific sensor scan that signaled the absence of the being that had brought them here, yet each felt more alone somehow, less... complete... than mere moments earlier.

The feeling that they were now *less* than what they had been with the Keepers frightened each of them, though they would not admit it, even to themselves. Staring above the battlefield, peering down at the victor of the horrible duel, Optimus Prime wished that he could take some course of action that would turn back time and prevent this madness from ever unfolding. But he could not.

And below, the devil bird was in a frenzy, along with all of its brethren. Inflicting death was not enough, it seemed. The winged creature was ripping apart the carcass of its victim with primordial intensity.

The Keepers intimated that there was a purpose to all of this. Yet what he had just seen, the savage, brutal conflict... what purpose could there be, other than the amusement of the Keepers, and, perhaps, others who watched from the shadows.

And yet...

Something within him had responded to the visceral action he had witnessed. Something buried deep had flared, if only for an instant, as the aliens attempted to kill each other.

Something within the Matrix.

CHAPTER FOUR

Franklin opened the aircraft hanger's metal door and ushered Spike into a military ad hoc wonderland. Their first glimpse of what lay inside revealed a central command center dominating the interior of the huge hangar. The center was comprised of a half-dozen high-tech workstations. The largest occupied the middle of the hanger and was enclosed behind what appeared to be a circular wall made of a dark, opaque Plexiglas. Upon closer inspection, Spike could see that the walls were neither opaque nor made of Plexiglas. Inside of that enclosure, what *appeared* to be a wall was revealed to be a 360° projection screen that provided instant data to the occupants inside of the command center. Topographical maps, real-time satellite images, windows filled with information, radar data and electronic communications beamed from a hundred remote locations—along with live broadcasts from CNN, Fox News, Nippon Broadcasting, Reuters and the BBC in large-screen television sized windows—all scrolled across the mammoth digital multi-viewing screen.

In the exact center of that central command area, hovering over what appeared to be a small radar dish, floated a holographic image of the wrecked Ginza District of Tokyo. This holograph was being diligently studied and accessed by several military intelligence officers. A second, smaller holographic image projected next to the first had an ominously familiar shape.

Starscream!

The Decepticon stood on a pinnacle of jagged rock that rose from the desert floor. His wings were outspread, and his arm blasters were aimed.

In a concentric circle around the holographic projector were dozens of computer workstations, each one a beehive of furious activity. Dozens of techs monitored the huge, high-definition screens that ran along the wall, as well as a host of smaller flat screens at each of their duty stations. Young women in battle dress fatigues moved carts stuffed with reams of paper—print outs from surveillance satellites monitoring electronic data transmissions worldwide. Other young officers—men and women—all raced back and forth between workstations, clutching PDAs like old-fashioned clipboards and displaying their data as requested by several duty officers who seemed to take the flurry of desperate activity in stride.

Beyond the enclosed central command station, Spike could see other work scattered throughout the large hanger, and in tiers of underground levels below it, too. Spike realized that there were probably underground corridors and high-tech facilities that reached well beyond the exterior confines of the hangar itself.

Each interior work area was a universe in itself. The entire hangar was teeming with activity, and by the time Spike noticed the single Black Hawk helicopter he was surprised. Not by the fact that the Black Hawk had been retro-fitted in a Pave Low configuration with night vision flying sensors, geo-positioning navigation system, and FLIR (forward-looking infrared radar) equipment for nape of the earth flying, but by the mere presence of the single chopper tucked into one corner of the expansive interior—the only aircraft visible in what was supposed to be an aircraft hangar.

Instead of airplanes, all around him Spike saw flat-screen computers that flickered with electronic life. Instead of the roar of aircraft engines, he heard the atonal warble of red, black, and blue phones. Trained by Optimus Prime to be intensely observant, Spike's keen ears instantly detected that each color phone rang with a slightly different sound—one that was instantly distinguishable to the highly-trained battle staff.

Security was tight within the high-tech facility. The doors to each work area were guarded by Marine Corps officers clutching M-16s. Each one of them wore dark colored battle gear and black body armor, and each one checked the electronic identity card dangling around the staff's neck before admitting them to a particular work area.

Spike wanted to ask what was happening with Starscream, but the Decepticon didn't appear to be doing anything at all. From the background conversations he quickly sorted out, Spike learned that Starscream had been standing out there for over an hour, as if he had simply been waiting for someone to make contact with him...or meet the silent challenge he was offering. The military was holding back, waiting on the arrival of some mysterious "package" before they would approach the steel goliath.

In short, they were playing "who blinks first" with a Decepticon who had *always* wanted leadership of his rogue faction of Transformers...and was now in a position to claim it. Only the Decepticon called Shockwave might challenge Starscream's claims to leadership, but no one had heard any communications from Shockwave in months. Soundwave might be a different matter entirely. He was a loyal puppet who worshipped Megatron, resorting to any means necessary, even the blackmail of his fellow Decepticons, to make himself look better in his master's eyes. To serve Megatron's ends, Soundwave preferred to subtly guide the path of the subordinate Decepticons with a whispered word here, an offhand suggestion there. With Megatron missing in action, presumed *dead* by many, would Soundwave simply transfer his loyalties to another? Or would he work from within to protect his true master's interests?

"So, do you feel better after those calls you made on the way over here?" Franklin asked, shocking Spike out of his automatic situational threat assessment.

Spike looked around, doing his best to seem unimpressed. Truth to tell, this place was incredibly impressive. That begged one major question: What in God's name was it doing in *his* hometown?

"You knew I'd have to check you out," Spike said.

"Of course. And you know with what we did with voice simulators that we could have rerouted every one of those calls to phonies. You think the President is that hard to impersonate?"

Spike said nothing.

"The bottom line is that some things you have to take on faith, or trust your instincts about. I think that's what you've done here. You know I'm not Hallo. Your gut tells you I'm not out to screw you. I want to save those people. I want to make sure no one else gets taken. That's it."

"We'll see."

"Yes, we will."

Franklin clapped his hand over the shoulder of a meaty, curly-haired man with dark circles under his eyes. Spike paid close attention as the fabric of the tech's *Akira* T-shirt bunched and the man winced in pain. Franklin eased his grip quickly, his features immediately painting a portrait of unexpected empathy and sheepishness. The tech said nothing, but his whole body relaxed when Franklin withdrew his hand completely.

"Still butting horns with Craig on this whole outside recruitment deal?"

"You know it," the tech said, typing away, his face bathed in the soft blue glow of his flat screen.

"And how's that working out for you?"

"You know. It's a good thing the asshole I had wasn't doing the trick. Otherwise, getting torn a new one would have been a bad thing."

"But we've got authorization?"

"That we do."

Franklin winked at Spike. "That's a good thing. Means we don't have to put you in protective custody and dump you in a hole until this mess is cleaned up."

Spike took a step back. "Pardon?"

"Think about it. If you weren't working with us, there's a chance you could be coerced into working against us. We've got people watching out for your wife and son, as well as your brother. They've *never* been safer, believe me. And all those troubles you guys have been looking at are definitely going away when this is all over."

"Co-opted by whom?" Spike asked.

Franklin gestured broadly. "Whomever. The Followers themselves, most likely. But there are always paramilitary and terrorist cells out there who want their hooks in you. My job for the last six months has been keeping those wolves from your door."

Spike couldn't hide his anger any longer. "You've been spying on me?"

"Don't take it personally. We spy on everyone with your kind of profile."

"And what kind is that?"

Franklin smiled. "You hang with a dangerous crowd. Those Transformers... always causing some kind of ruckus."

Spike sensed that he wouldn't get any more answers on that subject, so he changed tactics. "Why set up operations here?"

"Mobility. We have aircraft standing by and can be on our way almost immediately if we get a lead."

"I mean in Cleveland."

Franklin looked around. "Come on. I confessed we were spying on you. What did you think we were spying on you *with*?"

They came here because of me, Spike realized. *And if hostile forces learn about this place, that'll put my home and everyone I love in the direct line of fire.*

"Leads," Spike said, exhaling through gritted teeth, his face flush. "Do you *have* any?"

Franklin ignored Spike's emotional display. "One. I take it that you've seen footage of the lights that appeared just before the disappearances. U.S. Navy submarine commander Hugo Fortuna claims to have seen a very similar display of lights in the depths of the Pacific Ocean not long before the Transformers and those in a five block radius of them were taken. What isn't commonly known is that he has been approached several times by the Followers, and that he may well have been compromised."

Spike was intrigued. "Wait, wait... before or *after* he saw the lights?"

"Impossible to say. He was the only one to see these

weird energies or whatever they were. They weren't picked up by any of the sub's equipment, either. It could be that he didn't see a damn thing. This could all be misdirection on the part of the Followers, an attempt to construct reasonable doubt in the minds of the public and assign blame to some outside force for their actions."

"Or the Followers could be working with that outside force."

Franklin shrugged. "We don't know what's true and what isn't. Our only options are to pick up Fortuna and lock him in a room with a team of experts to try to persuade him into talking...or you can have a go at him."

"Great. Some choice you're leaving me."

"That's the reality of it." Franklin raised an eyebrow. "Think of it this way. Even though you've agreed to help us, you still have free will. We're pretty much at your mercy at every stage of this operation. I'm just telling you what will happen to the commander if you say 'no.' Statement of fact, nothing more."

Spike rubbed at his temples. The first signs of a migraine were showing up. "You think he'll try to recruit me?"

"If he does, then we'll know he's with the Followers. Otherwise, just being in the presence of someone else who's seen impossible things, experienced stuff that normal people never even dream about...it could make him let down his guard and say things he's been afraid to talk about before, or jog his memory. It's a chance. In my opinion, we should take it."

A sudden commotion made them both turn.

The tech wearing the *Akira* T-shirt almost leaped out of his seat. "Sir! You better take a look at this."

Starscream had ended the detente. After setting

down his weapons and raising his arms as if in surrender, turning quickly, aiming his arm-mounted lasers and blew apart the first jet to come within range. Now the full force of the military was about to be brought to bear on him—and Sideswipe, an Autobot, had been called in to help.

Sideswipe had been the package Spike had heard them talking about earlier.

"Track all of this," Franklin said. "Somehow, I don't think it's going to be pretty..."

Nevada

A flight of three Northrop B-2 Spirit stealth bombers streaked at near-sonic speed and at low level, kicking up dust as they raced over the brown rocks and red sand of the Nevada desert. Black aircraft that resembled flying wings, the Spirits cast a dark shadow over the landscape flashing by beneath them. Though the stealth bombers were huge, with individual wingspans that exceeded 170 feet, the noise of the four General Electric F118-GE-100 turbofan engines was buffered by sound suppressors, so that only the whisper of the wind over the airfoils could be discerned.

Inside the bellies of each of these airborne behemoths, mounted on a high-speed revolving carousel, were three advanced, specially modified AGM-137 cruise missiles. All nine missiles were primed and ready to launch, the data configuration of their target already programmed into their computers through the B-2s GATS geopositional targeting system. Part of the 509 Bomber Group out of

Whiteman Air Force Base in Missouri, the B-2s had been scrambled just hours before to attack a specific and deadly target.

Now, just 200 miles away from that target, the bomb bay doors opened and the carousel rolled the first cruise missiles into launch position. In these tense moments during missile launch, the B-2 stealth bomber loses much of its stealthy characteristics—what had appeared like a tiny bird on enemy radar now looked more like a flock of condors. This hazardous situation would persist until all the AGMs were fired and the bomb bay doors retracted again.

Suddenly, with a brilliant white flash of plasma, the first three AGMs left their launchers. The B-2s shuddered as the missiles left the carousel, to streak at bullet-speed toward their deadly rendezvous. Less than five seconds later, the second flight of three AGMs were fired. And less than ten seconds later, the third flight was launched and the bomb bay doors retracted again. Their stealthy characteristics restored, the three Spirits scattered in different directions—standard operating procedure after launching missiles, and a precaution against enemy radar honing in on them.

The first flight of AGMs dipped closer to the desert floor after launching, until their air scoops and wings were automatically deployed. Then they rose in the air and surged ahead, guidance system and forward-looking radar tracking the topography and matching it with the virtual maps stored in their computer memories. Suddenly the turbofan engines in the first flight of three AGMs slowed to allow the second and third flights of missiles to catch up to them. In a few seconds, the nine cruise missiles had assembled into a tight formation, their computer brains receiving new navigational information from GPS satellites in orbit around the planet every nanosecond. As one, all the forward-looking radar systems in all nine missiles locked onto the distant target, now illuminated by virtual radar. The turbofan engines whined as the guidance systems increased missile speed, accelerating the missiles toward their killing zone at seven hundred miles an hour.

As the missiles raced along their trajectory, they approached a massive cloud of dust that hovered low over the desert sand. The cloud was created by the swift movement of two U.S. Army divisions of boxy M1A2 Abrams Main Battle Tanks. Across a swath five miles wide these tanks rolled at top speed toward the spire of rock where the Decepticon called Starscream stood towering over the Nevada landscape. Moving at nearly forty miles per hour, the Abrams were dabbled in a desert camouflage scheme that uncannily matched the landscape around them. Neither quiet nor stealthy, the rumbling movement of the tank treads shook the earth in a raw display of military power that seemed unstoppable. Hundreds of 120-mm smoothbore cannons loaded with Sabot armor piercing rounds or High Explosive HEAT rounds were trained on the colossal mechanical shape that shimmered in the desert heat on the distant horizon.

As the tanks slowed and maneuvered into position to flank the Decepticon, nine cruise missiles flashed over the tanks and converged on Starscream.

Starscream, the Aerospace Commander of the earth-bound Decepticons, sensed the onrush of the cruise missiles. Cold-blooded and cruel, he held only contempt for the puny humans who tried to dislodge him from his perch atop the mile-high pinnacle of desert granite. Though Starscream fancied himself a brilliant military strategist, and preferred to rely on guile and speed rather than sheer brute force, the attack by the human military inflamed his anger and he lashed out just as the nine cruise missiles made their final, fatal dive on his position.

Raising the weapon on his left arm, Starscream fired once.

A split-second later, a single cluster bomb exploded amid the cruise missiles, scattering the AGMs in all directions. Five of the missiles were instantly obliterated. Three more, their guidance systems scrambled by the force of the airburst, spun out of control and plunged into the desert sand. But the ninth cruise missile, one fired in the final flight of three that had been launched by the Spirits, managed to penetrate the blast radius of Starscream's cluster bomb and relock on its target. Though the AGM's computer targeting system was damaged enough to miss striking the Decepticon, the cruise missile slammed into the rocky perch under Starscream's mammoth feet. The cruise missile's five-hundred pound high explosive warhead detonated with devastating results. The Decepticon was bathed in smoke and fire, and the force of the blast nearly knocked him off his feet. As the cliff began to crumble under his massive treads, Starscream blasted into the sky on a plume of fire. But instead of retreating from his adversaries, the Decepticon dived straight down, toward the ranks of main battle tanks still closing in on him.

The earth shuddered under the weight of his robotic form as Starscream landed directly in front of the first line of tanks. His burnished white and blue metallic legs absorbed the massive weight of his upper torso, and his outspread feet sank deep into the desert soil.

Metal wings spread wide, weapons pointed at the tanks that rumbled toward him, Starscream gazed down at the main battle tanks, his eyes blazing.

Then the Transformer looked up. High over the shimmering desert, distant white contrails in the blue sky announced the arrival of two flights of three McDonnell Douglas F-15 Eagles, each armed with two Maverick AGM-65 precision-guided missiles and a brace of AMRAAM AIM-120 air-to-air missiles. Using his telescopic vision, Starscream saw that the jets had just begun their final attack dive onto his position, and would arrive in less than a minute. Already their targeting system had locked onto him. They were not alone. A shining Autobot flew amidst the formation, just as Starscream had anticipated. The Decepticon knew it would be prudent to deal with the tanks now, before the U.S. Air Force fighters—and their *mascot*—deployed their missiles, so he turned and faced the tanks again.

His weapons crackling with power, Starscream attacked the armored column. He had played with these toys long enough. It was time to end this.

He wiped out his earth-bound enemies in a quick, violent, and altogether satisfying burst of all out destruction that lasted no less than six full seconds. Then he turned his back on the fiery field of death he had created, his masterpiece of devastation, and willed himself to change. Sections of his metallic body slammed, crashed, and shrieked as he came undone, unfolding his wings, smoothing out his spine, compressing his skull, as he lifted off into the air.

Starscream, wings spread and jet engines roaring, now resembled a gigantic version of the United States Air Force jet fighter bombers that doggedly pursued him. Behind him dozens of tanks burned, their composite armor shattered, turrets, treads, and armored wheels scattered all over the desert. Closer still the four F-15 Eagles, their missiles spent, fired their M61A1 Vulcan Gatling cannons at the Decepticon. Depleted uranium bullets bounced harmlessly off his glistening metallic hide. Starscream scanned the geographical features around him, until he located a deep and twisting canyon that ran like a brutal scar through the Nevada desert. Blue nose down, the Decepticon dived into the mouth of that deep ravine, the Air Force jets right behind him.

Behind Starscream, behind and above the diving F-15s, Sideswipe also dived into the mouth of the narrow canyon. His robotic arms were thrust forward, his trithyllium-steel alloy and carbon fiber armor gleaming blood red in the desert sun. Though his indestructible boxy form seemed clunky and not at all aerodynamic, Sideswipe moved through the air with a grace that belied his ungainly shape.

Down in the canyons now, Starscream picked up speed. As he raced through the rocky canyon, the slipstream ripped shale and rocks loose from the cliffs on either side. Racing into the cloud of rocks, sand, and dirt, an F-15 sucked debris into its jet intakes. The jet shuddered and stalled, but before the pilot could eject the aircraft was enveloped in an orange blossom of explosive fire and burning jet fuel. Flaming debris rained down on the canyon floor.

The three remaining F-15s continued their doomed pursuit of the savage Decepticon. Sideswipe raced to catch up to them, to somehow warn the pilots away, but he knew that the airmen were defending their homes and families and wouldn't give up without a fight.

The Eagle in the lead nearly caught up with Starscream. Vulcan cannon blazing, the pilot fired all 940 rounds at the Decepticon without effect. Just as he was about to pull out of the canyon, a blast from Starscream's null ray weapon totally disrupted the fighter's electrical systems. Spinning wildly out of control, the pilot tried to eject, but his escape system failed along with everything else. Striking the canyon wall, the aircraft vanished in a red ball of fire.

With a seemingly impossible maneuver, Starscream negotiated a sudden twist in the deep canyon. One of the two remaining F-15s wasn't so lucky. It's wing clipped the rocks and ripped free. The pilot ejected just as his fighter rolled to the starboard, but instead of parachuting free, his rocket seat blasted the hapless aviator right into the side of the canyon.

Sideswipe breathed a sigh of relief as the final F-15 pulled up and out of the canyon, away from the fight. Now only he and the Decepticon raced through the narrowing canyon, as billowing clouds of brown and ocher dust marked their paths. Starscream increased his speed until he attained a speed of Mach 1—only about a third of his top speed, but the best the Decepticon could do in such tight quarters. Still, the Autobot called Sideswipe closed the gap, surging forward with his arms outstretched, metallic fingers groping for Starscream's twin tail fins.

Suddenly explosions detonated all around them. Chunks of rock and an avalanche of earth and debris plunged from the canyon walls and bounced off Sideswipe's composite-armored skin. The Autobot looked up to see twelve F-16 Fighting Falcons diving out of the sun, a second wave of missiles preceding them.

Sideswipe surged ahead, diving under Starscream's

belly. His chest plate scraped the bottom of the canyon, but Sideswipe didn't mind. Better that than what Starscream was about to endure—direct hits from a score of AMRAAM air-to-air missiles.

The universe turned orange as a dozen missiles slammed into Starscream's fuselage, wings, and engine. Sideswipe immediately cut power and dropped behind the Decepticon, which now spun out of control. With an explosion of rocks and dirt, Starscream bounced off one canyon wall, to strike the opposite side. At that moment, Sideswipe surged forward, raised his mighty fists, and brought them down on Starscream's wings.

Something snapped, and the Decepticon crashed to the canyon floor and was instantly engulfed in a cloud of dust. Sideswipe shot upward, out of the canyon. He looked down and was shocked to see Starscream rising out of the dust, too. The Decepticon seemed unharmed as it closed in on Sideswipe.

"This day has had its ups and downs!" Sideswipe quipped as he dived into the canyon again, dodging a blast of the Decepticon's null-rays.

"This day marks your end, Autobot!" Starscream cried as he brought all of his weapons to bear on his foe.

Meanwhile the Air Force jets had returned, and now pursued the angry Decepticon. More missiles streaked toward Starscream, even as he chased the Autobot.

Sideswipe was determined to lead Starscream away from the humans. He saw a wide gap up ahead, and inwardly breathed a sigh of relief.

I'll get him out of here and smash him to bits where the debris from his carcass won't harm anyone, Sideswipe decided. *This is almost over.*

As fate would have it, he would only prove to be right about the last part.

Devastator stood waiting at the end of the canyon, his weapons raised. Towering over the desert, the sixty-foot monster was an awesome and terrifying vision. Composed of six separate Constructicons, Devastator was an ungainly thing—a mechanical being whose sole purpose was destruction of any and all things that stood in his path. A creature of pure instinct, his reactions were usually simple, direct, and violent.

Emerald and purple armor gleamed in the dying sunlight as Devastator sifted through the data pouring in from his component parts. Each of the six Constructicons possessed a super intelligence but they lost their brains when they formed Devastator. When Devastator's six computer brains registered the existence of the fighter planes, they acted in concert. The creature loosed a wide-angle blast of his solar energy rifle—a 10,000° heat blast that burned and melted everything in its path. In an instant, every one of the Air Force fighters was incinerated.

As Starscream streaked over his head, Devastator aimed his weapon at the approaching Sideswipe. The Autobot made the perfect target, trapped as he was between the narrow walls of the canyon.

He fired as Starscream *transformed* in midair, spiraling to face back at his opponent while sheer momentum carried him forward. Starscream loosed every weapon at his command.

Sideswipe didn't stand a chance. Every pressure point, every vulnerable joint, every chink between the plates of the great metallic knight's armor was targeted by the carefully orchestrated attack. His mouth opened wide as his neck blew apart, his arms were shredded at the wrists, elbows, and shoulders, his chest was slit open wide with surgical precision and a rocket volleyed into the cavity of spitting severed cables and groaning iron ribs—

The rocket lifted the Autobot up and out of the canyon with its incredible propulsive force, then exploded, a fireball of blinding yellow and blood red energies that sent whirling shards of the Transformer flying as far and wide as a dozen miles away.

Sideswipe's head buried itself only a dozen feet away from the underground oil reserves of the only gasoline filling station in the area. The lone attendant, smoking a cigarette as he filled up a tourist's gas-guzzling tank, had no idea how close he had come to seeing yet another explosion, one that would have consumed him had it occurred.

"Put... put... *crrrkkkk-fzzzz*... put that out..." Sideswipe's smoking skull warned, the energies beyond his eyes nearly faded to black. "Gonna... it'll kill ya..."

The attendant's brow wrinkled and he loosed a derisive laugh, fired, in part, by relief. "My girlfriend says the same thing. Moron."

The attendant froze as he saw more debris rain down over the desert in the distance. He was taken completely by surprise as another piece of the metallic guardsman—the tip of a finger, perhaps—flew down from practically straight overhead, piercing the roof of the car he was gassing up. The sound and shocking *punch* of the collapsing automobile made him spin, stumble back, and spit out his cigarette in one clumsy, fatal motion. He slipped in the pool of gasoline that had been pouring from the nozzle in his hand—an item he had unconsciously withdrawn when the devastation from above began—and smelled only a mild fetid odor as the gasoline ignited and he was trapped within a fireball that might as well have been a solar flare, for it incinerated him, his customer, and the entire station in a heartbeat.

Listening to it all from patched in audio feed spilling from the speaker's in Soundwave's chest, a Decepticon who had been chronicling this moment until now, Starscream laughed until he fell on the ground.

Echoes of his mad, triumphant laughter wandered through the canyon, merging with the *thrump-bump-clump* footfalls of the mighty Devastator, who joined his fellows.

"That was *good*," Devastator said.

"One down," Soundwave added.

Starscream straightened up and rose to his feet. He turned to face his subjects.

What he had done today was a simple show of force. A chance for the world to see—and understand—that Starscream was now firmly in control of the Decepticons... and that things were going to be different from this point on.

It was also a chance for him to be blooded before his subordinates, an ancient ritual of ascension.

"Megatron is dead," Starscream pronounced. "The destiny of the Decepticons is now firmly in my hands. My rule binds us. Guides us. Our glory is at last at hand."

Devastator, now disassembling into his six smaller, component Decepticon "parts," asked, "But... where do we go from here? What do we do?"

"The where is easy," Starscream said. "As the humans would say, 'Vegas, baby... *Vegas.*'"

The other Decepticons nodded as they internally

gauged the distance to the glittering city that was immediately called up in their data banks.

"As to what we do when we get there..." Starscream shrugged. "Who needs to rule the world when you can be a *god* in a city that's a world onto itself?"

CHAPTER
FIVE

For once in his life, Bluestreak was speechless. He woke in a luminous white room, alone and unafraid. He couldn't remember the last time he had felt such a sense of peace.

Wait. He *could* remember.

It was the last day he had spent in Praxus, the city he called home. The last good day. The perfect day...

The day before the Decepticons came and destroyed everything and everyone he had cared about. He had been the only survivor of that devastating attack. Memories of the destruction threatened to explode within his mind.

Then, as he touched the wall, a sudden and almost startling sense of well-being flooded through him. The feelings stirred up by his thoughts of the brutal attack immediately vanished. In his heart, it was as if they no longer existed... and had *never* existed.

As he watched, three of the four shining walls transformed, along with the floor and ceiling, into his home. The illusion, which seemed like anything but an illusion, was alive, vibrant and complete.

Once, a long, long time ago, Bluestreak dwelled in a graceful high tower of cezium steel and shimmering glass. Now he was back, transported—he didn't know how—and in that brief second it didn't matter, either. For now he was enraptured by the memories that flooded through his mind. He was home! With his own kind, on a planet of beings just like himself.

Memories he thought he'd forgotten raced through Bluestreak's mind. He moved through the apartment he once called his own as if in a dream, marveling at the sight of his personal space, a home he thought lost in time that was now magically restored to him. Turning a corner, Bluestreak saw the rosy glow of the sun arcing through the windows of his balcony. As he approached the glass, it slid aside with a whisper, and the clean, fresh air of an Autobot city flowed into the room. At once Bluestreak heard the sound of hover cars, botmovers, and leisure scooters streaming just a few yards from the edge of his balcony. He stepped outside, to gaze at the towers rising all around him.

Praxus was a riot of graceful, curved structures—each one colossal, with spires and towers reaching miles into the brilliant azure sky. Shining ziggurats, their pinnacles laced with clouds, gleamed with a million arching lights. Delicate bridges connected the high structures to one another.

Stepping closer to the edge, Bluestreak peered down. Three or more human miles below his balcony, long supply trains with a thousand cars, each the size of an earth-bound cargo ship, carried goods to the dwellers of the bustling Autobot city. Bluestreak recalled that those supply convoys moved day and night, for if they ceased, the city would stop functioning.

With a flutter of delicate metal wings, a leisure scooter paused before Bluestreak's balcony. The door opened with a hiss of air, and the Autobot climbed inside. With a second, quiet hiss, the door closed and sealed, and the leisure scooter surged forward. A moment later, the scooter was moving along with the main flow of traffic, toward The Assembly—a massive circular, domed and spired structure in the exact middle of Praxus. The Assembly was a special place—a center of Autobot science, technology, art, philosophy, and culture. Autobots spent as much time as they could spare from their busy day at that place—they came there to attend classes, lectures, discussions, presentations, demonstrations, music concerts, the theater, holographic entertainment, or simply to make use of the many hundreds of libraries and archives that were open to all citizens of Praxus.

Outside the spotless window of his leisure scooter, Bluestreak saw a thousand other vehicles, all of them moving at a steady and constant speed, to converge at The Assembly. Still drifting along as if in a dream, Bluestreak scanned his surroundings, careful to note each and every detail, to store them away in his memory, where he hoped this vision of his home would remain vivid and real for all time.

As the leisure scooter floated through one of the gentle curves that ran between the colossal, cyclopean structures to form what passed for streets, Bluestreak saw hundreds of examples of Autobot architecture—white, blue, brown and gold towers that scraped the sky. Massive, bulbous structures that, though large, nevertheless seemed graceful and delicate due to their subtle design. Some buildings bore the mark of other traditions and shadowy ancient Autobot cultures. They mimicked many different styles. One building looked like a hundred massive, opaque bubbles stacked on top of one another. Inside, Bluestreak could see hundreds of thousands of Autobots moving along tiers of platforms inside each bubble.

Another building resembled a tall, shining pyramid, with a huge glowing orb on its pinnacle. This orb glowed blue, orange, then white, and Bluestreak recalled that the building's designer, whose name is lost in time, designed that orb to broadcast a greeting in every known Autobot language to any possible alien cultures elsewhere in the universe.

As the traffic approached The Assembly, Bluestreak saw thousands of other Autobots walking along the high bridges, moving past a million examples of fine art, design, and sculpture, as they boarded the moving sidewalks that carried them to The Assembly.

Then, in the distance, the familiar shape of the domed Assembly building appeared. Bluestreak sighed and closed his eyes, as the beauty and majesty of his home city overwhelmed him.

It all seemed so real. He could reach out and put his hands on any of it and truly believe the illusion was now his existence... except for that fourth wall. It remained a brilliant white, untouched by his desires.

He was drawn to it. The closer he came to the wall, the less comfortable he felt. Yet he had to know what lay beyond it.

Bluestreak touched the wall...and screamed. The brilliant light faded and beyond it he saw a terrible vista of unchecked annihilation. Beyond the wall lay the day of the attack.

Beyond the wall lay Megatron.

Megatron reveled in this, one of his greatest triumphs. He knew it was an illusion, but he didn't care. He was back on Cybertron, and he was one with death and devastation.

He was *home*.

With a cruel, alien emotion that most closely

resembled the human feeling known as *gratification*, Megatron watched the destruction of Praxus once again. The events unfolded exactly as he remembered them, and he joyously relived the elation he felt on that glorious day of absolute victory—the day of the final demise of the hated Autobots of Praxus, as well as all evidence of their culture and civilization.

As the buildings were blasted into oblivion or crumbled into dust, Megatron drank in the visions of doom as if they were a finely distilled wine. To the vicious Decepticon, the violence and destruction he witnessed were as intoxicating as wine, and far more satisfying to his cold and inhuman intellect.

As the city they labored to build toppled around them, the power and prestige of the Autobots had finally been broken, irrevocably and forever, when the Decepticons struck their final blow and achieved their ultimate victory. Suddenly a roar of cruel laughter burst forth as Megatron relived the triumphant moment of his mortal enemies' destruction.

Megatron continued to chuckle as he watched black smoke rise from a hundred smoldering, red-hot blast pits, to blot out the sun itself. He laughed uproariously as the reflection from a hundred thousand blazes stained the once azure skies above Praxus a glowing blood-red. Megatron's eyes blazed as he watched the steel and glass canyons of the mammoth metropolis engulfed in a sea of fire.

Graceful, curved buildings and high, vaulting domes shattered under explosive bolts that exploded with the heat of a thousand suns. Balconies shook loose and high, arching bridges broke, to rain fiery debris down onto those few surviving Autobots who attempted in vain to flee the conflagration. Delicate towers and ornate ziggurats toppled, spilling hapless

Autobots to the ground far below. Cluster bombs burst among hapless leisure scooters and botmovers racing over the burning streets in an attempt to escape the destruction. Under the vicious guns of the Decepticons, their delicate wings shattered. Helplessly these flying vehicles spun down to certain death as they plunged into the leaping caldron of fire that spread exponentially to devour everything in its path.

The beams from null rifles arced across the sky, cutting down Autobots as they tried to escape across high, delicate pedestrian bridges. Soon those same bridges crumbled and plunged into the fires below.

With a final, massive explosion, the very earth under the hated Autobot city split asunder, to swallow buildings, vehicles, and Autobots. The colossal structure called The Assembly, shaken by the earthquake, instantly imploded. A million chunks of debris blew outward as the core of the structure plunged into the newly opened crevasse. Within seconds The Assembly, and all of its contents—its museums, lecture halls, libraries, and archives—vanished completely in a cloud of billowing black smoke and brilliant orange fire.

Then, like fluttering, burning insects, hundreds of Autobots rose above the ruins in a last ditch effort to reach the shelter of the open skies. But before they had a chance to escape, a thousand Decepticons dived out of the rolling red skies, null rifles, cannons, and blasters blazing. Like moths who flew too close to the candle flame, the damaged Autobots burst into flames, then plunged back down into the ocean of destruction far below. As the Decepticons darted between the tall buildings, firing at anything that moved, the structures themselves began to shake from a hundred internal explosions. As one, a whole brace of buildings toppled and fell like houses of cards.

With a last, deafening blast of light and heat, the center of Praxus melted as a mushroom cloud rose miles into the sky above the burning ruins. Megatron barked one last peal of laughter. The holocaust was now complete.

One of his lieutenants approached, a white, black and scarlet armored Decepticon named Ramjet. "One has survived. We sheltered him from harm, though he did not know he was being protected, exactly as you ordered."

"Of course," Megatron said, repeating the words he had spoken so very long ago. "What good is a cautionary tale if no one if left alive to tell it?"

On the other side of the wall, Bluestreak hammered away helplessly. This couldn't possibly be real. If it was, it meant he owed his *life* to Megatron. It meant that he had been spared to serve the Decepticon's plans, and thus, everything he had believed about the day his life was changed forever was a lie.

It was real. He knew it. He could feel it. Megatron had cheated him out of an honorable death in battle, and had used him in the process. Every time he told the tale, every time digital recordings were broadcast about their world of the destruction, images lifted from his own retina storage banks, he had spread terror and furthered the cause of his hated enemy.

"I'll kill you... I will..." Bluestreak said, his voice trembling with unbridled fury. "Bastard... you *bastard*... I'll see you dead."

His fist striking the invisible wall so hard that sparks flew and bits of scraped and damaged steel fell from them, Bluestreak screamed and screamed.

Megatron, his back to the Autobot, never seemed to notice.

Megatron felt an aching sadness as the vision faded from view. Then, picturing the greatest city he had ever known, Megatron changed his new environment into a replica of Kaon, the Decepticon power base and home city.

Now Megatron was truly home.

Contentment of a different kind flooded his being as Megatron again gazed at his homeland.

Everywhere machines belched smoke as thousands of weapons poured forth from the automated Decepticon factories. The sky over the city was black from the soot of a million furnaces. Bursts of fire and flame lit the night with brilliant flashes, illuminating the landscape beyond the city, which was scarred and ravaged by the six massive, crawling Constructicons that ripped away all useful ores and minerals in order to feed the insatiable maws of the teeming industrial plants.

Spidery buildings reached into the dark skies, their tentacles of steel, glass and stone spreading like a cancer across the ravaged planet. Leprous coils of metal dug into the ground like gigantic worms, tunneling deep into the core of the Cybertron in search of more useful materials to feed factories that continually spewed out more Decepticons, and their weapons of mass destruction.

With a tug of what humans would call nostalgia, Megatron longed to walk the dark streets of his home city once again.

"Keepers!" he called. "You must know that I am not like the others you have taken. Show yourselves to me. *Reveal* yourselves in my presence. I sense that we are very much alike, and we may help each other in many ways."

There was no reply, yet Megatron was undaunted; he would give it time, and, ultimately, what he desired would come to him.

It always did.

Moments later, several new sounds lazily drifted to him. He heard the clanging of Autobot feet moving with deliberate purpose in the area outside his chamber, and, somewhere distant, the roars of a bloodthirsty crowd rose up with an evil vigor that seemed musical to the Decepticon.

A fight was coming. At least *one* of the Autobots would soon be forced to do battle. Megatron wished he could see it, but the distant voices faded and he was left alone in the virtual construct of his home, a private paradise of dark roiling clouds and eternal, raging fires.

He would learn the outcome of the battle soon enough, he decided. And the data would be delivered, in person, by a Keeper.

Soaking in the stench of the thick, fetid atmosphere of his new world, Megatron stood alone and waited with near infinite patience... while elsewhere, a Transformer prepared for a battle that just might mean his life.

This was worth pardoning the Keepers for their offense against his person, for the affront of dragging him, against his will, to a world he could not yet quantify, for keeping him bound up in this cell—which it was, no matter how pleasant the scenery—and for treating him as little more than a toy for their own amusement. They would see their mistake and they would recognize him as an equal. Then, once their

guard was down, and their knowledge was his, he would crush them. It's what he did.
 Megatron laughed...
 And two minutes later, a Keeper appeared.

CHAPTER SIX

The arena Optimus Prime was brought to seemed little different than the last one—though it was far larger, and its architecture was more ornate. The exterior walls were organic—a form of durable, superhard bone-like shell that was smooth and pale ivory in color. Tiers that held the audience members rose from the floor of the arena in whorls that swirled gently around and upward, ringing the entire interior of the cone-shaped, mile-high structure. The arena's flat battlefield was also formed of the same bone-like substance.

Prime soon noticed a difference. In the center of the arena floor, separated from the combatants by a crackling force field, there stood a dozen delicate, bony structures. Some resembled curved musical instruments with fluted openings, other looked like gigantic antlers of some unimaginable wild beast. Most prominently, a tall, central spire resembled a complex antennae array made of ivory-hued bone.

That looks ominous, thought Prime, his fighting instincts instantly alert to new danger.

He had been led here with Jazz, but his friend stood frozen near the doorway: a backup, perhaps, in the event that the primary combatant proved inadequate to the task of providing suitable entertainment—or so Prime surmised.

As was typical of Keeper arenas, the battle area was

sliced in half—each half separated by a semi-invisible force field. Those same force fields also protected the audience from collateral damage that might result from the mayhem on the arena floor. Prime heard the roar of a hundred thousand beings, yet the audience didn't cheer or applaud wildly. Rather, the beings who watched emitted a steady rumble that sounded like an single tense and angry murmur.

With Prime in his half of the arena were the humans. Beyond the force field that shimmered in the center of the combat field, Prime got his first look at his newest opponent.

The creature Prime faced was massive, saurian, and bipedal, with a thick gray hide and a shower of bony, overlapping plates running down its shoulder and covering its back. Two parallel lines of long spikes ran down the center of the creature's back, the tip of each spike capped with cezium-steel, razor-sharp blades the size of telephone poles. The creature stood poised on two mammoth legs as thick as the stumps of redwood trees. Its upper limbs were short, with six fingers and an opposing thumb—each tipped with curled claws. A short tail ended with a massive and heavy-looking spiked club. As Prime watched, the tail twitched and the club struck the bony surface of the arena.

The creature's head was small and angular, with a pointed snout crested with a sharp bone-yellow horn. Two wet, gleaming eyes—black as obsidian—were set on either side of the horned snout. They burned with cruel intelligence. A mouth with thick, slavering lips and razor-sharp, protruding teeth seemed to smirk at Prime. The beast opened its wet maw, and a long blue tongue wagged in its lower jaw. Prime heard a roar, then an animal snort. The sound was followed by a long hiss, then several clicks and grunts.

"Now they send me a pile of *nuts and bolts* to destroy," the creature said, it's sibilant voice—translated by some alien technology and boomed throughout the arena—was laced with an almost-human contempt.

"You can try," the gleaming steel giant said.

"Five days of combat, five deaths to mark my lobes," the saurian hissed.

Only then did Prime see the five gold rings that adorned the bony crest on the left side of the creature's head—each a badge of honor that marked an arena kill.

Suddenly a loud, unearthly piping sound filled the arena—what passed for fanfare music to the Keepers.

Prime's opponent donned a huge battle helmet the size of a house. The gold metal headpiece covered the creature's entire head. Two slits that revealed the eyes, and a hole for the protruding snout horn, were the helmet's only openings. Another strange unearthly blast of alien music filled the stadium, and an opening appeared in the arena floor in front of Prime and his opponent in a place where no visible crack appeared before. From the pit rose a crackling weapon, hovering on a suspensor field. It was a spear made of unimaginable blue energy. As he grasped the haft, the weapon crackled with power and split into two. Now Prime not only gripped the spear in his right hand, but he also held a net made of the same blue crackling energy in his left.

At that same moment, Prime's adversary reached out to seize a curling whip made of what looked like crimson fire. The whip writhed and shimmered in the creature's grip, and the creature snorted appreciatively.

Raising its massive arm, the beast lashed out once, snapping the whip against the force field. It struck with a loud explosion, then split in two. Now the creature held a whip in one claw, and a shimmering scarlet scimitar in the other.

Watching his adversary, Prime knew that this creature had used such weapons before, and probably successfully, too.

Suddenly the even voice of a Keeper filled the arena. *"I am the Judge of the Games and it is my duty to announce the rules of engagement. The crimson whip and scimitar can cut through any substance save the net and spear the Autobot holds. And the Autobot's spear can pierce any object save the whip and the scimitar."*

The crowd's angry murmur grew in intensity.

"The opponents begin on equal footing," the Judge continued, *"but the longer the contest continues, the more obstacles will be thrown at the opponents..."*

The roar of the crowd became deafening. But only Prime understood the true context of the Judge's announcement: The longer the fight lasted, the worse things would get for him.

"Let the contest begin," said the perfectly modulated voice. Suddenly, the force field that separated Prime and the saurian vanished.

With a roar, the creature charged.

The attack was calculated to throw Prime off balance, and it did. The saurian led with a feign, its scimitar flashing. But it was the whip that lashed out, wrapping itself around the shaft of Prime's spear. The Autobot ducked and lashed out with his net. The saurian jumped backwards, its club-tail flashing to keep Prime at bay. The saurian's massive size did not diminish its speed, and the creature easily dodged the net. But the whip dropped away from Prime's spear, and the Autobot thrust it at the Saurian. The energy spear flashed sparks as it made contact with a metal-sheathed spike on the creature's spine, and it splintered and broke.

With a roar the saurian knocked the spear aside with its scimitar. The two energy weapons met with a roaring crackle of power and a shower of sparks. Muscles strained and servomotors ground as monster and machine strained to gain the upper hand. Prime dropped his net. It landed in a heap at his armored feet. Then, still clutching the spear, its shaft the only thing preventing the scimitar from ripping through his living metal body, Prime raised his blue fist and smashed it against the creature's helmet. Metal slammed against metal with a booming, deafening clang. Prime raised his fist and struck again... then again.

Finally, the saurian spun away, the death grip broken.

Prime snatched up the net and it swished through the air. The saurian ducked and slipped behind the bristling array of bone horns and antennae, the strange structures and the force field that surrounded them between Prime and itself.

Prime heard the sibilant hiss, then the translation.

"A worthy foe," the creature said. "A machine with a warrior's spirit."

"This fight is pointless," said Prime. "We should not fight for the pleasure of the Keepers."

"No fight is ever pointless," the saurian said. "It is cowardice to say such a thing."

The saurian charged again. Again it feigned—this time with the whip. But Prime was ready. Lashing out, his red armored forearm cuffed the saurian's head, knocking the helmet free. It landed on the hard arena floor with a deafening clang.

The creature's club-tail flashed, to collide with Prime's armored legs. The Autobot tumbled as his legs were cut out from under him.

Lips slavering, the saurian towered over Prime, scimitar raised. Prime kicked his legs out, and caught the creature under its jaw. The saurian was lifted into the air, to fly backwards. It crashed against the force field that surrounded the antennae, bounced away, and struck the ground. The arena trembled under Prime. The Autobot rose quickly to his feet.

Now a steadily increasing hum beat against Prime's audio sensors, flooding his cybernetic brain. Through an electronic haze of static, the steel gladiator could see the antennae arrays inside the force field begin to tremble and glow. Above the tallest spire, a whirlwind of crackling power began to form—a magnetic storm!

Suddenly, energies crackled and surged around Prime's robotic body. His servomotors became sluggish, as his cybernetic nervous system was assaulted by powerful beams. It was like the blast of a hundred null-rifles, all set on stun. The magnetic energy that whirled around Prime didn't destroy him—they only caused his cybernetic synapses to misfire, and mechanical systems to weaken and slow.

The advantage now belonged to the saurian, and the creature quickly exploited it. The energy whip lashed out, to wrap around the crimson armor of his right forearm. The whip crackled with energy, cutting into the Autobot's near indestructible armor. Power—and pain—surged through Prime's cybernetic nervous system.

Yanking sharply, Prime managed to rip his arm free, but the armor that sheathed his forearm was pitted and scarred from the power of the saurian's whip. He knew he could not allow that whip to catch him again.

Meanwhile the hum of the antennae seemed to intensify, as did the power of the magnetic storm. As a funnel of energy swirled around the arena, it began to flash with bolts of energy. One bolt struck Prime's armored chest plate, scoring his gleaming red armor.

Prime leapt aside to dodge the energy bolts. Moving quickly, he circled the arrays in the center of the arena, brushing the force field, which sparked against his armor.

Now the central arrays were between Prime and the magnetic storm. Another bolt fired from the energy cloud, and Prime ducked to avoid it—just in time, too, for the saurian was back, striking at the Autobot with the energy scimitar. The weapon shimmered eerily as it swished past Prime's head.

Suddenly the Autobot was free of the effects of the magnetic storm. Had he passed beyond its range? How? The answer was hammered home quickly. The field of energy still swirled, but Prime saw that it remained on the other side of the antennae.

I must be out of the magnetic storm's range! Prime thought, realizing now that he could exploit that knowledge.

The saurian barked and grunted.

"Afraid to fight?" the creature demanded.

Prime chuckled, and his amusement was not feigned. Now he had a plan to defeat his opponent. He only had to implement it to achieve victory.

"I have already won this contest, creature," Prime announced. "You are just too stupid to know when you have lost."

The Autobot hoped that the translation had the same arrogant nuance he put into his words.

When the saurian heard the translation, it roared in rage.

Good, thought Prime. *Now the beast is angry, and will make a mistake.*

Sure enough, the creature charged Prime again, whip swishing through the tense air of the arena, the scimitar forgotten in its grip.

Instead of dodging, Prime ducked his head and plunged it into the saurian's belly. The creature, still surging forward, flipped over the Autobot and landed on its back—right in the center of the magnetic storm.

Prime stood erect and reached out, grabbing the saurian's helmet where it lay. He raised the helmet above his head, and the metal began to attract the bolts of lightening still flashing out of the center of the magnetic storm. In a nanosecond, the helmet began to glow with heat and power.

Then, with all the strength of his powerful servomotors, Prime slammed the helmet down in the center of the saurian's belly. There was an explosion of sparks and fire and the saurian howled.

Prime didn't need a translator to understand that the creature was screaming in pain. The Autobot released the helmet, which had nearly melted from the powerful forces surging through it. Then he raised the energy spear above his head.

Energy bolts crackled around them both as Prime brought the spear down, point first, on the helpless saurian.

With a crunch of bone and the wet sound of tearing flesh, the spear point penetrated the saurian's shoulder, ripped through its back, to bury the tip in the bone-hard surface of the arena. The saurian struggled, but was pinned like an insect to the arena floor.

Planting one foot on the creature's belly to hold its writhing mass in place, Prime yanked out the energy spear. It left his opponent's flesh with a dripping *slorp* and a crackle as it chewed through even more bone and plating. The creature writhed and howled in agony as Prime lifted the spear once more—

And waited.

"Why do you hesitate?" the Judge demanded. *"The victory is yours. Make the kill."*

"I will not," Prime said confidently. To kill in wartime was one thing, to take life when it was the only way to stop an enemy—*that* he could accept. "Find your amusement elsewhere."

"As you wish."

Suddenly, one of the human spectators cried out in alarm as invisible pincers yanked her high into the air, holding her tight by her midsection.

"Wait!" she screamed. "No, I have a family, don't—"

The pincers snapped shut with a sharp hiss, spewing gore and a rain of blood over the heads of the crowd. The two halves of the still twitching corpse tumbled to the ground and terrified people darted like animals to avoid them.

Prime stared in horror at the wreck that had been a young human woman with a life still before her only seconds before. Her severed spine jutted from her torso, and entrails uncoiled and slowly snaked out from her body, slippery and eager to stretch out and relax.

"Kill them," the Judge suggested.

Startled back into the moment, Prime registered the Keeper's words instantly too late. Before he could react, five more people from the swelling, huddled mass of hostages were hauled into the air by invisible forces. Crackling lattices of energy whipped through them, slicing off heads, arms, hands, legs, and feet. This time a crimson tide washed over the closest humans and body parts flopped down on the rightfully terrified crowd.

"All of them next," the Judge said wistfully. *"Your choice."*

Prime panicked. His programming rebelled at the idea of being made a slave of the Keepers, of granting them this pleasure, but those people—

"Coward!" the saurian hissed, reaching up and grabbing hold of Prime's arms, driving the spear down with the last of its strength, straight through its throat.

Staring down at the dying creature, Prime felt every last convulsion ripple up through the energy spear and into his arms. A sudden and unnerving sense of strength and well-being flooded through him, and he wavered for a second, overwhelmed by the sensations. It was as if he was taking the lifeforce of his victim into his own body, benefiting from the searing currents of its final exploding energies.

Optimus looked to the shaking, frightened herd of humans, many of whom were frantically tearing off their blood sullied clothing, modesty be damned, or clawing at their hair to rid themselves of flecks of brain or bone. They wailed as one...and behind them, a gigantic, shadowy figure Prime thought he recognized took two silent, hulking steps away, then glanced back at the Autobot with glowing cinders for eyes.

Sentinel Prime. Optimus could feel the disgust of his predecessor, but he did not know if it was because he had participated in the battle at all, because he had taken the life of the creature, or because, in truth, he had been frozen into inaction, and the Keepers had no responsibility in that, it was all a result of his own inability to act authoritatively.

Then his predecessor was gone. Or maybe he'd never been there at all.

"That will do," the Judge said. *"Optimus Prime is the victor. To the victor go the spoils."*

Yet... no reward arrived. Unless the Keeper meant the surge of power he had received as the alien had died.

The thought sickened him.

Tossing the energy spear away, Optimus Prime trudged toward Jazz. He was unable to block out the screams of derision, of just rage and misery directed his way by the traumatized humans. He said nothing to them. What was there to say?

No, his words would be for Jazz alone, and thus they waited until he reached his friend.

"I am no longer fit to command the Autobots," Optimus Prime said solemnly. "Jazz, until I am able to properly name my successor, I would like you to serve that function. Will you consider it?"

"I... I don't know. I'm not sure how to answer that. I don't know what the right thing to do *is*, Optimus."

"A good commander never does. Not until it is too late. What matters is taking action when lives depend on you. Any action, sometimes. There is something wrong with me. Something the Keepers did not repair. Possibly something that is beyond even their abilities, I don't know."

"They act like they made us," Jazz said softly.

"We are defined by what we do in this life. In that way, it doesn't matter one damn bit who designed and manufactured our forebears, or even our world.

The purpose they were meant to serve is meaningless now."

"How can you say that when you don't know what it is? Maybe we still—"

Optimus Prime brushed past his fellow Autobot, only now aware that he was tracking blood from his slain opponent.

The blood was on his hands, on his chest plate. It dripped down to land in the thin crevices over where the Matrix was stored inside his body.

Prime walked alone into the steel-bone corridor, soul weary, yet determined that no further innocents would die in this alien world... *determined* he would have his vengeance on the Keepers.

CHAPTER SEVEN

Las Vegas

The city's lights glittered against the starless sky.

Any first time visitor passing the borders into the city might well have felt as if he or she had crossed into a nightmare of pulsing lights, twisted art deco architecture, and monstrous, self-perpetuating glitz. Casinos and hotels rose up into the dark desert sky like monolithic elder gods wearing blazing, sequined jackets. It was as if the set designers from a science fiction epic had channeled the spirits of the mad Roman emperors and together they had designed a city that sported more excess than any other place on the planet. The streets were packed with traffic. Pedestrians massed outside the various hotspots and congealed on the sidewalks.

Within the Grand Royale casino, the many of the people crowding around looked as if they had been sleeping in their clothes and had not even thought to bathe for weeks. Almost everyone carried plastic buckets that chinked with quarters, dimes, and nickels as they walked past, their eyes empty, looking more dead than alive.

Endless rows of slot machines stretched ahead,

three quarters or more occupied by people who stared, entranced, at the prize screens and seemed completely detached from reality. Mechanically, they dug their hands into their buckets, fed money into the machines, and pulled the levers. Occasionally they would collect a jackpot and immediately scoop those coins into their buckets and begin the cycle again. Or they would get up, their change evaporated, and stumble off to get more.

Handsome men and women dressed in the blinding costumes of another age's plunderers walked past, carrying trays of drinks they would distribute for free, helping the clientele to get thoroughly plastered so they wouldn't care how much money they lost.

The casino was a factory with desperation as its major product. Chronic gamblers darted here and there, anxious for their next chance to recoup their losses. If Walt Disney had opened a theme park in Hell, this would have been it, complete with loud, obnoxiously dressed, rude-beyond-*belief* tourists.

The gamblers were practically robotic; it seemed nothing could shake them from their trance. There had been a fire at the MGM Grand recently, and people had been burned alive with their arms still raised, their hands fused to the grips of the slot machines.

Outside, only hours earlier, a drunk driver who had ecstatically broke even that night jammed his Jaguar through a red and collided with a bright Ferrari, caving in the driver's side door, killing the driver instantly, and spinning both sports cars into armloads of recklessly speeding oncoming cars. A dozen cars were totaled in the pile-up, half that many again sustaining enough damage that they would need to be towed, another dozen getting off easy with bent fenders, dented chassis, or busted windows where a head, limb, or torso may have burst against the glass.

One guy in the small crowd that gathered to watch the frantic rescue effort and bloody aftermath of the pile-up referred to the incident as "the only free show in town."

That was before he looked up and saw two towering Transformers peering down at the carnage.

Starscream stared down at the mass of humans approvingly. Their thirst for the blood of their own kind was heartening; it gave him confidence that his assessment of their kind had been dead on from the beginning, and that his plan would indeed meet with overwhelming success.

"You have their attention," Soundwave said, broadcasting on a frequency no human ear or recording device could detect. "What do you plan to do with it? If I may suggest the approach Megatron might use, an initial show of force, perhaps the leveling of—"

"You are welcome to suggest *nothing*," Starscream retorted. "There will be no misunderstanding between us on this score. I made my bid for leadership of the Decepticons, and though your loyalty to Megatron is unquestioned, now that he is dead—"

"Or he has disappeared," Soundwave said with a hissing sibilance. "We have no proof he's dead."

"He's not here and that's all that matters. Let's be quick about this, the scurrying humans are gathering cameras and using their communication devices to draw more of their kind to this spot, as I knew they would. Our time—and my patience—is short."

"Agreed."

"You had your chance to challenge me. You elected not to do so. Therefore, you follow my orders now."

Soundwave bristled. "I have *always* been loyal to the power."

"You have always twisted yourself and the rest of us into knots to impress that fool Megatron. I will not have his spirit impinge on my authority, particularly not through you."

"Starscream, you have never struck me as the type to think long-term about anything. You blunder into action without thinking, you defy any reasonable course of action, your logic circuits are as limited as that of—"

Soundwave tensed and barely withheld a shriek as a sonic pulse tore through him, an ice pick jamming into his cybernetic brain.

The agony fled as quickly as it arrived. Below, the humans were pointing and gathering. The time would soon be upon them.

"What—what did you do?" Soundwave sputtered.

"Did it ever occur to you that perhaps I have aspects to my personality core that you and all the rest have no idea even existed? No, apparently not. Of course I challenged Megatron at every opportunity, defying his will and infuriating that pompous rusting fool in the hopes that he would make a mistake and give me the opportunity I needed to take what should have been mine in the first place: leadership of the Decepticons. But what of all the times I have been silent, watchful? Did you really think that not a single thought had gone through my head?"

Soundwave chose not to answer that question, fearing the sonic weapon Starscream had used on him.

"The answer to my question is clear," Starscream said arrogantly. "Thus all is as I arranged."

"Wait... the taking of Megatron and the others...are you saying that you—"

"I am saying that I have the means to keep you in line, Soundwave, and that I have plans I will not see disrupted. You will serve me or you will die. Choose now."

Soundwave took a halting step back, and fell to one knee before his new liege.

"Good choice," Starscream said. Switching from the private to a public frequency, Starscream addressed the crowd.

This should be highly amusing, he thought.

Then he spoke.

Considering the city's proximity to Los Angeles, those who flooded to Las Vegas were even more accustomed to life on the edge than ever before. Many even sought out danger, welcomed it with open arms. Fallout? Radiation sickness? Worry about crap like that was the business of lesser beings. Anyone with any stones at all could get themselves to actually believe the daily "clean" reports from the half-dozen environmental agencies set up to monitor L.A. and the entire western portion of the United States. It was business as usual in Sin City—until the booming words of Starscream erupted on every loudspeaker, every phone, every Karaoke machine, every computer with the sound turned on—every machine in the vicinity with the capacity to broadcast his words.

"You may think you know me and my kind," Starscream began, "but you do not. Just as every human has a separate identity, separate motives and objectives, so it is with us. Megatron, leader of the

Decepticons, has left us. I have assumed his station. I am here, because I have ambitions to assume a much greater role in the affairs of mankind than he had ever cared to consider. In short, though this may be difficult for many of you to believe, I come with the means to fulfill the goals of every human in Las Vegas, to make each of you wealthy and famous, and all that I ask in return is that we forge a relationship of trust and non-violent coexistence."

In any other city, immediate panic would have detonated in the hearts of every denizen, ripping open the calm and complacent core of their everyday existence. Not here. People angrily whacked cell phones against dashboards, ovens, or any other blessed thing available to them, and hollered in rage at their radios or computers for delivering up this unwanted noise. Only a select few actual listened. Of that minute slice of the populace, only some paid any real attention. Their eyes gleamed with fear or excitement—or both.

Naturally, the police were already mobilizing. Across the world, the indifferent words of Bumblebee and the angry threats of Prowl had a engendered a cataclysmic backlash and caused most nations to put their protectors on the highest levels of preparedness. Then, with the attack in the desert, and the sudden, and frightening disappearance of the Decepticons from any known surveillance and tracking equipment, nerves among the law enforcers of Las Vegas were heightened to white line fever.

Yet the police, and the Decepticons, knew there wasn't a thing that could be done to stop this takeover.

Especially not if the public wanted it...

"We have ultimate plans of course," Starscream

went on. "What you are witnessing is little more than an opening movement in what is sure to be a complex and interesting drama set to unfold here... *and* before the eyes of your world. I would like to make what I consider a legitimate business offer to everyone who dwells in this realm. You seek diversion, you seek riches. We can provide you with both."

Word spread slowly. The few who were awake, alert, always looking for an angle, shook others out of their lethargy, and at the feet of the living metal behemoths, the immediate crowd surged closer, ignoring the victims of the intense wreck whom rescue workers still worked over, the lure of fast cash and fame drawing them ever closer...

"We wish to transform this area into a city that will be hospitable to our kind and to yours," Starscream said. "There is the capital that can be legitimately drawn here, pulled from secret, untraceable off-shore accounts which thousands upon thousands of your denizens possess. This will allow us to finance the project. Think carefully. Imagine what I'm offering. For some, this situation would be a curiosity. Others would feel duty bound to offer opposition. Thus there would be conflict. And conflict equals cash..."

In the casinos, in the streets, more people listened, more hungry eyes turned toward the Transformers who stood at the heart of the city, sirens blaring in the distance.

"The phrase I am ultimately looking for here is what I believe you call Reality Television," Starscream said benevolently. "We will allow your cameras to record everything we say and everything we do. Select members of your cast, as you would call it, will be focused upon to add the human factor as we chronicle the drama that is sure to come here. That, in and of itself, is sure to be an income generator of epic proportions."

A long, low murmur of excitement flurried about the city. Many even stopped gambling to hear the pitch.

"Which of your networks would not pay every cent they have for such rights? Many would devote one of their existing cable channels to this venture. Thus far, there has been no destruction, no bloodshed. There is the potential that it might stay that way, at least within the protected boundaries of this city. Outside, we can offer no guarantees of course. And if the assembled might of the world is foolish enough—no. If the Autobots are reckless enough to come and attack, we will do whatever is necessary to protect those within these borders."

The sirens grew louder. The police would come. They would make noise and try to show their strength.

They would fail.

"I come from a city called Centurion," Starscream announced. Far above the humans, the steel giant spread his arms wide, emulating "showbiz" entertainers he had seen from video feeds of this city. "This will be the new Centurion. The Vegas Centurion. Everyone here, should they decide to accept my offer, is about to become, as you humans put it, gut stinking, filthy rich. While my offer does not technically adhere to the letter of human law it is certainly agreeable in the context of human commerce, capitalism, exploration and expansion. So then, my question is simple. Are you in—or are you out?"

The people of Las Vegas talked. This situation would not last forever and when those who participated were eventually freed, they would be rich, famous, and *powerful.*

What's not to love about this? many asked.

The sirens raged and Starscream's glowing eyes fixed on the convey of police cars heading down the strip. He ignored their sounds. The sweet noise of assent was all he wanted to hear.

It was there, too loud and strong to be ignored, or to be drowned out by high pitched wails of the coming enforcers.

The people had spoken, and they were *in*.

"Anyone who wishes to leave may, of course, do so. We simply cannot guarantee anyone's safety beyond the immediate perimeter of this city..."

Her hand trembling, Janie Whitmore punched up another channel on her car radio. The broadcast was running on every station. She killed the radio.

The steady *thrummm* of the *James Bond* sanctioned BMW her husband had insisted they buy brought little comfort as they cruised out of the city. Craning her neck, Janie looked back at her husband, Paul, and whispered, "I don't know if we should be doing this."

Paul sat in the backseat next to their five-month-old son Hendry, who was securely fastened in his baby chair. "I don't care what they're offering," he said firmly. "It's a load of crap."

"That's not what I mean. What if—"

A sudden grinding warned that all was not well with the road beneath them. Paul shouted, "Honey, look where you're going!"

Janie turned back and pulled the steering wheel hard to the left. She had almost run them off the road. "Sorry. I'm sorry. It's just... some of them can even become *cars*, right? What if this isn't a real car? What if it's one of them and it... eats us?"

"I don't think this model was around back then. Don't worry about it."

Janie wasn't satisfied with that. "You really think they're going to just let people go?"

"Why not? Most people didn't even notice. Most of the ones that bothered to pay any attention didn't really care. Look at what's in front of us, sweetie. It's dead out here."

Paul was right, of course. There were no other headlights anywhere else in sight. Still, she wished he could have phrased things a little differently.

Janie and Paul were a handsome couple. Janie was a natural redhead, a real rarity in Vegas, and that, coupled with her sparkling green eyes, perfect shining smile, hourglass figure, and winning personality, made her one of the most popular hostesses at Vivaldi's, the trendy Italian restaurant off the Strip where she had been working for three years. Paul—raven-haired, thin-featured, intense in a young Pacino way, as he himself described it, and blessed with a perpetual five o'clock shadow and highly expensive tastes in suits, was an "idea man." He drifted from club to club, casino to casino, freelancing in marketing and publicity to pay his share of the bills, partying for pay 'til dawn then rising again at ten to craft another of his big schemes that never paid off—was a caring dad who had sworn to never put his child in harm's way... unlike his own father. Paul had been raised among mob guys, con artists, extortionists, arms dealers—the works. He would forever carry around the scar of the bullet that burst through their kitchen window one fateful night, ripping through his shoulder as he sat on his dad's lap, and turning the man's head into a mass of gore that spray painted every surface in its reach. He had been nine. His life had been a horror show. Now it was fun and games.

He would be damned if he would let his son grow up in a war zone. They were leaving and that was final. Nothing would stand in their way.

"What about what that thing said about not being able to guarantee our safety if we left?" Janie asked, her voice close to breaking.

Paul was already regretting his decision to let her drive. It was just that he wanted someone calm with his little boy. No reason to panic his best guy. And Hendry was behaving himself, too, the happiest baby Paul had ever seen, always curious, rarely ever crying. The lack of wailing in the night had frightened them both on many occasions, causing them to rush, breathless, to his crib, only to find him sound asleep, or happily looking at the lights of the city through their bedroom window.

Those lights were fading fast behind them…just not fast enough for Paul's comfort. The Transformer's warning was, more likely than not, just an empty threat. Why would they care if a handful or three left the city?

A shining yellow sign off to the side of the road urged caution, there was construction work up ahead. Delays should be expected.

"You better slow down, sweetie," Paul said, hating himself for those words. He wanted to get his son out of here *now*. But he had to keep them all safe first and foremost.

Some rocks kicked up from the road, one big enough to *smack* and clatter against the underside of the car for several seconds and cause Janie to go even paler than usual. He talked softly to her, reassuring her that everything was going to be all right, urging her to take little glances in the rear view mirror so she could see her guys and how much they loved her...it was going to be fine...

He only caught the next construction sign out of the corner of his eye. For a second, he *thought* it said, "Don't say you weren't warned. Time for fun and games."

That was crazy, of course. Janie's fears were getting to him, that was all...

Suddenly, a huge bright-green bulldozer rumbled onto the road before them, blocking both lanes. The truck's roars, as it lumbered back and forth like an impatient animal waiting for its prey, deepened, and seemed to turn into mocking laughter. The front scoop rose and fell as if it were powered by the impatient heart of a beast itching to strike. Janie hit the Beemer's screeching brakes, and yanked hard on the wheel. She screamed as the car spun and skidded to one side, her door suddenly racing for the brilliant lights of the truck.

The lights blinked out. *Something* grabbed the BMW's chassis while its passengers wailed in terror... and brought the car to a safe, peaceful stop.

It was several moments before the shaking couple left the car, stunned to find all four wheels still filled with air and viable, the chassis scraped and dented, but otherwise unharmed. Paul held his son tight as he stared uncomprehendingly into the cool blanket of the Nevada night and the endless, featureless expanse of the desert.

"It saved us," Janie said at last. "It was one of them, but it *saved* us."

Paul was still trying to think of some way to respond when the true terror began.

Bonecrusher had never developed an active appreciation for the concept of restraint. Working from the shadows to create chaos and destruction was unsatisfying, and the only thing he could take his frustration out upon was the road itself, tearing it to pieces, sending chunks of concrete high into the air like shrapnel. Spotting a few buried boulders, he trudged to them and tossed them around, making sure everything landed close enough to the humans to make them wet themselves, but not to inflict any true danger.

By the makers, I can't even trash the car, he thought. *What good is being a Decepticon if they don't let you maim, ruin, and kill?*

Digging his huge hands into the sand and roaring in frustration, he dragged his finger-like scoops through the desert and raised them suddenly, flinging an impromptu sandstorm at the screaming humans. He hated having to find ways to hide himself from view, not an easy task when, even in robot form, one's boxy steely body was bright green.

Soundwave had performed a few modifications on him, equipping him with technology that bent light around him, helping to camouflage him from anything *but* a direct beam of intense illumination. All indirect light, like that shining down from the moon, cascaded around him and was absorbed by the night.

Bonecrusher didn't give a crud about the technobabbly stuff. He was baffled when it came down to explaining the mass displacement principles that allowed two story steel fighters to become tiny little cars or, in Soundwave's case, a stupid little boom box!

Heh.

He continued with his task, creating the illusion that two unseen behemoths were clashing in the desert.

"Get out! Go back now!" Bonecrusher hollered. "I'll hold them off as long as I can!"

Them. What a crock. It was just him, making noise from all sounds, putting on a magic show. He was conflicted about this action. Pretending like this was unsatisfying, he was being reduced to tasks better suiting mindless drones, yet the overall plan that had been outlined to him seemed to be sound.

Bonecrusher had made his choice, he had sworn fealty to Starscream. That meant he would his give new leader's plan a chance. If all went well, he would be content in the knowledge he had made the right choice.

Otherwise, he would simply kill the officious jerk and take command himself. Who could stop him?

Below, the humans were jackrabbitting into their car, pulling out, spinning, and flooring it to get back to the city. Oh, the stories they would tell... and unbeknownst to them, they would be carrying out the will of the Decepticons, spreading the word that there was danger in the desert...and a Decepticon had saved them!

Yes, they would be prophets for a new age, furthering the case well. And one day, if Bonecrusher had his way, once their usefulness ended, they would become intimately acquainted with the flat, bus-sized bottom of his foot just before he ground them into paste, reveling in the sounds of their spines and skulls smashing apart.

The headlights of another car approached, and Bonecrusher's victims cut the car off, the driver jumping out, pointing back to where he stood, cloaked from view. Soon, both cars were pointed back at Las Vegas.

The prophets had begun their work ahead of schedule—and despite the way he bristled at the task he had been made to perform, Bonecrusher felt deeply pleased.

The second age of the Decepticons had begun.

Arlington, Virginia

Spike and Franklin sat in the operative's car, an innocent looking GTX on the outside, a high tech extension of central command within. They had pulled up several houses short of the dignified colonial two-story that rose imperiously from the stately neighborhood surrounding it. Roman columns, the statues of lions, a flag waving high beside the tennis court and beside the pool. It was like seeing a Capitol building tucked neatly away in the midst of a mildly embarrassed housing community.

"So," Spike said, "is this car hot?"

"I like to think so."

"Stolen, I mean."

Franklin frowned. "Don't think so. Really wouldn't care."

"Still got that new car smell. So do you, for that matter."

Franklin stared dead ahead, watching the moving vans slowly cruising by, as if looking for an address.

In the back of each van was a team of commandos who could be scrambled at a second's notice.

"So...what kind of enhancements did they rig you up with?" Spike asked.

Franklin's smiling face didn't change a bit. Finally, he asked, "What gave me away?"

"Back at the hanger. You squeezed that guy's shoulder so tight you might have broke something. You're still not used to them."

"You never get used to them. And they hurt like hell."

"Plus there was the tilt in the chopper on the way over here, always to your side. The way floorboards creek like they've being punished whenever you take a step on them. The reinforced soles of your shoes. The way this car turns into a lowrider when you get in. I expect they had to reinforce your whole spine and at least 45% of your body to handle the weight of the grafts, making you literally a five-hundred-pound gorilla. Except for the gorilla part. Should I go on?"

Franklin sighed and looked away. "Right. I got it. Yeah, I know. This kid just can't get out of his own way."

Spike's stomach tightened into hard knots as he realized that Franklin wasn't talking to him—and that the cybernetic enhancements the man sported went far behind some added strength in his grip.

"Communications wetware," Spike said. "GTS tracking in your brainpan? Cameras in the corneas? Seriously, what kind of weird stuff did they hook you up with?"

"You'll find out," Franklin said dryly. "At some point. Now don't you have a job to do? The nice man you spoke to on the phone is waiting."

Spike got out and walked away. Each step he took in the direction of Hugo Fortuna's house was more difficult than the last. Dogged by the unshakable feeling that he was leaving one life and beginning another, Spike opened the latch on the white picket fence (there *were* such things?) encasing the submarine commander's snow-covered front lawn and drifted along the pristine path to the front door, bracing himself against the chill of the night air and the even greater cold now settling within his heart.

He had to push away his fears, drive off any thought of his son back home, who was scared and surrounded by strangers, and what it would mean for the boy if Spike never returned from this assignment.

You're a strong man, Optimus Prime had once told him. *You can survive anything.*

But Spike had just been a boy when those words had been spoken. Now...

Steeling himself, he strode up onto the porch and rang the doorbell. A very short man with a military buzzcut answered. He wore tan slacks and a green sweater, and heavy bags crowded under his otherwise kind gray eyes. Taking Spike's outstretched hand, Hugo Fortuna gave it a healthy squeeze and told him to come in out of the cold.

"I'm glad you called," Fortuna said as he closed the front door behind them and maneuvered himself to take Spike's jacket. The foyer was lined with hard wood panels and paintings of the sea. A small case was devoted to sports awards earned by his teenage sons, who were off visiting friends, according to Franklin's intel. His wife was on holiday. "Pretty dreadful business, this whole situation in the desert, wouldn't you say?"

"I guess that depends on your point of view," Spike

said as he stretched both arms out behind him and allowed Fortuna to tug at his sleeves to slip off the jacket.

Suddenly, the commander slid his hands up to Spike's forearms and planted a knee in the center of his back, thrusting his full weight against the younger man, who *oof*ed as he was sent crashing down to the hard wood floor, his skull and chest taking the brunt of the fall. Pain exploded behind his eyes and he was only dimly aware as Fortuna gathered the ends of both sleeves in one hand, preventing him from using his arms to fight, if he'd even had the presence of mind to swim up from his shock and fear to think to do so, while using the weight of his body to pin Spike in place and hold his legs in place. Something slipped from the waistband of the man's sweater and Spike heard the unmistakable sound of a hammer being drawn back as the icy muzzle of a revolver pressed tightly against the back of his skull.

"Endgame," the commander said—and pulled the trigger.

CHAPTER
EIGHT

Parked on the side of the road, on the edge of a small private airport outside the Mexican town of Mesa Verde, a yellow Volkswagen Bug and a what might have been a sleek, two tone sports car—or a police patrol car—sat unoccupied, gathering a patina of brown desert dust on their polished exteriors. It was almost noon, and the hot sun of Central Mexico beat down on the dusty town, sending the occupants scurrying for shade. But despite the shimmering heat that rolled off the concrete runway, there was a flurry of activity in at least one part of the airport

Atahulpa Aeropuerto de Mesa Verde wasn't very large. There was a main terminal about the size of a Denny's restaurant, with a walk-up tower attached. The control tower was not much higher than a suburban water tank, and wasn't state of the art, either. At the other end of the field were two hangars—Numero Uno and Numero Dos—of which Dos was the larger. Hanger Number Two was locked up tight, but the doors to Hanger Uno were wide open. Through the waves of heat rising from the concrete, Prowl could clearly see an aircraft parked inside.

"It's Thundercracker, for sure," the Autobot told his companion.

"Right," said Bumblebee, transformed into the

undistinguished yellow Bug that was gathering dusk nearby. His headlights flashed with excitement.

"We got him. Now let's get this over with," Prowl said impatiently.

Bumblebee noticed his partner's irritation and decided to say something.

"Listen, Prowl—I'd rather be somewhere else, too," Bumblebee insisted. "But since nobody can figure out what really happened to Prime and the rest—not to mention a sizable chunk of Tokyo—we can't do a thing to help on that front."

"And with the media and half of the human population turned against us, I guess there's not much we can do about the chaos in Las Vegas, either," said Prowl.

We really only have ourselves to blame for that, Bumblebee thought, recalling the soundbites he and Prowl had given the reporter in Tokyo—and the flurry of anti-Transformer sentiment they had kicked up around the world. The words "callous," "unfeeling," and "threatening" had appeared beside their names. Like, a *lot*. It wasn't fair and it wasn't true, but that didn't seem to matter. People wanted someone to blame, they needed a target for their aggressions over the latest incident in Tokyo, and Bumblebee and Prowl had done the world the favor of spraypainting huge bullseyes on their chests then looking down stupidly and saying, "Bummer of a birthmark, dude!"

"There's plenty we could do in Las Vegas," Prowl said. "Have you seen that show they're broadcasting? It's an aberration. We need to get in front of the eyes of the world and set the record straight."

"We can't. Not without defying a United Nations mandate, anyway. But I'm still itching to get into the fight—to do something. Well, at least we can bag this

Decepticon," Bumblebee said, his voice chipper. "If we can stop Thundercracker, then I'll consider my glass half full."

Prowl agreed.

"What is he up to?" Bumblebee wondered, focusing on the task at hand—the capture of Thundercracker.

Prowl used his telescopic sensors to hone in on the light-blue, silver and black aircraft inside the cavernous hangar. He noticed that a fuel truck was parked outside, but no hose had been deployed—no surprise there, Thundercracker didn't need jet fuel to get around. It was probably a prop, to make the process seem normal and not attract undo attention.

Piercing the shadows in the hanger, the Autobot noticed that Thundercracker had his loading bay doors open, and his fuselage was being packed tight with plastic bundles the size of barrels. So far everything seemed to be routine. The men who loaded the airplane were dressed in standard Atahulpa Aeropuerto-khaki uniforms.

But there were others inside the hanger, and outside, too. A dozen men stood about watching the loading process, but they were definitely not luggage handlers—unless the handlers South of the Border down Mexico way had a habit of wearing black skintight uniforms, Kevlar body armor, wraparound sunglasses and carrying automatic weapons!

Something that required a private army to protect it was going on inside of that hangar.

Prowl activated his array of internal sensors, and directed them toward the hanger. A moment later, data began flooding his cybertronic brain.

"That tanker truck is indeed full of jet fuel," he announced. "Those guns the guards carry are fully loaded, too. And they have grenades."

"More of a challenge," said Bumblebee, unperturbed.

Prowl got quiet as more data was sifted through his processors.

"Those bundles," the Autobot said after a long pause. "They are full of weapons."

Bumblebee sighed. "Weapon smuggling, huh. If it's dirty, trust Thundercracker to get involved."

"We have to hit him hard and fast," Prowl said, shutting down his sensors. "Otherwise he'll just fly off and we'll lose him."

"Over there," said Bumblebee. "A break in the fence. Maybe we can just drive into the airport and right up to the hanger?"

"I doubt we'll get far with those armed guards watching," he said grimly.

A moment later the two Autobots watched as a rickety pickup truck rolled past the terminal, out onto the runway, and right up to hanger Uno. In a cloud of dust the truck chugged and stopped, and an older, bearded man stepped out. He looked up at the beating sun, doffed his broad hat, and reached into the back of his truck.

"Cerveza!" he cried, lifting a Styrofoam container and offering everyone bottles of cold beer.

The loaders tossed the last of the plastic bundles into the cargo hold and raced to the truck. The armed guards relaxed their vigilance too, as each grabbed a cool bottle and drank deep. Soon the men were laughing and joking—and paying absolutely no attention to their surroundings.

"Well, well," Bumblebee chirped. "Looks like the break we've been waiting for. Let's roll."

As one, the two Autobots motored down a slope, through the break in the airport fence, and along the side of the quiet runway, closing in on the hangar and the unsuspecting Decepticon within.

Kicking up a cloud of dust, the two Autobots raced toward the hanger. At first no one noticed. Then one of the guards pointed at the approaching cars and shouted something in Spanish. Dropping his bottle, he fumbled for the automatic now hung over his shoulder.

"We've been made!" Prowl cried.

"Transform," said Bumblebee. "Maybe that will scare off the rent-a-terrorists."

As they raced forward, the Autobots shape-shifted until they were in robotic form. Prowl leveled his blaster at the guards as automatic fire began to erupt from the hangar.

"Finish the guards," commanded Prowl. "Pronto!"

But before the plucky yellow-armored Autobot could make a move, there was an explosion of activity inside the hanger. Men in khaki uniforms came racing out into the sun, some shouting, others screaming in fear. A black-clad armed guard flew out of the hangar a moment later. His body slammed against the ancient pickup truck with a meaty thwack, and the man landed in a bloody heap on the tarmac.

Thundercracker emerged from the hangar, a blur of light blue, silver and black. His component parts were shifting even as he emerged into the bright sunlight. With a roar, his burning eyes focused on the Autobots. Then the Decepticon trained his drone rocket launcher, armed with a weapon similar to a heat-seeking missile, on Prowl's gleaming ebony chest plate.

"Come and be destroyed!" Thundercracker cried defiantly.

Bumblebee looked at his partner.

"Well, at least he isn't flying off," the Autobot quipped.

On the tarmac, the security detail had reformed and began spewing automatic fire at the Autobots. Grenades began exploding around their feet. None of these weapons were likely to do harm, but they distracted the Autobot's attention.

Suddenly, there was a fountain of fire and a loud blast!

A missile left Thundercracker's tube and streaked toward Prowl. The Autobot easily dodged the projectile and it raced past his broad shoulder. The Autobot stepped forward, metal fist raised to strike down Thundercracker. But unnoticed by Prowl, the missile made a sharp curve behind him and aimed itself at the center of his broad robotic back.

"Look out!" Bumblebee cried, leaping.

With unbelievable speed, the yellow Autobot clipped the missile with a quick karate chop, deflecting it away from Prowl. The projectile wobbled in the air, then flipped end over end—to impact against the brimming fuel section of the tanker truck.

The truck, its cargo of fuel, the black-clad security detail, the pickup truck, the khaki-clad loaders, and most of hanger Numero Uno were devoured by a brilliant, white-orange fireball that rose into the afternoon sky in a large, rolling mushroom cloud. Bumblebee and Prowl were knocked flat by the force of the blast. Thundercracker was swallowed by the explosion. A nanosecond later, the hot wash of blastfire washed over Prowl.

Bumblebee was tossed like a leaf in a storm, to land with a crash in the center of the runway. As the rolling black smoke and fire engulfed the rest of the hangar, he rose unsteadily and crawled out of the pit of shattered concrete his body created when he struck. Bumblebee's yellow armor was scorched and blackened in spots and some of his internal servos were scrambled.

"Prowl!" Bumblebee called, "are you all right?"

The Autobot used his optical sensors, attempting without success to pierce the smoke, heat and fire. Through his overloaded audio sensors the Autobot detected the sound of distant sirens, and movement in the center of the roaring flames. Something was still alive and functioning inside that holocaust of fire

A colossal silhouette appeared in the middle of the roaring inferno. Soon the silhouette formed a familiar shape.

Bumblebee groaned, losing hope for the first time.

It was Thundercracker that emerged from the conflagration. Though his light blue, silver and black armor was blackened too, the evil robot was otherwise unharmed, and was ready for combat.

The same could not be said for the form clutched in the Decepticon's mighty metal grip. It was Prowl, and the Autobot seemed stunned. The robot's limp form was held by Thundercracker, who shook the Autobot like a rag doll.

With a roar, Thundercracker turned and spotted Bumblebee. He raised the unconscious Prowl over his head and prepared to hurl the stunned Autobot at Bumblebee.

Then, suddenly, miraculously, there was a second explosion, and a new cloud of smoke. This blast was louder than the first, but lacked the brilliant pyrotechnics. With a blast of hurling debris, the walls and doors of Hanger Number Two—which had been locked up tight—now burst apart in an avalanche of shattered steel and broken masonry.

Out of the center of that blast, a silver shape rose. Massive jaws lined with cezium-steel teeth opened wide and a booming roar louder than any sound yet heard in Mesa Verde that day echoed over the entire town.

Bumblebee recognized the fierce form of Grimlock, the leader of the Dinobot's, as he transformed itself into the shape of an angry *Tyrannosaurus rex*!

Facing the new threat, Thundercracker dropped Prowl like a forgotten sack of potatoes. The Autobot struck the hot tarmac and didn't move. Bumblebee raced to his partner's side as Thundercracker turned to battle Grimlock.

It was no contest. The Dinobot was undamaged from the explosion, and spoiling for a fight. Thundercracker was running on rage, his servomotors and sensors still somewhat scrambled from the force of the jet fuel explosion.

With a flash of its long metal tail, Grimlock cut the legs out from under Thundercracker. The Decepticon hit the concrete with a crunch. Before it could rise again, Grimlock leaped onto the evil robot, smashing him into the pavement.

Bumblebee lifted Prowl and carried him away from the battle.

Thundercracker was down but not out. His metal fists shot out and grabbed Grimlock's tail on its second pass. The powerful appendage didn't even slow in its arc—instead the tail lifted the hapless Decepticon and tossed him through the air. Thundercracker landed on his back and slid fifty feet, to crash into the now evacuated terminal building. The entire structure—including the control tower—folded like a house of cards, to collapse on top of the flailing Decepticon. When the smoke cleared, Thundercracker was down, his cybertronic brain scrambled, his internal workings scrapped.

There followed a series of secondary explosions as the gas mains that fed into the terminal blew up. With a grunt of animal satisfaction, Grimlock turned away from his fallen adversary and faced the Autobots.

Bumblebee had managed to revive his partner, and Prowl had risen to his feet in time to see Grimlock finish off Thundercracker. Now he and Bumblebee faced the determined Dinobot.

"Me not see you, either you, in long time," Grimlock said in his distinctive guttural dialect that belied his great intelligence. "With Prime gone, me am taking command of all earthbound Autobots. Me have the rank, and with it me have responsibility to put end to things in Las Vegas."

"We have orders to stay away from that fight," Bumblebee said. "The humans are concerned with collateral damage."

Grimlock grunted. It sounded like an angry roar.

"Me say the humans short sighted," he rumbled. "Me sure there will be more collateral damage if me do nothing and Decepticons gain a foothold on this continent—and allies to help them conquer all Earth."

Bumblebee and Prowl regarded each other cautiously. They had a history with this particular Autobot, and it wasn't a pretty one. During the conflict that led up to the climactic battle in Los Angeles, Grimlock, along with Bumblebee and Prowl, had been captured and reprogrammed by a nefarious human named Lazarus.

But afterward, when free will had been returned to them, Grimlock had stunned all by tearing off his Autobot symbol and siding with Megatron. Even after the conflict, when Optimus gave Grimlock the chance to come back, his transgressions forgiven, his slate wiped clean, Grimlock had spurned the chance.

Now, his scarred chest gleaming, Grimlock was announcing his plans to take Prime's place. The Dinobot leader was on his way to Vegas whether they joined him or not, that much was certain.

But if they went with him, and he had some kind of double-cross planned, at least they would be there to attempt to counter it.

Nodding, they turned back to the Dinobot.

"Maybe you've got a point," said Prowl.

"Yeah," said Bumblebee. "So what are we supposed to do about it?"

"Follow me," Grimlock declared. "Me refuse to be hampered by the humans' commands. Negotiations, warnings and sanctions accomplish nothing, except play into Starscream's hands."

Suddenly the sky above was filled with black helicopters—dozens of them. The choppers were clearly military-issue, as they were brimming with weapons. Hellfire missiles, Vulcan-cannons, machine guns. Some of the choppers were Black Hawks. Others where AH-64 Apache attack helicopters. None of them had national markings.

Grimlock turned his gigantic head to study the two Autobots with a single burning eye.

"Me have help," the Dinobot announced.

"Looks like it," said Prowl. "Who are they?"

"Never mind," said Grimlock quickly. "Only one thing important. Those that join me choose to fight—so do me."

Bumblebee and Prowl exchanged glances. Though the secret army, and the question of Grimlock's ultimate fealty troubled them, they also saw Grimlock's leadership as a chance to get some payback for the crap they have been forced to eat lately.

"Sign me up," said Prowl, his chin out-thrust.

"Me too," Bumblebee said. "All the real action is in Vegas now—and I want to go where the action is!"

CHAPTER NINE

The energy sphere pulsed in a heartbeat rhythm; now flashing sapphire blue, now crimson, now back to blue again. The strobing light reflected off Jazz's armored body, washing him in color, leading him once more through the dark corridors that tunneled through the Keeper's world.

The corridor's ribbed walls seemed to absorb most of the light, as if feeding off it. A few glossy patches glistened like black obsidian, reflecting back just enough to provide direct visual imaging. The cast-off light wrapped around bulbous nodules and sharp ridges, long, ropey strands that circled the corridor like petrified muscle, stalactites of organic metal. Jazz felt as if he were passing through the knotted intestines of a long-dead creature, one that had choked while attempting to devour this world from the inside out.

"Van Gogh would have gouged his eyes out in this place," he said, his words bouncing flatly off the walls, dying down on the sculpted floor. "H. R. Giger would set up a studio."

And the Roman emperor Caligula would have saluted the Keepers for their ultimate Coliseum.

The energy sphere dipped and turned, following a series of paths, until the corridor finally fed into a much larger—but no less grotesque—version of itself. The flashing colors pulsed more frequently for a moment... or so it appeared. Then Jazz stepped wholly into the new corridor to see two energy spheres hovering side by side, pulsing out of synch, one speeding up to match the other.

"Jazz! Man, is it good to see you!"

Bluestreak waited in the corridor, his ion-charged disperser rifle pointed at the floor, left hand clenching and unclenching in nervous repetition. His black and silver armor changed into different hues as the energy spheres continued to race through their color shifts.

"Bluestreak! Optimus and I wondered where they kept you."

The Autobot recoiled from the question. "In a cage. A tower cage. I woke in Praxus, or at least I thought it was Praxus, and then I watched it die again. Megatron was there, and he was talking to others, about me. He said that I was left alive on purpose. It felt true, but I don't know that it was."

Blue. Red. Blue. The two energy spheres pulsed in concert, and merged, becoming a single sphere of no greater size than before. Still flashing sapphire and crimson, showing no more intensity or speed. Simply a beacon, and now only one was necessary to show the Autobots the way forward. It moved along, and Jazz and Bluestreak followed.

Jazz walked to the left and slightly in front of Bluestreak. "It may be true. The Keepers seem to know a lot about us." Too much, in fact. More than the Transformers knew themselves anymore.

"I saw Megatron," Bluestreak said again. "He was enjoying the show I was forced to watch. I want to destroy him, crush him..."

"You may get the chance. But later, Bluestreak. Later." Jazz outlined the Keeper's basic plans for the Transformers. "If this is like before, one of us will be forced to fight once we reach the battledome, while the other is forced to watch. Most likely it will be me fighting since Optimus Prime fought and I watched last time. That is the way of things. We'll have no choice." Well, that might not be entirely true. They had a choice, didn't they? "The Keepers will put people in danger—kill them—if we choose not to participate."

And people could likely die during the contest as well. Learning when to sacrifice the few for the many was the kind of decision Optimus Prime had to make all the time. It was a skill Jazz might have to learn as well. Soon.

Whether he wanted to, or not.

Bluestreak perked up. "Optimus Prime. Is he all right? When we were taken, he looked like hell. Megatron nailed him pretty good."

"Optimus Prime has recovered quickly," Jazz assured the other Autobot quickly, trying to calm him, "with the Keeper's assistance." So many of their internal functions seemed to work better in their presence, in fact. Jazz himself felt stronger, faster...

Wiser? He hoped so.

"People." Bluestreak picked up on what Jazz had said earlier. "So these... Keepers. They took humans as well. Then maybe Megatron *is* here and I wasn't just looking at some illusion. Maybe we'll both get the chance to face him."

Jazz hoped not. Not until Bluestreak had a chance to calm down, to collect himself. "We will be finding out soon, I think," noting that the energy sphere had finally led them up to the massive doors which opened onto the battledome. Both Transformers waited, staring at the polished steel. Then the energy sphere pulsed once more, bright crimson, and then winked out of existence just as the door's seam split down the middle and let in a shaft of normal light.

The light fell across Jazz's vizored face, opened wider to cover his entire chest and Bluestreak's face which looked over his right shoulder. With a dull grinding sound the doors rolled all the way back until light poured into the dark corridor, reflecting off silvered visors and grills, warming painted armor. With combat instincts on high, Jazz and Bluestreak stepped forward, through the opening.

The battledome stretched out before them.

Thanks to Jazz's description, Bluestreak had some an idea of what to expect. The massive arena offered no view of the alien sky. The cone-shaped dome was organic, a smooth shell of pale ivory that was no doubt thick and very hard. The battlefield floor was the same, smooth and unbroken, looking like it was paved with the bones of a thousand dead. A million.

A semi-visible force field protected the audience, who sat in tiers that rose in a delicate whorl around the inside of the mile-high dome. The cheers of the many alien races the Keepers had brought here assaulted Bluestreak like one loud and continuous shout of anger, wrapping his mind with a dark veil he could not dislodge. He felt strength surge through his systems, raw and powerful, and yearned to move and fight and break...

Who?

Scanning the battledome floor, tracking his disperser rifle along the entire horizon, Bluestreak found no adversary. No crackling force field split the dome into two halves, as Jazz had described. No alien creature waited for battle. "I don't understand. I see the people." They stood in three clumps of four or five, with another handful of singles who had been scattered about the arena seemingly at random. The rest of the abducted humans waited in a protected alcove, surrounded by a force field crackling with pent up energies. His senses jangled with over-stimulated input as he reached for a conclusion to fit the facts. "Jazz? The people are here. We are here. Who is it you're supposed to be fighting?"

Jazz shook his head. "No."

That was all he said. *No.*

No he wouldn't fight? No, there would be no fight? Bluestreak clenched his left hand into a fist, his right around the rifle's trigger stock.

"The contest is about to begin," a voice thundered through the arena, sexless and with hardly any emotion at all. The Judge of the Games, as Jazz had described this Keeper. *"The opponents will move away from each other."*

"Jazz?" Bluestreak shuffled from one foot to the other, watched as his friend backed slowly away from him.

"It's us, Bluestreak." Horror bled through Jazz's voice. "The Keepers are pitting us against *each other.*"

He would fight Jazz? To the death? "Or humans will be slaughtered," Bluestreak whispered aloud, understanding now the stakes the Keepers were willing to put up to ensure the success of their gladiatorial games. Reluctantly, one measured pace at a time, he separated from Jazz, mind racing as he searched for ways out, ways to avoid...

No. Ways to win. He hated himself even for the thought.

"Not this, not even a nightmare of this," he said, talking mostly to himself. "I cannot fight Jazz, I cannot let innocent people be killed, I cannot stand here and be destroyed with Megatron still to deal with."

Or maybe he could. If he was truly Megatron's tool, did he deserve any less?

"Any determined or continued avoidance of battle, and a penalty will be incurred."

As if summoned by the Judge's threat, an energy sphere of bright crimson appeared over the captured humans. Four more appeared at strategic placements around the arena, spinning whorls of energy that hovered only fifteen feet above the floor. In a dozen places the bone-paved arena split open long, thin fissures where before Bluestreak had not detected even a seam. Sinewy ropes of metallic tentacles squirmed up out of half a dozen fissures. The others vented a sooty gray smoke.

"Begin."

And not knowing what else to do, Bluestreak ran for the far side of the dome, disperser rifle laying down a covering fire while he sought to put distance between himself and Jazz. Two bursts of the rifle's blue lightning leapt wide from Jazz, pulled toward one of the crimson energy spheres. It ricocheted the shots, like a perfectly reflective surface might return a laser, bouncing the first one toward the caged humans. The force field protecting them hissed and spat, but held. This time.

The second bolt of lightning bounced off the sphere at a different angle, throwing it straight back at him!

No where else to go, Bluestreak spread himself full length over the arena floor, scraping along and then rolling off his left shoulder top come up into a ready crouch. Jazz had leapt into a powered glide, circling around behind, away from the caged human audience, photon rifle swinging around to track him. Buying himself time as well?

Not that much time. An amber stream of energies flowed from the photon rifle, lancing over the battlefield at Bluestreak.

The Autobot tried to sprint aside, and suddenly found himself unable to move. One writhing mass of tentacles held him around the legs and waist! More coiled up his side, securing his right arm. Jazz couldn't miss. The energy stream blasted in against Bluestreak's right side, cutting through the tentacles' thickest part, slicing many of them in half and blasting apart others as internal fluids flashed into superheated plasma. Metallic joints burst and released, and Bluestreak managed to pull himself away to take only a glancing blow against the side of his chest, knocking him off his feet and away from the hazard.

He landed hard, and only a few hundred feet from where a lone human woman ran a wide berth around the arena hazard, trying to gain the relative safety of one of the tight knots of people. Bluestreak was staring right at her when a large rope of metallic segments fell from the sky, landing right in front of her. The tentacle spasmed, whipping one end around in its dying throes, and caught the woman in the head and shoulder.

She flew ten feet through the air, and landed in a crumpled, lifeless pile.

Bluestreak did not know who to blame. The Keepers. Fate. Jazz. Himself. The hapless victim had died for no reason. He reacted against the only target available, before he had much time to think about it, rolling over onto his back and sitting up with shoulder-mounted rocket launchers already tracking and locking on to Jazz.

He didn't want to fight his friend. It was painful to fight, he was anguished over this. They were battling because they had to, because the Keepers were making them do it...

Because more innocent humans would die if they did not fight.

Two shells launched on snap-shot aim, each bursting in the air at half the distance to Jazz to disgorge four independent warheads. Eight missiles slammed in at Bluestreak's friend, who jinked and rolled and dove to avoid the fatal spread. Blossoms of orange fire erupted beneath and to every side of Jazz, filling the arena with deadly shrapnel of ivory bone. At least two missiles hit on target, one scorching the small of Jazz's back and another tearing along the expanse of his right aileron. His trythilium armor held up, but the concussive force shoved him down into the floor. Hard. He rose slowly.

He rose cradling the bloodied body of another human victim, still alive but wounded from the splintered shrapnel thrown about on that side of the battledome.

Bluestreak locked down his rocket launchers, regaining control. Thoughtless action would only end up hurting more civilians. He and Jazz had to be more careful. Had to be certain.

Had to make sure that they hurt only each other.

Streams of energy lanced back and forth between the two Autobots, photon rifle answering for each blast of blue-tinged lightning, both careful of the whorling red energy spheres and the human prisoners scattered about the unprotected interior of the battledome.

Jazz knew they'd been lucky so far. Only two human lives had been lost. That was nearly miraculous, especially after he'd used his full-spectrum light-and-sound blast to disorient Bluestreak and buy himself some time. Bluestreak's rocket launcher had snapped back open, and four warheads went streaking out at random targets including a small group of four humans.

Taking back to the air again, Jazz had tried to put himself in between the warhead and its intended victims, detonating the warhead against his chest and nearly suffering another hard-hitting crash into arena floor. He had carried the mortally wounded human with him the entire time, hoping to drop the dying man among some of the others who could care for him. The concussive force of the explosion nearly tumbled the Autobot, forced him out over one of smoking fissures which erupted in a sudden wall of plasma-bright flame.

Jazz had swept up, trying to get above the white-hot fire. He nearly managed to do so. The highest licks of flames blistered his armored chest and legs. No flame reached his hands, but the searing heat above the fire did its job and broiled the fragile human. Jazz had glided on without realizing the man had already died. Only later did he managed to set him down near others, and nearly took the full force of Bluestreak's disperser rifle in doing so.

The scar left Jazz's right leg too damaged for sustained use, and the Autobot had to rely more and more on his aerilons. He ducked and rolled away from the writhing stalks of tentacles and avoided the plasma-charged crevices. His photon rifle splashed golden fire across Bluestreak's chest, throwing his friend backward and nearly into a cluster of human participants. He backed that up with another quick blast, glancing a stream of glowing energy off the other Autobot's shoulder.

The several hundred humans caged inside the force field cheered madly as it looked like one of the combatants had finally gained an upper hand. Jazz heard their bloodthirsty cheers over and above the muted roar from the alien crowd, making him their champion—and never mind that Jazz and Bluestreak were friends or that two of their own already lay dead on the battledome floor. They shook their fists. They screamed for him.

Jazz took a step in their direction, distracted only for a moment and failing to press his attack against Bluestreak.

"Penalty," called out the Judge of the Games.

Three deep crimson laser blasts fell down from high overhead, slamming into the battledome floor seemingly at random. One fell close to Bluestreak. Another vaporized a human victim about two hundred feet to Jazz's left.

The third hit one of the crimson spheres, which absorbed the laser into its body and held it for a whispered second. Then it spun out of the energy sphere's center, traveling in a three-bounce course between spheres as it worked its way toward the caged humans and then finally slammed down into the force field that held them. The field crackled and shimmered and nearly collapsed. People shrank away from the walls. The field held, though dimmed and obviously weaker than before. It might hold against another blast, it might not. The caged humans rallied and shouted their curses on Bluestreak and on Jazz, disparaging both and at the same time encouraging one or the other to victory over his friend. No anger was spent on the Keeper's. Or at least, not as much as was spent on the two Autobots.

For all his study of Earthen culture and ways, Jazz doubted that he would ever truly understand humans.

Hoping to improve his maneuverability—and to buy enough to think his way out of this deadly scenario, Jazz transformed into a white sportscar with blue and crimson markings. Using his 180 dB stereo speakers and his front grill beacon, he created a light and sound show that disoriented Bluestreak for only a moment—before his friend also transformed into a sleek two-door automobile and ducked and dodged Jazz's attacks. In car mode, Bluestreak could move at 150 miles per hour, making him the fastest of all the Autobots when moving on four wheels. Jazz saw the effect his "special effects extravaganza" was having on the human crowd and desisted, quickly changing back to robot mode. Bluestreak quickly followed suit.

Bluestreak was back on his feet, running a slanted path away from Jazz and away from the human bystanders trying to draw fire away. Crimson bolts now sizzled down at irregular intervals, always striking near humans or Autobots or one of the energy whorls. Jazz dodged away from one, fired at Bluestreak and missed. He kept up a steady stream of fire that chased his friend across the entire battledome, his aim always off as he fought against a surge of confidence inspired by the presence of the Keepers.

When he stopped firing, another crimson laser struck down from the top of the dome. This one took Jazz high in the left arm, spinning him around and throwing him roughly to the ground.

Jazz put it together as he stumbled back to his feet and raced off after Bluestreak, who had gotten himself entangled in another mesh of segmented tentacles.

Keep firing, and the overhead lasers hold off. Stop, and they retaliated with increased accuracy and possibly increased regularity as well.

Another bolt careened off the energy spheres, hammering in at Jazz who leapt up into a powered glide that barely escaped the laser. He began firing again, now juggling Bluestreak's position and his own, the people, the location of tentacle traps, plasma vents, and the reflective spheres, all in his mind while he circled around the domed arena waiting for any chance to end this—for better or worse.

Bluestreak had managed to free himself again, and his ion-charged disperser rifle crackled out three long streams of lightning that snaked across the battledome to strike just behind Jazz, above him, and down into the pale ivory bone beneath. Jazz knew that his friend's aim was off. He saw Bluestreak trying to keep all the dangers in sight as he snapped off wild shots and worried for the nearest human as well, head turning left, right, back again.

Another hasty blast. This one passed well in front of Jazz, and fed itself right into one of the energy spheres. Jazz sensed—more than saw—that the ricochet would come right for him, cut back toward the center of the arena, rolling up, over and around the returned ionized beam to let it slip by and back toward Bluestreak with himself right after it.

No. *Close* to Bluestreak, but not *at* him.

The disperser rifle shot would angle past Bluestreak, right into a knot of five humans who huddled together in the open area between plasma vent and a whirling mass of the metallic tentacles. Jazz saw this, calculated it out in an instant's time, and knew there was nothing he could do to stop it. His photon rifle readied, he triggered a golden blast right at Bluestreak.

But the other Autobot was already on the move, acting out if instinct and with reflexes that made him a silver-and-black blur as he raced to the side and thrust one hand into the charge of lightning, trying to slap it aside, letting the destructive energies blast into every seam and joint to rip away digits, armored skin, and finally take off the entire hand at the wrist.

Bluestreak hit the ground, scraping and rolling along toward the humans he had just saved, sliding to a stop just in time. One of the humans broke and ran, sprinting away from the Autobot while racing too close to the tentacles. Jazz saw it. Bluestreak too, as he released his disperser rifle and lunged forward, trying to put himself between the human and death.

Driving forward as fast as his aerilons could carry him, diving in at Bluestreak with photon rifle at the ready, Jazz had the shot. Perfectly framed. It would core Bluestreak right through the back and doom the other human to a crushing death. It meant sacrificing his friend and another innocent, but that terrible cost had to be balanced against the lives of a couple of hundred humans who would pay the price if Jazz and Bluestreak did not end this soon.

He had the shot, and a split second to make that call.

Golden fire lanced out of his photon rifle, spearing ahead of Jazz like a lance from the sun's own heart as he punched megajoules of energy into Bluestreak's back. The force of the blast lifted the Autobot further from the ground, propelling him forward. Golden fire washed out through Bluestreak's chest as the rifle's discharge punched all the way through, catching the Autobot in a glowing halo and then dumping him to the ground, smoking and still.

Jazz braced up into a quick and easy swoop, stepping down to walk out of his glide.

The tentacles waved over Bluestreak, capable of grabbing on to him but holding back. His one remaining hand was stretched out, cupped to the ground. Jazz knelt at Bluestreak's side and grabbed his arm, lifting it off the shaken but very much alive human. He picked the man up carefully, moved him back out of range of the tentacles and then rolled Bluestreak over onto his back.

"S... S... Safe?" Bluestreak asked.

"Safe," Jazz told him. "Thank you, Bluestreak. I don't think anyone else could have moved fast enough. I..." He wasn't certain what else to say.

"Y... You," Bluestreak said. Sparks flared inside the wound gaping in his chest, and dribbled from his lips like human blood. "You needed to win, J... J... J... zzz..." His voice caught and stammered like a skipping music disk.

"Finish him." The Keeper's voice thundered over the battledome, coming at them from all sides. *"Complete the victory."*

This was a victory? Jazz had been forced into it... no... he had seen the shot, and he had made the choice to take it. Not because he'd wanted to, but because it was the lesser of the evils presented before him. Now he had to make good on the choice he'd already made.

"Prom... promise," Bluestreak said. "K... kkk... kill Megat... t... t... kill Megatron. For me, Jzzz."

"Gladly, Bluestreak. When I get the chance." It was a promise Jazz would pay most anything to keep, in fact.

"Finish it, or suffer the penalty!" The protective force field that protected the human prisoners from death

faded out of existence. There would be no safety wall between them and the overhead lasers this time.

"Do i... t... t... tchk." It was the best Bluestreak could manage.

Jazz stood up, towering above his friend, and brought his photon rifle down to rest the muzzle against Bluestreak's chest. One more full-strength shot next to the existing wound. That's all it would take.

"You needed... d... t... t... to win."

Jazz triggered the rifle shot, and Bluestreak didn't say another word.

The guiding energy sphere flashed into existence off to Jazz's right, pulsing sapphire and crimson again, to an irregular, alien heartbeat that the Autobot would have given most anything to permanently still. It drifted back toward the battledome entrance, and he followed, but his eyes were left, now right, now searching into the furthest reaches of the arena. There would be a weakness, and he would find it.

The humans railed and cheered as he walked past their open cage, calling out to him as their champion, already having forgotten Bluestreak. Jazz paused near the massive doors and studied them, trying and failing to understand. They cheered him for destroying his friend, even as the humans they had failed to save were surrounded by lattices of blue and crimson light and incinerated on the spot. The prisoners had forgotten them already as well.

They had to be forgiven for this. They were only human, after all. That *was* the Earthen phrase, wasn't it? Or did their reactions stem from something deeper, more primal, something savage that was being brought out of them here, by the Keepers themselves?

One last survey of the battledome, the force fields and stands, and Jazz turned to follow the energy sphere into the dark, grotesque corridors, back to his cell. There would be a weakness. Jazz would find it, and find a way to use it to get at the Keepers and bring their games home to them in a most punishing way imaginable. Vengeance was a part of his programming, after all, and if being near the Keepers helped the Transformers to optimize their systems, then Jazz would put some work in on this area. It needed refinement.

He stepped through the doors, which began to roll shut immediately, shrinking the corridor light down to a thinning bar that sliced over his shoulder and into the darkness. As the heavy clang echoed past him, dying against the walls, he vowed that he would see the Keepers brought to justice for the choices they had left him today.

His justice.

CHAPTER
TEN

Deep within the hollowed out world many had come to call Labyrinth, close to a hundred human beings were quartered in a single glowing chamber the size of a half-dozen football fields. They had no one but one another for company. The Keepers did not speak with them or send thralls to keep them in line, but the humans were cared for very well indeed. The room itself served as a silent, but limitless provider. Any one of the hostages had only to *think* of a thing he or she desired, and it came into being, delivered from the walls, floor, or even the ceiling.

Banquet tables rose up from the featureless and cool material at their feet and fed them with elaborate meals. Sections of wall fell away and became motion picture screens playing favorite films or television programs. Even more detailed fantasy scenarios might come into existence around them, allowing some to relive their glory days of high school as they raced across football fields and were cheered on by crowds, while others took moonlit strolls over quiet bridges in pastoral settings. Privacy could be granted at any time, allowing for the more human or base needs such as the disposal of internal waste, or simply to get away from it all, to be alone in an environment one found safe and happy.

One man in particular felt neither safe nor happy. His name was Paul Charteris. Wendy, his last girlfriend, a six-foot-tall Nordic-looking model with an MBA from Harvard, had called him an empty shell of a man in the note she left to announce that they were over. He didn't disagree. He was forty-one, tall, dark, ruggedly handsome in a Joe Millionaire kind of way—as he had been told by the last four women that hit on him, each openly wondering if he might not indeed be that celebrity whom no one would even remember in ten years. Hell, even in the midst of his day job in law enforcement, he'd come across perps—whose heads he loved cracking—later talking among themselves in the holding cells about how weird it was to get the snot beat out of them by some guy who looked like he should be modeling Calvin Klein underwear on billboards.

Paul had a couple of scars from his eleven years on the force, sliding from vice to homicide to major crimes and back, but those marks only added to his attractiveness, making him more... real, somehow. He had learned that his looks could be an asset or a liability depending on the circumstances, such as if he wanted to draw a crowd—or blend into one. Right now, in the vast white room the aliens had provided for the humans they had scooped up along with the Transformers, Paul was drawing a good deal of unwanted attention. He wasn't sure if so many of the people who kept watching him had simply sniffed "protector" or "cop" on him, or what the deal was, but one thing was certain: unlike so many here, he was calm, observant and seemingly ready for anything.

Since their arrival, he had counted exactly how many people had lapsed into catatonic shock, collapsing under the weight of their circumstances. He had catalogued and segregated those men and women he felt he might rely on in a crisis. He had pulled out the whiners, the instigators, the opportunists. He had looked long and hard for leaders but, with the exception of one olive-skinned woman, had found only frightened people, looking to be led.

He could not think of them as "followers," however. In this age, that phrase had a very different connotation, one that was practically sacred to Paul.

He was a Follower... and he had been made.

The attractive, olive-skinned woman sauntered his way. "It's really crappy the way they never let one hand know what the other is doing. I think if this hadn't happened, we both would have thought we were the only ones sent to Tokyo from the *Organization*."

The Organization. Another way of saying that she, too, was a Follower. Somehow, he wasn't at all surprised.

She was 5'5", dressed in tight black jeans and boots, a ribbed olive sweater clinging tightly to her ample chest. Her long, silky black hair fell in waves to her shoulders, framing her beautiful but thankfully not perfect face. Her green eyes, slightly protruding nose, rich, full lips (that an untrained eye might have thought were collagen enhanced) added to her beauty, but it was her neck that got to him, her long, inviting, perfect neck.

That... and her scent. Unlike so many here, she hadn't sweated once since this started.

He couldn't see the sense in maintaining the pretense that he was not a Follower, and clearly she had come to this decision as well.

"Yeah, I really wish they would let us read each other's dossiers," Paul admitted. "How the hell are we supposed to make any kind of coordinated effort—"

"Well that's just it. I don't think we are. I'm Melony, by the way."

"Paul Charteris."

They shook hands. "I should say, Dr. Melony Dodds."

"Medical doctor?" he asked.

"Yep," she said in a Texas drawl that was at odds with her East Indian heritage.

"And, if I'm not mistaken, you pardner, are the local sheriff?"

"I'm a cop, yeah. Vice, currently."

They fell silent as the sounds of an argument rose up from the far side of the room.

"Gonna do something about that?" Melony asked.

"Not sure if this is my jurisdiction."

"Do something about it," she said softly. "I want to see you in action."

He had the distinct idea she was coming on to him, so he called her on it.

"Yeah," she admitted. "Danger turns me on."

"How about we talk about it another time?'

"Are you feeling intimidated? Does it bother you when women are the aggressors?"

"Nah, I just don't like the idea of either of us letting our guard down like that. We don't know what to expect from these *things* that took us. It might not pay to get that close."

"Who's talking about close? I'm just thinking about a quick tumble to relieve some tension."

"Talk about it later," he said with a sigh, and went to see what the trouble was.

Paul sorted out the difficulty quickly and easily. Two young Asian men were arguing about the proper use of the Paradise Room. One had been leaning towards visceral vistas of vainglorious violence. Bloody boxing matches, human gladiatorial games. The other wanted to play quiet problem-solving video games. Their patches of wall and floor overlapped a little, causing the fighters to sit around and have philosophical discussions, and the adventurers digging about in ancient crypts for mysterious clues to launch into fistfights.

Paul rubbed his temples. It hadn't taken long for the hostages to realize that the perfect sedative of the horror they were facing was right at their fingertips. They only had to touch a pillar, a podium even a stretch of floor with their bare hands and anything they could imagine would come into existence and become their lives. Even after the slaughter of the half-dozen during Optimus Prime's match, the herd had quickly immersed themselves in unreality, allowing the room to supply them with showers, fresh clothing, and disposals for any stray bits of brain or bone they found upon their persons.

Paul separated the two young men who'd been arguing, finding new stretches of unused wall on opposite sides of the room, and quickly allowing each of them to get lost once more in their private paradises, and he did so without ever having to raise his voice.

Back at his "place," he found Melony waiting for him, leaning back seductively, thrusting out her chest, shifting her weight from one perfect hip to another. Her inky hair fanning against the unblemished piece of wall that Paul had currently made his own.

"So you're not using their hologram tech or whatever this is?" she asked her voice throaty, husky, oozing with wantonness.

"Are you going to keep doing that?" he asked, in no mood to play games, particularly with a fellow Follower. The way she kept coming on to his was distracting.

She laughed. "No, just messing with yah."

Then he understood. "You're *testing* me," he said, smiling despite himself. "Why?"

"Because I didn't get 'cop' the first time I saw yah. There was something else. I wanted to find out what it was."

"Priest."

She did a double-take. "Oh, now you're just having fun with me."

"True. What I'm saying is very, very *true.*"

Her eyes widened. "You have a personal relationship with our lord and savior?"

"It felt a lot more personal and made a lot more sense when the question of the possibility of life in other parts of the universe was still just a question."

"Theology," she said excitedly. "A crisis of faith. That's what led you into, you know..."

Being a Follower, he thought. "Yes, I want answers."

She shrugged. "I hear the Rock'em Sock'em's have a religion of their own—or they did. This guy, Optimus, has some connection to it, like a messianic figure. That's why I was in Tokyo." She smiled, turning on her seductive charm once more. "That... and to have some fun."

"Okay, we were getting somewhere for a minute there. Why'd you go back into Aaron Spelling vixen-of-the-week mode? I know I'm good-looking and everything, but you're an educated woman. Why act like this?"

"You think being smart makes me any less in touch

with my own needs? Just the opposite. I'm a lot more aware of things. But, uh, the truth is, it makes sense to me that eventually these guys might want a couple of us to fight, and while it might be funny to watch some of these losers. I'm pretty sure there's only two people in this room with real training. Us."

"You want to know how easily I can be distracted?" he asked. "If a little cleavage or some male machismo 'protect the little woman' instinct would make me an easy target in the arena?"

"I think it might be in everyone's best interests if we end up knowing as much as possible about each other. Maybe it'll never happen, but the people they culled from the herd..."

He thought of the six that had been chosen for horrific executions. "No. I got it," he said. "They were at the bottom end of the warrior scale."

"Yeah. If you have to dispose of someone, choose the ones that are disposable."

"I thought as a doctor all life is precious to you."

"I'm not here as a doctor."

"So you're not looking for some alien miracle cure to HIV, cancer, whatever? The dummies guide to regenerating limbs? Stopping the aging process completely? All that good stuff? That's not why you're chasing after the Transformers?"

"I'll take any and all of that if it comes, and if it I had to make a choice, my life so that all of humanity could benefit like that? Fine. I'd put my issues aside."

"So you had other reasons for joining up?"

She smiled but there was nothing behind that smile. Or so it seemed. Paul found it incredible how even her eyes could go dead at a moment's notice.

"There are *some things* that I'd give up because it's no big deal for me," she said.

"Like sleeping with a stranger."

"A good-looking one. But there's other stuff, well..."

"You're not going to tell me why you became a Follower."

Her expression did not change. "You gave up all your personal information way too easily. That makes me worry about you. And worry for everyone here."

"We have different opinions about when to keep secrets," he said. "Certain things that you think are weaknesses I might consider strengths."

Her hand touched the wall it became black, shiny and began to curve around them as if to enfold them in an embrace. "We could have a little privacy here. No one would have to see or hear."

"No thanks," he said, walking away. "I think it might take the edge off my game."

He nodded towards a large opening forming at the far end of the Paradise Room. An archway large enough for a giant to pass through.

"I have a feeling that I'm gonna want to stay *very* sharp for this," he waited, observing from the periphery of his vision as every corner of the white room took on its original dull white glow once more.

The din of voices died down, and were replaced by the clanking, metallic footsteps of one some in his organization considered a god. The footsteps echoed in the outer hallway, coming closer...

Closer still.

Then a shape appeared, filling nearly all of the high, wide doorway that had been created.

It was Optimus Prime.

The weird, angry buzzing that the Keepers took for applause intensified as Megatron was led to the forcefield gate that opened onto the arena floor. The dome was packed, with tier after tier filled with spectators rising into the darkness. Though all cheered in their traditional manner, only the humans—seated in the lower decks—clapped, hollered, and waved handmade signs much as they would at an earthbound sporting event. The opaque force field gate shimmered as Megatron approached it. When he was visible to the crowd, strange musical piping blared to announce the commencement of the next contest.

Megatron noted that the lights in the arena were bright—unnaturally so—and the illumination was tinged with an odd, crimson glow. So intense was the glare that Megatron was forced to activate his internal wide-spectrum visual filters. He wondered if the illumination was meant to imitate some faraway sun, and thus favored the opponent or opponents he faced. The Decepticon chuckled with amusement at the notion. These Keepers were certainly clever, and Megatron thought he understood them. He also felt an affinity for the overarching cruelty and arrogant superiority of the Keepers. Indeed, were the situation different, he might ally himself and his Decepticons in a mutual cooperation and conquest pact with this race... which the Keepers *believed* he had already done. But under the current circumstances—in that the Keepers forced him to come to their world against his will, and then made him perform like some trained animal for their amusement—Megatron vowed revenge. Though he enjoyed the carnage of the arena, the Keeper's control over his every move angered the Decepticon, and Megatron decided that the Keepers would feel the pain of his wrath just as soon as he got the chance to inflict it on them.

Once he had what he needed from them, that is.

The exact limits of the Keeper's control were being

felt by the Decepticon. They were reaching deep inside him, programming in subroutines that would make it impossible for him to call upon his fusion cannon or his Energon Morning Star. Another attempt, apparently, to even the odds during the battle... or to make things more interesting, in any case.

Beyond the shimmering force curtain, Megatron saw the arena floor, and two more gates on the opposite ends of his position. He guessed he would face two foes this day, and relished the thought. Suddenly, the force gate vanished as if it were never there, and Megatron stepped into the arena. As soon as his massive metal feet touched the surface of the battle area, Megatron felt a crippling weight press down on him. The force was relentless, as if the Decepticon had tripled in weight. He deduced correctly that the gravity inside the area had been adjusted, making it impossible for the Decepticon to move with accustomed speed, strength, and agility.

Piercing the glare, Megatron saw two opponents exit the gates. The first was a gigantic saurian, a biped with gray armored skin and overlapping plates of bone on its shoulder, back and upper tail—and the tail ended with a giant, bony club as large as a human house. Two parallel lines of spikes ran down the center of the saurian's back, starting at its angular head and ending at the base of the tail. Those spikes were tipped with long, curved, razor-sharp metal blades. The creature hissed and glared at Megatron as it swayed on colossal legs that were thick and rippled with powerful muscle. The creature's forearms were short, and tipped with curled claws that raked the air. The gleaming red eyes were separated by a long white bony horn, the end of which had been snapped off in some previous contest. As Megatron appraised the creature, he heard a booming animal snort and a long series of growls that echoed off the walls of the arena, but if that was actually a language that the creature was speaking, then no translation was offered by those who controlled the games. Megatron noted with satisfaction that this creature also seemed to move sluggishly, as if the gravity was impeding his movements as well.

When the force field that blocked the final gate was deactivated, Megatron and the Saurian turned to face the third contestant. Both were surprised when a strange, totally alien creature slithered into the harsh light, to glare at Megatron and the Saurian through purple, multi-faceted eyes.

The monstrous thing vaguely resembled an earthly insect—a centipede, or cockroach—with a thirty-foot-long body that was flat, wide, and quite low to the ground. The tittering creature's flesh was shiny black, and it walked on hundreds of stout, short legs that rippled like a field of wheat when the beast moved. From a gigantic, ivory-colored circular shell on the bug's chest, three opaque tubes emerged, to run up the bug's neck and along a bony ridge between the bulbous, faceted eyeballs. The tubes converged, to enter the bug's skull at the forehead just above the eyes, and each was filled with liquid—the tube on the right had a core of bubbling blue, the tube on the left glowed smoky red, the one in the center bubbled with a brown, thick and viscous fluid that resembled mud. The creature had no mouth, only a large pair of sharp, ebony pincers tipped with purple that opened and closed spasmodically.

Megatron's attention was soon drawn to the armor on the bug-like creature's broad back, armor that bristled with strange metallic appendages—hundreds of them. Megatron saw claws and spikes and club-tipped robotic arms, and spiny arms that ended with saw blades, alongside what appeared to be cannons and rocket launchers, that stuck out like the quills on a porcupine's back. Yet despite the crushing weight of these snapping scythe-like appendages and claws, the bug moved effortlessly. Obviously the creature was unaffected by the crushing gravity that slowed both the Decepticon and the saurian. Nor did the harsh light bother the Bug's faceted, lidless eyes. More ominous, this monstrosity had myriad weapons, while Megatron and the saurian had none beyond the power of their own limbs. Indeed, the whole situation was heavily weighted in favor the armored and armed insect-like nightmare.

Suddenly, the voice of the Judge of the Games filled the arena. *"Three go in, two come out,"* the Keeper announced.

The saurian roared, and Megatron chuckled. So an alliance of some kind was to be formed! That was fine with Megatron. He was good at forging alliances—when they suited him—and the Decepticon was equally adept at breaking them off once his interests had been satisfied. In this contest, Megatron had only to decide which creature would provide the better ally—the Bug, or the Saurian.

Megatron's thoughts were interrupted by the booming of a gong. Suddenly, the crowd went wild, with the angry buzzing of the Keepers intensifying, and with the screaming and yelling among the human contingent growing louder and more frenzied.

"Let the contest begin," said the Keeper.

Megatron looked at the saurian, then at the Bug. Both creatures stared back at him. For a moment, nothing moved as each creature appraised the others.

Then, with an angry, clacking sound, the Bug surged forward, slithering between Megatron and the saurian, its array of weapons and appendages bristling threateningly. Tube-like spikes on the Bug's back flopped sideways and pointed at Megatron's chest, even as others aimed at the saurian. Before either could react, there was a blasting roar as hundreds of spinning metal plates the size of manhole covers shot out of tubes.

Though the whirling discs had edges that were razor-sharp, they bounced harmlessly from Megatron's titanium steel armor. The saurian was not so lucky. As the beast threw up its forearm to protect its face, hundreds of the metal discs buried themselves deeply into his thick gray hide. Blue-white blood gushed from a score of wounds, and the saurian roared in anguish.

Megatron reached out and grasped one of the tubes. Using the incredible power of his servomotors, the Decepticon snapped it off. The human spectators cheered and leaped from their seats—first blood had been drawn, then countered.

But the Decepticon felt hamstrung, like he was moving in the depths of the ocean. Just grasping the tube and snapping it free required vast amounts of energy from Megatron's many systems. Moving laboriously, much slower than he was accustomed to, Megatron managed to flip the tube around in his hand and plunged the sharp tip into the Bug's back. The tube broke yet again—far too fragile to penetrate the Bug's formidable armor. Megatron grabbed two saw blade arms and held on tight.

Sparks flew as the Bug's mechanical arms, which were tipped by spinning razor-teethed circular saw blades, raked Megatron's chest plate with a ripping sound. The sparks quickly turned from blue to red, as the incredible friction generated began to melt a furrow in the Decepticon's metallic frame. Reluctantly Megatron relinquished his hold on the bug and jumped backward—but slowly and awkwardly, and the Bug managed a glancing swipe at his faceplate with a sword-like arm, causing another shower of sparks but little damage.

Then, with a roar of rage and defiance, the saurian turned and struck the Bug with its clubbed tail—once, twice, three times, on the insect creature's head, neck and arms. The Bug shrugged off the blows, then it's pincers snapped, seizing the saurian's tail and causing a howl of pain and anguish to emerge from the reptilian biped.

The crowd jumped to its feet and roared with excitement as the Bug dug its powerful pincers into the saurian's flesh, snapping through the bony plates that guarded the soft, tender muscle and fat beneath. More blue-white blood flowed, to gush onto the arena's floor. In a mad frenzy to escape the Bug's grip, the saurian twisted in its grip, only to slip in a large pool of its own blood. Down the saurian went as its tree-trunk legs flew out from under it. The reptile landed with a spat on its side.

Immediately, the Bug opened its pincers and released the tail, then turned and swarmed over the saurian, its many legs rippling over the reptile's upturned belly as it crushed the biped with the weight of its insect body. Each tap of a black, stout leg tore a new furrow in the saurian's exposed flesh. The creature howled and kicked helplessly, but before it could move the pincers closed around the saurian's throat.

Quickly, the saurian redoubled its efforts as it tried to escape, but the insect hung on, its pincers closing tighter and tighter. The saurian gurgled as its legs kicked out spasmodically. Its forepaws ripped and tore at the Bug's face, seemingly without inflicting damage. As Megatron watched, the saurian turned its red, pleading eyes to the Decepticon. Within a few moments, those same eyes rolled up in the saurian's skull as the creature began to wheeze and gasp. More blood flowed as the Bug squeezed tighter.

The crowd was on its feet now, wild cheering and indistinguishable cries filled the arena. Megatron knew it was time for him to choose an ally, before the choice was made for him. He studied the powerful and formidable insect-like armored creature—mere moments from victory—then the struggling, gasping reptilian near death. Finally, Megatron made his decision.

Instinctively, Megatron willed his fusion cannon to fire before he remembered he was unarmed. Instead, the mightiest of the Decepticons raised his heavy metal arms. Then, closing his hands into huge pummeling fists, he brought them down onto the Bug's armored spine.

The first blow shocked the Bug, and its pincers opened to release the saurian's throat. But instead of retreating, Megatron brought his fist down a second time, then a third, a forth, a fifth. Finally, on the seventh blow, the crowd heard a loud crack. The previously impenetrable armor on the Bug's spine had actually shattered on a single stress point, sending the creature fleeing into one corner of the arena.

The saurian rolled clear. Still clutching its ravaged throat with one hand, the biped rose to its full height with Megatron's help. The Saurian stepped backward, to lean against the wall. As it gasped, blood leaked from a dozen wounds.

It was a standoff now. Only Megatron hadn't yet been injured, and the insect creature knew that the robot had taken sides against him. The three combatants eyed one another warily. Then, unexpectedly, several of the Bug's bristles shot forward. There was a blast of fire, but instead of spinning disks, hundreds of globs of some hot, molten material emerged from the tubes. Megatron managed to dodge most of the fire, but a few globs struck his head, shoulder, arm and chest plate—along with the wall of the arena.

Wherever the liquid splashed, the damage was immediate. The substance burned like acid, scoring Megatron's armor and threatening to melt through to his interior structure. The Decepticon staggered back, to slam against the saurian. The robot rubbed some of the scorching acid from his faceplate in time to see the tubes trained on him once again.

But this time, as the Bug let loose with another torrent of burning globs of acidic magma, the saurian threw himself in the liquids path. There was a splash as almost the entire stream washed over the reptilian biped's body. Megatron watched, fully expecting the saurian to die very quickly and in acute agony. Instead, the creature merely shook the dripping magma from his body. Then it turned and faced Megatron and the Decepticon was sure that the creature was smiling!

"Immune to the substance, I see," Megatron rumbled.

The saurian did not reply. Instead it turned to see the Bug surging forward, ready to strike Megatron. The reptile tried to jump, but gravity was its enemy and it failed. Instead of leaping, the saurian simply fell on the Bug, grappling with the waving appendages on its bristling back. The Bug rolled and slithered around the arena, trying to shake the angry saurian that held on to its back with one claw while it ripped robotic arms free from the armor with the other.

Bellowing angrily, the Bug turned and shot more hot globs at Megatron, who managed despite his war with gravity to dodge them. The Decepticon knew it could not dodge forever—not with gravity so dense—and he envied the saurian his acid resistant hide.

Only then did Megatron see that there was a connection—though the environment clearly favored the insect creature, both the Decepticon and the saurian possessed natural countermeasures against its weapons. Megatron shrugged off the disc attack as easily as the Saurian shook off the magma attack.

This creature must be vulnerable! Megatron decided, appraising the creature for any signs of weakness.

While the Saurian rode the Bug like a bucking bronco, it continued to tear appendages free. Soon broken blades and shattered metal claws littered the floor of the arena. Megatron studied the Bug's movements, which still showed no sigh of exhaustion despite the fury of the battle. The only change the Decepticon noticed were within the three tubes that ran up the Bug's neck and plunged into its skull. The fluids inside were glowing and bubbling violently, as if the creature somehow required the substances inside those tubes to live.

"That's how it breathes!" Megatron cried.

The Keepers had given the Bug weapons, and an environment that suited it—except for the *atmosphere.*

Just as Megatron reached this revelation, there was a loud cry from the audience as the saurian was finally thrown clear. The reptile hit the arena and rolled. When it was out of reach of the Bug's pincers, the saurian staggered to its feet, the broken blades from the Bug's armored spine in each claw-tipped hand.

The Bug twisted around to face Megatron. Its purple eyes burned with an evil intelligence. But Megatron would not meet the creature's gaze—his eyes were fixed on the three tubes that ran up the Bug's face and into its skull. As he suspected, the fluids inside of all three tubes bubbled wildly.

Then the Bug charged. But this time, instead of avoiding the attack, Megatron embraced it. As the Bug's vicious pincers closed on Megatron's metal thigh, the Decepticon reached down and grabbed at the tubes. The Bug closed its grip, crushing Megatron's titanium steel leg. But the Decepticon ignored the damaged, fumbling to grab hold of the three tubes.

The saurian moved forward and thrust out with the steel blades in its hand. One blade sunk into the black exoskeleton of the Bug's neck and broke off. But the other plunged through the glassy membrane of one purple faceted eye, to erupt in a shower of steaming black inky blood. Still the saurian thrust, plunging its claw wrist deep into the Bug's ruined eye.

The Bug opened its pincers, releasing the Decepticon. But Megatron did not retreat. He was now grasping the three tubes, and now he began to squeeze them.

It was the Bug's turn to squirm helplessly under the grip of the mighty robot. Hundreds of legs kicked as the insect creature tried vainly to free itself. Still Megatron held on, to tighten his grip. When he could no longer crush the tubes more, he began to pull at them—causing the Bug to mew and howl, the remaining appendages on its back waving and snapping helplessly.

Stepping backward, Megatron released one hand.

He reached out to grab an arm with a circular saw blade on its tip. As the Bug activated the saw, Megatron ripped it free with a loud metallic snap. With the saw blade still spinning, the Decepticon plunged the tip into the untouched eye. It exploded in a shower of black blood that washed over Megatron's armor. The Bug backed up with all its might to escape the cutting blade, and in so doing ripped the three tubes Megatron still grasped out of its own skull. There was a shower of blue sparks, a cloud of red smoke, and brown mud spewed forth—followed by the Bug's brain matter. The creature staggered and turned over on its back, black legs kicking in its death throes.

Suddenly, the saurian was back, fist raised. Flashing down, the reptile brought the tip of the broken metal spike down in the center of the tube-hole in the Bug's head. The monster cried out once, its pincers opened and closed. Then the bloody head sank to the arena floor as the last of the insect-creature's life flowed onto the floor of the arena.

The crowd was in a frenzy now, with people cheering and Keepers buzzing. The humans were jumping up and down and falling all over themselves to get a better view as Megatron stepped back and raised his gory hands high in a victory salute. In one robotic fist he gripped the shattered saw blade, in the other the twisted ends of the shattered tubes. A moment later the saurian was at Megatron's side, arms spread high.

The cheers became deafening as the scarlet glow vanished and normal light beamed down from on high. Megatron felt his metallic form rise to its full height as the weight of gravity was removed. The saurian felt it, too, and seemed to look on Megatron with grateful, triumphant eyes.

In front of the victorious contestants, a gate opened. But as the saurian took his first step, Megatron whirled and plunged the sharp edge of the saw blade into the already-ravaged throat of the saurian. Megatron twisted the blade as he stabbed out, ripping through muscle, cartilage and bone. The reptilian biped gave the Decepticon a look of puzzled confusion before the red eyes rolled up into its head a final time.

Megatron released his grip on the blade and the saurian plunged forward to land in an expanding pool of its own life's fluid. The saurian twitched once, its tail flopping. And then it was still.

The crowd that had been shocked into stunned silence when the Decepticon stabbed his ally, now began to roar its approval. As the cheers and calls grew in intensity, the voice of the Keeper filled the arena.

"Even better," the voice said, brimming with bloodthirsty satisfaction.

Megatron chuckled. Then he shook the blood off his metal hands and strode arrogantly through the gate and out of the arena.

The cries of the frenzied crowd continued to swell long after he was gone.

Optimus Prime was confused. Jazz had never returned from his battle, and Prime had no idea if that meant his friend had been sent to other quarters, or had fallen during the fight. A seeming eternity had passed, then the lights came for him, leading him to what he believed would be another fight in the arena.

Then glowing lights had vanished suddenly. He'd wandered until finally he saw a door appear, a glowing white door, and heard sounds beyond it. Jazz, he assumed, had returned from his match and was taking some comfort in the pleasures offered by the room. Prime felt that he could not judge his friend on this issue, he simply, and fervently hoped his friend had fared better than he had in his challenge.

Now he stood before the people he had fought to protect, and they stared at him as if he were the most heinous criminal they had ever seen. Some humans cursed him, others cringed from him.

All he could think about while staring down at them was the cruel humor of the Keepers, and their difficult-to-fathom reasons for any of what they had done.

Then images of the six humans who had been horribly slain exploded in his mind, and he looked away in shame.

Suddenly, another door opened, this one only a few feet behind him. But... that had been a corridor only instants before. Now he saw a familiar, hulking figure, and behind him, the other hundred humans quartered in this place.

Megatron. And the crowd behind him was cheering!

Spinning, Prime raced at his enemy—and was instantly rebuked by a practically invisible wall of force, a partition separating him from the Decepticon leader.

Megatron's laugh was hearty. "Look at them, Optimus, you poor, deluded *fool*. They adore me. They worship me. They know I will keep them safe, and they don't care that I act strictly out of self-preservation and the pursuit of my own goals. Your intentions are pure, but your follow-through is little more than a joke. They fear you, and with good reason. You don't have what it takes to protect them. You never did, and you never will."

Optimus flinched inwardly. Sentinel Prime had delivered a similar sentiment.

Listening to the cheers and jeers of the humans surrounding him, he hung his head, wondering if it was all true.

He didn't notice the pair of humans standing on his side of the partition, a calm, attractive man and woman who eyed him with interest that went beyond their concerns over their immediate survival.

No, that wasn't quite true. He hadn't noticed them consciously, but his scanners had recorded their images, and his cybernetic brain's deep subroutines would eventually ferret them out.

For now, all he could take in was his mortal enemy, who slammed the partition hard enough to make Optimus look up sharply.

"One more thing," Megatron said. "The Keepers? They've revealed themselves to me, and I've made my deal with them. When this is over—and it will be over, Prime—I will be on my way back to Cybertron with the means to create as many Decepticons as I so desire, and the firepower and fuel to wage the war as it should have been waged four million years ago. Your precious Earth, on the other hand... it will be a charred husk. Such is the price for mining *all* of its Energon at once. Pity that, I suppose. Or possibly not. I think it's more than high time that these talking monkeys of yours are put out of their misery...and there's not a damn thing you can do about *any* of it."

CHAPTER
ELEVEN

A U.S. Army Black Hawk helicopter raced over the Autobots' heads at low level, it's electronic sensors activated, all gathering data on the mysterious military force that suddenly appeared out of nowhere on the Army's right flank. Prowl watched as the chopper passed his position and dipped low over the Nevada desert. Cautiously, the Autobot raised the photon rifle he clutched in his powerful grip, but did not pull the trigger. Instead, he lowered his weapon and, unmolested, the Black Hawk made a graceful turn to avoid a rocky spire, then flew nape-of-the-earth back toward the U.S. Army's front lines.

"They're just checking us out," said Bumblebee, who crouched between two giant tables or rock. "Trying to figure out just who we are."

"So am I," said Prowl, still uneasy over his choice of allies.

Despite his hesitant tone, the Autobot called Prowl didn't regret joining forces with Grimlock, despite the Dinobot's past treachery. That was because the savage Grimlock at least offered a course of action—as opposed to a course of *in*action favored by the United States military and the United Nations Security Council. But Prowl did have misgivings about the secret army that Grimlock allied himself with.

Grimlock was not exactly forthcoming with the details, and the few human soldiers from this military

154

force that Prowl came in contact with were civil, businesslike, and closed-mouth.

"I just wish I knew where this mysterious army came from, and who commands it," Prowl said.

Bumblebee chuckled. "What difference does it make in the long run," he said. "We made a deal with the devil we knew—Grimlock—so why worry about a devil we know nothing about? Heck, we don't even know if they *are* devils. Did it ever occur to you that we might all be on the same side?"

"Not really," said Prowl dubiously.

"You really are a half-full kind of guy... er, Autobot," Bumblebee said, still chuckling.

"Nothing funny here," a gruff voice rumbled. "Many humans move to stop our movements."

The Autobots turned to see Grimlock lumbering toward them. The massive Dinobot trod the desert like a prehistoric beast of old, its huge metal claws digging into the rock and sand with each step.

Stomping up a slight incline to their position near the Army's front lines, Grimlock halted and dipped his massive head. His jaws opened and the Dinobot spoke in its halting, stilted style.

"Human army has moved between our forces and Las Vegas," Grimlock growled. "Our allies do not want a fight with the United States Army. They want you to take the Army out, open a road through their lines so we can attack the Decepticons."

"What about negotiations?" Bumblebee asked. "Hasn't anyone asked the Army to maybe step aside and let us through?"

Grimlock roared. "No negotiations! Already the Army moves to flank us... block our path."

"Okay, okay," Bumblebee said, "you made your point."

"We must attack now, before the Army can move all of its forces to stop us," grunted Grimlock, his eyes burning.

"But we can't just indiscriminately kill American soldiers!" Prowl insisted.

"Kill or don't kill," Grimlock rumbled. "That is Autobot's choice. But move them out of the way or I will."

On that ominous note, Grimlock turned on his heels and stomped away, his metal tail flashing angrily.

Bumblebee and Prowl exchanged glances.

"Well," Bumblebee shrugged. "Better us than that crazy Dinobot. We can use a little restraint, anyway."

"I still don't like it," said Prowl. "Maybe we can buy some time, convince the Army to let us pass."

Bumblebee looked up, to see contrails in the blue vault of sky. Military aircraft, approaching their position.

"I think time has just run out," Bumblebee said, pointing.

Inside the cockpit of his A-10 Thunderbolt, United States Air Force Lieutenant Vic Mellors scanned the boundless desert racing by under the belly of his straight-winged, twin-engine close air support attack plane. The desert camouflaged A-10 Lieutenant Mellors was flying into combat that day was old by military standards. First designed to stop Soviet tanks in the event of a Third World War, the ungainly A-10 was left without a mission when the Soviet Union ceased to exist in the 1990s. Fortunately for the formidable warplane, the A-10—dubbed the Warthog by its crews because it was just so damned ugly—found a new military role as a tank-buster during the first Persian Gulf War. It was a role the Warthog was suited for because in reality she was nothing more than an airplane built around a cannon—the GAU-8/A-30-mm multi-barrel cannon that ran through its fuselage and stuck out of the aircraft's chin. That gun could fire over a thousand rounds of dense, depleted uranium shells that could penetrate any type of tank armor. Add to that capability the eighteen Mark 82 500-pound bombs the A-10 carried—nine under each wing—and you had an aircraft that could deliver what is known in military parlance as the "knockout punch."

Lieutenant Mellors was too young to have flown in the first Gulf War, and he was just beginning his training when the second one started, so he missed that war too. Now he was leading a flight of four aircraft on an attack against an enemy that his superiors in the United States Army and Army Intelligence knew absolutely nothing about.

"Well, orders are orders," Lieutenant Mellors had told himself. Of course, the world had gotten a little crazier lately, and so had the orders he received. Like the ones he got just that morning—orders to attack an army that wasn't supposed to exist.

"This is Uberhog One. We are within range," Lieutenant Mellors announced, breaking radio silence. "Everyone check in."

"Uberhog Two present," said Lieutenant Vern Fox, his voice tense.

"Uberhog Three reporting in," Lieutenant Antoine Debussy said in his lazy New Orleans accent.

Uberhog Four checkin' in," said Lieutenant Dave Langer in thick Brooklynese.

"I'm going to pop up for a peek over the ridge," Lieutenant Mellors said. "If all is clear, we'll attack."

Lifting the nose of his A-10, Mellors surged over a rocky ridge. A quick check of the desert and Mellors was oriented. He saw the mystery army a few miles ahead of his position—a dark line of tanks in the brown sand.

According to the intel briefing Mellors and his unit received that morning, the enemy—if that's what they were—had top of the line military equipment of American manufacture, including M1A2 Abrams main battle tanks with reactive armor, Bradley armored personnel carriers and fighting vehicles, Crusader mobile artillery, and, ominously, M48 Chaparral short-range surface-to-air mobile missile launchers, with missiles quite capable of bringing down all four A-10s.

"This is Uberhog One," Lieutenant Mellors reported. "Tally-ho. Enemy sighted. No SAM radar yet. Maybe they don't know we're coming."

The others clicked the mikes to acknowledge their commander.

"Form up behind me for the first pass," Lieutenant Mellors commanded, his heart racing in anticipation. The twin General Electric turbofan engines hummed behind him as Mellors took his Thunderbolt up to attack altitude, to rendezvous with the rest of his flight for the final attack dive.

The A-10s were deployed for a lateral attack, and were now poised to zoom down along the entire line of enemy vehicles, dealing death with bombs and the deadly Gatling gun. But before his squadron mates could form up on his wing, Lieutenant Mellors sensed movement out of the corner of his eye.

He turned in time to see a streak of *something* race past his cockpit. It was gray, flat and looked like a big slab of rock! Lieutenant Mellors heard a terrible ripping sound as the entire aircraft shuddered and seemed to stall. Swiveling his head around, Lieutenant Mellors was horrified to see that the entire tail section of his Warthog—including the rear stabilizers and the two turbofan engines—had been torn away. As the aircraft began a fatal dive, the young flight commander had no choice but to punch out.

A second later the cockpit blew away and Mellors felt icy cold blast of air hit his chest. Then the rocket under his seat ignited and he was shot into space. As he tumbled toward the desert far below, the lieutenant's parachute deployed. With a jerk, his rapid decent slowed and Lieutenant Mellors was dangling from his chute.

On the ground, Bumblebee hesitated before hefting a slab of stone just like the one he had thrown at Mellors' plane, his amazing visual acuity, the best of all the Autobots, allowing him to spot exactly where to throw the stone to do the precise type of damage necessary.

"Have a nice day," Bumblebee said with a smart salute.

Mellors turned to see the Autobot focusing his attention on the other three A-10s circling the sky.

Bumblebee's quick, precision throws caused instant confusion among the three remaining Warthogs. The wing of one aircraft—bombs and all—was sliced clean off by the volley of rocks from Bumblebee far below and sent fluttering end over end, to crash into the desert sand below.

"This is Uberhog Three!" the frantic voice of Lieutenant Debussy cried. "I'm going down."

A second later the pilot punched out and floated to the ground as his A-10 slammed into a hillside in a fireball.

"We're under attack!" Lieutenant Fox cried from Uberhog Two. "Take evasive action."

"I'm beginning to think you don't like me," Bumblebee quipped as he hurled another projectile, ripping free the tail section off Lieutenant Fox's aircraft. Like the others, the aircraft went into a spin. The maneuver was so violent that the pilot's head struck the canopy, and Lieutenant Fox was knocked unconscious.

Bumblebee sensed something was wrong when the pilot didn't bale out right away. Turning away from the final A-10, which had turned tail and was heading back to the Army's front lines, the Autobot zoomed in on the cockpit of the stricken Uberhog Two.

Delivering another volley of rocks with precise surgical strikes, Bumblebee tore through the aluminum skin of the A-10's fuselage, severed the bolts holding the canopy in place, setting it free, and, with a final rock, nailed the button for the ejection seat with the precise velocity and impact necessary to tap the release and set the pilot loose. Seconds later, the stricken A-10 hit the ground, its unconscious pilot drifting downward, parachute open.

"Your turn," he said to Prowl.

"On it," said Prowl, surging forward into battle.

In desert warfare, mobility is the key to victory.

German Field Marshall Erwin Rommel knew that fact in World War II, and used fast action to conquer all of North Africa. So did his nemesis, British General Montgomery, who used mobility to take North Africa back again. General George S. Patton also realized that mobility was the key to victory and urged his tanks forward in Sicily and the Ardennes, no matter how much resistance they faced. General H. Norman

Schwarzkopf also knew the importance of mobility, and beat Saddam Hussein's elite Republican Guard by moving his tanks around them in a bold flanking maneuver that cut the Iraqis off from Baghdad and safety.

And General Ben Fellows, West Point, 1968, knew the importance of mobility too. That was why he was moving an entire tank battalion around the mysterious enemy force to attack them from the rear. General Fellows was counting on the A-10s to create enough of a diversion to move his force into position. Unfortunately for General Fellows, things didn't go as planned.

"Keep moving!" Fellows said from the turret of his command tank, an M1A2 Abrams in the very center of a two-mile line of tanks racing to engage the enemy.

Dust rolled from the treads of a hundred tanks as the clanking main battle tanks rumbled across the flat desert landscape. By the general's estimation, his tank force was less than five minutes from being in range of the enemy's guns, which also meant that his own tank force was less than five minutes from being in range themselves.

"Button up!" General Fellows commanded.

In all the tanks the commanders ducked inside their hatches and closed them up. Only the general himself remained exposed—the better to see what the enemy was up to.

"Sabot!" Fellows commanded. "Lock and load!"

Sabot—the French word for "shoe"—is a special type of armor piercing tank shell. The sabot projectile has two stages. The first stage strikes enemy armor, then instantly melts—creating a hole in the armor with a super-hot jet of molten plasma. A nanosecond later the second stage—the actual warhead—detonates inside that hole, blowing the tank and its crew to kingdom come.

General Fellows checked his watch. In three minutes they would be in range. He planned to have his tanks fire as soon as that happened.

Suddenly, through the shimmering waves of heat that rose from the desert floor, General Fellows saw a colossal shape rise up in front of his tank. It was a huge robot, its armor black, white and silver. Intel had warned General Fellows that Autobots were working with the mysterious army, but he refused to believe it. Fellows wasn't one to believe the worst in anyone, and he had pretty much dismissed the media reports of Autobot treachery.

But now, as Prowl blocked his way, General Fellows could not deny the evidence of his senses. He didn't hesitate.

"Target that Autobot and fire at will," he cried into his mike.

A dozen muzzles spit fire as the tanks opened fire on Prowl. As the first shells struck his armor, the Autobot swayed on his feet. A half-dozen explosions burst on his chest plate, his arms, his legs and even his head.

"That hurt!" Prowl cried, then he leveled a huge weapon on the lead tank. With an electronic crackle the Null rifle fired, its burst striking General Fellows command tank. Inside the turret, all electrical systems went haywire, and sparks filled the tank's cramped interior. Within seconds a dozen small fires broke out.

Nothing frightens a tank crew more than fire, and as soon as the crew realized that the Abrams' built-in fire-extinguisher system had gone blooey with the rest of the electrical systems, they began to bale out.

General Fellows hesitated for a moment, trying to give final commands to the rest of his tank force. But like everything else, the radio was dead.

Reluctantly, the general abandoned his multi-million-dollar vehicle. As he hit the sand, he ducked behind a pile of rocks. While his command tank burned, the Autobot called Prowl moved past the wreckage to attack the rest of the battalion. General Fellows watched helplessly as Prowl engaged the rest of the tanks.

With each blast of his Null rifle, Prowl took out more tanks. Some burned where they sat, their crews abandoning them. Others just stalled and halted in their tracks as all electrical systems—including those that aimed and fired the main cannon—shorted out. In a few minutes, twenty tanks were disabled. Another twenty turned away from Prowl and retreated.

Unseen by the fighting Autobot, three M1A2 Abrams had moved into flanking position behind a shelf of rocks. Moving into position, they fired as one. Instead of targeting the Autobot, the tank commanders had aimed at his weapon.

No one was more surprised than Prowl as the Null rifle exploded in his hand.

"Ouch!" he cried, dropping the now-molten weapon.

The Autobot turned in time to see—but not avoid—the three tanks as they moved out of cover and fire again. Once again the Autobot had no time to duck. Three shells struck his faceplate, the force of the unexpected blast knocking Prowl head over heels. He landed hard on the sand, and a cloud of dust rose to obscure his massive form. The tanks moved inexorably forward.

Suddenly a yellow form landed on the back of the lead tank. Bumblebee reached out and grabbed the turret in his powerful grip. Bracing his legs, Bumblebee pulled. His metal fingers dug into the composite armor, which shattered like glass. Then, with a final sound of tearing metal, the turret ripped free. Bumblebee held it over his head and shook. One crewman spilled out, tumbled into the sand, stumbled to his feet and ran to safety. The rest of the crew of the now ruined tank ran around Bumblebee's massive legs and scampered for cover, too.

Hurling the turret at another tank, Bumblebee leaped into the air just in time to avoid a round fired from the second tank. The turret struck the other tank a moment later, snapping the cannon muzzle in two. The crew abandoned ship. The third Abrams turned tail and retreated, firing a few shots to cover its escape.

"You okay?" Bumblebee asked, helping Prowl to his feet.

"Rescuing me is starting to become you life's work," Prowl quipped.

Bumblebee laughed. "I could think of worse jobs."

"Like the one coming up," Prowl said. "Duck!"

Bumblebee threw himself onto the sand—and not a moment too soon. A flight of six AH-64 Apache attack helicopters had unleashed a torrent of Hellfire missiles at the two Autobots.

Explosions burst all around them, kicking up rocks and sand and striking their robotic forms. The shells were, of course, ineffectual, but they prevented Prowl and Bumblebee from attacking.

Prowl rolled behind a mound of boulders, and dragged Bumblebee with him. More missiles struck the rocks, shattering some. Then the Apaches opened fire with the chin guns, and machine gun bullets bounced off their tough hides.

"This is humiliating," said Bumblebee.

Suddenly the torrent of bullets ceased. Poking his head up, Bumblebee saw the reason—Grimlock had jumped in front of the helicopters and was taking their steady fire.

As they watched, the Dinobot lashed out with his tail, shattering the rotors of an Apache that got too close. Helplessly the combat helicopter spun out of control and crashed to the ground. Prowl was relieved to see the crew exit the burning craft.

The rest of the Apaches pulled away, their ammunition spent.

But the second line of tanks was moving closer to their position. As Prowl and Bumblebee watched, their cannons opened fire and shells rained down on the Autobot's position.

For the next three hours, the Autobots fought off assault wave after assault wave. The burning wreckage of a hundred tanks, helicopters, Bradley fighting vehicles and Armored Personnel Carriers littered the Nevada desert.

But as the afternoon continued, the attacks slowly abated.

Prowl and Bumblebee, their armor scarred and scored from a thousand hits, approached one another from opposite sides of the battlefield. From between two peaks, Grimlock appeared. He stomped toward the battle-weary Autobots, shaking the ground.

"Humans retreat," the Dinobot announced. "Way is clear to Las Vegas."

As he spoke, Prowl saw a line of tanks behind the Dinobot—the mysterious army was moving now, heading across the desert through the gap in the American lines.

"We destroy Decepticons now!" Grimlock said in a deep rumble.

Bumblebee sat down on a wrecked Abrams tank.

"I need a rest!" he declared.

"No time to rest," roared Grimlock, his eyes burning as he waved the crackling energy sword he clutched in his grip. "We fight."

Bumblebee sighed and stood up. He wavered unsteadily, his interior systems still a bit scrambled by all the fighting. Slowly, almost painfully, Prowl moved to Bumblebee's side.

"I know I wanted this fight," the plucky yellow Autobot said. "But I am discovering that at least one earth saying is true."

Prowl tilted his head. "Oh? What's that?"

Bumblebee chuckled. "I've discovered that payback *is* a bitch!"

CHAPTER TWELVE

Spike heard the blast, felt something slap against the back of his skull, and had been rocketed into oblivion. It wasn't the first time he had died; his body had been trashed pretty badly when he was a child, and the Transformers had saved him, draining his consciousness from his mortal frame and "downloading" it into the hulking metal body of a giant robot. He recalled the power he had felt looking out through visual sensors instead of eyes, being able to curl his hands into fists and smash through solid rock, and so much more... but he also remembered the loneliness he had encountered within his living metal shell, the feeling that there was no place in this world for what he had become.

Prime had ultimately saved his body, bringing it back from death itself, and made Spike whole again, *human* again, but he had never forgotten the experience; he never would.

So, what's dying like, Dad?

Well, it hurts like a mother, I can tell you that much, son—at least, the first time it did. This time it was more like having someone rap me on the back of the skull while a stick of dynamite blew up a few inches away from my head—deafening, scary, then... nothing.

No, Spike thought. *Not nothing. There were dreams this time, thoughts and recollections.*

How was that possible?

A sudden light seared into his right pupil and Spike registered that he was awake, aware, alive—laying on the floor of the commander's entryway, Franklin and a handful of medics crouched over him. There was a smoking crater in Franklin's palm, tiny wires and bits of circuitry hissing and sparking from the damaged area.

A ringing came to Spike, and he thought it was a result of the gun going off so close to his head, but no, it was Franklin's cell phone.

"Of course he'll live," Franklin said, clearly annoyed. "No one dies on my watch, you know that." The agent hesitated. "Uh-huh. Right. Yes, we have them both. Full report to follow, I've got to bring our boy back on his feet and bring him up to speed first."

Franklin hung up, rolling his eyes. Then he fixed his gaze on Spike and smiled. "Hey, kid, ready to get this party started?"

Two of the medics helped Spike into a sitting position, though his head throbbed and he felt sick to his stomach. The heat in the commander's house was oppressive, a stark contrast to the chill outside. Franklin sat next to him.

"Probably wondering what the hell happened, right?" Franklin asked.

Spike nodded, though it pained him to do so.

"I like to keep every base covered. While you went in the front door, I came in through the back. I was only a few feet away when Mr. Rogers over there decided to evict you from his neighborhood...permanently."

Spike turned his head, another painful mistake, and saw Hugo Fortuna sitting in a wooden chair, his ankles handcuffed to the legs, his wrists bound to the arms. The man's face was flush and his sweater-bound chest rose and fell with manic, rhythmless speed. Fortuna's eyes darted back and forth wildly, yet not out of panic, or so Spike decided from the quick glimpse he'd attained of the man, but more from a desperation to find some weakness in the defenses of his captors, a desire to find a way out and do what he had wanted to do in this first place:

Kill Spike.

There was no questioning, in the split-second their eyes met, that there was murder on the man's mind. No, the real question was *why* did he want Spike dead?

Spike shifted his gaze to the mess that had been Franklin's palm. "Okay, so you were nearby when he tried to pop me. Then what?"

"I can be pretty quick when I have to be," the operative said. "What you felt smacking into the back of your head was the back of my hand. Knocked you out, but it didn't do any real damage. Must be the thick skull..."

"You got between the gun muzzle and my head."

"Right."

"In the time it took for him to pull the trigger and the bullet to come out. As in, faster than a speeding..."

Franklin blushed. "Aw, come on, newbie. You don't have to flatter me with the comparisons. I just did what anyone with my skills—and my agenda—would have done under the circumstances."

Finally, the commander chimed in. Though gritted teeth, he snarled, "You're both freaks. How can you live with yourselves, all that... contamination... in your bodies?"

Franklin's eyebrows flashed happily. "Woo-woo, first words he's spoken since I tore him off you and sat him down in that chair and forced him to get all civilized like."

Spike couldn't help but notice the manic, fast-talking change in Franklin's manner of speech. "What's all that tech pumping into your brain? Organic stimulants? Pure adrenal gland extract?"

"Naw." Franklin raised a can of diet soda in his undamaged hand. "It's just the caffeine. Makes me wired."

Now the two med-techs—who looked a lot more like no-neck military types, or bouncers, were hauling Spike to his feet, helping him over to a couch across from the chained man.

"Gugh," Spike mumbled as they deposited him on the lightly cushioned couch and took up stations on either side of the commander.

Franklin waved his hand at his side, like he had pins and needles and was trying to shake it out. Little sparks flew as he addressed the prisoner.

"You know, I have nerve sensors in there. That actually hurt," Franklin said.

The commander glared up at him, sweating, grinning. "Thanks for sharing."

"He's talkative already," Franklin said with an over-the-shoulder glance at Spike. "That means he's probably going to tell us everything we need to know without the least little bit of persuasion, which is great. Save us all a lot of time and effort."

"Sure," Fortuna said. "That's just how it'll go down."

Franklin knelt before him. "You realize we're on the same side, right? This doesn't have to get... unpleasant."

"Being around traitors like the two of you is unpleasant enough," Fortuna said. "You mean it gets worse?"

"Lots worse. So talk. Tell us why you tried to kill our buddy Spike, here."

Fortuna said nothing.

The operative was undisturbed; he looked like he expected the silence. "Tell me, why do you think Spike is like me? Augmented, I mean."

Easing back in the chair, Fortuna said, "Can't blame a dog who likes to fight, likes to bite, for his nature. All you can do is put 'em down."

Spike shook his head. *Ow!* Another big mistake. "Now he wants me in a kennel."

"So you believe Spike is augmented," Franklin said calmly. "Why would you hold that belief? Did the lights tell you?"

Fortuna looked up sharply. "The lights?"

"The ones off your ship. The ones you reported seeing, that looked just like the ones that appeared before the Transformers and all those people were taken."

The light in the commander's eyes darkened. "Killed, you mean."

"No, I don't, and I don't think you do, either." Franklin frowned. "We're going to have to move this along..."

With that, Franklin slipped his damaged hand over the commander's chest, stopping right above his heart.

"Yaghh!" Fortuna gasped, his spine going ramrod straight in the chair, his teeth rattling, his head bobbing.

"Microwave emissions. Plays hell with anyone who's gone and had a pacemaker put in."

The commander gasped for air, his hands twitching, eyes flitting wildly.

"That's enough!" Spike hollered.

"Not your call," Franklin said, pressing his hand a

little harder against the commander's chest. He leaned in closer. "I've read all about you. You remind me of my dad. I mean, a lot. Unfortunately for you, my dad and have *never* gotten along."

Fortuna kicked and spit. Spike could tell the man was in agony.

The operative gripped the back of the man's head and forced him to look his way. "You self-righteous, sociopathic son-on-a-bitch. You decide who lives, who dies, and it's based on whether you approve. There's nothing you would stop at to get your way, is there? Right, wrong... doesn't mean anything to you. Alien concepts."

"Y-yuh... you know more about... aliens... than me!" Fortuna said, wheezing, struggling for breath, his body thundering, looking nearly ready to break the chair.

"Stop it!" Spike yelled, bolting to his feet—and getting forced back down by one of the medics.

Fortuna smiled and looked at the younger man. "You're... weak. Take shortcuts." He coughed. "I'm not afraid of anything you can... do... to me!"

"Guys," Franklin said. "Hook up the monitor."

One of the medics pulled a laptop computer from a black bag and cracked it open, holding the screen upright so that the images playing across it were in plain view to both Fortuna and Spike. Three women were mall-walking... no, two teenage girls and their mom, a woman about a decade younger than Fortuna.

The first teenager spoke in hushed tones to her sister. "So I'm like, first date, first base, that's it. Them's the rules. He got all confused, like no one'd ever turned him down before."

"Yeah? Was that it?"

"Oh, oh, you'll love this. You know what he said then?

The other teenager shook her head.

"He goes, 'Don't be hatin' on me, dog. I needs what I needs!' I mean, can you believe it? I just thought his dimples were cute and I heard he was a really good kisser... What I should have been doing was listening to what was coming out of his mouth. I think some people shouldn't be allowed more than two hours of MTV a week. This boy thinks he's Eminem? He's Em-in-ain't."

Fortuna's face paled. "Hurt them and you get nothing."

"Who's looking to hurt anyone?" Franklin said, clutching a little harder at the commander's chest and making him stifle a scream. "Oh, right. Me and you. But that's different. You're an attempted murderer, and God knows what else."

"Leave... leave them..." the commander sputtered.

"We're just keeping an eye on them for you," Franklin said. "You're not there, lots of things can happen. People have enemies. Folks get put on lists all the time and don't know it. Believe me, so long as you cooperate, we'll keep your family safe as houses."

Spike felt a chill. Franklin's people were also watching those he loved. Is this what would have happened to him if he had failed to cooperate?

Fortuna squeezed his eyes shut and hissed, "It's himmmm... what's in his head. Can't come out. Mean the end... end for us..."

"Says the man who tried splattering young Spike's brains on the floor," Franklin observed, raising an eyebrow.

"Things he knows... doesn't know he knows..."

"Lovely. More mysteries." Franklin turned, tapping at his ear, cupping it. "Really? Another of the Followers? Armed? Huh..." He looked down at Fortuna. "Take a good look."

A bald man in his fifties appeared, pushing his way through the crowd at the food court where Fortuna's wife and daughters had appeared. His long black leather duster swept the ground dramatically, and he had one hand in a long, deep pocket.

"Recognize him?" Franklin asked, his hand pressing even harder into the commander's chest.

For the first time, Spike was certain he registered fear in Fortuna's eyes.

"Read his file, didn't you? Just like I read yours. You know he's a cleaner, and not the kind that takes care of offices late at night."

"Stop... himmmm!" Fortuna pleaded.

"Tell us what we want to know and we'll intercept. Otherwise..."

Spike's gaze darted from the screen to the operative. Franklin was serious. He would let this assassin attack Fortuna's family. "Just tell him!"

Fortuna hesitated, then acquiesced with a single, sharp nod.

"Take him out," Franklin said.

Suddenly, a middle-aged couple broke from the crowd, each snagging one arm of the surprised bald man, leading him forcefully away.

"I've shown you mine," Franklin said, removing his hand from the chest of the heaving, gasping man. "Your turn."

"The basement," Fortuna said quickly. "It's down there."

"We've thermal scanned your house and I've been through the place twice myself. There's nothing in that basement except boxes of old magazines and a work station where you've been trying to repair some old TV."

"Look beneath... like with you people... more than meets the eye, right? Heh... you always have to... look beneath." His chest beginning to slow to a normal heart rhythm, the commander recited a string of numbers to the operative, then slumped back in his chair. "God forgive me," he whispered. "God forgive me..."

Sickened by what he had just witnessed, Spike nevertheless allowed himself to be led by one of the medics to follow Franklin to a door in the vast kitchen that took them down to the musty basement.

"What do you expect to find down here?" Spike asked.

Franklin shrugged. "Answers, I hope. Here's my read on what just happened: Fortuna isn't a part of the Followers. In fact, he's terrified of them. He's been keeping track of them, finding out who the major players are, what their goals are... and he's decided it was safe to do that, because if someone has a problem with anything he's doing, they'll come see him about it. He wouldn't even conceive of them going after his family to get at him. Honestly, that's usually the case..."

The operative popped on a low hanging amber light and surveyed the basement once again. He stopped when he came to the torn up television and went to it, fishing around inside its chassis. For Spike, it was a little like watching his dad ferret around in the torn open carcass of some big catch on their fishing boat.

"He clearly perceives you as some kind of threat and wants you gone, that's for sure. As to why he thinks you've been augmented, I dunno. We've checked you out—"

"Excuse me?"

"Just the usual. Thermal scans. And that last time you were at the dentist and they had to put you out..."

Spike's gaze narrowed. "You're just messing with me, aren't you?"

"Maybe." Franklin fished out a remote control from the inner works of the twisted TV set. "Let's see what this can do."

Moving in a wide arc, Franklin aimed the remote at the floor and punched in the sequence the commander had recited. At first, nothing happened. Then there was a groan that sounded from all around them, and the worktable, seemingly riveted to the floor, slid to one side, revealing a darkened stairway leading down to a subbasement.

"It might be booby-trapped," the medic who had accompanied them said.

Franklin nodded. "Good point. Spike, you go first!"

"Yeah, right."

Smiling, the operative breezed past Spike, crouching at this new opening. Behind him, the medic was fishing for something. "I have a flashlight here—"

"Don't bother," Franklin said, touching the side of his skull. Bright beams of light tore from his eyes like something out of a comic book—and Spike, who had flown thousands of feet high on the backs of living robots, jumped back with a whispered curse.

Regaining his composure, Spike said, "Now you're just showing off."

"Probably," Franklin agreed, the eerie luminescence streaking into the darkened lair below. "Now let's see if we all go boom."

The operative carefully navigated the stair, quickly

disappearing from view. Spike and the medic exchanged glances, each nervously awaiting Franklin's call... or some tiny sound that might precede weapons fire or the explosion of an incendiary device.

An astonished whistling came from the darkness. "Hoss! Little Joe! Hitch up your horses and come on down here for a looksee, why don'tcha?"

The medic, whose bright red buzz cut gleamed in the amber light, the edges so clean it look like someone had gone at it with hedge clippers, muttered, "I hate when he goes all TV Land about this stuff."

"I heard that!" Franklin called.

"You were meant to."

Spike followed the medic down the stairs, still feeling a little wobbly. It seemed like they were descending forever, Franklin's eye-beams guiding the way. Spike could see that the steps were made of solid steel, but all he could make out of their surroundings were large, bulky, vague shapes. Soon, they were at the base of the stairs.

"Ready, boys?" Franklin asked.

Nerves practically shot, Spike growled, "If you've got something to show us, then just—"

Click.

Brilliant overhead light flooded the room. Spike heard the man beside him gasp, and remembered how it felt to gaze upon the strange and impossible for the first time. Only a few of the things collected in this place surprised him. He felt substantially more disoriented at the thought of such a bizarre menagerie existing beneath an otherwise normal looking house in an unremarkable community.

"How... how... This isn't possible!" the medic said, stumbling back, then turning and racing back up the stairs.

Spike nodded. What the medic had said was true. This *wasn't* possible. The house was older than most in this area, a good hundred years if Spike had guessed correctly, and the idea that it's foundation was hollowed out like this and lined with an alloy that seemed all too reminiscent of the gleaming metal of the Transformer's metal flesh... no, none of this made sense, none of it could be real, or possible.

Yet here it was.

Beneath the commander's house was the largest single collection of bits and pieces hewn from the mighty Transformers over their many years of battle. Giant hands, torn open thighs, curling steel ribs... and against the far wall, the scorched black face plate of the hero Spike had mourned since his death in the California incident:

Superion.

In other areas, there were chunks of tech that looked something *like* Transformer designs, yet different in hard to pinpoint ways... rounder, sleeker, almost organic—and if it had an organic element, it *couldn't* have been from a Transformer. Where had *this stuff* come from?

"I'll take it there are no records of this guy having work crews out here, no major deliveries of crates the size of elephants or busses, nothing like that," Spike ventured.

"Nope. And there's no way in or out except for that door up above, which isn't big enough to allow for getting this stuff through. Underground tunneling is a possibility, the Constructicons might have pulled this off..."

"But why?" Spike asked.

"You want to be more specific?"

"Take your pick. Why would Fortuna be interested

in all of this? What was he trying to accomplish with it? And if Decepticons helped him, why would he have allowed such a thing? Why work with Transformers of any kind?"

"Hmmm," Franklin said, stepping up to the visor of the fallen Superion. "We combed the ocean for any debris left after the nuke went off... Fortuna's boat wasn't one of the salvage vessels, but he might know some of the crews. On the other hand, whoever grabbed Optimus used a highly selective form of matter transfer, something we could only define as teleportation, crude as that term might be. Fortuna could be hooked into this half a hundred ways. I agree, too many questions, we'll have to talk to—"

A single, muted gunshot rang out from above. Spike and Franklin dashed for the stairs, the steel buckling slightly as the augmented agent stomped onto the steps. Before they reached the landing, another shot sounded.

Upstairs, they found Fortuna's body slumped forward in the chair, blood dripping from a wound in his forehead. The medic who'd been left with him lay on his side, his weapon held near his own head.

The jarhead who had ventured downstairs with Spike and Franklin, then left, was gaping anew at this grisly sight. "He... Paul Buckley, my partner... he was crying, and he told Fortuna, 'God may forgive you, but I don't'...then he shot him... shot himself."

Spike's stomach twisted into knots as he turned to the operative. "You're compromised. There are so many factions, so many splinter cells—"

"All I'm seeing is opportunity," Franklin said calmly. "Paul, Fortuna...they must have been involved in the same business. Paul must not have thought Fortuna would crack. Once he did, there was no going back.

Paul couldn't have moved fast enough to kill me, and everything I see and hear is being broadcast, recorded. This was the only course left to him."

"How do I know the people protecting my son aren't on *their* side?" Spike said, slamming his hands into Franklin's shoulders... and not budging him an inch.

"You don't. Just like I can't know with one hundred percent certainty where your loyalties lay, or you mine. We just have to deal with it. Take our chances."

"I don't have to do anything," Spike said, moving for the door.

Franklin was before him before Spike could get more than a few steps. The gouge in his hand was sparking again. "Yes, you do. We both know what the deal is here."

Staring into the cold eyes of the operative, Spike wondered how much of Franklin that had been flesh was now machine, and if the man still had a soul—or ever did.

"We'll pull everything we've got on these two," Franklin said, nodding back at the corpses, then returning his gaze to Spike with an uncharacteristic intensity. "We'll track their inner circles, their closest friends, acquaintances, who they each dated in high school, for heaven's sake, see where they overlap, and take action from there. It will bring us closer to where we need to be. I know it."

A car crushed the snow and gravel in the drive, squeaking its brakes as it pulled up to its familiar spot.

"If that's the family, keep them out," Franklin said. "If it's hostiles..."

"Right, right," the surviving medic said, sprinting for the door and nearly slipping in the slick twin pools of blood. He took a quick peak out a side window. "The wife and kids."

He opened the door, went out to keep them at arm's length.

"Interesting thing with that one," Franklin said, referring to the man who had just left. "Paul has all this time to turn out Fortuna's lights, but it doesn't happen until *he* comes back upstairs."

"Maybe they wanted a witness," Spike said dully, still trying to comprehend how Franklin could be so unaffected was by all of this.

"Or maybe he killed them both. Someone with enough skill, and enough mech, could blur the evidence beyond the best forensic investigator's abilities. I say we keep him with us, see what he does, force him, if he's going to make a move, to do it right in front of us."

"You're enjoying this," Spike said, even more horrified than ever.

"Yeah," Franklin replied bitterly. "You believe that if you want. Spy versus spy. My favorite game growing up. Or maybe I'm just trying to get your friends and those innocent people back, and the only means open to me are the ones I'm—"

On a small table in the corner, the phone rang. Without hesitation, Franklin blurred past Spike and snatched it from its handle, immediately checking it for whatever its LCD Caller ID readout might tell him. "Unknown caller," Franklin said, biting his lip and grunting as the wires in his hand snaked out and jammed into the side of the phone.

He hit the talk button. "Fortuna residence."

Whoever was on the other end hung up immediately. Franklin cursed under his breath, then closed his eyes, controlled his breathing, and nodded for several seconds. Then he put the phone back in its cradle.

"All I could get was an area code," Franklin said quickly, smiling slightly, despite the horror of what surrounded them. "Pack up your surfboard, Spike... we're going to big, bad El-lay!"

CHAPTER
THIRTEEN

From his sentry platform atop the giant pyramid of tinted glass that was the posh Luxor Hotel and Casino in Las Vegas, Nevada, Soundwave activated his built-in array of thousands of sensors and began to *listen*.

Using super-advanced, ultra-sensitive data processors built into his Cybertronian brain, the Decepticon monitored all electronic chatter flowing in and out of the occupied city of Las Vegas. Radio and television broadcasts, land-line telephone calls, satellite transmissions, digital and coaxial cable systems, cell phone signals—all possible lines of earthly communication including human brainwaves themselves—could be intercepted and interpreted by Soundwave's powerful, built-in surveillance systems. Once gathered, the raw data was filtered through Soundwave's computer systems and converted into raw intelligence data almost instantaneously.

Through the complex haze of conflicting data streams, Soundwave detected a signal that was not of human origin. Turning to face west, the Decepticon increased sensor intensity in an effort to locate the source of the unusual signal. Immediately the signals originating from the city of Los Angeles, hundreds of miles away, began to bombard Soundwave's sensor arrays and threatened to overwhelm his critical, intelligence-gathering capabilities. Soundwave instantly activated more filters to screen out useless data. Finally, he narrowed his sensor beam to an area about thirty miles outside the Las Vegas city limits, near a mammoth man-made body of water called Lake Mead.

Soundwave smiled when he finally honed in on the strange, yet oddly familiar signals, and he almost laughed out loud when he positively identified his targets. Mission accomplished, Soundwave activated his internal scramblers and sent a coded transmission to Starscream.

"Someone approaches," Soundwave said. He was gratified when the new Decepticon commander replied immediately.

"Autobots?" demanded Starscream.

"No, commander," Soundwave replied. "They are fellow Decepticons. Two of them. They lurk thirty miles west of the city, at a place called Hoover Dam, and they are approaching Las Vegas—but warily."

"They come, as I knew they would," Starscream rumbled. "But are they here to pledge their allegiance to the New Decepticon Order, or do they come to challenge my dominance?"

As he spoke, Starscream rose from a colossal, ornate, solid gold throne he had commissioned for himself shortly after he took over the human city. Since that time, the new Decepticon commander dominated occupied Las Vegas like a Roman Emperor of ancient times, ruling from his command center located— appropriately—in the main gaming hall at Caesar's Palace Hotel and Casino. There, Starscream was served by a retinue of humans and Decepticons whose only task in life was to fulfill Starscream's every command.

"I only know they come," Soundwave replied. "I

cannot know their intentions until we establish communications..."

Soundwave paused dramatically. "So far these two have been ignoring my signals."

"I already distrust their motives,"Starscream said. "So we will confront them where they stand. "Truth to tell, I am bored and look forward to any distractions from the burdens of absolute leadership."

As the Decepticon commander stepped down from his elevated throne, human servants scampered to get out of his way. Ignoring them as if they were ants, Starscream strode to the entranceway and stepped outside, into the hot desert morning. His armor unfolded and began to take on a new design and purpose. Moments later, Starscream had transformed himself into a jet aircraft. Soundwave likewise transformed into a cassette player which fit into Starscream's cockpit. Starscream leaped into the sky on a fiery plume.

At 25,000 feet, they banked and headed west toward Lake Mead, two fast-moving blips in the blue cloudless sky.

Right on the border of Nevada and Arizona, situated in the middle of the sprawling Black Canyon on the Colorado River, sits the 726-foot high concrete water barrier known as Hoover Dam. A major engineering achievement, the dam is 1,244 feet long at its crest, with a wide roadway on top. The reservoir formed behind the dam is called Lake Mead—one of the largest artificially created bodies of water in the world. Lake Mead covers an area of over two hundred square miles, and has over five hundred miles of coast.

The hydroelectric generators inside of Hoover Dam create over a million and a half kilowatts of power to provide energy to Arizona, Nevada, and parts of Southern California. Since the occupation of Las Vegas, any power generated by the plants at Hoover Dam had been diverted away from Las Vegas in an effort to disrupt the Decepticon's occupation—to no avail as it turned out, for Starscream and Soundwave cleverly devised an alternative power generating system using Decepticon technology.

Nevertheless, since the crisis began, Hoover Dam—because of its strategic importance to the infrastructure of the West Coast—had been guarded by a battalion of M1A2 Abrams tanks from the Nevada, California, and Arizona National Guard, as well as an infantry division from the regular army. So it was that the people who lived and worked around Hoover Dam had become accustomed to seeing military vehicles, and as the late morning sun rose overhead, the single armored tank that rolled along the roadway atop Hoover Dam attracted little attention.

Which was just the way the Decepticon called Spyglass wanted it. Through long-range sensors, Spyglass detected the presence of his partner in this risky endeavor, the Decepticon called Skywarp, who waited nearby, prepared to teleport in at the proper moment.

"Soundwave has stopped hailing us," Skywarp announced via their private comm. "Perhaps he has given up. Or perhaps he no longer wants to speak with us."

"Or perhaps he is about to attack," said Spyglass.

"Let him," Skywarp replied. "Forcing him to come here, to us, to venture this far from his new imperial surroundings to challenge us in this place is a victory in and of itself. It shows we have power over him, that he is afraid of us."

"And if he isn't? If he wants to fight?" Spyglass asked.

"Then we fight Starscream, or any Decepticon he sends against us," cried Skywarp passionately.

"And don't forget," Skywarp added with an evil smirk. "We are not alone, either."

"No indeed," said Spyglass, remembering their secret weapons, waiting to pounce if needed. "But if this can be resolved without conflict, if Starscream can be made to see reason—"

"Damn Starscream to the blackest pits of Charr!" Skywarp growled angrily. "His blind ambition endangers us all! The challenge must be met, and Starscream must be judged on the field of battle!" Skywarp shouted. "For he is a plague on all Decepticons."

"Enough!" cried Spyglass, who was sick of listening to Skywarp and his angry tirades.

"But Starscream must be deposed and Megatron restored to power," Skywarp insisted. "And, until his return, a more fitting temporary leader, like myself, must rule."

But Spyglass said nothing, perhaps because he was not yet convinced Megatron would return, nor was he ready to fully condemn Starscream's actions. Spyglass never wanted to be the leader of the Decepticons, nor did he much care who led his robotic race. Perhaps Starscream would make a worthy leader, perhaps not. Who was Spyglass to judge?

Skywarp simply could not hide the contempt he felt for Starscream, whom he judged to be a pretender to Megatron's position as commander and a traitor to the Decepticon cause. Unimpressed with the new Decepticon "capital" in Las Vegas, and disgusted with Starscream's recent addiction to the outward trappings of power, Skywarp longed to face his foe in just combat, and put the Decepticon Aerospace commander in his place once and for all.

But suddenly Skywarp's angry words were interrupted by a flash of light, and the instantaneous appearance of a fiery crimson streak shooting across the sky just above the eastern horizon.

"Spyglass—"

"I see it," Spyglass replied, his laser rifle aimed at the fast approaching objects.

Teleporting onto the scene, Skywarp landed on the concrete roadway right next to Spyglass. His mammoth legs were spread belligerently, his weapons—two heat-seeking missile launchers and variable-caliber machine guns—at the ready.

"Do not fire," Skywarp said to Spyglass. "The protocols must be followed. But be ready to attack if set upon."

Spyglass generally preferred to shoot first and not even bother to ask any questions, but in this mission, by mutual consensus, Skywarp was "in charge." Spyglass was one of three Decepticons who joined together to become Reflector, a camera. The other two were here, as well, ready to join the action if necessary.

As the first object streaked across the sky, it ejected a tiny cassette player that changed shape. Soundwave landed on the rocky cliff high above the top of the dam, to stare down at Skywarp and Spyglass. The communications Decepticon eyed Spyglass's laser rifle warily—a fact that made Spyglass smirk.

The streaking jet rocketed between the canyons then, in a blur of motion, unfolded and transformed itself into the formidable Starscream. The heavy legs of the powerful warrior robot slammed down on the roadway, cracking the pavement. His imperious gaze stared at Skywarp and Spyglass, locking them in its magnetic grip, as he strode arrogantly forward.

"Bow down your heads," Starscream roared. "And swear your allegiance to your new ruler: Me!"

Skywarp seemed to waver, then stepped forward, to gaze right into Starscream's ruthless, cold-blooded eyes.

"You are no leader," Skywarp said boldly. "You are a traitor to Megatron."

"Who won't be coming back," said Starscream.

Skywarp shot Starscream a look of pure malice. "You lie! You are a prince of lies," Skywarp cried.

"You forget," said Soundwave from his high perch. "My reach is far. I have listened, but there is no sign of Megatron. He is gone."

"Lies!" Skywarp screamed, his weapons at the ready.

Starscream chuckled. "Perhaps I should allow you two to settle the score between yourselves."

"No!" shouted Skywarp. "I challenge *you* to relinquish the role you have no right to claim, Starscream. Surrender your leadership, or face my wrath."

"A challenge it is!" Starscream cried, leveling his two null rifles and firing.

Skywarp ducked and the blasts went wild, striking the lock control tower at one end of the Hoover Dam. Blue sparks flew, sending bolts of force into the air. Explosions erupted throughout the structure. The staff—six men and a female programmer—had been watching wide-eyed as the giant robots landed on the dam. Now they fled the lockedcontrol room in panic as blue electricity crackled all around them. From somewhere deep within the bowels of the dam, emergency sirens began to blare.

Starscream fired again. This time the null bolt

smashed into Skywarp's chest plate. With the brittle shatter of stressed metal, Skywarp's torso housing broke, sending deadly shards in all directions. A few of them accidentally struck Spyglass, hitting him with "friendly fire" and throwing him off balance.

Suddenly a purple streak shot out from behind the cover of some rocks, null rifles blasting.

"Spectro!" the self-appointed leader of the Decepticons shouted in surprise.

Null bolts struck the concrete roadway around Starscream. Each shot blasted out chunks of cement the size of watermelons. The entire roadway on top of the dam crackled with eerie energies.

"Yes, Spectro!" Skywarp cried, swaying unsteadily on his legs from the damage to his core systems. "Like me, he will take joy from your destruction."

Another Decepticon with silver and purple armor appeared: Viewfinder. He likewise joined the assault.

"I told you of my powers," Soundwave cried from high above the dam. "Now witness them."

Soundwave raised his hands, which folded into his wrists, then two high-powered radar dishes unfolded to emit powerful sound blasts. He aimed the dishes at Spectro. Suddenly two focused beams of pure energy emerged from Soundwave's dishes. Like lasers, the beams lanced out and struck Spectro. At first nothing happened. Then, suddenly, Spectro fell back and was blown in reverse by the powerful energies. Desperately, the Decepticon tried to regain control, but flipped over instead. As Spectro raced toward the edge of the Hoover Dam, he tried to deploy his air breaks. Like most of Spectro's internal systems, the Cybertronian brain was sending out the message, but it wasn't being received—the beam from Soundwave had successfully nullified all of his systems.

Skywarp and Spyglass watched helplessly as Spectro spun circles in the air, then struck the water. The Decepticon began breaking apart upon that first impact, even as the main body of the robot cartwheeled right into the side of the dam. Spectro exploded into an orange ball of fire that blasted the damaged Skywarp off his feet. Spyglass spun away too, barely dodging flying debris.

A moment later, Spyglass leaped to his feet and turned, in time to see billowing black smoke swirling above the rippling surface of the burning lake—the only thing left of the Decepticon called Spectro. No, that wasn't true. Upon closer examination, he could see the torso, head, and at least one limb of the Decepticon. It appeared that Spectro had, on the other hand, been sent into stasis lock, making him useless for the rest of the battle.

Skywarp staggered to his feet a moment later. As he did, he felt a powerful grip seize his neck.

He turned to see Starscream. The raging Decepticon stuck his face into Skywarp's shattered visage. Starscream fired against Skywarp's chest plate.

There was a loud, metallic shriek as the plate burst out in a shower of blue sparks. Skywarp howled in agony, then doubled over.

For a moment, Skywarp was suspended over the edge of Hoover Dam, kept from plunging to the rocks far below by Starscream's powerful grip. Then Starscream released his hold and Skywarp plunged over the edge, bouncing off the concrete side of the dam three times before he struck the rocks below.

Horrified, Spyglass peered down at his fallen comrade. Amazingly, Skywarp stared back at him, his Cybertronian brain still functioning despite the awesome amount of sheer punishment his systems endured.

Suddenly Spyglass felt a presence at his side. He turned to see Starscream glaring at him.

"Me or Megatron?" Starscream said, null rifle raised.

"What did Megatron ever do for me?" Spyglass quipped before falling on bended knee before his new lord and master. Viewfinder approached and did the same.

Starscream smiled.

"My sentiments exactly," he said. Then Starscream chuckled. Two more Decepticons won over. And so it will go, on and on, until every Decepticon had pledged his allegiance, or been destroyed.

And then it would be the Autobots' turn to pay!

CHAPTER
FOURTEEN

Vegas PD Officer Ryan O'Brien woke with a bad taste in his mouth and drool covering his UH-HUH, IS THIS IRISH ENOUGH FOR YA? T-shirt. Nudging Vi, short for Violet, his hulking black lab, awake and off the bed, Ryan did a careful search for his wife.

Her side of the bed was cold.

The bedroom, too cramped for his taste, but this apartment was all they could afford on his salary, smelled like well worn dog, that fine old sweaty mutt smell that covered up the odor of stinky socks piled up in the corner and the rank fragrance drifting off the half-eaten onion-covered Burger Slime meals he and Ginny had attacked, a bite here, a bite there, while tearing each other's clothes off after he'd gotten home from shift last night. Life as a cop in this city had always been tense, but the tension had grown practically unbearable ever since the Decepticons arrived. No one knew what to expect on a day-to-day basis. Was today the day that the city itself might become a war zone, or when the robots might just march everyone out into the street and say, "hey, that whole thing about making your lives better? Just kidding!" then roast them all with their practically invincible firepower.

Beige shower curtains had been nailed up over the main bedroom window, allowing a flow of gentle golden light. The fabric was nice, they were cheap, and, at some point, they'd be able to afford those curtain rods and do the job right...

Living on a cop's salary was hard. Sure, you could go on the take and rake in the bucks, but then you became a criminal, you would be no different, really, from the scum you became an officer to put away. There was no way in blazes that Ryan would start taking bribes. He'd rather be struggling to pay the bills and have his conscience clear.

Vi whined a little, her nails click-clacking on the bare wood floor as she circled by the door a few times, then whacked her snout on it, whimpering, stumbling back, and whining again.

"You're a silly dog," Ryan said.

Sighing, he got up, wondering if he was late. As if the alarm clock next to the bed could read his mind, it popped off immediately, a big blast furnace of Lilith Fare wannabe noise firing from the speaker. He *had* to talk to Ginny about changing that radio station.

A female announcer said, "It's SHE-101 coming at you live from New Vegas—or Dirty Vegas as some are now calling our fair city... at least those who've seen the premiere of last night's reality TV ratings blockbuster *Real Life—Transformers Style*. Following the lives of seven lucky 20-somethings who've been chosen to live and work in the very casino that Starscream himself has made his base of operations for Project: Renewal, this show featured more bleeped out words, full-on naked craziness—all appropriately pixilated out, natch, and hook-ups galore. Glynnis and Kimberly are both going crazy over Jamal, and he only has eyes for Bethann, though his hands... well, *that's* another story!"

"Yeah," Ryan said, jabbing his finger at the off-switch. "And that's got a whole lot to do with what's going on out there."

He opened the door, letting Vi bolt from the room, and followed her out. On some level, he knew it was the beginning of the afternoon, but, to his brain, it was first thing in the morning. He'd been on night shift for two years now, and was wondering if a time ever came when you were done paying your dues. On days like today, it just didn't seem like it would.

In the living room, Ginny was curled up on the couch, underneath their Andy Warhol-style painting of four highly irked Puffins. Blonde and busty, wearing a cleavage exposing white tank top and a pair of tight jeans, Ginny was working nights at the supermarket to pay for the degree she was slowly amassing in marine biology.

Puffins had put them together. He had been wearing a little plastic one on a chain, a present from his six-year-old niece, she thought he must have had cast iron *cajones* to walk around in public with such a thing, and they'd rolled the dice on love—and won.

Pretty much.

"Butch told me he has a line of some King Puffin memorabilia on eBay," Ryan said softly.

"King Puffin for a day," she said distractedly, putting one hand up behind her head, making the little feathery sign with a wiggling of her delicate fingers, a must whenever royalty was mentioned. It was funny, they never really argued, not once in the five years they'd been together.

Ryan stopped, wondering why he had thought of that here and now. Something was wrong, but he could identify exactly what it was. Ginny's face was trained toward the second floor patio and the view of the city beyond. They couldn't see much, this was a low-rent neighborhood, but the Royale rose in the distance, one of the Transformers standing sentinel-like on its roof.

The sight made Ryan tense up, as it always did. Ginny, too... normally. Right now, she was sprawled into the couch, looking comfortable as could be.

Then he caught the glittering.

"What the—where'd that come from?" Ryan asked, his attention now firmly fixed on what might have been a diamond ring on the little toe of her left foot. It was probably a gag, a cubic zirconia, something from a kid's game, maybe, like the kind Ginny's niece played... but it looked real.

"I hit the ATM around lunchtime," she said, stretching and slipping a receipt from her tight back pocket.

Ryan took it from her, staring for a good long time at the numbers. Ten thousand dollars had been deposited in their account last night—from the same source his regular pay came from.

"This has got to be some kind of mistake," Ryan said.

She shook her head, her bangs falling into her eyes, smoky and sexy. "Nuh-uh. Real deal."

He nearly tripped over Vi, whom he hadn't even heard padding up, and snapped at her for the first time in months. Growling in the back of her throat, she backed away.

Ginny glared at him. "I knew this was going to be a problem."

"It's just... honey, this is wrong. We can't think of it as real. Someone in payroll must have screwed up, that's all..."

She shrugged, her lower lip threatening to jut forward in as much of a pout as she ever achieved. "Uh-

uh. I was watching the local news. You got a pay raise. Every cop in the city did. It's because of all the licensing fees and the cash the Decepticons are bringing into the city. The Governor said each officer would be getting a nice fat bonus check to start with, then double the pay after that. The mayor was talking about it, too. This is *real*, Ryan. You guys are heroes and you're being rewarded. Best of all, we don't have to be begging and scraping any more."

Ryan shook his head. This just didn't track. The Decepticons didn't do *anything* just to be nice.

Staring at the ATM statement, Ryan felt his stomach tying itself into knots. The money felt like a *bribe*. The only question was... a bribe for *what?* What did the Decepticons expect him and his fellow officers to do to earn this money?

"Look, Ginny, I'm sure the mayor and the governor said whatever they felt they had to say to keep any trouble from breaking out with the Decepticons. I wouldn't be surprised if the President and the U.N. say it's okay for us to keep the money, too. At least, they're saying that for *now*. They'll say anything at this point to avoid having L.A. happen again. That's the leverage the Decepticons have on us. No one can really say 'no' to them because if they do, it could mean another fight, it could mean hundreds or thousands of people getting killed."

Ginny's gaze narrowed, but she said nothing.

"When the Decepticons are gone, when this is over," Ryan said, "and it's *gonna* be over, the government's going to want the money back."

Ginny's foot slid beneath the cushion. "Forget that noise. We're married. This is a joint bank account. I'm keeping the money, keeping the ring, and everything else, too."

Everything else? he thought. Then he caught the time, realizing he was going to be late if they kept this up. "Come on, sweetie, don't put me in this position."

"It's legal and we've earned it," she said resolutely.

"I'm not talking about this," he replied, storming off.

"Fine. It's not going to make things any less real."

Ryan took his shower, ticked off, and emerged, ready to do battle. So what if he was late? This was important!

But Ginny was gone.

"A ten grand bonus! Can you *believe* that? Did you see what they're raising our salaries to?"

"It's dirty money," Ryan said.

"That's not what the letter they're passing around says. All the transactions are clean. Big business, investing in our getting rewarded for what we do."

"How much product placement's involved?"

"We could get shot any day. I got three kids, Ryan. Think about it."

Ryan shrugged, not looking his partner in the eye. He didn't want to argue with the man. Phil Brodaker was six foot-three, a former linebacker, former marine, and a member of three male dance reviews before joining the force. Ryan knew all his weak spots and could fold him up like a little kid with a couple of punches if it came to it, he'd thought about it once or twice with the hot-head... it just didn't seem worth it. His partner had that same, "you just don't get it" glare that his wife had paraded around this morning.

"Just need some time to get used to the idea of being appreciated, I guess," Ryan said, backing down.

Yeah, back down, he thought. *Because* that *is what you do...*

Not always.
Right. Just most of the time...

During roll that afternoon, Soundwave and his cassette tape minions cameup a good dozen times or more, and it wasn't because they had done anything wrong. Just the opposite. They were the new eyes and ears of the street. Today alone, seven outstanding warrants had been taken care of, seven scumbags driven out of hiding and taken off the streets because of the city's new watchers.

"It's incredible," Sarge said, pounding his meaty fist on his podium while his assistant handed out assignments. "So long as we have voice tapes of these guys, if they've ever been questioned, if we've ever run a tap on their lines, if they're even sung karaoke and been fool enough to let someone lay it down on audio, these guys can track them. The technology is amazing, and I hear there's talk of sharing it directly with us and with law enforcement outside the box. I know these guys have a bad rep, but they seem to be making for it now!"

Ryan sat at his well worn desk, the kind they made for kids, for heaven's sake, with its little half desk top carved with messages from thirty years back, and thought about that phrase: Outside the box. New Vegas was now "the box." You were either in or out. Getting with the program, or being left in the dirt. He looked calm enough, but inwardly, he was seething.

They're Decepticons, people. Emphasis on the deception part? We're letting them run us around like they own us. Damn machines!

Then a sheet of paper fluttered onto his desk from the assistant's hands and he saw the list of perps that had been brought in this morning. As much as he hated to admit it, he couldn't help but be glad that these guys were off their streets. Two were known killers, the others gun runners.

"At this rate, New Vegas will be the most crime-free city in America before you know it," Sarge said proudly. "And don't think that means we'll be out of a job when that happens. Starscream and Soundwave have big plans, and just like they're watching our backs now..."

Ryan tuned out of recitation. He hated that Sarge had let himself be so easily led, that this man, whom he had looked upon as a hero and a firm upholder of the law, had embraced the quick and easy route the Decepticons had provided, even seeding the Earth for future developments. Ryan agreed with Sarge, he was sure the Decepticons had plans for their private peacekeeping force... how else would they quell civil unrest and disobedience when their plans no longer seemed to benefit the common people of this city, when the truth of this came out?

Not that Ryan knew what Starscream was really planning—how could he? He was just going with his gut, something Sarge taught him.

Looking around the assignment room, into the faces of his fellow officers, Ryan felt his heart sink. Everyone looked like Sarge: placid, accepting, focused on the temporary good, not giving a second thought to a future in which they lived, powerless, under the merciless monarchy of a metal scrapheap on legs.

Or was that the present, and he had simply not managed to catch up?

Ten minutes later, he was on his way to the men's room when the silver-haired officer approached him. The man's name was Buckingham; Ryan had seen him around but never spoken to him before.

Like Ryan, Buckingham walked around like Donald Sutherland in *Invasion of the Body Snatchers*, trying to fit in, but wary of those possessed by all the propaganda.

As they passed one another, Buckingham whispered, "You're not alone. If you want to do something about all this, be at the parking garage of the Palms Grayson Hotel, two o'clock, level G-2."

Ryan didn't have a chance to question, no time to react in any way. Buckingham was swallowed up in the crowd before the officer had a chance to recover from the surprise offer and turn back to face the man.

Soon, he was in his patrol car, Brodaker at the wheel. It was looking like a quiet afternoon, on the whole. Soundwave had reported over the police broadband trouble brewing in several areas, nothing immediate, just spots to keep an eye on, certain people who bore *watching*, and this they did, among their usual rounds.

Above, the Flying Elvises leaped from an airplane, and near the Mirage, the four P.M. pirate battle raged before Treasure Island in the choppy waters of the lagoon. The British frigate HMS *Britannia* defended itself against the pirate vessel the *Hispaniola*, cannons booming, masts toppling, sailors plunging into the drink.

Their radio crackled. "Car 112...um—preventative maintenance required at the blackjack tables of the Mirage. Please respond."

"Preventative maintenance," Ryan said sourly as he took the radio and poised his thumb over the red send button. "Now we're mechanics."

His partner grunted and rolled up on Valet parking, sirens off, as Ryan took down the particulars.

Within the casino, the officers passed a gaggle of

brides gambling at the slot machines in their wedding dresses, senior citizens wheeling oxygen tanks in one hand, clutching their walkers with the other, cheap plastic buckets filled with tokens dangling from their necks and *chink-chanking* against their bony chests, laid bare by half-open Hawaiian shirts on the men, neon tube tops on the over-tan geriatric women. The rules of the house had changed at the Mirage and all the casinos: They were now in the fulfillment business, distributing wealth to those who desperately needed to believe they had some form of control over their lives, engineering winners, pre-selecting losers based on careful psychological profiling, the funds they paid out instantly replaced—with bonuses attached—by the New Vegas business consortium. It was still a game, and the visitors were still being played...only the rules had changed.

As promised, a sweaty man in his late 40s was quietly turning beet red near the center blackjack table, the female croupier eyeing him with calm reserve—and caution.

"You're always so good to me," the man said, his voice a hair's breath away from a desperate whine, "I never lose with you. Don't you see what that means? It's like fate. We're meant to be together!"

"This is for hotel security," Ryan whispered.

"Laserbeak reported to Soundwave that a police presence was needed," Brodaker countered. "That's good enough for me."

At the table, other patrons were taking their winnings and clearing out. The croupier, a beautiful redhead in her late twenties, calmly asked the small, balding man if he wished to play another hand.

Shaking as if he were about to have a fit, the older

man lost it. "I love you! I love you and you don't care!"

His hand came up swiftly and what appeared to be a cheap watchband *transformed* as Ryan surged forward, suddenly quite certain that Laserbeak had been right, casino blue would not have been able to handle this.

The wristlet worn by the screaming man, which had been camouflaged as a simple watch, sprouted silver cables, glowing crimson energy tentacles, and long, crystalline blocks. The assembly snapped together in milliseconds, forming a cannon the size of the man's forearm.

Ryan's eyes went wide. He'd read reports about strange devices and weaponry clearly influenced by Transformer technology showing up on the black market ever since the Decepticons had taken over the city. Honestly, he hadn't given them a lot of credence—until now. If a guy like this, some dumb lug, could get a hold of this kind of weapon so easily, then his job had just gotten a lot more complicated and a lot more dangerous.

Maybe *this* is what the extra money had been for: hazard pay!

It was then Ryan noticed the camera crew that had conveniently chosen a position a half-dozen yards away for a standup interview of the casino owner. The camera was now pointed right at the slaughter about to commence, and the two officers ripping through the panicking crowd, valiantly seeking to prevent the disaster.

Ryan's every nerve flared with horror as he realized they wouldn't get there in time.

Brodaker leaped onto a table, aimed two empty fists at the perp, and hollered, "Shield!"

Suddenly, an amber energy sphere burst into existence around the older man's weapon arm as he fired at the terrified croupier, containing his blast. The man threw his head back, screeching in agony as crimson light filled the sphere, consuming everything inside it. He dropped to the ground, pale, in shock, the sphere still attached to his arm—or what must have been left of it under the protective shield.

Ryan looked back at his handsome, smiling, camera-ready partner, who had rolled down his sleeves to reveal a pair of wristlets glowing with amber flames.

"Don't worry, people! New Vegas PD has this all under control," Brodaker said, the line phony, the delivery clearly rehearsed.

Standing off to the side of the media frenzy that followed, handling the messy details of getting EMTs to the scene, the perp secured, and so on, Ryan occasionally took in the sight of his partner, the hero, posing for photo ops with the adoring croupier, the casino owner, and regular casino patrons. When questioned by the media, Brodaker said that New Vegas was a city of the future, and that meant its protectors had to be prepared for anything.

And they were.

An hour later, as the sun was beginning to set and the sweltering humidity finally thinned for the onset of night, Ryan slipped back into the cruiser with his partner, who was now politely declining autographs...he had work to do, after all, and two or three dozen was all he could do at one time before his trigger finger started to feel it.

They pulled away, the news camera still on them from the driveway.

"When were you going to tell me?" Ryan asked, nodding at the weird tech his partner wore.

"Times are changing partner," Brodaker said. "Change with them or get left behind. That's the best advice I can give you."

"You knew about this whole thing ahead of time, didn't you? It's like it was all arranged, this jerk getting his hands on weaponry he shouldn't have been able to get anywhere near, you getting to the scene with exactly the mech needed to stop him, the camera crew right there, in place, just waiting... the Decepticons moved everything around just the way they wanted it!"

"No," Brodaker answered too quickly, his forehead wrinkling up, the lines around his mouth deepening. "This shield tech is going to be standard issue, along with a lot of other improvements the Transformers are sending our way. Sarge told me to keep it on the Q.T. unless there was a need for you to know. We just had a need to know, that's it."

Brodaker was driving faster than usual, cutting across lanes, smiling to himself.

He was a lousy actor and a worse liar.

Didn't he understand what this meant? Soundwave wasn't only listening to the conversations of the bad guys...he was listening to everyone!

No, that was paranoid. The Decepticon couldn't process that much information, no machine could, not even a Transformer, from what he'd read. The intelligence they'd gathered on this guy must have come as an unexpected bonus to their normal patterns of observation.

Ryan thought about *why* the Decepticons might have manipulated events to produce the end result he'd witnessed. Well, it had been the perfect publicity opportunity to get footage of a New Vegas police officer rigged up with weird alien tech in action. And so long as the bad guys had even worse and scarier weapons, which this footage showed, then the average person on the street wouldn't be so wigged out seeing a cop with this gear. It would be comforting.

Then more gear could be added... and more...

Were the Decepticons looking to *transform* the police department into their own private army? And was this their way of doing it so that the public—and even the cops—would accept it as natural in some way?

"Who cares about any of it?" Brodaker asked. "We're safer than we've ever been, and it's all about choices. Our buddy back there could have decided not to make a move, and we wouldn't have had to move in. But he broadcast the whole thing in advance, he didn't want to do this, but he couldn't help himself. He needed help, and we were there. Nothing like this would have been possible back in the day."

Back in the day... in other words, a few days ago.

"If Laserbeak knew he had that weaponry, why not let us know ahead of time so we could pick him up on illegal weapons charges before he even reached a crowded area?" Ryan asking, pressing the issue with his partner for what he decided would be the last time. "Why not send some of us to bust up the black market ring selling this stuff?"

Brodaker shrugged. "He must not have known. Probably just went around, shooting his mouth off that the redhead was going to pay him some respect—or things would get nasty."

Then why not leave it to casino blue? Ryan thought.

"Right," he said. "I guess I hadn't thought of that."

Brodaker smiled, reaching over and jostling Ryan

by the shoulder. "Don't worry about it, partner. You can't think of everything. None of us can." He nodded to a casino in the distance, where another Transformer was addressing a crowd of schoolchildren. "That's what we have *them* for."

The words chilled Ryan. Thinking machines... *thinking* for them.

He stared into the gold and reddish tinged clouds hiding the setting sun, wishing the light was strong enough to burn away the thoughts in his head.

Something has to be done. Some *one* has to try and stop this.

He didn't want to be that person. He might have been ticked off, and in a crisis, he could turn off his own fear of being wounded or killed, think only of protecting others...but now, when he had nothing but silence, nothing but time to think, he was very, *very* afraid of taking a stand.

That night, they were cruising a low-income area far from the strip. Ryan might have felt he was visiting his aunt and uncle in Brooklyn with all the pawn shops, dry cleaners, mom and pop restaurants, bail bondsmen, and liquor stores in plain view, but there was always one detail that brought the difference between this urban crawl and most others home for him:

It was a green-free zone.

No grass, no trees, no gardens or hedges of any kind. Sure, they lived in a desert, but one really didn't have a sense of that when tooling down the Strip, the great green inviting lawns, swaying palm trees, and oasis-like "set-building" everywhere in sight. Here, where the bangers did their business, where drugs and guns and pimps and whores were in an ever burgeoning supply, there was only brick and mortar.

"Over there," Brodaker said, nodding toward the corner, where they were stopped three car lengths before a light.

A tall man wearing a black windbreaker dug his right hand into his pocket and bounced nervously in place, his head turned in such a way that he seemed to be targeting the convenience store across the street.

"Our old pal Bernie Klaus," Ryan said, feeling himself slip into combat mode. "Just released last week."

"Isn't that the *same* store we busted him in last time?" Brodaker said idly as he quietly slid into a diagonal parking spot.

"Point of honor for him, I guess," Ryan said, unbuckling his seat belt. "If at first you don't succeed..."

Ryan couldn't believe he was actually glad to see a bad guy in the opening stages of doing something really stupid, but this was what he had signed on for, it was a bright, shining moment of normalcy in an otherwise upside-down day, and so he was determined to hold onto it, savor it while he could. Plus, his partner was acting like his old self: cocky and enjoying this a little too much, a real glory hound, but back to feeling like part of the same family of cops that Ryan belonged to. There was no question that every family was dysfunctional in its way, and they might go at each other like crazy people within the boundaries of that family...but no one from the outside had better mess with any one of them. In that, they were al ltogether, or had been, until today.

A great humming sounded from above. Ryan and his partner looked up and saw a titanic machine hover into position atop the three story high roof of the building housing the convenience store.

Buzzsaw.

He looked like a great steel hawk, his black steel skull tipped by a golden-tinged beak, his crimson eyes glowing in the darkness. His wings were sleek and aimed back, blue steel with yellow patches, and his visual sensor apparatus rose on his back like twin towers.

Ryan had read up on every Decepticon that had come to the city, and he knew this one could travel at 250 miles an hour without every making a sound. The humming, then, was intentional. A warning.

Buzzsaw's beak, with its diamond hard, micro-serrated edges, swerved in Bernie's direction, the garish glow of neon signs glinting of the living metal. The hold-up artist's hand darted from his pocket, absolutely empty, and he spun, scurrying away from the corner, disappearing down a side alley.

"We should go after him," Ryan said, vexed.

"Why bother? We've got the watchbirds to tell us when there's trouble. It looks like Sarge was right, too—they're working as passive deterrents."

Ryan couldn't see anything passive about the Transformer.

It was close to midnight, shift's end, when the real trouble began. The call for backup sent them speeding, siren blaring, toward one of the busiest intersections in town. Three of the "most wanted" from the Decepticon's list of "unfriendly citizenry" had been spotted by another pair of officers, and they had given chase. The high-speed pursuit had culminated in a pile up, with at least four vehicles overturned, and shots had been fired after that. There were no officers down, not yet, but this was a nasty one, and it had just gotten started.

Brodaker yanked the wheel hard, angling them to one side behind a pair of smoking wrecks at the outskirts of the accident, solid cover providing no innocent motorists were trapped inside those cars. Ryan felt his dinner lurch in his stomach as they screeched to a stop, then, still in the passenger seat, did a quick head count of the ruined pickup and Camry in front of them.

Bodies, bodies everywhere... He couldn't be sure, but there didn't appear to be any survivors.

"If we had thermal scans now, we could know for sure if anyone's hiding in the backseat, or still breathing down on the ground," Brodaker groused.

The hollow *pops* of weapons fire sounded, and Ryan saw the cops who'd radioed for help about sixty feet away to the left, the trio of criminals a hundred feet from there on the right. A mad collage of busted bumpers, twisted chassises, sparkling shattered glass, ruined, severed body parts, and pools of blood separated the two camps of shooters. Car alarms honked automatically, survivors screamed and onlookers crowded close, many with digital cameras so they might nab some amateur footage and sell it to the news service later.

Brodaker flexed his fingers, the alien tech wristlets flaring to life. "I am *so* ready for this, I—"

The world was ripped up by its foundations as something rammed into the tail end of their squad car, spinning them around—another car!—then headlights blossomed before them and the officers had no time to react as brights blinded them and a second car collided head on with theirs, mashing in the front of their patrol car, cracking the dash, and folding, with a hideous scraping noise, the side doors and molding in on them as they rocked and smacked foreheads first onto the car's innards, which were being forced into their laps.

Their car smashed against the two behind it, the impacts tearing through Ryan as he desperately tried to get his bearings. Then the rocking stopped and the hits ended, and Ryan heard laughter.

The bad guys had backup of their own.

"Little pigs, little pigs, come on out!" some kid yelled, his voice accompanied by the *SHH-SHKKK* of a shotgun being primed.

Ryan's head cleared and he looked down to see he was pinned in place, unable to twist around and reach their shotgun. He heard footsteps and more pops of weapons fire in the near distance, and decided he had time to draw his handgun before this new crew of arms runners opened up on the car, but not much more.

He left the gun, and turned to his partner.

Brodaker was unconscious, the wristlets still glowing. Ryan reached for them, but they had security protocols in place to keep unauthorized users from extracting them. At first, they sprouted metal tendrils that bore into Brodaker's skin, holding them tightly in place. When Ryan kept yanking at them, a flashing LCD cautioned him to desist—then the defense shields themselves activated, two impenetrable spheres of energy that cut off all egress to the tech.

A tapping at the driver's side window told him time was up. A thin, Snoop-Dog wannabe smiled in at Ryan, his teeth pearly white, the barrel of his shotgun quickly rising.

This is it, Ryan thought wildly, his hands out of control, his fear so great he couldn't quite recall how to unholster his gun, not that he would have had time to do so, even if his brain wasn't already failing him.

Shades. Dark shades and a dark cap. That's what death came dressed in—that and a basketball jersey.

He wouldn't even see his killer's eyes...

An explosion sounded and Ryan jumped, the roof of the patrol car sinking down, pushing against the top of his head, and the shotgun blast went wild, blowing out the already cracked front windshield, releasing a torrent of shattered glass that thankfully sprayed outward, glittering in a bright white field of light that was streaking across the scene like a spotlight.

He heard the shooter scream, and turned to see the head of a great, sleek, metal cat reach down, maw open, and throttle and horribly dismember the man.

Bloody sneakers with bone stumps slopped to the ground. Other shots rang out, his car was hit again, this time by the body of the Decepticon called Ravage, whose deep black hide easily provided cover for the downed police officers as the Transformer growled, hissed, swatted, and pounced on the guys who had attacked, then bounded over the top of their car, right into the midst of the first group of shooters, flattening them under its gigantic body.

Looking back, the Decepticon lowered its gaze to Ryan, then, with a flick of its snarling head, bounded off into a darkened street, immediately disappearing from view.

The onlookers cheered, and Ryan saw the officers who'd been pinned down, the two he had been sent to protect, emerge from cover, weapons raised, joining in the whooping and hollering.

Ryan leaned back, waiting for help to arrive. He knew that a corner had been turned, his life had been saved by the very machines he had been considering allying himself against, and the decision that had seemed so difficult earlier was now an easy one.

When the EMTs got there, he checked out with only some bruises and contusions, refusing the "mandatory" ride to the hospital for x-rays and other precautions. He left the area, grabbing the first cab he could find.

He had somewhere else to be.

At ten minutes after two in the morning, Ryan dragged himself up the ramp to the casino's parking area. His gun was holstered, but he was sharp, filled to overflowing with adrenaline, ready.

The gray-haired cop stepped from the shadows. "Make up your mind?"

Ryan nodded. This man was one of those who wanted to destroy the hold the Decepticons had on New Vegas. He was a threat to all the good Ryan had seen today. If he wanted to prove himself, to gain access to the inner circle that had been wisely, cautiously, keeping him out, he had only to bring this man in with him.

"I want to take down these things," Ryan said. "I know I would have died tonight if not for them. I've seen what they can offer. But I also see the price."

"That's your final answer?" the man asked, tonelessly.

Ryan almost chortled. What the hell was this, a game show? "Yes!"

"Pity."

Three more figures emerged from the shadows on every side of Ryan.

They were on him, clubs in hand, drowning him in a rain of killing blows before his fingers ever got near his weapon.

One more threat to the supremacy of the Decepticons had been eliminated.

CHAPTER
FIFTEEN

The summoning light came for Optimus Prime in the cell he shared with Jazz.

He stirred even before it appeared, sensing an air of expectancy suddenly hanging over the room with its glowing white walls, ceiling and floor. Humans might have named such a feeling as déjà vu, or perhaps a premonition. Jazz would know the correct term. Optimus Prime attributed his untangible feeling to the Matrix that he held inside his chest. Integral, yet not completely *of him*.

Perhaps not even meant for him at all. He rose to his feet.

"What is it, Prime?"

Jazz was instantly on his feet, ready. His massive hands opened and closed, wanting something to fasten onto. He'd focused on the need to plan, to act, with engrossing need since his forced battle with Bluestreak. Determined to find a weakness in the Keeper's designs, he had not even been tempted to indulge himself with the illusions offered by their cell. Did that bother the Keepers? Stark, white walls continued to glow on all sides, showing no details from Cybertron or, even more to Jazz's credit, not a scene or hint of activity from Earth. An accomplishment, Optimus Prime judged. They could not afford such distractions.

Studying the walls to their cell, Optimus Prime

sensed the first tangible change to their environment. The walls glowed a touch brighter, as if running on a surge of power. The change was subtle, but there nonetheless. Then they all flashed, once, disgorging a swirl of energies that colored and coalesced until one of the Keepers' energy spheres pulsed between him and Jazz. Even though Jazz's body and his own reflected back a pale wash of color as the sphere strobed blue, then red, then blue again, Optimus Prime noted that the walls still reflected nothing.

What did the summons mean this time? Who would leave? Who would be allowed to return? Optimus Prime saw Jazz's hasty step forward, and held up a hand. "Wait," he said.

"Wait for what? For the Keepers to decide which one of us to sacrifice for their games this time?"

Optimus Prime simply nodded. "Yes." His answer struck Jazz speechless for a moment. "What we reveal through our actions only gives them more control over us." Optimus knew the value of denying an enemy any assistance in their plans.

The energy sphere glided forward, passing through the wall just in front of Optimus Prime. So he was to proceed first. Very well. He stepped forward, expecting Jazz to immediately follow no matter what he had commanded. And the other Autobot tried. He moved for Prime's half of the cell only to freeze at the midway line, held immobile by an unseen force.

"Prime! I can't move."

"Then you are not meant to follow this time." Even though Jazz so obviously struggled with the idea, Optimus Prime was partly relieved. Whatever the Keepers' plans, they would not involve a deathmatch between himself and Jazz. He strode forward, passing through the glowing wall as if its substance had always been an illusion. And perhaps it was.

On the far side of the wall he found himself once again in the corridors of dead techno-organic matter, ribbed with a network of exposed musculature turned gray and rigid with time. It was as if the walls and floor had been sculpted to represent something once alive. If Jazz was correct in his belief that there must be a flaw in the Keepers' world—in their plans or in the Keepers themselves—then the Autobots' goals had to include finding that flaw, exploiting it, and getting everyone back to Earth.

But nothing was to be gained by resisting now, or by questioning the Keepers, so Optimus Prime walked along in silence, following the pulsing energy sphere which chose a path through the dark tunnels and finally led him, alone, to the massive doors that sealed the arena off from the corridor.

This is where his vaunted leadership abilities brought him. Facing the inevitable. Then the doors split apart and rolled open on a dimly-lit arena that seemed only half-formed.

The floor was made of the same thick, bone-like material as before, smoothed to a perfect finish and showing no signs of any previous combat. But there the similarities ended. There were no hostages, caged or otherwise. Not a human to be seen. And no alien spectators. No roars of challenge or encouragement, no Judge of the Games. The lights were very dim, and even with enhanced vision Optimus Prime could not see the far side of the arena, but so far as he could tell—turning in a slow circle—there were no hazards and no opponent to fight.

What new deceit was this?

Something darker and more shocking than he had

ever faced before, Optimus Prime learned then, turning again to find himself no longer alone.

He stood face to face with another Transformer. The specter which had appeared to him so recently. His predecessor, lost to the millennia but waiting before him here and now.

Sentinel Prime.

"If you are waiting for your orders, Optimus, do not bother. There are no Keepers here. No Judge of the Games."

Sentinel's voice was as Optimus Prime remembered it, deep and commanding and all but shaking the ground on which they stood. The other Transformer stood taller than Optimus Prime. A massive chest which had once protected the Matrix now a part of Optimus, blocky legs and arms, full of strength, and a large helm that bent down into a mask around the eyes. Two visored lenses stared at Optimus Prime, waiting for him to answer.

"The Keepers sent for me," he said.

"I sent for you, Optimus. I wanted a private audience with you, and now I have it. This is between you and I. No one else."

Optimus Prime ran through dozens of possible scenarios in his mind, trying to find the flaw in his reasoning. Sentinel Prime could not be here, yet he was. Everything that was a part of Optimus said that this was the Prime who championed Cybertron before him, a warrior destroyed over four million years ago.

"What is between us?" Optimus asked.

"What you already know. This role, that of Prime, was not meant for you, and I intend to demonstrate that. Your time is at an end, Optimus."

Sentinel Prime, here to prove that the vision's words were accurate? Optimus Prime had been worrying such thoughts in his mind, trying to discover the truths for himself. Was this, then, an illusion, manifested in the same way that the Keepers' cells could provide any scene desired by the Transformers?

Optimus thought of Megatron. He had betrayed something to Optimus Prime earlier. He'd said that the Keepers had revealed themselves to him, they had appeared in the "flesh." Was *this* a Keeper? In the guise of Sentinel Prime?

How could they build—or recreate—Transformers, if the Keepers were not indeed the progenitors? Or was all this another trick? This half-formed arena, Sentinel—it could all be in his mind.

Anything was possible, Optimus Prime knew. It *could* all be an illusion. But illusionary or not, Optimus was soon shown the futility of such arguments when Sentinel quickly stepped forward, bringing both fists up and slamming them into Optimus Prime's shoulders before the Autobot leader could do any more than register surprise at the lightning-fast attack. The raw force of the blow hurled Optimus Prime hundreds of feet backward. Before he landed, Sentinel had already tracked him with his shoulder cannon, slamming out gyro-inhibiting shells in rapid-fire bursts. The shells exploded against Optimus's arms, his legs, tossing him through the air like a piece of thin metal caught in a tornado of wind and fire.

Optimus Prime slammed down into the arena floor, limbs splayed and back scraping along the smooth surface. His combat instincts kicked in as he rolled up and off his left shoulder, pulling himself out from under Sentinel's sights as the other Transformer followed up with shrapnel-needle shells that exploded into the pale ivory bone right where he had been laying.

Still reacting by reflex, Optimus came down on one knee in a three-point stance as his right hand reached back over his shoulder. The armory built into his back split open, and the stock of his laser rifle thrust up into waiting fingers. He pulled the rifle over, armed it, and fired in one smooth motion, the sapphire lance spearing directly back at Sentinel, piercing him through the head.

Piercing Sentinel's electro-disruptor *image* through the head!

The defensive illusion blurred into basic colors, and then fled through the air as it snapped back to cover Sentinel's actual position fifty feet on the left. The larger Transformer had pulled out a solar-energy rifle, cradling it across his body. He snapped it forward, a stream of golden fire blasted across the short distance, tracking in as Optimus Prime leapt to one side and fired again.

Sentinel launched himself into the air, jumping out from under the sights of Optimus Prime. His solar beam clipped Optimus in the knee, cutting through armored skin and spinning the Autobot back to the ground again.

Slow to regain his feet and favoring his injured leg, Optimus ran for what he assumed would be the closest wall of the arena. Something to get his back against.

Too late. Sentinel fell out of the sky and landed with his knee caving into Optimus Prime's back, driving the Autobot to the ground—which shook under the impact of such titans.

"You were never meant to be a warrior, Optimus. Whatever made you believe that you could take my place?"

Because the Matrix chose me. Optimus struggled to

regain his feet, his overtaxed body beginning to slow. He expected to feel the solar beam cutting into his back, or perhaps an Energon-charged sword lancing into him. Instead, Sentinel drew back his foot and kicked Optimus with all his might in the hip, picking the Transformer up off the ground and sending him spinning through the air again.

Somehow Optimus managed to hold onto his laser rifle. Crashing down and rolling over, he spread out one arm and levered himself into a grinding slide that pointed him back toward Sentinel, who again unlimbered his solar-energy rifle. Sentinel moved faster. Optimus Prime had the keener eye, and so took an awkward shot with only one hand on the rifle.

The laser sliced clear through the focusing barrel on Sentinel's rifle, ruining the weapon, and then shattered against the Transformer's breastplate. Trithyllium alloy, impregnated with irradiated carbon fibers. It would be nearly impossible to breach except at point-blank and a highly accurate strike.

Sentinel wasn't about to lay down for Optimus. Discarding the ruined rifle, his shoulder cannons snapped around again and dished out a pounding assault of magnetic inducers and shrapnel-needle shells. He fed round after round into the air, fouling Optimus Prime's ability to track and target, to do much more than dodge to one side or the other.

Optimus's balance teetered on his bad leg as more shells burst against his hip, his legs, his shoulders and arms. He fought against the destructive swath being layered all around him, his shattered confidence warring with the opening Sentinel left him by not replacing the solar rifle. But his predecessor refused to concede anything, pressing his cannon attack as his electrodisruptor cast false images left, right, back to center—appearing real in almost every way and never overlapping with his actual position. Optimus Prime hesitated. He backpedaled out of the cannon's immediate firing path. And then he did something that he had never done before.

He turned. And he *transformed,* his body unfolding into that of a truck's mighty cab, as he fled. His wheels spun and he barreled ahead, picking up steam, performing every defensive maneuver he could think of in this mode, but it wasn't enough. Sentinel Prime lobbied weapons fire at him, denting his chassis, nearly shattering his rear window, twice almost shredding his tires. Detecting a blast that he knew he would not be able to survive in cab mode, he transformed back into his robot form.

Feet pounding against the arena's ivory floor, right leg unable to fully extend and every joint in his titanic body stressed to the limits of their capabilities and beyond, Optimus Prime fled before Sentinel's punishing assault. Cannon shells chased after him, chewing up the once-smooth landscape. Sentinel's voice called after him, taunting him for the poor replacement that Optimus acknowledged himself as.

But even with that being so, what did Sentinel Prime fear?

It was the thought—the question—that had sent him into flight. Sentinel was faster, stronger, with nothing but confidence in his voice. Yet still, his lashing attack had felt desperate, and desperation was only born of fear. Sentinel was no coward. Such a thing was not possible. Even if the Matrix had been at fault with Optimus's selection as Prime, it would never have installed a coward as leader. So either this was not Sentinel, not truly, or Sentinel feared as a natural reaction by his programming. The same programming which Optimus now shared through the Matrix placed inside his chest.

Optimus Prime planted his left foot, spun into a wide-legged stance, and fired his laser rifle back in Sentinel's direction. This time the ruby-edged beam sliced through the electrodistruptor's torso, scrambling the illusion into its constituent points of light again which briefly fled back to cover Sentinel's true location.

A second, rushed shot glanced off the larger Transformer's shoulder, shoving him off center as more shells spat out from his shoulder cannon. Shrapnel shells tracked in at Optimus, bursting along his left side, spraying him with quills like some Earthen beast.

Optimus shuffled to the side, measuring out uneven steps as the two Primes circled and feinted with each other. He was quick to trade distance for time, trying to come to grips with Sentinel's now-obvious hesitation. Sentinel switched to magnetic inducer shells, trying to foul Optimus's reactions with the disruptive warheads.

That was another thing. Shoulder cannons firing shrapnel-needle and gyro-disrupting shells. Electrodisruptor imaging. Solar-energy rifle. Trithyllium alloy. These were all weapons that Optimus Prime—that the Keepers—had seen before. Abilities taken from other Autobots and Decipticons. Optimus was not fully cognizant of all of Sentinel Prime's abilities, but certainly there had been something else to make him unique.

Well, there had been one thing.

If there was an advantage unique to any Prime, and one advantage Optimus now possessed over Sentinel, it was the Matrix.

Was that what Sentinel feared? Optimus had been given the Matrix, had been named Prime, and now it resided safely within his chest? It was possible that Sentinel—or this recreation of Sentinel—without the Matrix was no longer the leader *he* had been either. And if such was the case then Optimus himself did not need to hold back at all because he was the one empowered!

Gathering his strength to him like a second skin of armor, Optimus crouched and then leapt forward with his laser rifle blasting away at Sentinel. His launch wasn't nearly as impressive as Sentinel's earlier skybound leap, and it carried him right into a hellfire storm of shrapnel shells that he weathered with arms held up protectively to guard his head, his chest.

He cleared his vision and fired again, catching Sentinel before the Transformer's electrodisruptor could generate another false image. The ruby lance shattered and glanced and washed fire over Sentinel's chest, out over his left shoulder and into the barrel of one shoulder cannon. The weapon shattered into a mangled twist of living metal, and for the first time Optimus had wounded Sentinel.

He landed scant yards away from Sentinel, laser still held ready, but was momentarily blinded by a magnetic inducer shell fired out of the remaining shoulder cannon and detonating against the side of his helm. Gyro inhibitors struck him once, twice, three times, staggering him. Sentinel threw himself bodily against Optimus, using his faster reflexes and much greater strength to wrestle away the massive laser rifle. Optimus let it go, balled up his fists into two hammer-like squares, then drove forward with both arms working like pistons.

Twelve thousand pounds per square inch caught

the laser rifle against Sentinel's chest with crushing force, smashing in, hurling the larger Transformer backward further even than Optimus had jumped. Still holding onto the wrecked weapon, he slammed down into the ground with a jarring blow that left it trembling.

Then, climbing back to his feet, Sentinel cast aside the mangled rifle and launched himself straight up into the veiled sky.

Optimus did not try to chase after Sentinel or even follow with his eyes. He held his right arm up at an angle, and *transformed* it. His hand pulled back inside. The bulky forearm slimmed down and split into a square haft, and the great Energon axe head powered into existence in place of a hand. He stood alone on the arena floor, staring straight ahead with his Energon-charged weapon readied.

And it came again, just as it had back in his cell. A feeling of expectancy that charged through his limbs and tensed him for action. Optimus let it build, his instincts wavering on edge, and then he leapt up and to one side, swinging his energy weapon with all his strength.

To smash into Sentinel, who dropped like a meteor from the heavens.

The electric-blue axe caved into Sentinel's hip, even as Optimus caught a foot into the side of his left arm. Both Transformers fell back to the floor, landing poorly. Both were on their feet again at once, hammering at each other in a fury of cannon fire, arms, legs, and axe.

"You are slow," Sentinel said, sidestepping another axe blow and delivering two magnetic inducer shells into Optimus's right shoulder. He caught hold of the

Autobot leader's right arm, held the Energon-charged blade away from his body. "You are weak."

Optimus jacked the heel of his hand into Sentinel's midsection, throwing the larger Transformer back again. *This* was the specter who haunted his thoughts? This is who he held as the impossible standard, never to be reached, only aspired to?

"That may be," Optimus admitted. There was no shame in the truth. "But I am Prime."

Sentinel came for him in a blaze of desperate speed that made lightning look slow, pummeling with fists and feet, striking at him with his remaining cannon. Optimus's first blow blasted through only empty air, striking through Sentinel's defensive illusion, and he took a hard chop to the side of his neck as the light reformed around the older Transformer. It was the last blow Optimus Prime allowed to land.

He used his block-like forearm and the haft of his Energon axe to fend off one strike after another. He struck back with a solid punch into Sentinel's damaged hip—tired of dwelling on what he did not have. Smashed into the remaining shoulder cannon with the axe—past caring about what he hadn't achieved. Another hammering blow, and another.

He remembered with greater emphasis an unspoken answer of his from earlier. What made Optimus feel worthy of being leader? Because there *was* no other. HE was Prime! And he was through torturing himself with of what he *might…not…be*.

And as he made that promise to himself, his great Energon-charged axe rose and fell, and fell, and fell. It hammered deep gashes into the trithyllium armor, bit into Sentinel's neck, and finally caved in and through Sentinel's chest.

Light flared deep within that wound; brilliant, silver

force that bled out in a glittering stream and then bulged and ruptured through the shoulder joints, hips, along the waist and around Sentinel's neck. Optimus Prime swung one last time, putting the axe head into the deep gash, throwing Sentinel back like a tin man struck by lightning, who then burst apart into pieces, parts and scrap.

Optimus Prime was left standing alone over the battlefield, surrounded by the bits and pieces of the one who had been his superior. Perhaps Sentinel still was, in a way, but Optimus would not let it hold him back again. He would work through the last of his doubts and put them—finally!—aside.

It was with this renewed sense of purpose that Optimus Prime stepped over the scattered wreckage of Sentinel. He'd accomplished a lot of good as leader of the Autobots. He'd be around to do a whole lot more.

But first there were the Keepers to deal with.

CHAPTER
SIXTEEN

The sleek, twin-engine Cessna Citation V sliced through a steel gray cloudbank, emerging into a blinding golden explosion of afternoon sun. Spike clutched at the soft leather cushions of his armrest, refusing to allow himself to enjoy the many comforts of the luxurious flight. Only eight seats lined the small cabin, a bathroom behind the door at the back, the cockpit beyond a steel door up front. Every chair was an ergonomic recliner, and every manner of distraction had been made available to him: magazines, books, a computer, Playstation, TV and stereo...even the flirty attention of an attractive female flight attendant.

Joe Torres, the medic from the commander's house, sat alone in the front row, headsets on, watching a film. Spike had been thinking about Franklin's words about Joe for some time, and he had a hard time believing that Torres had shot the others. Considering all the tech Franklin and his people had at their disposal, his guilt or innocence should have been easy to establish. One thermal scan recreation and the whole business would have been behind them.

That wasn't the way Franklin wanted it, though—or so Spike had gathered. No, Franklin wanted Spike edgy, paranoid, not trusting anyone. Or perhaps he just wanted Spike's attention focused on Torres, making him susceptible to some other form of misdirection. Plots within plots...his body was so tight he had to fight off muscle spasms in his legs, side, and back each time they hit the slightest turbulence.

"I wouldn't think *you'd* be scared to fly," Franklin said, lazing in the window seat on the other side of the aisle.

Spike forced his hands to relax, watching his knuckles go from sickly white to their normal tanned shade. He shrugged. "Maybe I had more confidence in the guys that used to fly me around."

Sighing, Franklin fished around in his suit jacket pocket, withdrew a slimline cellular phone, and tossed it into Spike's lap. He jumped as if someone had unexpectedly deposited a flopping, gasping grouper upon his legs.

"Call him, if it'll make you feel better," Franklin said. "I understand."

Somehow, I doubt that, Spike thought. He picked up the phone and called the number Franklin had given him earlier. An answering machine with a factory-made generic message picked up. He waited for the beep, identified himself, and, two seconds later, felt his heart leap and his tensions ease as Daniel picked up the phone.

"Daddy! Daddy!" Daniel yelped excitedly.

"How's my little trooper?" Spike asked.

Daniel paused. "This place stinks."

Leaning forward, resting his elbows on his knees, Spike's brow furrowed with concern. "Really? Why's that?"

"Well, they've got comic books..."

"That's a bad thing? You like comic books."

"Yeah. And they've got movies and Sega and there's other kids I can talk to, and we played basketball, and we won, and this house is really big, and that's cool, and they made us cookies and I taught the cook how to do a cheese melt on pasta like you do, and it didn't come out right but it still tasted good, and it's not real cold here, and I like that, and they got motor cross bikes and there's hiking trails and a swimming pool and everyone's really nice and..."

"It stinks."

"Yeah!"

"How come?" Spike asked. "Was anyone mean to you, did someone—"

"It stinks 'cause you're not here."

Spike settled back, smiling, his tensions soothed. "I love you, Daniel."

"Bleahhh!" Daniel said, following the insightful commentary with a series of raspberries. It was his way of saying, *I love you, too, Dad, but let's be grown-up about it, okay?*

"Are you in a bus?" Daniel asked.

"No."

"I hear noises in the background."

"I'm on a plane."

"Are you coming *here?* Are you? *Are* you?" Daniel asked breathlessly, the words all running together: *Areyoucominghereareyouareyou...*

"No. I wish I was. I'm just on my way to see some people, that's all."

"When are you gonna be done? When can we go home? Mommy wants to know, too, even though she's not here—she's takin' a shower. But she said it before."

"Soon," Spike said. It was the only answer he'd been able to give since this had started, and soon couldn't be soon enough, as far as he was concerned. Still, he had seen the danger he was in first hand... unless, of course, the whole thing had been elaborately staged, including the murder/suicide, for the sole purpose of making him think that.

Plots within plots. He just wanted answers.

"How soon is soon?" Daniel asked, refusing to be put off. "A half-hour soon? Tomorrow soon? How soon?"

Spike smiled and shook his head. "I love you—"

The raspberries came in a steady stream now, and went on until Spike got a nod from Franklin and said he had to go.

"Why aren't you coming here?" Daniel asked. "When are we gonna be together?"

Spike didn't want to say 'soon' again. "You know."

"I'm gonna get chef to try the cheese melt again," Daniel said. "By the time you get here—"

"The two of us'll show him how it's done. I'll call again."

"'Kay." Another hesitation. "See ya."

The line went dead.

Spike handed the phone back to Franklin without even looking at the operative.

"He sounds like a good kid," Franklin said.

"You got any?"

"Kids? Hell, no. They're cute and they're fun to play with and I'm all for them, so long as they're not mine."

"Why's that?"

"Not married, for starters."

Spike grinned inwardly, thinking of how Daniel would always get him with this one. "Why's that?"

"Not interested in being married. No woman's going to put up with me."

Waiting for it, Spike asked, "Why's that?"

"The job, the hours... not being human any more.

Not like I was. Not—" The operative swiveled his way. "Hey!"

Spike smiled smugly. Another poor victim taken down to Chinatown by the "why's that" game.

His son was brilliant.

"So you want to know more about me," Franklin coaxed.

"You know everything there is to know about me. Seems only fair."

"Everything I tell you could be a lie. I'm not saying it would be, it's just, if I were in your position..."

"Sure. But even if it is, just looking at the story you have to tell might let me know something about you I don't already."

Franklin considered this. "All right, the short version. My family's rich—DuPont level wealthy. When I was growing up, no one ever expected anything out of me, nothing was ever made a challenge, and I just kind of went along with it, like I was sleepwalking through life. I liked video games, so my family gave me the money to start a video game company. I went into the office whenever I wanted, did as little work as I had to, drove everyone crazy, changed the rules all the time... I could, y'know, so why not? Then I met a girl."

"So, you fell in love and she straightened you out."

Franklin shook his head. "No, I mean literally... a girl. Ten years old, dying, and she had more going on in her head than you could ever believe...you just looked into her eyes and it was like she was living her entire life in the months she had left, she had accepted what was going to happen to her and was focused, disciplined, in a way I never had been. She won a contest to come see our facility, where the 'magic' happened on the gaming front. After I met her, I couldn't get what I saw in her eyes out of my head. Two weeks later, I enlisted. And right now, my family, my friends, everyone who knew me in my old life, just thinks I'm off wandering somewhere, spending the family's money. I send a postcard now and then, drop an email, and no one thinks twice about it."

"That's what you think," Spike said.

"Pardon?"

"How do you know *what* they're thinking? Your family, I mean. Let's say what you're telling me is true. I'm not saying I believe it, I figure there's probably some truth in it, enough to make it convincing, but let's say the part about your family is real. Just because they're not out looking for you, just because they're not begging you to come home, doesn't mean they don't miss you or want you back."

Franklin looked away, staring out at the soaring clouds slicing past his wing. "You lost your father and you can't understand how someone could just walk away from family."

"Nice try. The stuff your story skips right over is, why enlist? Why let them augment you? Make you not human any more, like you said."

This time, Franklin returned Spike's gaze, the agent appearing momentarily confused. Then understanding struck him. "You think it's the tech that doesn't make me human any more? That *that's* what I'm saying?"

Spike nodded.

A thin smile appeared on Franklin's guarded face. "Oh. Okay, you can take it that way, if you want."

Giving up on any chance of getting a straight answer from the agent, Spike changed the subject quickly. "Let's go over the mission parameters again."

"It's simple. Doing overlapping traces of the commander's and our turncoat operative's recent movements, we narrowed the field regarding mutual acquaintances who may have had means and opportunity to salvage bits of Superion, people who work in Los Angeles. Agents in the city found three locations where calls were made to the commander's area code at the exact time the phone rang in his house. We check those locations one by one."

"Your field agents could do it."

"But they're not you."

"I'm bait again."

"Exactly."

"And if you screw up again, if another of your people isn't to be trusted, my son ends up without a father."

"Same deal if we do nothing. Listen," Franklin said, "I did some reading up on professional gamblers one time. You know what separates the professionals from the amateurs?"

"No idea."

"The amateur believes in the possibilities. The amateur goes in looking for the big score, the one-in-a-million shot, because it *is* possible, it can happen. The professional knows better. The professional goes in looking at the probabilities, understanding the house advantage, knowing full well how much has to be lost or sacrificed before you can win anything. What we're doing is gambling, yes, but we're going based on the probabilities, not the possibilities."

"And the probability is that there's a bunch of people out there who want to blow my head off because of something I know, but don't even realize I know."

"Yes. We need to know who they are, and why they want to keep you away from the Followers."

Spike winced. "You don't think they *are* the Followers?"

"I think this whole thing lays out a lot more directly than it might seem, but not that directly, no."

"So what do you—"

A scream from the rear of the passenger compartment arrested their attention. Spike and Franklin looked back to see the flight attendant staring out the window on Spike's side of the plane. Franklin unfastened his seatbelt and was leaning in next to Spike, looking out the window with him.

A boxy shape was bulleting up at them, crimson eyes glaring, faceplate, arms, fists, and body gleaming in the harsh light of day. A Transformer, certainly, but its colors were... wrong, somehow. Spike saw blue and red, purple and orange, gray and green, all on different parts of its body. The incoming projectile looked like a patchwork creation of fused together parts, Autobot here, Decepticon there. One hand was steel gray, the other red and black.

Those hands were aimed at the wing.

The plane lurched and Franklin was sent tumbling as the pilot banked sharply, attempting to avoid a midair collision with the giant robot, but there was a jarring impact, the sound of metal screaming, and a sudden implosion as the emergency door was torn away with the Cessna's wing and a howling vacuum drew the air from Spike's lungs and tugged at him so hard that the chair he'd been strapped into shuddered but did not yank free of its moorings.

Instead, the floor cracked open wide and the plane split in half, tumbling side over side, a Transformer hovering behind them, wing in hand, waving "goodbye" instants before the clouds swallowed him whole and the world was drawn into darkness.

When Spike woke, he was on a patch of high ground, gasping for air, his fingers clutching at the seatbelt that was no longer biting deeply into his chest, no longer threatening to crack open his ribs or pulverize his heart. Franklin stood nearby, shrugging off a parachute, and a crackling rose up from the woods in the distance. Yellow and red flames wavered as treetops served as torches, bits of the downed plane scattered everywhere.

Franklin looked back over his shoulder as he gathered up the parachute. "I said I'd keep you safe. How are you feeling?"

"Everything hurts," Spike said, sitting up slowly, his breathing coming under control, his panic subsiding.

Franklin knelt, hauling a huge and very heavy stone from the ground, and jammed the parachute into the space left before it. He let go of the rock and it landed back in its spot with a loud *thump*, pebbles and bits of earth spat in every direction. "Good. Means you're alive. I checked you out, nothing broken, nothing ruptured. Probably have some pulled or torn muscles, which will slow us down, some really nasty bruises, but no head trauma, vertebra's still in one piece, you should be able to get moving, and you need to."

"What the hell was that thing?" Spike asked.

"An unfriendly. There are more unfriendlies on their way here, standard mop up. We have to get moving."

Spike tried to rise, but his head was still foggy. Franklin blurred to his side and helped him up.

"It wasn't like any Transformer I've ever seen," Spike said. "Was it with Starscream?"

"Doubt it. We were way clear of New Vegas air space. And yeah, I got the Frankenstein's monster bit, there's been a lot of unrecovered material from

Transformer battles over the years. Someone's found a way of building their own."

They headed down the slope of the plateau toward a patch of woods in the opposite direction from the wreckage.

"Shouldn't we check to see if anyone else made it?" Spike asked.

"Have to deal with the immediate crisis first. The other unfriendlies will go for what's left of our ride. That means we should be as far from it as we can be. I've already called in for ground and air support, but we've got to survive until they move in. I spotted a cabin about a mile from here when we were in the air. With any luck, it'll be defensible."

"But the others—"

"I don't think any one else made it, Spike. I'm sorry."

"You're not sure."

Franklin's eyes went dead, emotionless. "My job is to keep you safe. Everyone who was with us knew the risks, and if I could have saved them, too, I would have. Now—I'll knock you out and carry you, or you can come under your own steam. Those are the only two options. Your choice."

Spike saw a tiny needle spring from the tip of Franklin's finger. The agent wasn't bluffing.

He went with him.

The woods were thick, with heavy, wide-bodied pine trees rushing into the sky, their ropy upper branches magnanimously spread wide to provide a canopy of spotty cover. Sunlight streaked through the openings between the branches, stabbing at the soft, musky ground, and tiny rustlings came here and there, squirrels rushing about, curious, wary.

As Franklin had guessed, Spike was slower than he

would have liked to be, his muscles burning and straining as he forced himself to keep pace with the agent.

"I don't hear helicopters, jeeps, anything," Spike said, already out of breath. "How do you know there's a team on the ground? The plane could have hit anywhere. They couldn't have been in place ahead of time."

"Agreed," Franklin said coldly. "They're here. I can hear them and they're moving fast, a lot faster than they should be able to on foot, and they're on our trail. None of that's good."

Spike couldn't hear a blessed thing and said as much.

"They're augments," Franklin said. "Not as good as me, but there are more of them."

A clearing loomed and Spike broke through it with Franklin, who rushed for the door to the cabin's storm cellar. Kneeling, he shattered the rusty lock holding its chain in place, slid the chains free, and hauled open the doors. A terrible and ripe odor assaulted them.

A bug whipped past Spike's ear—at least, he thought it was a bug, and suddenly, Franklin's hand was on his shirt, spinning him toward the darkness below, shoving him down the steep steps as another *zzzhhhrrr* came, followed by a *thwack* of impact, and Franklin came stumbling down the stairs after him. They struck the stairs, bouncing, grunting, Spike's elbow smashing on a step, Franklin's weight pulverizing several of the steps as he tumbled down, grunting with each impact.

Spike hit the floor and rolled free as the agent thundered down with him, face pale, his natural grace gone as he was flung ass over heels into the darkness.

In the shimmering sunlight dancing down across the shattered ruins of the steps, Spike could see Franklin's face and chest.

Franklin had been shot, a gory exit wound the size of a small fist a few inches to one side of the man's heart. He wasn't moving. His chest was still, his eyes wide and staring.

"Oh, Jesus," Spike whispered, specks of blood on his hands.

From outside and above, he heard the "mop-up" crew Franklin had talked about. They were shouting, barking orders he couldn't quite make out. All he did know was that their voices were getting louder, and he had no idea if there was anywhere down here where he could hide, any way that he could reach the storm cellar's open doors and pull them closed and barricade himself from within...

For all he knew, everything he needed was sitting around him, but he couldn't see much of anything, just vague outlines of beams and stacked boxes and the handlebars of a couple of bicycles... and there was that terrible smell, like something had died in this place a long time ago and been sealed in here, sealed up *tight*.

He was in a killing box.

A shadow pierced the long, slanting rectangle of light reaching down from the open double doors. Then another.

He thought of his son, and he wished he knew what these people wanted from him, why they were so determined to reach him, to take his life.

Something in your head...

The figures at the top of the ruined stairs flickered back and forth wildly, then one halted at the entrance.

Suddenly, a huge, hulking man in a strange combat

suit leaped down from the opening, the sunlight revealing a reinforced exoskeleton, cables glinting and bulging around his collarbones, shoulders, and ribs. His head was shaved, and his goggles, probably infrared and capable of picking up heat and other signatures, glowed scarlet, like the eyes of a Transformer.

Spike fell back into the shadows as the man silently advanced—then his world became a chaotic jumble. The face of the man in the augmentation suitwas before him in a series of blurs, one second snarling as if to move in for the kill, then eyes rolling back in surprise, the next sinking away. Then others were around him, a sea of faces, all disguised by masks ofpoorly designed mech,darting at him. He heard grunts, screams, hissing that he now knew was silenced weapons. The walls and boxes and tables and bicycles and everything around him leaped and recoiled from the starting strength of the weapons fire, but he felt no pain, no fear—only a strong sense of purpose. A cold, inhuman determination to perform a task, complete an operation.

He was doing something he didn't understand, something his brain couldn't fully comprehend, not on a conscious level. His hands were on the bodies of the killers, striking, stabbing at them with any objects in reach—a fork, a screwdriver, *anything*—and their numbers were dwindling, the tiny rectangle of light from above growing from the patchwork quilt of illumination as seen beyond the attacking figures, until finally the light was all there was, and all was silence, all was still.

When he returned to himself, he was looking down at a dozen armored soldiers, all unconscious and disabled, several with suits that sparked with white wriggling lines of energy, their weapons scattered about the floor, their suit's coolant fluids pooling at his feet.

Impossibly, he was the only one left standing. What had happened?

Spike turned suddenly as he heard a choking cough from across the room. It was Franklin, one hand covering his chest, as he attempted to rise. Spike went to him, and was about to tell him to lie still, when Franklin's hand came away, revealing a metal plating over the spot where his flesh had been torn asunder.

"How—how did you—" Spike began.

Franklin shook his head and cut the younger man off. "I didn't do anything. It was you. You took those guys out. You healed me."

"I... I don't remember."

"There's a lot you don't remember," Franklin said as the steady whipping of chopper blades sounded in the distance, the rescue team finally arriving. "A lot you don't *think* you remember."

Spike was shaking, the enormity of what Franklin was saying threatening to overwhelm him.

"You were one of them," Franklin said. "Your mind was inside the body of a Transformer. That means, for a time, you not only had awareness of everything that's inside them, you knew how it all fit together, how it worked. The people that made me...and them...only know bits and pieces. Everything there is to know is stamped in your brain. I think that's why the Followers want you, so they can know what you know, and I think that's why these guys, whoever they are, want you dead. They don't want to know, and they don't want the knowledge in anyone else's hands."

Drawing back from the operative, Spike said, "That

can't be right." He took another breath and nearly gagged on the horrible stench in this place.

"What?" Franklin asked.

"That smell. I've been smelling it since we fell in here."

"There wasn't any smell then," Franklin said.

"Yeah, there was."

"A combat smell? Some blood, lots of sweat, residue from weapons fire?"

"Yes."

Franklin nodded. "Some part of your mind telling you what was coming, trying to prepare you."

The operative's mouth quirked to one side. He looked over at the closest augment, reached in his direction, and whispered, "I'm picking up a control beacon. Some kind of signal feed." He touched his ear. The voices in his head, the ones who were always listening, always talking to him. "All right," he said abruptly.

"What?" Spike asked. "You were talking to the home office or whatever, right?"

"They were talking to me. They've pinpointed the signal. We don't need to worry about L.A. anymore. Whoever's getting in touch with these guys is in Vegas."

"Starscream."

"I don't think so. It's coming on the one frequency we figured out a Transformer can't send or receive. And...well, here's the part that doesn't make a lot of sense: the signal isn't meant to give these guys orders, it's supposed to scramble them, make it impossible for them to think, to function." Franklin met Spike's gaze excitedly. "Whoever's sending this was trying to help save you. And that means it's the Followers.

Damn it all to hell, I can't believe it. We've got 'em. We're closing in on an exact fix."

The choppers landed somewhere close.

Franklin grinned. "And we're going to pay whoever's behind all this a little visit."

CHAPTER
SEVENTEEN

Chaos ruled the white room. Paul Charteris did what he could to stop the arguments, the fights, the violence threatening to erupt among the hundred or more prisoners, but he was only one man, and the insanity spreading through the crowd was too powerful and all consuming for him to stop on his own. Melony had been little help; she'd decided early on that there was nothing to be done except to protect herself from the chaos, and that meant staying apart from it. Paul simply couldn't do that.

"It won't give me my games!" a man shouted, frantically touching the walls, the ceiling. "I was... I was complaining because all the games were old ones I'd already played, I wanted something new, and then the games were gone, and I was back at the office, and it was that day Hiro came, Hiro and his gun..."

The story was the same all over, only the particulars had changed. The pleasure the white room had doled out had turned to pain. Instead of allowing each of the prisoners to become lost in his or her fondest memories, to watch movies they loved again or again, to re-experience falling in love for the first time, to once more be transported to times and places that had provided safety and security, the room's manifestations were now of the private terrors each person wished with all their hearts to avoid. Paul saw people experience the deaths of loved ones, terrible arguments resulting in the loss of lifelong friends, heart-wrenching break-ups with lovers, and worse. Whatever shames they had were laid bare, whatever secret acts they'd performed were now public knowledge. Their lies were their lives.

Yet they went back to the walls, they tried again and again to reclaim paradise. It had been there once, why couldn't it come again?

Their only reward had been more misery.

Soon, cliques had begun to form. Groups from one part of Hong Kong blamed those from another part for the change in the white room. Those who worked in offices sided against those who worked in factories. Even whatever part of the room one had resided in played a part: one group had divvied up the room like a chessboard, referring to those who resided in each square with a different designation, assigning each another motivation and agenda.

They would be killing each other soon. Paul was certain of it.

Paul knew that he shouldn't have been surprised at how quickly it had all fallen apart. Civilization, order, common courtesy and decency...these were all abstract concepts when human beings had experienced ultimate pleasure and escape—only to have it taken from them. In his time as a police officer he had seen behavior like this many times, usually when he'd worked vice. Melony had, too. These people had a dependency on the soothing effects of the room, and now that their sole comfort had been taken from them, they would do anything—to anyone—to get it back.

"We were wrong about the Keepers," Paul said as Melony stood with him, watching yet another disagreement between factions grow more heated.

"How so?" she asked calmly. Her clinical detachment was in high gear.

"They're not just interested in the Transformers. We're under the microscope, too."

Crossing her arms over her chest, she said, "I think these people are doing this to themselves. They've gotten bored. There's nothing new on the happy side of things, so they've gone the other way. The room's just responding to what's on their minds."

"Heaven or hell," Paul whispered. But it just didn't feel right. The Keepers had wanted to keep the crowd motivated, cheering on their champions, or so it had seemed. Why would they *let* the room do this to these people?

"Have you used it, yet?" she asked.

Paul shook his head. "Not going to, either."

"We could find out for sure. You could try for a happy memory..."

"No way." He gestured at the unruly crowd before them. "I'm not going to risk becoming like *that*."

"All right, then explain it to me. Why do you think the Keepers are torturing these people?"

"For the same reason no one can get anything new, anything they haven't experienced in the past: the Keepers are studying us. They want to know what makes us tick, what gives us pleasure, what brings us pain. Not just physical pain, either, that's easy. They want to understand us."

"Why would they bother?"

"Maybe because they don't have anything else to do," Paul said. "Maybe because it serves some need they have, I don't know. But we have to do something, or this place is going to turn into a slaughterhouse."

"He's quite right," a voice said from behind the pair.

Paul and Melony turned to see an elderly man *emerging* from the white wall behind them. He was covered in an elastic, ivory substance stretching outward from the wall. His features were only partially formed.

Yet they could see he was smiling...

"You're one of them," Paul said in a small, uncharacteristically wavering voice. He trembled, taking a step back despite himself.

"A Keeper? Not exactly. Think of me as a servant, a manifestation, whatever your limited mind has the capacity to accept."

"You want us to fight," Melony said, voicing the concern she had held from the beginning of the incarceration.

"In a manner of speaking, yes. But not against each other." The featureless man gestured at the wall behind him. *"You are Followers, and we wish to know more about you. Yet you remain hidden."*

"So you can't just take whatever you want," Paul said with increasing boldness. "You're not gods."

"We believe in freedom of choice. We seek to lead only by revealing paths to those who seek them." He gestured again, and an opening appeared in the wall, a darkened space behind it. *"The path to what you want is here."*

"The hell with you," Paul said, his fear plain.

"No. I believe that hell for you is to be powerless to prevent these people from tearing each other to shreds. Yet you do have power. Indulge our curiosity and we will restore the white room to its former function. Refuse, and it will go much worse on these people. The room can feed their paranoia, enforce their delusions."

Paul knew that he was being offered a choice; in a way, the same choice Optimus Prime and the others had been offered: fight or innocents would die. But this battlefield would be different, he sensed, and there was no way to win, no way to change what was done.

Melony was the one who turned away. "You think you're getting in my head, forget about it."

A white wall rose up before her, cutting off her escape. Others rocketed to the high ceiling, luminescent, warm.

"We have our hooks into you already," the featureless man said. He gestured again, and the walls sped forward, *absorbing* Melony before she could even scream. Then he turned to Paul. *"The choice is yours. Save her, save these people, or don't."*

"Free will," Paul said bitterly.

With a laugh, the creature from the wall nodded. *"Free will."*

Paul stepped into the darkness.

The years melted away. He was a teenager again, living in a nightmare. He could barely eat or sleep, and when his stomach was empty, he was wracked by dry heaves. His waking life felt like ground zero just before a nuclear explosion. Second by second, his existence seemed normal, the same as always, but there was a sense of imminent change, disaster and destruction, a future that had been reasonable and assured, calm and structured, a lifetime of caring for others and being cared for in return in the service of the almighty that, he was certain, would soon be taken from him.

It didn't matter if he was sitting alone or with a crowd of people, in the room he shared with two others or in Saint Michael's mildewy library or commissary or cathedral, he was always alert, always waiting for a rapping at the door, or the slow, solemn approach of one of the Fathers, who would tell him it was time for him to go, he wasn't fitting in, he didn't belong. His belief wasn't strong enough, this seminary school and the path to God's grace on Earth was not for him.

There was almost nothing worse than that: the calm, the silence...the fear. A part of him wanted out, wanted it to be over, but he had nowhere else to go, no family to speak of, no friends outside of these walls, no one he could *trust*.

It was a golden, sunny morning, a Saturday, when it all fell apart. He woke in the little room atop the no longer used bell tower, technology, electric bells and whistles, having replaced tradition, and heard shouts of excitement and alarm. Paul had come here to be alone with his thought, a skinny, spindly teenager, frightened all the time, secretly wishing to be rescued, to be comforted, to be brought into a circle that everyone told him he already belonged to, though he never felt it was entirely true.

"You're every bit as welcome in the presence and spirit of love and forgiveness as any of us," Father Simon had told him often enough, smiling comfortingly, letting him know that many students had felt as he had, awed, worried that he might not live up to expectations, filled with need for approval, desire for acceptance.

Yet the words had seemed false, somehow, spoken as if by rote, perhaps meant to set him at ease so that the crushing blow yet to come would not be met with much resistance.

He hadn't always felt this way. In fact, until *they* arrived, he had fit in perfectly. Now the world was changing, there were aliens among them, living machines, and nothing in their books had prepared them for this, nothing warned them...and these beings had no concept of the almighty, not in the sense that anyone could grasp. They were an abomination, an affront, possibly even a test.

And they were accepted. Following statements released from Rome, Father Simon had preached understanding. Paul couldn't understand it. How could these creatures be a natural part of existence? What did their existence say about the laws of the universe by which they had all governed themselves?

They frightened him...their images, their words, their terrible conflicts. He tried to take comfort in words. Words, he reasoned, would not betray him. They could not magically change on the page, they might as well have been written in stone.

Yet what those words meant to him, and to others in this new age, *did* change.

It was all he thought about; that, and how the plan of the almighty seemed to be *changing* somehow, interpretations desperately rearranged to accommodate the existence of these godless things. How could ancient words change? No, more to the point, if the way those words had been taken had changed once, if a single error could have been made, then how could anything anyone said about the tenants of their faith be correct?

Paul went to the window, looked outside. At first, he couldn't understand what he was looking at. Here, several stories high, he was gazing out at the rear of an edifice that hadn't existed when he'd accidentally fallen asleep in this tiny room last night. Huge metal blocks, cylinders, something from an industrial complex—

That *moved*.

Paul stumbled back, the perpetual knot in his stomach tightening to an excruciating level.

It was one of them. A Transformer. Worse, as the giant robot turned, he identified it from his many researches into these inhuman things:

The Decepticon known as Starscream stood on the great lawn of the seminary school, looking down and turning slightly to address the silver-haired Father Simon.

No, no! Paul screamed silently in the confines of his mind, his chest rising and falling madly, his breath caught in anguished wheezes. *They'll kill us all, they're here to destroy us!*

"This conversation is now private," Starscream said. "No one beyond fifty feet of us will hear anything that is said."

Paul was within the radius, unknown to the Decepticon and the priest. He heard everything.

"What brings you here?" the Father asked.

"I wish to learn. I need to understand what it is that drives humans of your designation."

Paul watched, chilled by these words. Yes, how can you defeat an enemy if you don't understand your nemesis completely, if you can't understand their weaknesses and how to exploit them.

But—what could he do? What could he say?

How could he stop what was going to happen?

"There are many in this world who are afraid of you and your kind," the Father said boldly. "I know at least one of them is here, among my students."

"Only one?"

"The exception that proves the rule. Those we follow tell us you are not to be feared. Respected, yes, for you have power beyond that which we can currently understand. But fear solves nothing. It simply debilitates."

The Decepticon seemed amused. "Interesting. Then you are akin to soldiers, following the edicts of your generals?"

"We are servants."

"And if I were to command the one you serve?"

"Impossible. Though, as I said, there is one here, to my shame, who does not feel that way. I think he sees your kind as a challenge to the existence of our lord and savior, your presence as an invalidation of our beliefs."

He's talking about me, Paul realized. But...how could he know? Paul had only told two people, two friends, whom he trusted, each of whom he had sworn to silence. He hadn't even spoken a word of this in confessional.

In his mind, he was falling into a tunnel, while his body inched closer to the wide-open window, a large rectangular opening with no glass. He wanted to see, he wanted to hear all of it, he wanted to defend himself, defend the others... he understood, much later, that Father Simon had been placed in a very difficult position. The man had no idea what the Decepticon wanted, and when it turned out to be a better understanding of theology, a glimpse into the heart and soul of human belief, a thing he couldn't simply assimilate through conventional research, the Father had chosen to be open, and to pray that some measure of their beliefs might inform upon the actions of this killing machine, perhaps sway it, as so many before it had been swayed, to the path of light rather than darkness.

He knew this later... after he fell.

Paul hadn't realized he stood so close to the edge,

he had been without more than an hour or two of sleep in any given day for close to a week, and his appetite had failed him, leaving him weak, sickly. He told himself later that he had misjudged where the edge of the window had truly been, that he had meant to anchor himself on the frame and that, instead, his hand, bearing all his weight, had passed into empty air—but he wasn't sure.

Paul tumbled, the concrete below reaching up, ready to dash his brains, when a blur came and his fall was arrested, the breath knocked from his lungs as he struck something huge and metallic instead. He rocked back and forth, dazed, and realized he was still far above the ground, *resting* in Starscream's hand.

"Please," the Father said. "Put him down."

"I know mercy," Starscream said. "And forgiveness. If I close my hand, I might crush this being. Would you then offer me forgiveness?"

"If I believed you were truly aware of what you had done, that it had been wrong, that you had repented and were heartily sorry, yes. But if you take his life simply to test my reaction, then no, forgiveness would not come to pass."

Paul looked out at the steel fingers, any of which might stab the life from him with blinding speed.

"Mercy, on the other hand, would be sparing the life of one I could destroy so easily, is that not so?" Starscream asked.

"Not entirely," the Father said. "If you spare him, it may also be to gauge my reaction, to see what it benefits you. That is not mercy. Or you may set him down and let him run away as a sign of strength, to show you are beyond petty displays of power. Mercy is something one often grants one's enemies, and this boy is no threat to you."

The hand in which Paul had been cradled quickly sank to the ground, the fingers springing open like ramps the size of alligators. Paul raced to the ground, nearly passing out, but somehow managing, despite his terror, despite how numb he had become, to stumble onto the grass and wobble away from the Decepticon and the priest.

"He doesn't run," Starscream said.

"In his heart, he does," the Father said. "And, I fear, he always will."

Paul looked back. He had so much to say, so many questions to ask, but he was frozen. Somehow, he resisted the fear, and he spoke to the terrible machine. "I... I need to know..."

Starscream bent low. "Ask. One question."

"Paul," the Father warned, but it was too late.

Standing as still as he could, despite his fear, Paul asked, "Have you looked upon the face of God? Out there, in the emptiness, have you seen Him?"

Starscream laughed. "Only in my *reflection*, child."

The Father hung his head.

Paul, shattered, aware that he was being mocked, manipulated, stood trembling before the behemoth.

"BOO!" Starscream hollered.

Paul *ran*. He allowed himself to fall into a life of confrontation and conflict. Bitterness, pain, and isolation colored his existence from that moment on, making him stronger, tougher, fearless—or so he made everyone believe. Yet, inwardly, he was always staring up into the face of something that dwarfed his perceptions, something that terrified him for what it might be, the hidden knowledge it held.

Is this all there is? he had wondered, and that had

been the question he'd truly wished to ask, and it had haunted him. Perhaps these things, these living automations, perhaps they knew, perhaps the stories of the stories they once saved whose essence—whose soul—they had drawn from their body and into one of their own hollow shells then returned again, perhaps that story, if true, held the answers humans had been seeking all their lives.

The trail to those answers was one he was determined to follow.

Paul heard a scream. He suddenly became aware that his surroundings had changed. *He* had changed. The city spread before him was on fire.

Transformers fought and buildings tumbled or burst wildly into flames.

A twisted chunk of twisted steel, mortar, bone, and more, fused into a projectile the size of a Buick struck the ground next to him, chewing through a concrete sidewalk, exploding the window behind him. Shards of glass tore through him, but he felt nothing. This wasn't real to him, it wasn't his memory. Debris ripped into his body and departed harmlessly.

Not so the woman ten feet to his left.

"Jenny!" someone screamed. He recognized the voice even before the figure who'd cried out that name darted into his field of view.

Melony knelt over the ruined body of the woman she had called Jenny, staring down at her with absolute horror. Jenny was dead, there could be no question. Glass shards the size of swords jutted from her throat, her chest, her stomach and her left arm, which had nearly been severed.

Paul watched as Melony's features changed, her emotions running out of her, a calm, clinical detachment overtaking her as she surveyed the damage her companion had suffered, then her gaze seemed to turn black, and a hatred more chilling than any he had ever stood before overtook the woman.

"This was her sister," the featureless man said, appearing beside and a little behind Paul. *"Oh, don't worry. She can't see you. She can't see or hear either of us. It was interesting to experience the memories she shared before you arrived. She was actually quite neglectful of her sister throughout their lives, paying to have her placed in boarding schools when their parents died, seeing her only grudgingly and at times of her choosing after that. In later life, they had a chance to reconnect, and so they came to this place—Baltimore, I believe it is called, near the college Jenny attended. Jenny's death was a relief to Melony, though she cannot admit it. She feels shamed, and thus she is angry. She will not accept responsibility for her actions, she must focus her rage on others. On them."*

The man swept his hand at the battling behemoths above. *"Fate does not have a face. Neither do random acts. She hates, but for all the wrong reasons. We find that... useful."*

"You said I could save her. You said I could rescue them all."

"Ah, yes. That. There's a simple explanation, of course. We lied."

Paul watched as above, the robots fought, and below, the streets ran red with blood and fire.

He said nothing, but inwardly, he swore he would find a way to save Melony and the others.

And maybe even himself.

CHAPTER EIGHTEEN

On the eastern outskirts of Las Vegas, all was desolation. The once-cozy suburban homes, the apartment buildings, the miles of highways, the strip malls, fast food restaurants, bars, mega-stores and motels were all utterly deserted, their once glittering neon signs now dark. The homes were dark, too, and so were the apartment buildings and restaurants. Only the security lights burned behind the locked doors and shuttered windows of hundreds of small businesses hurriedly abandoned in the wake of the Decepticon invasion.

The stores were empty thanks to the new city administration, headed by Starscream, Soundwave and the rest of their Decepticons, no one in Las Vegas showed up for work anymore. No one had to. According to their new lords and masters, the denizens of Las Vegas were the kings of the new world order.

Downtown, the casinos and hotels were still garishly bright with gleaming neon, and the slot machines and roulette wheels still worked just fine. But in this particular suburb, only the traffic lights still worked, blinking red to yellow to green as they mindlessly directed traffic that no longer flowed.

It was high noon on the outskirts of Las Vegas, and not a creature was stirring.

"Looks quiet," Prowl said from his vantage point behind a deserted Exxon station.

"Too quiet," Bumblebee observed, recalling the line from an old Western he'd watched on television. "Well, Pilgrim," Bumblebee added, getting into the Western spirit. "We knew it was a trap when we came here. This is the only part of Las Vegas that was completely evacuated, so there's no chance of inflicting collateral damage in a knock down drag out fight."

Prowl nodded. "Logically speaking, the Decepticons know we want to avoid hurting humans, so by clearing this suburb out, they might as well have sent us an invitation."

"Let's let them know we're here, so the party can get really started!" quipped Bumblebee, moving from his hiding place behind a darkened Wendy's sign.

Prowl hesitated, then nodded. They were there to scout ahead for the secret army that was following on their heels. Scouts were supposed to find trouble, not avoid it.

"Yes," said Prowl. "Let's go."

In their robot form, the two Autobots, ran into the middle of the deserted stretch of highway. A few broken down cars, trucks, and delivery vans were scattered about—looted of all cargo. Prowl and Bumblebee ran among them, seeking cover wherever they could find it.

Now that they weren't battling the United States Army, Prowl and Bumblebee decided to take off the kid gloves—they traded their relatively harmless null rifles and stunners for full-bore laser blasters and cluster bomb cannons. The Autobots were hunting for Decepticons, now, and subtlety in their choice of weapons was not a prudent option.

"Downtown Vegas is straight ahead," said

Bumblebee, pointing to the tall tip of the dark pyramid that was the Luxor Hotel and Casino peeking just above the rest of the hotels and gambling palaces.

"Let's see how far we get before they try to stop us," Prowl said.

"Not far at all, Autobots!" boomed a cruel and arrogant voice.

Whirling on their heels, Prowl and Bumblebee were greeted by a familiar form—Bonecrusher, one of the six components that together made up one of the most powerful and dangerous Decepticons in the universe, the gigantic creature called Devastator.

"Well, well," Bumblebee quipped. "Does the right arm know what the left arm is doing out on its own?"

Prowl actually chuckled.

Poor Bonecrusher was low man on the Devastator totem pole—his left arm module—and as such was almost totally subservient to Devastator's right arm component, along with his head and torso modules. In fact, Devastator's left arm was probably his least critical and most expendable component—and Bonecrusher knew it, too.

"Another crack and I'll smash you to smithereens," Bonecrusher cried, his pride injured. To emphasize his statement, the Decepticon's fists crashed down hard, flattening a McDonald's restaurant like a house of cards. After just two blows, only a cloud of dust and debris and the famed Golden Arches remained as testament to the once-thriving business.

"I'll attack on the right," Prowl commanded. "You take the left."

"Got it, but—"

Bumblebee didn't finish his sentence. He was forced to dodge an SUV hurled by Bonecrusher. Diving to the pavement, Bumblebee turned over on his back in time to see the vehicle whiz over his head.

"Hey, did you do that?" Bumblebee said, further taunting Bonecrusher. "You know SUVs are prone to rollover!"

"I'll tear you apart!" the enraged Decepticon cried, lunging toward Bumblebee.

Suddenly there was a hissing *WHOOSH*, followed a split-second later by a loud *BOOM!* Bonecrusher staggered as his robotic form was enveloped in smoke.

A cluster bomb fired from Prowl's shoulder-cannon had struck the Decepticon in the middle of his chest plate insignia. The detonation sparked off his armor, and Bonecrusher was blasted backwards, to fly all the way across the street.

The flailing, helpless Decepticon tore though two telephone poles and ripped out their attached power lines, then slammed into the façade of an Outback Steak House. The building collapsed on top of Bonecrusher, and the sparking power cables met the natural gas escaping from the ruptured gas mains. There was another, much larger explosion, the force of which nearly knocked Bumblebee and Prowl off their feet even though they stood over a hundred yards away. The windows in the buildings all around them shattered. A burglar alarm in one of the small businesses was tripped and rang urgently.

Debris was blasted high into the air by the terrible force of the gas explosion, to crash down onto the street and all over the deserted parking lot. It looked as if nothing could survive such a blast, but in the middle of an orange and scarlet ball of fire the angry Decepticon called Bonecrusher rose from the rubble and raised his fists in defiance. His impenetrable cezium steel armor had protected him from the force of the blast and the heat of the roaring flames.

"Good! GOOD!" Bonecrusher cried. "You brought *real* weapons this time, not puny null rifles and stunners. Now we can really bring down this house!"

Before either Bumblebee or Prowl could move to stop him, Bonecrusher took off running. With a speed that belied his great size, the Decepticon raced across an expansive parking lot in front of a Wal-Mart store. Then, without hesitation, he crashed into the building itself, to wade through it like a wave on the beach, scattering debris and consumer goods in every direction.

"Catch me if you can, Autobots," Bonecrusher cried over his cyclopean shoulder. "Before I kill more humans."

"He's trying to get around us," Prowl shouted. "He's trying to destroy the secret army...The allies we're supposed to protect."

"Don't worry, I'll stop him," said Bumblebee, leaping at the Decepticon.

In a single bound, the Autobot leaped high into the air, arched over Bonecrusher's thick head, and landed right in front of the startled Decepticon.

"Remember me?" Bumblebee said.

He punched Bonecrusher right in the robot's steel plated jaw, just as hard as his hydraulic system and servomotors would let him.

"ZEEEZZZZ!" Bonecrusher cried, toppling backward and hitting the pavement hard, his Cybertronian brain temporarily scrambled.

"Ouch. That hurt!" Bumblebee said, shaking his metal fist.

"Watch out!" Prowl warned his partner—but was it too late?

Amazingly, the Decepticon had recovered almost immediately. He pointed his laser rifle right at Bumblebee's face and fired!

A bolt of red flashed past Bumblebee's cheek, but the Autobot managed to avoid the deadly beam. Prowl's warning had come just in time.

"No you don't," Bumblebee cried, seizing Bonecrusher's arm and trying to wrestle the laser rifle free. Bonecrusher resisted, throwing the Autobot around like a rag doll. But the stubborn Bumblebee wouldn't let go of Bonecrusher's arm.

Bursts of laser blasts fired randomly, striking a Jimmy Dean's restaurant, a Seven Eleven, and an Office Max—all of which disappeared in violent eruptions of burning doom and destruction.

Suddenly a wave of black camouflaged AH-64 Apache attack helicopters flew overhead—the first wave of soldiers from the secret army. With a final wave of his mighty arm, Bonecrusher tossed Bumblebee aside. The Autobot crashed onto the pavement and slid across the parking lot to come to rest halfway through the plate glass windows of a Hallmark store.

Then the Decepticon looked up, aiming his laser gun at the approaching helicopters, their rotors beating a staccato rhythm in the hot desert air.

"Too soon!" Prowl cried, trying to wave the helicopters off.

Bonecrusher's laser rifle barked. The lead helicopter blew into burning chunks that tumbled to the street below. Prowl knew that no one got out of that chopper alive—more humans died because he failed.

In an attempt to distract Bonecrusher, Prowl fired his shoulder-mounted cannons again and again, striking the Decepticon in the chest, face, and shoulder before Prowl's ammo was exhausted. Bonecrusher was dazed for a moment, but quickly shook off the effects of the explosions.

Frustrated, Prowl triple checked that he was out of ammunition in his cannons and drew his laser blaster.

Bonecrusher laughed and aimed at Prowl, but before he could fire Bumblebee's leg lashed out and kicked the rifle out of the Decepticon's grip. A second kick struck Bonecrusher in the chin. A third hit his chest plate, lifting him off his feet. Staggering helplessly backwards, Bonecrusher tripped and fell onto a Dairy Queen, utterly flattening the building and its contents.

Prowl looked into the sky and felt relieved. The helicopters got the message after the first one was shot down. The rest turned tail and retreated back to friendly lines just as fast as they could fly.

When Prowl turned to face Bonecrusher again, he saw that Bumblebee and the Decepticon were once more locked in mortal combat—with Bumblebee once more on the receiving end of a vicious pummeling dealt out by his much stronger and far more ruthless adversary. Blow after blow rained down on Bumblebee, striking his helmet, his chest plate, his shoulders and arms. Soon his Cybertronian brain was sending off sparks as Bumblebee reeled.

"That's enough out of you," Prowl declared, uprooting a telephone pole and waving it at Bonecrusher like a baseball bat. With a powerful leap, Prowl launched himself at the Decepticon. He landed between Bonecrusher and the fallen Bumblebee. Before the Decepticon could react, Prowl struck him again and again with the stout telephone pole, until the thick bole splintered and broke over Bonecrusher's spine.

HARDWIRED

Dazed, Bonecrusher crashed to his knees, his head low.

Prowl dropped the pole and put his fists together. Then he brought them down on the back of Bonecrusher's thick neck. With a crash, the Decepticon pitched forward and slammed into a Pier One Imports, knocking down the front wall and caving in the roof.

With a second leap, Prowl was at Bumblebee's side. He helped the struggling Autobot to his feet.

"I think we're even now," Bumblebee said, rising on shaking legs.

"Not yet!" an angry voice said.

Prowl turned to see Bonecrusher, on his feet again, fists raised.

"Duck!" Bumblebee cried. Too late, as it turned out. The mighty metal fists of the vicious Decepticon came down hard on Prowl's shoulder, knocking him sideways. Prowl dropped his laser rifle, and Bonecrusher stomped on it. In a shower of sparks the weapon exploded.

Bumblebee, still weak from the beating he took, tried to pull Prowl away from Bonecrusher. But Prowl wasn't helpless yet. As the Decepticon reached for his throat, Prowl kicked him with both legs. Once again Bonecrusher was lifted off his feet. He flew backward and slammed down hard in the middle of the deserted parking lot, his colossal form leaving a pit in the shape of a giant man in the pavement.

Bonecrusher rose, but slowly. Prowl crawled to his feet and closed on his fallen foe in an effort to finish him off. Bumblebee moved toward Bonecrusher as well, intent on finishing the cruel Decepticon.

Crab-walking backward until his back crashed

against the wall of a Michelin Tire Garage, Bonecrusher sought to escape Prowl's grasp.

Then, unexpectedly, the Michelin Tire Store crumbled into dust and from the center of the smoke and wreckage another Decepticon rose to face Prowl.

This time it was Scrapper, an ingenious Constructicon who was a veritable wizard at designing fortresses for the Decepticons, and equally talented at disguising his creations to blend unnoticed into any surroundings. Indeed, the garage Bonecrusher had retreated to wasn't a garage at all, but one of Scrapper's ingenious booby traps.

Scrapper was in robot mode now, a laser pistol clutched in one fist.

Then the earth began to open near Prowl's feet. He leapt into the air and the ground under him bubbled and boiled as it was reduced to liquid, molten magma. The Constructicon called Mixmaster rose from that surging pit, his burning gaze locked on Prowl as he landed far enough away to be safe. Bumblebee had also jumped into the air, and now watched from the roof of a supermarket on the opposite side of the parking lot.

Mixmaster and Scrapper formed a wall to protect the still dazed Bonecrusher. They both trained their laser pistols on Prowl.

"First we'll finish you," Mixmaster declared in a growl. "Then we'll finish off your little yellow buddy."

"Me think you speak too soon," a voice boomed. Then the earth began to shake as Grimlock charged down the center of the highway, knocking abandoned vehicles aside with each powerful stride.

"Fire!" another voice boomed. "Fire at the Autobots now!"

Prowl looked up to see the brains of the outfit—the

Decepticon called Hook. When Devastator was fully assembled, Hook, a highly intelligent and skilled Constructicon, served as the head, shoulders and brainpower of the formidable, 60-foot tall Decepticon. As usual, Hook was in command—giving orders to Mixmaster and Scrapper.

Suddenly red bolts of burning energy flashed all around Prowl as Mixmaster and Scrapper opened fire.

Fortunately for Prowl, after a few short bursts, the Decepticons were distracted from their target by the charging Dinobot. Tail flashing, Grimlock cut the legs out from under Scrapper. The robot pitched forward, right into the pit of still bubbling magma created by Mixmaster.

With a hiss of steam and a screech of tortured metal—followed by an agonized scream—Scrapper tumbled into the pool of molten rock. Instantly Scrapper's Cybertronian brain was shorted out by the tremendous heat. With an electronic groan, the Decepticon went limp and began to sink in the superheated muck.

Mixmaster dropped his laser pistol and grabbed his partner, dragging Scrapper clear of the magma before the damaged hulk sank like a stone in the white-hot quicksand of melted rock and concrete. Unfortunately, that move turned out to be a mistake, for Grimlock's powerful steel jaws closed on the Decepticon's head before he could resume his attack.

There was a crunching sound, and a shower of sparks. Mixmaster was lifted into the air, still trapped in Grimlock's jaws. Then the Dinobot opened its maw, and Mixmaster—limp and broken—dropped to the ground. He kicked spasmodically and clutched his broken throat as energy bolts poured from his wound.

Grimlock roared and looked up from his fallen prey, fixing an angry stare on Hook, who still hovered in the sky high over the others.

The Decepticon was about to fly to safety when, with an amazing burst of speed, Prowl leaped skyward to crash right into him. With a clang of steel, Prowl and Hook slammed together, grappling as they both plunged toward the ground.

At the last second, Grimlock leapt aside as Hook crash landed right at his feet.

The Decepticon looked up to see Grimlock's gigantic metal foot crash down on his head. Then all went black as his Cybertronian brain was temporarily scrambled.

"Good timing," Prowl declared.

"Bad timing for them," Grimlock grunted.

Prowl looked at the fallen Decepticons. "Four down," he said.

Suddenly an earsplitting explosion rocked the parking lot. The force of the blast kicked up desert dust as it buffeted the Autobots.

"And one to go!" cried Bumblebee, his voice stricken.

Grimlock and Prowl turned to see Bumblebee locked in a fighting grapple with yet another stubborn and angry Decepticon—the formidable supply and transport Constructicon known as Long Haul.

While Dinobot and Autobot watched, the two combatants struggled for a moment, exchanging blows, before their combined weight collapsed the roof of the supermarket they were standing on. As one, Autobot and Decepticon disappeared in a cloud of smoke, fire, and flying debris.

Grimlock and Prowl took off in a run to help their comrade. The ground quaked under the considerable weight of their metal feet. Halfway across the parking lot, Prowl paused to uproot a thick metal pole topped with a giant neon cowboy on top, the logo for a chain of retail stores called The Electronic Roundup. Prowl hefted the object like it was a spear, checking the balance.

"This will have to do," he said.

But before Prowl or Grimlock could reach the shattered supermarket, the back wall of the building exploded outward and a yellow and white blur shot from the wreckage. In a shower of bricks and canned goods, Bumblebee tumbled helplessly through the air, his headlong flight ending only after he smacked into six or seven semi trucks and trailers that were lined up behind The Electronics Roundup store. With a sickening sound of tearing metal and crumbling concrete, the Autobot came to rest in the center of a broken trailer, the wreckage of big-screen televisions, stereo components, DVD players, and personal computers scattered all around him.

"I see a fire sale in *this* store's future," Bumblebee groaned, shaking his metal head to clear his Cybertronian brain.

From the center of the wrecked supermarket, Long Haul rose, a heat-seeking missile launcher in his grip. He aimed at the very center of Bumblebee's chest plate and squeezed the trigger.

Shaking himself from his stupor, Bumblebee quickly transformed into a yellow VW bug and sped away—just as Prowl hurled the sign pole like a spear, only instants before Long Haul could fire!

Even Grimlock froze in his tracks to watch the flight of the two-ton steel pillar tipped with the plastic and neon figure of a happy cowpoke spinning an electronic cord in lieu of a lariat.

Prowl's aim was true, and the pole struck Long Haul's shoulder just as the missile left the tube. The projectile hit a truck behind the Autobot, blasting it to atoms. The neon cowboy disintegrated on impact, but amazingly the pole actually punched a hole through Long Haul's armor in a burst of blue energy.

The Decepticon howled in shock and surprise and the missile launcher dropped from his now limp hand. Blue energy waves flowed from the wound as Long Haul flailed at the shaft that still projected from his back.

Finally, his only functioning hand seized the spear and yanked. Instead of ripping free, the pole snapped, leaving part of the shaft still imbedded in Long Haul's body. Bumblebee, transforming back into robot form, jumped to his feet to attack the Decepticon, but before he could make a move a series of ripping explosions blew up around Long Haul, destroying what little was left of the supermarket.

Prowl turned to see that the Apache attack helicopters had returned, but this time they were armed for bear. Hellfire missiles poured from the launchers mounted on the Apache's stubby "wings," enveloping the helpless Constructicon in smoke and fire.

With an angry roar, Long Haul transformed before their eyes.

Metal refolded itself, and what was a giant robot became what looked like an average-looking dump truck. With a squeal of tires, Long Haul pealed away too fast for Grimlock or Prowl to chase him.

They didn't have too. The helicopters roared over their heads in pursuit of the retreating Decepticon, machine guns blazing and missiles firing. Within a minute, the truck raced down the center of the highway, knocking aside abandoned vehicles as it went. Hot on its heels came the helicopters.

Bumblebee trotted over to his partner. Prowl stood, legs braced wide, watching as the Decepticon and the attack choppers faded andwere lost in the distance.

"Nice throw!" Bumblebee said.

Prowl shrugged. "I was lucky."

Bumblebee chuckled. "So was I!"

"None of us lucky," Grimlock roared. "We let Decepticons get away."

Bumblebee and Prowl followed Grimlock's gaze. On the other side of the vast parking lot, the pit of lava still bubbled, but there was no sign of Bonecrusher, Mixmaster, Hook, or Scrapper. Like Long Haul, they managed to make their escape.

"And we didn't even see hide nor hair of Scavenger," Prowl said grimly.

Bumblebee and Grimlock said nothing. They knew that the presence of these Decepticons was an ominous development, for Bonecrusher, Mixmaster, Hook, Scrapper, Long Haul and Scavenger had the potential to come together to form the awesome Decepticon called Devastator!

"We go," Grimlock growled. "More fighting ahead."

"That, my good friend, is an understatement," Bumblebee replied.

The sleek black Scorpion M515 touched down gently in the blazing desert, its blades lazily chopping through the hot, humid air. Spike and Franklin emerged, their boots sinking into the sand.

"This is as far as I can go," the pilot, a rail-thin man named Chuck "Chubby" Cherwonowitz breathlessly informed them. "Sorry. I know it's about a mile east of the drop, but…"

He waved at a flickering control panel. Green radar circles and other sensor devices revealed multiple bogies in the sky.

Franklin was a highly-placed United States government agent tasked with learning all there was to know about the disappearance of the Transformers and the possible role of the Followers in that incident. He had multiple divisions of fellow operatives assisting him at all times. Naturally, he was well aware that Bumblebee, Prowl, Grimlock and some private militia had battled U.S. forces on U.S. soil. News of that encounter had been instantly transmitted to him via the "voice"—or "voices"—he heard in his head. Global satellite imaging had kept his people well aware of what was happening in the desert. And Franklin, in turn, had informed Spike of the situation.

Spike had expressed mixed feelings about the actions of Bumblebee, Prowl, Grimlock, and their companions. Like everyone else, he did not want anotherLos Angeles incident. On the other hand, Starscream was becoming *entrenched* in Las Vegas. What if other Decepticons who had not yet come to Vegas decided to take over other cities either in the U.S. or abroad? By allowing Starscream to remain in place, the citizens of the world were opening the door to possible "copycat" takeovers. And yes, the people of Vegas had agreed to Starscream's terms—or, at least, some percentage of them had—but what choice did those people truly have? Spike was certain that some who had sided with Starscream were acting out of pure greed, but that many others were living in occupied territory against their will.

He had considered contacting Bumblebee—such an act seemed possible, at least, with Franklin's connections and the technology at his disposal, perhaps by means of a cell phone call routed through a private audio channel to Bumblebee—but he had chosen not to do so. He wasn't sure what we would say to Bumblebee. Would he say, "Hey, fella, back off from there?" Or, "Kick their butts!"

If he couldn't answer that question, he decided, he had no business attempting to contact the Autobot.

The current push by Bumblebee, Prowl, Grimlock and the private militia against the Constructicons had been reported to Franklin, and then to Spike—practically blow-by-blow—by the people with whom Franklin worked. The attack had opened up a narrow window of opportunity for Franklin and Spike. Starscream's forces were being diverted from their standard border patrol, allowing this small craft to enter hostile airspace and land here.

"Get the hell out of here," Franklin said. "No one will notice us, keep yourself safe."

Hauling their equipment, they cleared out of the chopper's way, their heads low, hands on their hats to keep them from whipping off as the breeze kicked up, intensified, then faded as the Scorpion rose high into the sky. For the first time, Spike really noticed that the bubble-like front window, which was split in two, truly made the speck disappearing into the sky look insectoid.

"So now we walk," Spike said.

Franklin's smile was thin. "Unless you expect me to carry you."

They trudged, their tan fatigues blending with the lazily churning sand.

"Question for you," Spike asked.

"Uh-huh."

"All that stuff you told me about that girl helping you find a sense of purpose…any of that true?"

"Yeah. Why?"

"What happened to her? With all the money you had, with all this tech that's floating around, it just seems like—"

Sweat poured into Franklin's eyes as he cut the other man off. "She died. Nothing could stop it."

"Um." Spike wasn't much of a poker player, but he knew enough to look for tells. Franklin always looked down and off to one side when he was hiding something...just like he was doing now. "What about those voices in your head? Keep you up nights."

"Only one voice. Sometimes, it keeps me sane." The operative nodded at standing stone in the distance. "Talking like this can drain you. Let's hold off on any more talk until we get up there."

They reached the standing stone, each soaked in sweat. Franklin dug around in the sand, found a chain, and yanked it up with both hands.

The sand shifted, whispering, and a huge rectangular plank, ten by eighteen feet, was torn from the earth. A trapdoor. Sand hissed as it dove into the darkness below. Franklin asked Spike to wait as he walked down a ramp into the abyss.

Spike was halfway through a refreezeable water, his body sweating out the liquid nearly as quickly as he could drink it when he heard a rumbling and saw the black and gray Desert Rover jeep emerge, Franklin behind the wheel.

"We're gassed up, loaded up. Let's go!" Franklin said.

Looking to the sky and seeing no signs of Transformers or the military, Spike nodded and got inside. Franklin tapped a button on the dash and the doorway into the sand passage closed by itself. The wind churning the sand would cover it over quickly enough.

"Nice timing," Franklin said, the air turned up high. "Your friends getting involved, I mean. Bumblebee, Prowl...but Grimlock? I'm not sure I'm getting that one, or who those guys are who are with them."

"What are you saying?" Spike asked, the jeep slicing through the sand.

"I'm suggesting that we *may* have just lucked out on several fronts—or that we're following someone else's gameplan." Franklin gripped the wheel tightly as the spires of Las Vegas appeared in the distance. "We've got to be careful, because from this point out, it gets really, really tricky."

CHAPTER
NINETEEN

Megatron slaughtered the last of three aliens the Keepers had set him against in the arena. His energy sword, supplied by the Keepers, raised high, he took in the wild applause of the humans gathered to witness his victory—and felt nothing. These humans were pitiful, unevolved creatures, and he would gladly kill them all, if only to shut them up.

At his feet lay a biped with slightly more potential, a crystalline lifeform whose body had properties reminiscent of Energon, the substance that powered the weaponry and the living metal forms of the Transformers themselves. Megatron wondered if this shattered creature had the power to absorb Energon emissions and perhaps process and output these energies in greater quantities, a trait it had displayed with other energy emissions when he'd run it through with the energy sword. Ultimately, he'd had to tear the creature limb from limb to kill it, which had been a crude display, but highly satisfying. If these aliens could boost the power of Energon, they might make a useful slave race after Megatron conquered Cybertron, then spread his influence into the galaxy.

Yes, at long last he would be the conqueror that destiny had always intended for him to be. That knowledge made his current circumstances easier to deal with. He knew there were greater satisfactions ahead. In fact, he sensed that those developments might be imminent.

"Keepers!" he called out boldly. "A word."

A hush fell upon the arena, and no answering voice immediately sounded to Megatron's request. The Decepticon knew this was a risky gambit. The Keepers were prideful beings, like himself, however, they had promised him a partnership of equals, not a master and slave relationship. Why should equals not be allowed to call upon one another whenever they so desired?

Yet...there was still no answer to his summons.

Megatron felt the slightest flicker of something like doubt—then a cone of darkness appeared, cutting him off from the view of the human and various alien audiences. A Transformer—or a thing that looked much like a Transformer—stood silently a dozen yards away, a brilliant light, bright as a blue-white star, descending on his crimson, gray and black metallic form as he surveyed the ruined bodies of Megatron's latest kills.

"You serve us well."

Megatron chuckled inwardly. The Keeper was testing him, and perhaps displaying some minor annoyance at Megatron's imprudence. "I serve no one but myself. It is fortunate that our goals coincide."

The Keeper looked up at him, blue-white eyes blazing. *"What is it you want?"*

"A battle is coming," Megatron said.

"A battle has just been fought." The Keeper swept his hand, indicating the savaged alien forms around them.

"This was exercise, little more," Megatron replied. "You know my potential as you know my *will*...and I know yours."

"Your chance to slay the one designated Optimus Prime will soon be upon you—this is true."

Megatron spoke freely, certain that the Keepers had cloaked not only their appearance, but also the sound of their voices from the spectators. He pictured the humans, so easily panicked, clinging to each other in fear at the very notion that a Keeper lay within this field of darkness. It amused him greatly.

"When I kill Optimus, I want to do more than destroy his body," Megatron said. "I want to see his spirit broken, I want him to know what he could have been, what all of his pathetic Autobots might have become, and now, never will."

The Keeper angled his head slightly, signaling Megatron to continue.

"I wish to be evolved," the Decepticon said. "This form I inhabit, while mighty, is far from all-powerful. This could not have been what you, the progenitors, had envisioned for us. Make me more than I am, Keeper. Unleash my potential, *transform* me into a nightmare with powers and abilities I could not even hope to imagine. Make me greater than any Decepticon or Autobot in recorded history. Upgrade me in your image."

A long moment of silence passed. Then:

"You... you appear to be confused as to the nature of our roles," the Keeper said.

This surprised Megatron. "In what way? We are equals. That is what you told me."

"Equals?" the Keeper asked, raising his hand and sending the startled Decepticon into the source of the light high above. Megatron flew, powerless to control his slightest movement. The light from on high was searing. Some form of radiation that Megatron's sensors couldn't identify scorched his metal hide.

He felt the heat reach into the core of his body and struggled in his own mind to understand what was happening—and why. He had done nothing but offered to *honor* the Keepers by achieving his potential, by assuming a form that was more suited to that of a conqueror of worlds. Yet the Keepers were punishing him... destroying him!

"Do not speak to us of equality," the Keeper roared. *"When you can stand unscathed in the heart of a star, when you can rain fire upon the surfaces of a thousand worlds at once, when you can do what you will, when you wish it, we will discuss our 'equality.' At present, you have overstepped your bounds, interpreted our past conversation in a way that suits your vanity and ego, and for that you wish us to endow you with power you cannot even define?"*

Megatron felt an invisible hand batter him down and away from the light, sending him crashing to the floor of the arena. He struck the remains of the crystalline warrior, smashing them to bits, sending sparkling diamond-like shards to rip through everything in the cone of darkness—including the body of the Keeper. He grunted, sparks tearing across his shadowy frame, and stumbled back under the assault.

Rising on weakened arms, Megatron saw the Keeper literally fall to pieces. The torso's upper half dropped to the right, its bottom half to the left, the head dropped in three slices, the appendages fell forward, back, to either side.

It was horrific, yet—beautiful.

"I... killed you," Megatron said, stunned.

An invisible wall of force smashed against him as a voice raged, *"We cannot die!"*

Megatron rocked and fought to stay on his feet as

he was pummeled from every side, the voices of the Keepers rising with the attack. They railed at him, derided him, proclaimed him a fool. Then, just as suddenly as the attack began, it was over, and the Keeper who had been destroyed stood directly before Megatron, whole once more, the cone of darkness still intact around them. Megatron looked down at his metal body and saw that the damage they had rendered to him had been repaired in the same nanosecond it took the Keepers to rebuild the hollow shell before him.

"Our interests align, it is true," the Keeper said, *"but do not confuse convenience for anything more than that. Know your place, respect it, and us, and one day, you may well earn the reward you seek, Megatron. Otherwise, the punishment you have just experienced will be little more than a taste of what is to come."*

The cone of darkness disappeared and Megatron found himself exactly as he had been before he demanded the presence of the Keepers: sword raised overhead, the human crowd cheering.

Did the Keepers possess the power to turn back time? Or had the onlookers—and he, himself—been placed in stasis, their bodies repositioned like storefront mannequins, their collective consciousness restored at the exact moment of the Keeper's choosing?

Megatron said nothing this time, he merely fulfilled his function as reigning champion, leaving the stage when his cue arrived. Yet he noticed the body of the crystalline alien was still shattered into shard, an indicator that it was the second of his two theories on what had occurred that was the more likely.

Back in his cell, surrounded by images of Cybertron in flames, memories recreated to soothe or lull him into a false sense of security, Megatron thought long and hard about what he had experienced. The Keepers said that they would not evolve him to the next stage of his logical development, the time had not yet come when such an act was appropriate, and they had tortured him when he had done nothing more than remind them of their own promises and proclamations.

Was the truth that he had overstepped his bounds, that, in fact, they could easily fulfill his desires? Or was the display meant to distract him from the simple truth that what they said they would not do, they, in point of truth, *could not* do?

Megatron had no answers, only suspicions. Yet in a mind as dark and malevolent as his, suspicions often equaled facts, and courses of action were often plotted on far less data than what he had culled from this encounter.

The battle was coming... but his objectives, and his plan of attack, were changing.

At the end of the long, desolate highway, New Vegas rose in the distance. The towering hotels and casinos seemed bare somehow in the harsh light of day, desperate and alone. Or so it seemed to Spike as he sat beside Franklin, his mind awash in panic at the more immediate sight that he would have preferred to put out of his thoughts completely: Half a mile ahead, four cars that looked like police cruisers evolved into something like Humvees, or even high tech tanks in compact packages—blocked the road. An armored patrol, a contingent of a dozen men and women wearing midnight blue fatigues and silver and black body shielding, each carrying weapons the size of small cannons, waited at the blockade.

"So what do we do?" Spike asked.

Franklin didn't answer.

"No, I mean it, what's the plan?" the younger man demanded.

"The only plan is that there is no plan," Franklin said. "Well, that's what a buddy of mine keeps saying in my ear. Actually, I think it's meant to annoy me, or something."

Spike felt his stomach muscles tighten as they cruised closer to the blockade, several of the cannons swiveling in their direction. "You mean you don't have a plan?"

"Didn't say that. Just don't feel like sharing."

Looking at the weaponry and armor of the Decepticon militia, or so Spike had inwardly named them, Spike wondered if *he* was the plan, if Franklin had simply decided that if they met with resistance it would be relying on TF-based tech, which Spike could somehow deactivate. If that was it, then the agent had come up with a lousy plan, because Spike still had no conscious idea how he had pulled off taking down the augments and healing Franklin when they'd been attacked.

Franklin pulled to a stop forty yards before the enforcers, making the closest walk the distance to their vehicle. Three approached, a woman backed by two men. Franklin kept his hands on the dashboard and urged Spike to do the same.

"I don't see diplomatic envoy tags," the woman said. She had auburn hair piled high and leading to a ponytail trailing into the back of her shirt. The mirror shades she wore had tiny flickering displays in bright green and amber.

"Well, we're certainly emissaries of good cheer," Franklin told her, his gaze trained firmly ahead.

The woman stepped back and fired two short energy bursts at their tires, blowing out the rubber with sharp hisses, bangs, and pops. The vehicle sagged on Franklin's side.

"Get out of the car," she said.

He acquiesced with that same annoying confidence he'd displayed from the beginning. "Since you put it nicely," he said, opening the door and stepping out.

"You, too!" she commanded, and all Spike could see were the barrels of two more energy cannons aimed at his chest. With shaking hands, he fumbled for the door handle, his mind going blank when faced with the simple notion of how to work it, then he got his fears under control, opened the door, and stumbled out. He kept waiting to hear a grunt, to see a blur of action, to know Franklin had gone into overdrive and taken out the militia. Of course, there were still nine or ten more near the barricade...

Standing away from the vehicle, Spike looked at it with a desperate, forlorn expression. He'd expected concussion cannons to rise from the fenders, or a white sound beacon to appear and emit a frequency so intense it would scramble the heads of the cops, or soldiers, or whatever they were.

Nothing.

Franklin was slammed to the hood, his arms dragged behind his back, heavy shackles attached to his wrists.

"You do know this city isn't going to be safe for much longer, I assume?" Franklin asked. "I mean, I'm sure there's a news blackout and everything, but that whole business with Devastator is something you guys must have at least heard from here."

Of course Franklin knew about what had happened

with Devastator in the desert. His people had kept him well informed through the "voice" in his head.

The question for Franklin was whether these cops—or private soldiers—had been kept in the loop by their new boss. He studied their reactions to his words, and had the distinct impression they had no idea what was happening and that his casual statement had unnerved many of them.

Good. Just looking at them, and how quickly they had fallen under the sway of the Decepticons, had unnerved Franklin. A little payback was certainly in order.

"Hey, he's just got our best interests at heart," the female officer said. "We got this guy all wrong."

Spike was still waiting for Franklin to do *something* when another of the militia grabbed him from behind and cuffed him. They were dragged to a revamped squad car, jammed into the back, and driven off.

As they entered New Vegas city limits, Spike wondered how had so much changed so quickly? Were the Decepticons really this efficient? How had they bent the populace to their will so easily?

"I doubt you're gonna like the holding facilities we've got for uninvited guests," the officer behind the wheel said. "They're down underneath one of the old casinos. Dark and scary, I'm telling you. I mean, if I were the two of you, I'd make up my mind to cooperate as much as possible. Maybe you can be put to some constructive use. Otherwise, you probably won't see daylight again for years."

Spike's heart was racing. Franklin had just *let* them be captured! What was he playing at?

As they reached a light, Spike found out the answer.

A silver van ripped through a light and spun their way with a loud screech of tires. Spike didn't even have time to tense up as the van struck the cruiser head on, sending them crashing back into the car behind them at the stop light. Spike and Franklin—as well as the officers up front—were strapped in with a seatbelt made of a fabric Spike didn't recognize, one that seemed to attenuate its properties directly to their bodies, restricting their movements and preventing whiplash, shattered knees, concussions, and so on, without causing cracked ribs or severe bruising.

The officers were out of the car in seconds, moving toward either side of the van, handguns that had been augmented into energy weapons held before them. Spike watched as each officer stiffened, hands reaching wildly for their necks, before they crumbled to the ground. Then a handful of guys in soft gray designer suits were breaking from the small crowd of gawkers on the street, racing their way. One slid behind the wheel of the cruiser, unlocking the back doors from the front, while others opened the doors and hurried the pair out.

Quick hands worked the chains binding their wrists, freeing them, then Spike and Franklin were ushered toward the van, which was driverless, but still under firm control.

"Hold on, wait a minute!" Spike said. "Who are you people? What's going on here?"

Franklin nudged him closer to the van. "All will be explained. Come on!"

The closest *GQ*-looking guy had what looked like a game control console in his hands, and he used it to close the doors once he, Franklin, Spike, and several of the other sharp-dress men were inside. Then he used it to haul the van back into traffic, and send them speeding off in the opposite direction.

Spike turned to the guy who seemed to be running

things from his jazzed up game console. "Those cops, or whatever they were," Spike said urgently. "Did you—"

"They'll be fine," the guy with the gaming device said without looking up. "They're all good people, just misguided. Happens easily enough in this city, especially when things get dicey."

"Where are you taking us?" Spike asked.

"To the guy that sent you an invitation with that homing signal," Franklin said, breaking in. "Don't you get it? These are *his* people. It's smart. Having them all dress and look the same makes it hard for anyone on the street to give individual IDs on any of them."

"So, were your people talking with the guy who sent that signal?" Spike asked.

"Of course not," Franklin said. "It was just a matter of trusting my instincts. I didn't think he'd let us be taken in and I was right. He had his people watching us, probably right from the second we hit the border patrol, and from that moment on, they were planning how to break us out."

"You got it," the guy with the game console said. "You folks got here just in time, too. From what *we've* seen, Vegas isn't going to be a great place for kicking back and relaxing much longer. There's a small army heading this way."

"And who's funding that?" Franklin asked.

"Could be our boss," the guy with the game console said. "Or it could be our guy keeping good tabs on things. Just hang tight. You'll be able to ask him yourself in just a little bit."

Paul stood alone, surveying those he had sworn to protect.

As the Keepers had promised, the white room had returned to its initial programming, providing pleasant distractions from the harsh reality that should any of their champions fail in a contest, one or all of them might die. The discord had died down, the splintered cells of dissidents among the populace quickly disintegrating as each person retreated to his or her comfortable world of more pleasant memories. This time, no one complained that there were no new joys to experience beyond those culled from their pasts; at least, no one had complained *yet*. Paul was certain that, given time, the grievances would rise again.

He was also certain, on some primal, instinctive level, that their time was short.

Paul and Melony had barely spoken to each other since their most private moments had been laid bare by the Keepers. He knew her secret, but had no idea if she was aware of this or not. A part of him wanted to talk to her and deal with this situation directly but then the door to the white room opened and his opportunity was lost.

The lights came into the room. The humans gathered together without even a command by their captors into a single file line in preparation for being taken to the arena to witness another battle. Once the humans were in formation, the door to the white room opened and the group of over 200 humans were guided down the long main corridor by the lights.

Paul realized it was different this time. There was a sense of finality to the proceedings as they marched that only a few of the other humans seemed to sense. Those who did sense it were extraordinarily quiet, walking with their heads down. Paul glanced behind him and could see tears in a girl's eyes as she glanced quickly up at the ceiling. He could see her mouth moving silently and forming words that appeared to be part of a prayer.

When the entourage got to the junction where they usually turned right to get to the main arena, they did not. Paul stared ahead and could see that the hallway was starting to go downwards. Paul could see nothing ahead but the descending corridor into darkness. It was like walking into an abyss. They dropped deeper and deeper, these new passages were darker and more twisting than any the lights had led them through in the past.

The lights had been leading the troupe for over an hour by Paul's reckoning and there was still no sign of their progress slowing as they marched into the nether reaches of the Keeper's domain. Terror gripped everyone as they continued their constant progress into the darkness. In front of him, Paul could see people shaking and hugging themselves as they marched.

Paul thought of a film he had seen once about prisoners of war during World War II being led into the wilderness to be slaughtered and buried in a mass grave. Was this what the Keepers had in store for them? Perhaps the battle had already been fought and the Transformers had lost so now all their lives were forfeit. But if that were the case then why lead them anywhere? Why not just kill them all in the white room? Why postpone the end? Paul shook his head, no. There had to be another reason for what the Keepers were doing.

He thoughts turned to Melony and the vision he had seen of her sister's violent death as a result of the Transformers. They had both seen the worst of the gifts that the Transformers had bestowed on mankind since their arrival on Earth. Melony felt betrayed by everyone in her life: by her parents for dying and leaving her responsible for her kid sister, by her past boyfriends who didn't understand how having such demands put on her made it hard for her to commit to a relationship, and by her sister who just had to die when Melony had finally made time for her. Paul could barely see Melony walking about ten people ahead of him on line.

Then Paul heard something, barely audible at first. He turned around to see if anyone else heard something but the others just continued their forced march. A voice whispered in his ear.

"A lifetime of betrayal. It's interesting to consider what that does to a person, don't you think?" said the Keeper.

Paul tried to ignore the voice.

"She will betray you. Her only interest lies in serving her own need for vengeance. When the time comes, she will prevent you from saving anyone at all if it means the survival of the Transformers. That is her nature, a thing she cannot, will not, transcend."

Paul put his hands over his ears but he could not stop the voice from reaching his mind. Melony had good reason to hate the Transformers—that was why she became a Follower in the first place.

"How do you save someone who doesn't want to be saved?"

He wasn't trying to "save" anyone, Paul thought. It sounded like a question that Father Simon would have asked when he was in seminary. But there were no easy answers to that question for Paul.

"The only way you can win is not to play the game."

Paul considered the last statement. What if the Transformers decided that they would not play along with the Keepers? Is that why they were not being taken to the arena? Did the Transformers decide not to champion the humans any longer? Were they no longer playing the game?

The voice continued. *"You have been an interesting specimen to observe. How do you feel about the finite nature of your existence? Do you fear its end? We have only to think about ending your life and you will be torn apart, like an animal. Doesn't the power we have over you, the ability to engineer your fate in any way we see fit, make you tremble?"*

The cop thought about these questions but honestly he was tired of being afraid of dying, tired of having someone else being responsible for whether he lived or died. These Keepers only knew about how to instill fear and terror in people. He had run up against plenty of people in his life who knew how to do the same things. One thing he had learned as a cop was that if you allow the criminal to have power over you because he can kill you then you better give up the force. There are always people in life who can have power over you, if you let them. But there was always a choice and the Keepers didn't seem to understand that choice.

"You have such a great need to believe in something, anything, greater than yourself. Why not believe in us as your gods? Our power dwarfs that of the Transformers, and our goals, and ways of achieving our goals, are every bit as mysterious as that of the deity to whom you once swore devotion."

And to think, he was once afraid of the power of the Transformers. Compared to the Keepers, they were simply robot versions of the old cowboy movies. Some wore white hats and some wore black hats but it was always the innocent town folk that got hurt and killed in the shoot outs, the towns they lived in that got raised to the ground and had to be rebuilt.

The Keepers were even further from any concept of God that he had studied than the Transformers. The Keepers knew nothing of the higher good or of devoting your life to the service of others. They knew nothing of love or sacrifice. All they understood was want and need. He could not believe in anything that didn't understand the complexities of the human condition.

"Your need is every bit as great as hers, but while she embraces her need wholeheartedly, you deny yours."

Paul snorted at hearing this statement from the Keepers. It just went to show that they really had no understanding of humans, especially someone like him. If he embraced every need that he had, then Paul would never achieve anything of significance. He would be ruled by his baser instincts and he would never have even thought of devoting himself to the church or to anything else for that matter.

Paul glanced ahead and could see that the lights were slowing down. The prisoners had reached their destination. Before the lights was an entryway from which no further illumination came. It appeared to be just an empty void. The lights moved forward and into the gateway. At first, Paul could only see the line in front of him being slowly swallowed up by the impenetrable darkness, then the crowd was moving faster, those in the back anxious to discover what lay ahead, the group surging forward into the blackness. Finally, Paul reached the entrance and paused for only a moment before following the others inside.

On the other side, there was a vast chamber that reminded Paul of photos he had seen of great underground caverns, yet what he was gazing upon had, to some degree, been engineered. The structure was enormous, Paul could not even see the roof. All he could see above was hundreds of enormous stalactites that descended from nothingness at least a hundred feet above the ground. Each one glistened with an eerie green phosphorescence which appeared to be the only light source.

The whole area was a huge spider's web of narrow stone paths, which were thirty feet above an enormous pit, broken up by occasional raised, larger areas where at least twenty to thirty people could stand comfortably. Paul maneuvered around people to get close enough to the edge of path to see down into the pit. What Paul saw didn't fill him with confidence about what the Keepers had planned for them. The entire pit was filled with boiling lava and unless Paul was mistaken, the lava was slowly rising closer and closer to the tops of the stone paths.

The only words that came into Paul's mind stumbled out of his mouth before he could stop them.

"Oh, hell."

Optimus Prime knew the time for final battle had come. He wasn't sure how he knew—he merely sensed it. Perhaps it was that connection he had felt to the Keepers that had given him awareness of what he would soon be facing, or it might simply have been finely honed battle instincts letting him know the fight was coming. In any case, the summoning lights had arrived, and the doorway to his cell had opened. His friend Jazz stood in the hall, waiting for him.

They walked a good distance silently, Jazz's usual light tone nowhere in evidence.

"For Bluestreak," Jazz said finally.

Optimus seconded the notion.

The spines of the world around them darkened as the lights turned down a tunnel ahead of them, casting the dead, hollowed, techno-organic shell surrounding them in even greater shadow.

They turned the corner, and saw the light of the arena in the far distance.

"Just one thing," Jazz said, slowing a little as he and Prime walked side-by-side. "Your naming your successor."

"I think that's pretty obvious."

"I just want you to know... I could do the job, but I don't want to. So if you decide to do something stupid, do me a favor and get us both killed, okay?"

Optimus nodded. "Consider it done."

Ahead, the arena beckoned...

For the last time.

CHAPTER TWENTY

Spike and Franklin left the van, which had pulled up behind a Porsche. He watched as an elegantly dressed woman graciously accepted the hand of the college-age valet intent on helping her from her car before the entrance to the opulent and towering Buccaneer Hotel and Casino. The handsome, dark-haired valet was dressed in the wardrobe of a sanitized cinematic pirate, complete with an eye patch, knee-high black boots and leggings, and a garish shirt open to the waist to reveal his well-defined chest.

They don't know, Spike thought. *They don't have any idea what's coming. Starscream actually made them feel safe.*

Realizing this was disquieting, but there was nothing he could do. He and Franklin followed the Gucci boys inside the hotel, which carried the pirate motif throughout the environs. The walls were curved wood, with panels that could be slid back to reveal views of a raging ocean or a pirate battle at sea. An authentic cannon was set in the center of the lobby, which was filled with people even so early in the day. Hotel employees wandered around in full pirate regalia.

Attached to the hotel was a large shopping mall covered by a vaulted sky. A placard told him that every three hours, the artificial sky changed from dusk to dawn. He'd spotted several people staring up longingly at the ceiling.

"You think this is something, the Forum at Caesar's Palace has seventy-four stores, including Louis Vuitton and Gucci," the "gamemaster" said enthusiastically.

One of his companions added, "I like the Animatrons of the Roman gods. It's funny with those sensors and stuff, it's actually like they're talking to you, or each other."

They passed through a long wooden hallway lit by electric torches. Floorboards creaked beneath their feet. Concealed speakers hissed the rushing sounds of the ocean. A gaggle of young women passed them, each drunk out of their minds. Fair game for any predator, human or otherwise.

Ignoring the signs for the convention center and meeting rooms, they came to the vast gambling hall, which had been styled to resemble a Daliesque version of Madagascar, one of the most notorious pirate havens in history. Sealed glass cases with relics from pirate ships dotted the floor, along with roulette wheels sitting on tables that looked like sections of shattered hulls rising from the floor. Hucksters passed out fliers concerning the next night's floorshow. Traditionally dressed blackjack dealers were intermingled with scantily clad women who proudly told everyone they were pirate "wenches."

This place could be coming down around their ears any second, Spike thought. "We should say something. Clear these people out of here."

Franklin shook his head. "They wouldn't listen."

The gamemaster agreed. "We have emergency measures in place, ground and air evac standing by... if we try and sound an alarm, the Decepticons will know it, and short it out before it can make a sound. As it is, we're pumping enough white noise in that frequency they can't pick up, along with false voice tracks on loops that eventually they're going to realize there's trouble here. But by that time..."

Spike nodded. By then, Grimlock and the others would be here, and the city would soon after be crumbling.

Then it was on to a narrow hall where a half-dozen elevators waited. The Gucci guys led Spike and Franklin to one marked 'private' and used a passkey to bring it to the lobby and open its shining, golden, double doors. They rode to the penthouse, and were led a spacious series of rooms decorated with gleaming plaques and trophies, garish posters for ultra-gory video games, and an incongruous selection of *Jetsons*-style Art Deco meets retro-futuristic furniture.

In the center of it all stood a kid who couldn't have been more than nineteen, so far as Spike could tell. He gestured to the Gucci guys, who scattered to the four corners of the penthouse, leaving them alone.

"It's nice of you to drop by," said the guy wearing his baseball cap turned backward. His navy blue and white football jersey was dotted with ketchup stains from the overstuffed hot dog he'd been eating, and his white satin sweats and shiny new Reeboks picked up the golden glint of the afternoon sun from the penthouse suite window. The brand name *High Rollahz* was emblazoned on his sleeve, the name of the boy band scheduled to do a satellite concert tie-in to the Transformers reality show. The guy caught Spike's gaze and tugged quickly on his sleeve with a short laugh. "Yeah, one of our franchises. I know the whole thing's a little like an inside job, but that's what packaging is all about. CAA puts together a movie, they're looking to attach actors, a director, everybody else, from their own stable. Same deal here."

"Hold it," Spike said, "am I supposed to know who you are?"

"Not if you don't follow the trades. "I'm Darren Norbert. Welcome to my happy home."

Outside, an explosion sounded in the distance.

"Well," Darren said, "my home for the next couple of minutes, anyway. I've been looking forward to meeting you for a long time, Spike. We're going to do incredible things together." He smiled, his teeth inhumanly white. "In fact, it's honestly well within the bounds to say that together, we're going to become gods..."

Optimus Prime and Jazz walked into the arena and found Megatron already waiting.

The Decepticon leader stood fast, looking ready for a fight. "At last, it comes to this. Optimus Prime, you and I—"

Prime surged forward, not giving his opponent the chance to finish. With a savage cry of rage, Optimus dug one hand into Megatron's chest and closed the other around his throat. With all his power, he *threw* Megatron into the air, then drew his pulse cannon and blasted at his mortal enemy's body with every salvo he had at his disposal, driving the Decepticon higher and higher into the air, until Megatron's body reached the high ceiling—and burst through it!

A wail sounded as the vacuum of space whooshed into the arena, dragging at the Transformers, a scream as if something *living* had just been stabbed, its flesh torn and violated.

Something that was *not* Megatron.

The Decepticon held fast to the steadily self-repairing tear in the arena's ceiling, and climbed back inside, tumbling hard to the ground as the rupture closed and the vacuum that had been tugging at the Autobots faded.

Laying on his back, his chest dented and penetrated by the force of Prime's unprecedented attack, Megatron laughed.

"It's good to know you'll meet your fate happily," Prime said, nodding to Jazz, who fingered his weapon and stood over Megatron, aiming his cannon at the Decepticon's head.

"Idiot…" Megatron said, still looking up at the wound in the ceiling, amusement still tingeing his words. "It's all in the timing."

A sudden wave of force swept Jazz and Prime away from Megatron, tossing them off their feet and smashing them against a far wall.

"HOW DARE YOU!" screeched the Keeper.

The voice was not only emotional—it was *pained*.

Suddenly, Optimus Prime knew why the Keepers never revealed themselves, except, perhaps, in mechanical husks. The truth came to Prime in a single, shattering instant,

What they had seen from space, the dead, inert bodies of techno-organic leviathans in myriad configurations…these had been the bodies of the Keepers. Of course the Keepers could never show themselves in a way that the Transformers or most life forms were accustomed. They had been hiding in plain sight from the beginning.

"That's right, Ahab," Megatron said, rising slowly. "Welcome to the belly of the whale."

Prime looked around at the vastness surrounding him. They had been *within* the Keepers all of this time!

By late afternoon Grimlock, Bumblebee and Prowl

had made considerable headway in penetrating the city of Las Vegas. Since their short but intense—and ultimately stalemated battle with Bonecrusher and the other Decepticons, the Autobots had not seen any sign of their enemy.

As they cautiously approached the downtown area, there were more and more signs of normalcy. Traffic jammed the roadways, and the busy sidewalks were thick with pedestrians. To avoid attracting undo attention, Prowl convinced the pig-headed Grimlock that maybe a fifty-foot tall robot that looked and acted like an angry *T-rex* just might not be able to move through the busy streets of an American city totally unnoticed—whereas both Prowl and Bumblebee could transform into innocent looking cars and move covertly and swiftly to the heart of Decepticon territory. From there they could send back data to the private army waiting to take back the city from its Decepticon masters.

"Grimlock no like this idea!" the stubborn Dinobot insisted. But in the end, sanity prevailed—of a sort. Prowl and Bumblebee were given permission to make an advance reconnaissance run down Las Vegas Boulevard to the center of the Las Vegas strip, while Grimlock waited in an abandoned parking garage on the edge of Fremont Street, where he could quickly respond to a distress signal from Prowl or Bumblebee, if necessary.

With Grimlock safely ensconced, Prowl and Bumblebee transformed—Prowl into a sleek, black and white patrol car, Bumblebee into a little yellow compact. A few minutes later they slipped unnoticed into the regular flow of traffic. As they approached Fremont Street, the crowd became thicker. Over the heads of the pedestrians, Prowl could see the glitter of a million lights just ahead of them.

"Looks normal," Prowl observed. "For Las Vegas, anyway."

"The humans in this town are behaving as if a war had never broken out in their back yard," Bumblebee replied. "Just how self-absorbed can you get? No wonder they call this place Sin City."

The twin Autobots pulled over to the curb and parked near the four-block long covered area of casinos, shops, restaurants and assorted adult entertainment establishments called Glitter Gulch, which runs along Fremont Street, the older, less popular part of the Las Vegas strip. Dubbed the "Fremont Street Experience" this area resembled a huge covered shopping mall filled with neon, with a multi-million dollar digital lightshow constantly projected onto the arched ceiling. From their vantage point, the Autobots could hear the oohs and ahhs of spectators, but they could not enter the "Experience" because the thoroughfares were all for pedestrians only.

Bumblebee and Prowl were both thinking the same thing. It was Prowl who first voiced his concern.

"There's an army of liberation roaring through the desert right now, and we're practically on ground zero. There's going to be a lot of collateral damage in a fight," the Autobot said ominously.

"True enough," said Bumblebee. "But maybe these people will gain some sense and surrender."

"They might want to surrender," Prowl replied, "but will their Decepticon masters permit it? That's really the question."

Prowl activated his communications array and began sending images of Fremont Street and its surroundings back to the secret army's command center, hoping that the commander of the military operation might rethink his strategy. He continued his surveillance activities for several minutes, beaming any information that might be valuable in the coming campaign—or valuable in stopping the invasion in its tracks if need be.

"These humans sure design some crazy looking buildings," Bumblebee observed. "Look at that casino over there. And that theme restaurant." Bumblebee chuckled. "And check out that nutty looking red building over there. I don't see any doors or windows... How can anyone get in or out."

Something in Bumblebee's statement bothered Prowl, and he focused in on the building in question, using not only his telescopic vision, but also his infrared scanners and his energy detection systems.

"There are a lot of unusual energies being emitted from that structure," Prowl declared.

"You're too suspicious," Bumblebee told his partner. "That's probably an electronic transformer or something—it takes a lot of juice to light up this town."

"No," Prowl grunted, his instincts alert to danger. "I don't think so..."

Spike heard the explosions growing closer. There were screams outside, followed by squealing tires, crunching metal, and breaking glass. He wanted to go to the window, wanted to see what was happening, but he felt it would have been suicide to turn his back on his host...or to stray too far from Franklin's side.

"So you're the one," Franklin said. "You bankroll the Followers."

The kid pshawed that idea, scrunching his features up in a *you've gotta be kidding* expression. "I like the networking, and I found a way to skim a hell of a lot off the top of whoever is funding all this craziness. The new technology possibilities are astounding, and someone needs to make a buck off that, sure. But no, I'm not that guy, or gal... I'm just a little ol' pirate, out taking whatever I can when no one's looking."

"Then you don't have anything to do with the disappearances... or with what's happening here?"

"Don't go hatin' on me, dawg! I didn't say that."

"Wait a minute," Spike said. "*You* gave Starscream the idea to take over Vegas?"

"A couple of distant signals, the right message in a bottle tuned to his wavelength... call it a suggestion. Or maybe it was in his head already, and I just made him feel like it'd be a really good idea."

"Why?"

Darren shrugged. "I do pretty good on the money front, but you know what they say: what's the definition of enough? A little more..."

"So they set up a media empire and you just happen to be here, their guy on the spot who can make it all happen and pirate off the profits," Franklin said. "Or maybe you just figured out what they were going to do and got yourself in place before they could show up."

"Either way, those upfront fees can pay for a heck of a lot."

"Like your own army?" Franklin asked. "The one that's backing Grimlock?"

"Could be," Darren said, "but you know what I'm all about, I'll take credit for everything, if you let me. Maybe it'd be cheaper for me to just find someone else with all that stuff and make him think going up against the Decepticons is a good idea. Anything's possible. Let's stick with what we know, a'ight?"

"What is it you want?" Spike asked.

"The same thing a whole lot of the Followers are after," Darren said, tapping the side of his head. "All that yummy data you've got crammed into your brain. The way I see it, you know—whether you realize it consciously or not—exactly how Transformers work. You could take one apart, put one together, kill them, bring them back to life, make an army of them...even figure out how to turn one of *us* into one of *them*. Like what happened with you, like why you know what you know."

"Fine," Franklin said, "we know what you want. What are you offering?"

Spike turned on the man in surprise. "Hey, hold on! Even if I wanted to do this—which I *don't*—I don't have any way of just flicking a switch and rattling this stuff off."

"Course you don't," Darren said. "Data extraction is hard work, and it costs big bucks. That's the other reason I needed funding, and lots of it. I started on the gaming circuit, designing—stealing, really—doing endorsements, all that, yo. Lots of good investments, including joining up with the Followers, and pretty soon, we're all standing here, which'll probably be a smoking hole in about ten minutes, so let's wrap this up."

"Lets," Franklin agreed.

Darren grinned. "Here's the thing: you walked right into it, just like I knew you would. You were curious, you wanted to help your friends. Not a problem. The whole thing with the ones who took Prime and all those people? They're like... well, they're not like vampires, that's not it, but you know that thing where with vampires, you have to invite them in? Same deal. Someone over here had to open the door so they could do their snatch and grab. That same person can open the door again so you guys can go all *Stargate* and try to rescue them. And, natch, that someone is *me*."

The kid dug into his pocket and took out a glowing, blue-white shard of crystal with strange pulsating marks lining its surface. "See this?" he asked, holding the shard up high. "This is all it takes. The thing is, you can take it from me—how can I stop you—but I'm the only one who knows how it works. The Keepers don't exactly share what they know freely, and I won't either."

Franklin smiled. "So all I need to do is knock the snot out of you until you talk and the problem's solved?"

Darren shrugged. "Well..."

Suddenly, a low vibrating thrum sounded, and Franklin doubled over.

"Same frequency that gave you the edge with the augments," Darren said, nodding to Spike. "But that was over a pretty far distance. Your pal here's getting a taste of it up close and personal. Don't expect him to be doing you any favors soon."

The sounds of battle grew even closer. "So here's the thing," Darren said, "I'm trying to be polite and make you feel like you've got a choice here. Even exchange. You come with me, I leave the garage door opener to the Keeper's world with your pal and later I send him instructions on how to use it. Make it harder on me than it has to be, and my boys take you down the way they did the Decepticops on the way over here, and the remote control stays with me. Which way's it gonna be?"

"Neither," Spike said, gripping Franklin's arm. "You know what I did to the augments that came after me, right?"

"Yeah, that was pretty damn cool. I'm looking forward to finding out how to do it myself."

"You're in for a long wait. There's a part of my brain that has all the information you want, and probably a whole lot more, that's telling me something is possible. You know anything about electroshock therapy?"

For once, the kid was quiet.

"Electro-shock wipes out short term memory." Spike concentrated, and a spark of energy leapt from Franklin's arm, making the operative's knees buckles, and lanced into the back of Spike's hand. "Imagine electroshock powered by Energon. That's what's inside Franklin and all other augments... has to be, how else would Transformer tech work? So here's how this goes: Either you give me that thing and get the hell out of here, right now, or I'll use what I know to fry my own brain with Energon current, and I'm pretty damn sure it won't just be my short term memory that goes. One good jolt and everything you want to take out of my head goes bye-bye. You decide, here and now: In or out, pal? My way—or no way at all."

CHAPTER
TWENTY-ONE

Optimus had no answer to the question plaguing him: How he could then take revenge on the Keepers, how could he destroy them... without killing everyone he wished to save?

"It's like Oz, and the little guy behind the curtain," Jazz said. "But in reverse. It's like the whole city is that guy!"

"The time for pretenses is done, it seems," came the booming voice of the Keeper. *"That doesn't mean we owe you anything. Our reasons are our own. Know this: The contest before you, should you choose to participate, will be unlike any other. Gaze at what we have done and despair."*

A single light appeared at the far end of the arena. It grew, illuminating something like a hive that grew above and below the arena floor. Prime could not see deeply into the hive, until, without warning, his vision sensors penetrated the deepest reach of the hive, allowing him to see a fiery pit at its core, where the humans were fleeing from geysers of liquid fire stabbing up high and dropping to scald or kill.

He stumbled back, Jazz at his side, steadying him, as the vision faded and only the hive, a single blocked up entrance glowing crimson, remained in view. It was a labyrinth, and the entrance to the maze was too small for Optimus or Jazz to fit through in their robotic forms.

"The humans you seek to protect are in danger. If

you fight among yourselves, you will lose the precious time you need to save them. Even if you do not, the only way to break the seal and reach them is beyond your basic natures. You are hardwired poorly. Designed for limitation, not expansion."

"Jazz, hit that thing hard!" Prime commanded. "I'll keep Megatron occupied."

Without hesitation, Jazz raised his weapon and fired at the seal. He blasted away at it, but he could not break it.

Megatron approached Optimus, his arms at his sides, his hands open, weaponless. "Is destroying me all that matters to you?" Megatron asked. "For time beyond measure, we have fought. Perhaps today we share a common enemy."

Optimus did turn his back on Megatron. He called, "Jazz, how are you coming with busting through that barrier."

"Nothing!" Jazz called. "I can't breech it!"

"I can," Megatron said. "If I transform, I can do it."

"Perfect," the Keeper called. *"Your enemy attempts to lure you with false promises."*

"What I say is true, is it not, Keeper?" Megatron yelled, challenging the voice.

Several seconds of hesitation came. Then: *"While there is even the slightest chance that his desires will be fulfilled, he will not aid you. He is hardwired to pursue his own goals at any cost."*

"The Keeper did not say that I couldn't help you, only that I won't," Megatron said. "It wants something. They all do. The Keepers promise much, but all that truly seems to interest them is taking."

Jazz called, "Optimus, people are dying, I can hear them!"

"All right," Prime said. "Transform."

Megatron laughed again. "Prime... first you try to kill me, then you want favors. It seems little changes."

"You mean you want something in return," Prime said.

Megatron nodded. "A favor to be named *later*."

"Done."

The Decepticon stepped back. "Your time of indecision seems to be at an end. But the role of leader calls for more than just fast calls. You must also be able to live with the consequences of your choices."

"I'm letting you remain in one piece, aren't I?" Prime said. "Every time it happens, I have to live with that."

Leaping into the air, Megatron *changed*.

Paul's earlier fears that this was a charnel pit had been proven true. The lava was rising. There was a platform at the top of the pyramidal structure large enough for all the humans to stand upon and escape the boiling flow of liquid, at least for a time.

"We have to reach the top!" he yelled.

Screams sounded from below as people faltered, tripped, and fell into the churning, hissing tide of fiery crimson lava. Paul wouldn't have been surprised to learn that some of the terrified herd had pushed others to their deaths to clear the way ahead for themselves, or to free themselves from those reaching and clutching at them out of fear, a need for reassurance and safety.

Ahead, he saw Melony, shaking, but not with fear. It was rage that consumed her, all encompassing rage at the idea that she would die in this place, so close to the very creatures she had followed for so long, so close to the vengeance she wished to take on them, if only she had the means...

He pitied her, and wanted to comfort her, to drive the anger from her heart.

As if sensing his thoughts, she looked up coldly at him. "Come anywhere near me and I'll kill you. I swear I'll do it."

And he could tell from the look in her eyes that not only was she serious, but that she knew. The Keepers had probably been whispering in her ear, too, and she *knew* that he had seen her living nightmare, he had walked in the world of her memory, and rather than sharing her lust for revenge against the Transformers, had, in fact, wished to save her from herself.

Things would never be the same between them again.

Prowl's sensors zeroed in on a strange frequency—which seemed to be coming from a lone human being listening to a tape on an odd-looking cassette player.

A voice filled with cruel malice crackled inside of Prowl's and Bumblebee's Cybertronian brains.

"You found me!" it said. "Good. Now the fight can begin."

A second later, the strange-looking cassette player began to shift and change. The man who had been listening to it dropped it and ran away as it grew quickly, reforming itself into something else—something evil, something monstrous.

The citizens on the streetlooked on in terror as tremendous legs unfolded, gigantic arms unwound, and weapons bristled, a pulse rifle appearing in the robot's hand and the blue barrels of multiple cluster missile launchers formed on the robot's broad mechanical shoulder. In just a few moments, the colossus known as Soundwave stood in the middle of the Fremont

Street Experience on wide braced legs. Panicked humans scurried for cover as Soundwave turned and faced the Autobots.

Prowl and Bumblebee had no choice but to transform. Laser rifles at the ready, they faced the arrogant communications Decepticon in the very center of the covered street. Wild lights flowing across the ceiling, and oceans of neon all around them made Autobot and Decepticon armor gleam eerily. Within a few minutes, every human had retreated from the scene. Glitter Gulch was suddenly deserted, to the relief of Bumblebee and Prowl.

"Your concern for these biological parasites is quite touching," Soundwave said, reading the thoughts that flowed through the Autobot's Cybertronian brains with his powerful electronic scanning array.

"Activate your internal scramblers!" Prowl commanded. "Now!"

Before the jamming was activated inside the Autobots, Soundwave could hear every thought they had and every statement they made. In the next moment, it was as if a dark curtain fell, cutting off their frequency. Now Soundwave couldn't hear anything the Autobots didn't say out loud.

"Scramblers working," Bumblebee announced, grinning. He fixed his stare on Soundwave. "Now you can fight us on equal ground, Decepticon," he said. "Without the benefit of knowing our fighting moves before we make them."

"I don't need to know what you are thinking to defeat you both!" Soundwave cried. To emphasize his boast, a brace of cluster missiles blasted out of the launcher mounted on his shoulder. The projectiles streaked toward Bumblebee and Prowl on tails of yellow fire.

"Yow!" cried Bumblebee, leaping through the glass

double doors of the Shangri-La Casino. Two cluster missiles chased him through the neon-lit entranceway.

Meanwhile Prowl dropped to one knee and ducked his head. The first cluster missile overshot its target, missing Prowl's helmet by inches. It flew on, to punch through the arched ceiling. Lights and electronics exploded in a shower of sparks and fire, and glass from shattered lights and metal support beams crashed down in the middle of Fremont Street. An entire block-long section of the ceiling went dark, but in other parts of the grid, the light show continued. Cartoon buffalo stampeded over the heads of the battling robots.

As glass and showers of electric sparks crackled around the hole, the cluster missile continued on in an upward trajectory, to detonate harmlessly seven hundred feet above Glitter Gulch.

But the fight wasn't over for Prowl. As more missiles streaked toward him, Prowl fired his laser pistol twice. Two red bolts of energy beamed through the air and two cluster missiles disintegrated in mid-flight.

Then Prowl fired off a desperate third shot—and missed.

The final cluster bomb struck Prowl's chest plate at an angle, tearing a scorched furrow along the Durabyllium-steel armor that protected Prowl's shoulder. But miraculously, the missile failed to detonate at the moment of impact. Instead it shot off at an angle, exploding in mid-air half a block down the street, to shower burning destruction onto a crowded Chucky Cheese. People fled the building in fear as fires spread throughout the damaged structure.

Inside the Shangri-La Casino, Bumblebee rolled over and crashed into a bank of slot machines. Coins flew everywhere as the two cluster missiles whizzed over the Autobot's head. The casino floor was packed with frightened people, many of whom took refuge in the gambling house when the fight started outside. Bumblebee realized too late that he had brought the fight right to them.

"Duck!" the Autobot cried.

Many people hit the floor. Many more did not. One cluster missile slammed into a giant statue of a Dalai Lama, penetrating its plastic heart. The missile's engine sputtered and died as the statue toppled over and crashed onto the roulette tables.

The last cluster bomb shot through a second doorway, to rocket its way deeper into the building. Bumblebee heard a rumbling explosion. The next second, a wave of heat and fire washed over him, spilling gambling tables and sending people out of the building and back onto Fremont Street.

The roof above Bumblebee's head began to collapse. He looked down to see frightened, screaming people still milling around his legs and bunching up at the exits. Smoke filled the room and the automatic sprinkler system went on, dousing Bumblebee. Still more people poured out of the building's interior, some were wounded and were being helped—or carried—out of the shattered casino by others.

"Prowl will have to fight without me for a couple of minutes," the Autobot decided. Then Bumblebee spread his metal legs wide and grabbed hold of the crumbling ceiling, holding it up in an effort to buy more time, so that more people could escape.

"Damn Autobots!" cried a man, shaking his fist as he raced between Bumblebee's legs. "You're all a menace."

A burning chunk of roof struck Bumblebee's faceplate. His knees wavered under tons of steel, but he quickly redoubled his efforts.

Outside, people were spilling into the street from

the crumbling Shangri-La Casino, and the burning Chucky Cheese across the broad street. Prowl wondered if his partner was all right, or if Bumblebee needed assistance—though there was nothing Prowl could do in either case. He had his hands full fighting Soundwave. And with the streets filling up with people again, the battling Autobot knew he would have to take the fight outside to avoid more collateral damage than had already occurred.

Prowl rose to both feet again, in time to see Soundwave leveling his sonic gun at his chest.

"Listen to their cries!" Soundwave said. "Their screams of fear and anguish are music to my ears."

"You have strange taste in music then," Prowl said, his voice more confident than he felt.

"So you say," Soundwave shot back. "Now listen to my greatest composition—my magnum opus."

The Decepticon fired.

Like a tidal wave, wave after wave of solidified sound slammed against Prowl, knocking him backward. He fought to keep his balance, but his legs got weak and his Cybertronian brain seemed sluggish. At Prowl's feet, humans dropped to the ground, clutching their ears and crying out in screams drowned out by a pounding, caco-demoniacal whine that destroyed all other sounds.

"Die, Autobot!" the voice of Soundwave boomed inside of Prowl's head. Vaguely he knew that his jammers—like many other functions—had failed. Prowl stumbled to his knees, fighting to stay focused. But it was a losing battle.

Suddenly the roof of the burning Shangri-La Casino burst outward, its neon sign tumbling into the street. A ball of burning wreckage—tons of it—flew into the air in an arc, to drop down again right on top of Soundwave's head.

In the center of the flaming mass of debris, Bumblebee—his audio systems deactivated—used his telescopic vision to aim at the Decepticon below. With a final push, Bumblebee burst out of the burning mass, to land beside the fallen Prowl.

The fireball of molten steel continued downward, to slam right into Soundwave's helmet. The Decepticon squawked once, then toppled forward and crashed into The Long Branch Casino Hotel. As tons of debris covered the disabled Soundwave, Bumblebee added to the mess by tossing any piece of shattered metal he could find. When Soundwave was completely buried under hundreds of tons of hot steel and crumbled masonry, Bumblebee turned to face Prowl.

The Autobot was on his feet again, his eyes scanning the area, his sensor arrays active and searching.

"We got lucky," Prowl said. "They're coming at us one at a time."

"You're welcome!" quipped Bumblebee. "Happy to help."

Prowl ignored his partner's levity, to focus on his surroundings. People began to flood back onto Freemont Street as soon as they sensed the battle had ended. Sirens wailed in the distance, as fire engines raced to the scene of the destruction.

"Let's get out of here," said Prowl. "Before we bring more grief to these people."

"Should we call Grimlock?" Bumblebee asked.

"Not yet," Prowl replied. "And only if we really need him. We've managed to do enough damage here without including a Dinobot in the mix."

Bumblebee nodded. "Point taken."

Spike stared at the teenager. He was certain he could back up his claim...the hidden knowledge in his head seemed to need extreme circumstances, life or death scenarios, to manifest itself. And that was certainly what he was facing now.

Darren smiled, then laughed out loud. "You sure picked the right city for a hand of poker, I'll tell you that much. I guess the real question is who's bluffing and who's really holding all the cards. If you fry yourself, I don't get what I want. Your kid, on the other hand, also ends up without a father. You know how much that hurts, Spikey. You sure you want to do this?"

"If I go with you, I'm pretty sure I'll end up dead by the time you're done with me, so what do I have to lose?"

Darren's smile faltered a little—just as the glass window on the far side of the room *imploded,* a hunk of debris the size of a Volkswagon slicing through the air, busting through the furniture, sailing right at him.

He didn't even have time to scream before it plastered him—and the object he held—into the wall.

"Understand, before you take this journey, what we would have of you," the Keeper said. *"You must become something more. Something different. Something new. You must transform yourselves in ways that go beyond your programming, you must reach for heights you may never have believed attainable and you must grasp them firmly, you must prove your worth to us or else we have no reason to continue your existences. Do this—or all will die."*

Optimus Prime held the weapon that had been Megatron in his hand.

Prime raised the gun with his right hand, aimed carefully at the barrier, and fired. An enormous bolt of energy hit the wall and chunks of debris flew in every direction. When the smoke cleared, Prime saw a hole the size of a diesel truck's cab had been created by the force of Megatron's firepower.

Jazz peered through the hole in the blockade and looked back at Prime.

"It's a maze. The only we'll be able to get through and rescue those people is in car form."

Prime nodded. He leaned the Megatron gun against a wall and transformed into a diesel truck.

Jazz prepared to transform as well and then pointed at the gun.

"We should bring him with us in case we need the firepower again."

"Yeah," agreed Prime.

Jazz secured the gun inside Prime's cab and then transformed into a white racecar.

"Let's go," said Prime.

"I'm right behind you."

The two Transformers raced into the maze. They had only driven a short distance when Prime had to slam on the brakes. Prime's visual sensors had noted that the floor of the maze dropped away and there was a bottomless drop into nothingness right in front of them.

"Jazz, we're going to have to find another way around. There's a huge drop here that we can't get around."

"Prime, my scanners indicate that there is no other way to get deeper into the maze other than following this path. We need to try and jump it."

"Alright, Jazz but let's move fast."

Both Transformers went into reverse and backed up far enough so that they could build enough speed to fly over the opening. Prime floored the accelerator and easily cleared the opening. Jazz tore across the maze and flew over the cavity landing hard but safely.

Prime took off deeper into the maze, almost hitting the walls a few times as he took the tight turns in his truck form. Jazz followed Prime closely but because of his smaller size and better maneuverability, he was able to easily avoid hitting the walls.

Jazz saw Prime ahead of him turn sharply to the left and disappear behind the wall of the maze. Suddenly, Jazz heard a loud crash and then a loud scream from Prime. Jazz raced around the turn and his sensors were completely disoriented at what they saw. Prime had again slammed into another wall when he completed that last turn but this wall was not like the others that he had hit. This one was hot, literally.

Jazz's temperature readings from the wall almost blew his temperature gauge. The right side of Prime's red cab was smoking from the heat, there were black scorch marks and some of the titanium had bubbled up in places where it had slammed into the maze wall.

"Prime! Are you alright?" asked Jazz.

"Yeah, I'm fine. Just going to need a new paint job when this is all said and done."

"Well, if that's all you need when this is over then I'd say you got off lightly."

Jazz checked inside Prime's cab to ensure that Megatron was still secure after this collision. Fortunately, Megatron appeared unharmed from the heat blast.

"We need to keep moving," said Prime.

"Right. All's secure and ready to go."

Prime sped through another section of the maze this time concentrating hard on the turns to not hit the walls again. Out of nowhere, spikes thrust out of the floor and pierced all of his tires. Before Prime had a chance to warn Jazz of the danger, he slammed into a wall as he tried to apply the brakes. Jazz also hit the spikes and spun into Prime as he skidded to a stop. All of their tires had been pierced by the spikes and they were both dented from their smash up.

"This maze is really beginning to get on my circuits!" shouted Jazz.

"Let's just fix our tires and get moving," said Prime.

Fortunately, all Autobots who can transform into cars are equipped with self-healing and self-inflating tires. Within a few minutes, the two Autobots were back on the road through the maze. They both drove cautiously through the labyrinth keeping careful watch on their sensors for any and all changes.

Jazz screeched to a stop as he picked up something on his auditory sensors. Prime detected Jazz's change in speed and stopped as well.

"I can hear them!" shouted Jazz.

"We're getting close, but there's another barrier ahead. We've only got one chance to bust through. Autobots—roll out!"

"Megatron—this means you, too!"

Jazz pulled Megatron out of Prime's cab so that he could transform back into robot form as well.

Prime barreled at the shining barrier ahead, *transforming* as he made contact with it, the energies he released as his mass and size altered searing through the molecular bonds of the barrier, shattering it, allowing first one, then two more Transformers to leap into the fiery pit where the humans were being held...

To leap straight into hell.

CHAPTER
TWENTY-TWO

The Gucci boys fled, and whatever silent alarm Darren had triggered to keep Franklin's telemetry scrambled died with him. Spike looked to the window and saw the conflict in its brutal glory, then turned to see Franklin striking at the debris that had killed the insane teenager.

"We've got to get out of here!" Spike yelled.

"Not without that device," the operative replied. He touched the side of his head. "I'm getting communications back. This rock coming through the window wasn't random. There are no other concentrated attacks in this area, and the trajectory and velocity was hand-selected."

"You're saying a Transformer did this."

Franklin kept digging. "Either on purpose... or because he was being controlled. Now come on. Someone wants us to bring back Prime and the others!"

A mile away, Soundwave chuckled inwardly. He had deduced who had summoned the aliens intent on studying their kind some time ago. But merely using his power and influence to open the doorway to the world where Megatron had been summoned and *perhaps* bringing back their leader would not have been nearly as satisfying as this—watching Starscream recoil as his plans fell to dust around him.

Now, when Megatron returned, he would find Starscream precisely where the arrogant fool belonged: down on his knees, broken, and buried in the flaming debris of all his schemes.

For the affront Starscream had performed, for the humiliation Soundwave had endured, this was the *least* he could do...

The most would wait for another day.

Cautiously, the Autobots moved up Las Vegas Boulevard South in their car forms. The Decepticons knew the Autobots were there, and that they were coming for them. The Autobots wanted as much speed and maneuverability as they could get if a sudden attack came!

There was much activity on the brightly-illuminated streets, but most of the pedestrians were moving *toward* Fremont Street, not away from it as Prowl and Bumblebee were doing. Most citizens of Las Vegas were still ignorant of the danger they faced, and curious to see what all the noise, smoke, fire, and fuss on Fremont Street was about.

Traffic soon became too heavy for the Autobots to move through easily, and so they took on their robot forms and practically played Twister among all the vehicles and pedestrians just to keep moving ahead. Most folks looked at the Autobots with open curiosity. Some gave them a friendly nod. But a few people shouted insults or shook their fist at them—another sign that the Autobots weren't particularly popular with humans at the moment. But at least no one tried to impede their progress as Prowl and Bumblebee moved toward the glittering neon heart of the Las Vegas strip.

Behind them, bringing up the rear, was a secret

army bent on liberating Las Vegas, no matter how the citizens felt about it. Prowl and Bumblebee still felt uneasy about that, and hoped they could stop the Decepticon plot before the army even arrived.

The Autobots continued their stroll down the neon-bright Vegas strip. Far ahead of them, the spire of the Luxor rose, the bank of searchlights mounted on top and aimed at the night sky created a column of light that could be seen from orbit. The air was clear and getting cooler. It was too beautiful a setting for war, Bumblebee thought.

He decided to act like a tourist instead of a warrior for a few minutes. Instead of making war, Bumblebee enjoyed the sights and sounds of America's most notorious and popular metropolis.

He saw The Sahara. Circus Circus. The Riviera. Legendary places he'd only ever heard about before he now saw first hand. He felt a thrill rush through his Cybertronian brain as the excitement filled his senses.

"These were the very street where the Rat Pack once walked," Bumblebee observed.

"Rat pack? Does that have anything to do with The Pied Piper legend?" Prowl asked.

"Never mind," Bumblebee said, shaking his head. Poor Prowl had trouble keeping his facts straight when it came to the subject of human culture and mythology.

As they passed Sands Avenue, the Autobots paused—as did hundreds of humans—to gawk in wonder at the water volcano show that ran hourly in front of The Mirage. Bumblebee marveled at the prodigious amount of energy and water being squandered to fabricate the appearance of an erupting volcano with lights and water instead of magma and fire.

"I believe it would be cheaper and more efficient to build a real volcano!" he declared.

"But I doubt local safety codes would allow for a volcano in the heart of downtown," Prowl replied.

"Ever the pragmatist!" sighed Bumblebee.

As the pyrotechnics finished up, Prowl's senses suddenly tingled with danger.

"Bumblebee!"

"I sense it, too!" the yellow Autobot said.

They turned and scanned the streets around them, little knowing that the danger they faced came from above.

Fifty miles over Las Vegas, in the dark, cloudless sky above the shimmering city, the Decepticon Aerospace Commander Starscream dived at a speed of Mach 2.8. He had transformed himself into the shape of a state-of-the-art military fighter jet, and, engines roaring, the descent to sea level took less than a minute. Though armed with an array of cluster bombs, each with a range of forty miles—bombs that could level a 10,000 square foot area—the urbane Decepticon chose not to use them. Not yet.

Instead, he trained his null rifles on the hated Autobots, who were still ignorant of the threat that would soon streak out of the sky and disable them. Starscream's plan was to hold the two Autobots hostage against the potential invasion that now had a distinct possibility of occurring—and soon. Starscream had just taken over control of the earthbound Decepticons. He had no intention of relinquishing his hold on power, or his central command center in Las Vegas.

Down on the street, Bumblebee restored his audio

faculties and increased their sensitivity. Only when Bumblebee utilized his powerful audio buffers to filter out street noise and human voices, did he hear the sound of airfoils cutting through the wall of atmosphere far above his and Prowl's head.

"Attack from above!" Bumblebee cried. At that moment null blasts lanced out of the sky, to strike the pavement.

"Starscream!" Prowl cried, raising his blaster. He fired a quick shot and struck Starscream's left wing. The Decepticon pulled out of his dive and leveled off barely above street level. As he shot past the Autobots, Starscream reached out with mooring lines and caught Bumblebee in his grip.

The Autobot felt himself being lifted, but instead of resisting he went limp, feigning helplessness. But as Starscream soared over Las Vegas Boulevard, he banked into a turn that would take the Decepticon and his prisoner right over the expansive man-made lake that lay on the grounds in front of the luxurious Bellagio casino and hotel. As they raced away from the crowded streets and jammed sidewalks and over grass and water, Bumblebee saw his chance and struck.

With all the considerable power of his robotic construction, Bumblebee bent his knees and kicked upward, smashing his metal heels against the delicate vectoring controls behind Starscream's engine ports. The jet staggered in the air and almost spun out of control. It took all the control Starscream possessed to keep his flight level after his control surfaces were so effectively attacked.

And Bumblebee wasn't finished. Once. Twice. Three times more, the Autobot kicked out with all his might, slamming his metal feet against the delicate, super-stressed control surfaces. As they raced over the pond, Bumblebee lashed out one last time.

Suddenly there was a sound of ripping metal and the jet that was Starscream flipped over in the air. Struggling to compensate for the damage, Starscream leveled off and righted himself. But it was time to rid himself of the bothersome Autobot. As he dived low over the water, Starscream let go and watched Bumblebee strike the water and vanish in a gusher that spouted higher than the top floor of the hotel.

Circling about, his vector controls trailing smoke, Starscream changed, transforming himself into robotic form and landing in the middle of Las Vegas Boulevard, right in front of Prowl.

Damaged servomotors smoking and throwing off sparks of blue energy, Starscream leveled his null-rifles and fired. The bolts narrowly missed Prowl, who transformed into a car and sped out of the way and down the street to The Venetian hotel. Prowl transformed into robot form and climbed the hotel's exterior until he was on its roof where he could get a better view to find out what happened to Bumblebee.

Starscream sneered and fired again. The bolt struck the hotel and shattered windows on three floors. Instantly the Venetian went dark, the null-rifle boltsshorting out its electrical systems. Prowl aimed his laser pistol and fired three shots. One struck Starscream's visor, the other hit the damaged area—inflicting more pain and injury on the enraged Decepticon.

"Where are you Bumblebee?" Prowl shouted.

"Right here!" screamed Bumblebee as he climbed out of the lake, transformed into a car and sped over to The Venetian. Then Bumblebee transformed back into robot form and scaled the hotel's outside. A moment later he stood on the roof of the hotel, next to his partner.

Then both Autobots ducked behind the building's façade and began firing laser bolts at Starscream. Most of the shots did no harm, but a few hit Starscream's damaged areas, doing further damage to the Decepticon's delicate internal systems.

"Surrender, Starscream!" Prowl cried.

"You think I'm finished?" Starscream shouted incredulously. "I have yet to begin my fight."

"You are hurt, damaged," Bumblebee called. "And alone."

"I am damaged, it is true," Starscream replied with a confident chuckle. "But I am hardly alone."

Franklin found the alien artifact amidst the horror that had been a human being only moments earlier. It was intact, seemingly undamaged by the blow that had killed Darren. He held it out to Spike, who took a step back from it in surprise.

"What?" Spike said. "I don't know how to use it."

"There's a lot of things you don't know... only, you *do*."

The building rattled as if it might collapse under its own weight. "There isn't enough time to get out of here unless we can stop what's going on outside," Franklin said. "You've got someone you don't want to leave behind." He touched the side of his head, and Spike thought, for a moment, that he could actually hear the voice that spoke to Franklin.

A voice that was electronic, not exactly any Spike had ever heard before...

The voice of a human child, a girl—who was no longer what she had been.

"Maybe I have someone like that, too," Franklin said, his lips pulling back in a snarl. "Now take it!"

Spike grasped the artifact, and almost immediately, something happened.

It, too, was talking to him.

Jazz had been struggling to grasp the concept that he had seemed to know intuitively upon his first look at the "world" that was, in fact, the gigantic bodies of the Keepers. He had sensed them within him, felt lost when they were gone.

At the same time, he despised them for what they had made him do.

Now, standing ankle deep in searing pools of lava, attempting to rescue as many human lives as he could from the pit, Jazz could not ignore the doubts that had assailed him for so long. *These are our makers. They've said as much. I can feel that it's true!*

As he went about his task, the fires reflecting off his shining metal skin, he chanted those words in his head, chanted them until a single voice broke through the screams and the chaos below.

"It's not true!"

Jazz shook himself, suddenly realizing that he must have been repeating the chant in his mind. Below, a single human stood apart from his frightened companions, a dark-haired man who stood near the edge of the structure, helping others to safety.

"They can't be your makers," Paul said. "They can't create anything. I thought all they wanted was to study us, and I think that's part of it, but why not pull our fantasies, our daydreams... why not find out what we want to become, all the things our imaginations make possible?"

"Because they *can't*," Megatron concluded, turning

to take note of the human's words. "How could they have made us? They can't make anything."

"We may have come from the same place as them," Prime said. "They may be searching for answers, like us."

Then, to everyone's surprise, a woman leaped at the man, dragging him from the safety of the structure's plateau toward the abyss, a primal scream of absolute anguish torn from her lungs as she sent them both flying to the hungry flames simmering along the boiling lava below.

For the second time in his life, Paul was saved by a Decepticon. Megatron had reached out with blinding speed, catching both humans in his giant hand. Melony struck her head against the hard steel of his forefinger, and sagged into unconsciousness. But Paul was alive, awake... aware.

This time, there would be no running, no trembling in fear. As the Decepticon brought the human close, he said, "I know what you are... and I wish to learn more about those like you."

He knows I'm a Follower, Paul thought. *Somehow, he knows.*

Megatron deposited Paul and Melony safely onto the plateau from which they had come in the first place.

"You may serve a greater purpose than you know."

Looking towards his comrade Jazz, and even the malevolent Megatron as they struggled to save the humans, Prime knew that there was only one course of action left to take. Looking about at the fiery inferno and the techno-organic walls that surrounded them, Optimus Prime realized he had listened to the Keeper's dialogue for long enough. He had been subjected to torturous events, watched his comrades fall, and been forced to ally himself with his life-long nemesis—the time for talk, thought and deliberation had ended. The time for action was now upon him.

Prime opened his chest panel, and a flood of crimson energies filled the cavity. Megatron and Jazz looked toward the stalwart Autobot leader in awe as he became encased in a silvery light, Energon arcing and pulsing around his massive form. As the iridescent radiance filled the fiery cave, everyone stood silently as Optimus Prime removed the Autobot Matrix of Leadership from his chest—and held it aloft.

Lacing his mammoth fingers into the slotted handles of the ancient Cybertronian artifact, Optimus Prime called forth all of the wisdom, all of the knowledge, and all of the *power* of every Autobot leader that came before him, and willed the Matrix to aid them in their time of need.

With a radiating light like that of a galaxy being born, the Matrix pulsed to life and expelled a pure, scintillating blast that momentarily blinded Jazz, Megatron, and the humans surrounding them.

As the purest light of Primus coursed through the bowels of the Keeper's techno-organic body, a wretched, guttural, animal roar of pain rang through the cavernous halls.

A wail even more anguished than the one that sounded when Megatron had ripped through the flesh of the Keeper came, a deafening roar that made humans drop to their knees, clutching at their skulls, a sound that registered on every wavelength known to Transformers, ripping through their bodies, ravaging their minds. Around them, the walls began to glow, and a terrible disintegrating energy raced through the body of the Keeper, a scourge that grew exponentially with each passing second.

"You don't have long," Prime said as the Matrix poured raw, beautiful Energon into the cavern, lighting it with a silvery, crimson glow, calling out to the Keepers over their horrid screams. "If we are *similar*, then this will destroy you. All of you. Take us back to our home or I will let it happen."

"You would," Megatron said, clearly impressed. "You would sacrifice all our lives to ensure that these creatures meet their deaths."

"So many innocents," the Keepers cried. *"Races, species you have not encountered, millions of lifeforms we are studying..."*

Stalactites fell, and Jazz brushed them aside before they could strike the humans. The world itself—the body of this Keeper, and the bodies of all those it had bonded with—was coming apart. Prime recalled his brief glimpse of the strange techno-organic shapes, the seemingly dead leviathans, and now pictured them writhing, stretching, frantically attempting to tear themselves away from the source of their agony, but there was no hope of reprieve—unless Prime willed it so.

Finally, Prime had the Keepers on the ropes.

"Our programming... we cannot go where we are not invited. We cannot do what we are not asked to do, not given leave to do. This is one of two critical limitations in our core coding that we wish to overcome."

"The other?"

"To create. To be the progenitors of new life, to reverse our own stagnation and become something new, something more..."

The encoding... in human terms, it would be considered DNA. A primordial programming code from which all parameters of behavior was derived. The Keepers had sought to force the Transformers to create, to *transform* into something new, something that went beyond their program. Because if they could evolve, the Keepers could reduce them to code, and steal from them whatever links were missing in the chains that made up their own primary encoding.

"Take us back!" Prime said.

"We are trying but it is impossible—only if one on your world wishes it, calls to us, can we do this. Give us time, allow us that grace, we beg you!"

"I can't trust anything that you say," Prime said, understanding that the full weight of leadership was now upon him, and he was not buckling beneath it.

Though he was about to die, along with all the others he'd sought to protect, he was now at peace.

"All things live and die by a particular code. Some may interpret this as a code of behavior, a code of honor. The life cycle of beings can be encoded into the basic building blocks of a living being, even one of mechanical origin, such as myself. As you see into me, I see into you, our coding aligns. Let our wishes, our wills, be one."

"Bring them back," Spike whispered, clutching the artifact.

And outside, the doorway to another world was opening.

Starscream raised his arms above his head and called out in a booming voice. "Devastator! To me!"

Suddenly the casino called Paris, France burst asunder, its wall collapsing in a cloud of dust and wreckage that obscured everything at street level.

Prowl and Bumblebee watched in horror as the fake Eiffel Tower crashed down to crush fleeing people trapped below. The tower was followed by the walls themselves, as the entire structure imploded.

From amid the smoke and rubble, a sixty-foot-tall robotic figure arose—Devastator, the mightiest of the Constructicons!

"We should have called Grimlock," Bumblebee said. "We sure could use him now."

"Not worry!" the Dinobot's voice boomed from many blocks away. "I coming!"

The Autobots heard the now-familiar sound of heavy, massive, earth-shaking Dinobot footsteps thundering toward them. It was the best sound Prowl and Bumblebee had heard all day!

Kicking aside rubble, Devastator stepped into the middle of the busy boulevard. Cars screeched to a halt, some striking his legs. People fled in all directions as, from the other end of the block, Grimlock appeared. With long, loping strides the brave Dinobot charged the mammoth Decepticon. From somewhere near, searchlights reached out, pinning the combatants in a halo of light.

The battle of the century was about to begin.

Prowl was gratified to see that Devastator's movements were slow and sluggish, and Bumblebee pointed out blackened patches that were heat scored, dents, and furrows on many of the Decepticon's component parts. The left arm—comprised of the Constructicon called Bonecrusher, was limp and practically non-functional. Prowl and Bumblebee were gratified that he still suffered from the defeat they had dealt him earlier in the day.

But just because Devastator had taken a beating, it didn't mean he wasn't ticking—or itching for a fight.

"Come to me!" Devastator cried, his voice echoing off the skyscrapers around him.

"I come!" Grimlock roared.

With a final, bounding leap, Grimlock attack his opponent. The sound of the two heavy, metallic bodies slamming together shattered windows for miles around. Sparks flew and energy bolts shot out, ripping through the sides of buildings and tearing up the pavement. Gawkers fled, fearful for their lives.

Decepticon and Dinobot staggered, but neither fell. Instead the two mighty robots glared at one another before launching simultaneous attacks.

Grimlock lashed out with his tail, raking it across Devastator's chest plate. The Decepticon leveled a cannon at Grimlock and fired, the shell striking the Dinobots throat.

Grimlock roared and jumped backward, crushing cars under his mighty feet.

Buildings shook from the epic battle, forcing Prowl and Bumblebee to hang on to the roof of The Venetian with both hands.

As the two gigantic robots continued their fight, Prowl sensed movement above him. To his shock and surprise, Starscream landed on one side of the Venetian's roof, a recovered Soundwave on the other. Between the two Decepticons, the Autobots exchanged glances.

"Not again," said Bumblebee.

"This is the end, Autobots," Starscream shouted. "I don't need hostages anymore. Your wrecked bodies will suit me nicely."

As he spoke, Starscream leveled a multi-barreled cluster bomb launcher on his left arm. On the other side of the roof, Soundwave aimed a similar weapon.

"Looks like this is the end," Prowl whispered.

"Never give up," Bumblebee said hopefully. "Who knows what could happen in the next second."

As if on cue, the face of The Mirage hotel several blocks away began to shimmer with an eerie, unearthly light. Suddenly an opening formed, a shining gate to somewhere else...

The battle came to a standstill as figures stepped out of the gateway.

It was Prime! He and Jazz...and Megatron. The humans were there, hundreds who had been taken, and beings from strange, alien worlds, as well, many of whom seemed to be suffering greatly in the atmospheric conditions they were encountering.

The Transformers had returned to Earth.

But... they were not alone.

Prime had replaced the Matrix into its designated chest cavity and was closing his chest plate, the crimson, pulsing energy spilling out then fading as the seals connected. Behind him, the door flickered shut—then a sudden, swirling array of blue and crimson lights overtook the city, and the door expanded, widening until dozens of strange shapes the size of skyscrapers seared themselves into this reality, techno-organic lifeforms that looked out at all they surveyed with glaring, malevolent eyes.

The Keepers had taken new forms—and had come to Earth. One of these forms was shockingly familiar to Optimus Prime. He recognized the body of his fallen comrade, though it was battered, broken, welded together with alien technology, a mad, mocking parody of the friend he had known:

Standing with the Keepers, his consciousness replaced by that of an alien techno-organic, was Bluestreak.

The battle was far from over, Optimus Prime realized with horror. In fact, it had only just begun.

To Be Continued